Woul.. .. Ask My Husband That?

Would You Ask My Husband That?

Kathleen Whyman

embla
books

First published in Great Britain in 2023 by

Bonnier Books UK Limited
4th Floor, Victoria House, Bloomsbury Square, London, WC1B 4DA
Owned by Bonnier Books
Sveavägen 56, Stockholm, Sweden

A CIP catalogue record for this book is available from the British Library.

ISBN: 9781471415715

This book is typeset using Atomik ePublisher

Embla Books is an imprint of Bonnier Books UK
www.bonnierbooks.co.uk

To the loves of my life,
James, Eve and Elena

(Just as a matter of interest, how many books do I need
to publish before this is considered 'a real job'?!)

Chapter 1

Sarah

'Mind if I have a quick word, Sarah?'

My stomach plummeted. Being singled out by the HR Director was never good, especially not at an event. I was supposed to be relaxing and letting my hair down, which everyone knew was code for 'getting sozzled'.

I nodded and Clara gestured to a quieter corner of the function room – well away from all the fun. The colleagues I'd been talking to gave me sympathetic smiles. I returned them with a grimace, picked up my glass and followed Clara. It wasn't that I didn't like her – she could be a good laugh – but one-to-ones were rarely laughing matters.

'I know we shouldn't be talking shop when you're trying to let your hair down' – see, even Clara knew the code – 'but it's hard to track you down in the office, so I thought I'd seize this opportunity, as you're here.'

So that's what this was about. Not being in the office enough. My face grew warm. This wasn't fair. It had been agreed that I could work flexibly when I came back full-time. It was the only way I could make it work with school drop-offs and pick-ups. And I worked most evenings, at my laptop or on calls to overseas clients, once Evie and Fred were in bed. I wasn't just meeting my targets, I was smashing them. It was killing me, but I was doing it. Clara's snide comment was completely unjustified.

Clara took me to an empty bar table so far away from

everyone else, we were practically in another building. I sat down and tried to zone out the laughter and general merriment going on in every other area of the huge room. Clara wiped the table with a napkin and smiled at me.

'I might not physically be in the office full-time, but I'm working at home when I'm not there,' I said defensively. 'You can contact me any time, including evenings and weekends. I'm always available.' Just the night before, I'd taken the children trick-or-treating while listening in on one of my team's marketing pitches. Thankfully, the blood-curdling screams in the background hadn't put him off.

Clara's sleek bob barely moved as she shook her head. 'That wasn't a complaint. It's hard to track you down because you're always in meetings. I've seen your calendar. It's crazy.' She took a sip of her wine. 'Speaking of time ...'

Oh no. She'd seen me sneaking into the autumn conference late that morning. Usually, Evie and Fred went to breakfast club on the days I came into the office, but Will and I were staying in a hotel tonight, so it hadn't felt right doing my usual drop-and-run when I wouldn't be seeing them until tomorrow. I'd made myself even later by dropping my case off at the hotel en route. But missing two hours was nothing compared to the number of extra hours I'd worked.

I nudged the side of my glasses up. 'Time?' I asked innocently. I'd pretend I'd been at the conference from the very start. Setting up even. Someone had to put out the name badges, corporate notepad and cellophaned croissants with the texture of a rubber band.

Clara nodded. 'You shouldn't have to work evenings and weekends regularly.'

Easy for her to say. I had no choice. If I didn't, I wouldn't be meeting my targets, let alone smashing them. It was impossible to work when Evie and Fred were home from school, and Will didn't get in until they were going to bed. Later, if he had to take clients out.

I forced a smile. 'Working evenings and weekends to get the job done means I don't feel guilty about spending time with the children after school on the days I work from home, or leaving at five when I'm in the office. I don't mind.'

I did mind. It was exhausting going back to my desk after falling asleep while reading the children's bedtime stories, or turning down the offer to watch Netflix and chill with Will. I meant that in the genuine sense, not with the expectation of sexual activity. We'd been together for twelve years, with children in our lives for the past seven. The prospect of watching something that didn't involve a puppet or talking animal was much more appealing than sex most nights. Not tonight, though. We'd booked that hotel for a reason. And that reason most definitely involved sexual activity. Although I wouldn't mind watching the next instalment of *The Crown* if we could fit that in too.

'I hear what you're saying.' She leant forward. 'I don't think you're hearing what *I'm* saying.'

Au contraire. I'd politely listened to everything she'd said. Despite the fact it was about as interesting as the house-rules section of the conference and I *should* have been 'letting my hair down' with my friends.

Clara motioned to a waiter. 'Could we get a bottle of champagne, please.'

I perked up. If I had to attend an enforced, impromptu HR meeting, I may as well attend it with a decent drink. Pre-Will, my friend Tonya and I had been known to endure some very boring conversations with city slickers who sidled over with a bottle of bubbly by way of introduction. If I could get through those conversations, I could get through this. Not only was Clara much more interesting than they'd been, but she was also unlikely to go off in a strop when she didn't get a hand job afterwards.

The waiter left and Clara smiled. 'Let me start again. I'm not explaining myself very well.'

I took a large drink of my wine. Partly to prepare myself

for her explanation, but mainly to get it out of the way before the posh stuff arrived.

'You're working long hours,' she said. 'Many more hours than a Manager at your level is expected to work.'

I gulped into my wine. Did I work too slowly? Did other Senior Managers achieve more in less time?

'Why not get paid for those extra hours?' Clara eyed me over her glass.

'You're giving me a pay raise?' I asked excitedly. This was unheard of mid-financial year without a promotion.

'No,' Clara said.

My excitement drained away even more quickly than I'd drained my glass.

'Then what—' The waiter arrived with our champagne and I stopped talking. Just as well, as the obvious next two words were 'the actual' and we all know what came after that.

My heart pounded with frustration while the waiter poured the champagne. Was Clara playing some sort of game with me? If so, what was her aim? To dangle the carrot of a pay raise to make me work even harder? To wind me up so much I handed in my notice? To get punched in the boob?

Clara handed me a flute. 'Cheers.'

I couldn't bring myself to return the 'cheers', although I managed to find it within me to drink the free champagne. I didn't believe in cutting off my nose to spite my face. I needed it to stop my glasses falling off.

'I'm confused,' I said. 'First you say I deserve more money, then you say I can't have it. With all due respect, what are you talking about?'

I love the disclaimer 'with all due respect'. You could pretty much get away with telling someone they were a total arsehole if you tagged 'with all due respect' onto the sentence.

Clara grinned. 'I think you should apply for the Director position.'

I gripped my glass. Director? Was she serious? Directors were only one down from Partners. They worked on the company's biggest and best accounts. Their roles involved wining and dining clients, jetting overseas to attend very important meetings, and basically living a life of prestige. Mind you, Will had been promoted to Director a couple of years ago and, having seen him in a unitard for a client's charity bike ride, I knew it wasn't all glamour.

'You're already working the hours expected of a Director,' Clara continued. 'You may as well get paid for them.'

The prospect of a Director's salary was massively appealing. If I earned the same as Will, we'd be so much better off. We could look into converting the garage into a playroom. As well as our annual family holiday, Will and I could have the odd city mini-break. We could take the kids to Center Parcs during school holidays. We could ... Actually, I'd have to check Center Parcs' prices. Even two Directors' salaries might not stretch to that. But the rest might be achievable.

Clara laughed. 'I'm guessing that look on your face means you're interested.'

I realised my expression was on par with Scooby-Doo's when he's presented with a giant Scooby Snack. I looked down to hide my eagerness and realised my wrap dress was gaping open, revealing my bra. Scooby-Doo wouldn't look so excited if presented with that view. I pulled it back into position and sat up straight.

'Yes, I'm interested.' That was the understatement of the year. Becoming a Director had been my long-term goal since joining the company fifteen years before. It had been tough watching Will become Director first, considering he'd started three years after me. But that was what happened when you took nine months' maternity leave twice and worked part-time until both children were at school.

'I didn't realise there was an opening,' I said. 'Is someone leaving?' This was rare. Becoming a Director was as out of reach for most people as the art of turning base metals into gold. If you were privileged enough to become one, you hung on tight.

Clara leant closer. 'Don't say anything, but Jasper's for the chop. He was caught on CCTV stealing stationery.'

My stomach tightened. I'd pilfered a few notebooks and pens in my time. Not to mention highlighters, Post-it notes, a hole punch and enough Tipp-Ex mice to open a laboratory. 'How much stationery?' I asked nervously.

'Some envelopes.'

I fiddled with the arm of my glasses. 'He's being sacked for that? Seems a bit excessive.' I was never taking anything again. If Jasper was getting the boot for pinching a few envelopes, I'd be put on death row for my haul.

'They were premium, A3 gusset envelopes.' I commended Clara's ability to give that sentence *gravitas*. 'But, between us, it was an excuse. He's been on borrowed time since he lost his work laptop.'

I relaxed slightly. I didn't have a blot on my copybook (not that anyone would know, as I'd probably taken that home, too) and Clara wouldn't be offering me Jasper's job if I'd popped up on CCTV too.

'What do you think?' Clara asked. 'Honestly.'

Honestly, the prospect excited me more than anything had for a while, even the time I got a *Pointless* answer – and I hadn't been sure anything would ever top that. If I became a Director, my years of experience and hard work would be validated. I'd have to work even harder, but that didn't faze me. I loved to be stretched and challenged. It brought out my creativity and drive. I knew I was capable of doing the job and that I'd love it. There was just one problem. Well, two actually: Evie and Fred.

I clasped my hands together. 'Would there be any flexibility with the hours? Could I work from home some of the time, like I do now, so I'm around for the children?'

'Afraid not.' Clara smoothed down her already-smooth bob. 'The big clients expect you to be there for them. Doesn't cast the company in a good light if their direct contact is on the school run when they need them.'

Well, that was the end of that dream then. The children already moaned about having to go to a childminder after school three days a week – the toilet paper wasn't as soft as what we have at home, apparently. They were clearly talking out of their bottoms (which weren't remotely chafed, despite the prison-like facilities they were forced to endure), but it wouldn't be fair to make them go every day and there wasn't anyone else to help. My widowed mum had relocated to sunny Spain when she remarried, Will's parents were elderly, and his sister Tonya, also my best friend from school, worked erratic hours as a chef. She was having them for a sleepover that night so Will and I could stay in London after the conference, but that was a rare Friday night off for her and it had been extremely kind of her to give it up to help us.

Without reliable after-school care, there was no way I could take the job. My disappointment must have shown on my face, as Clara reached over and refilled my glass.

'Please don't just dismiss it because of childcare. Bet Will didn't think twice when he went for it, did he?'

'No,' I admitted. 'But he had—' I paused. He had me to sort everything out and make sure our lives ran smoothly. It'd never cross his mind who was going to pick the children up if a meeting overran, or what he was going to give them for dinner because he hadn't had time to go to the supermarket. He could focus fully on his job, knowing that everything at home was taken care of. And when he had to travel, which he did fairly often, his only consideration, outside of what he needed to prepare for the project, was which box set to watch on the plane.

Will worked very hard. I wasn't trying to belittle that. But he could, because that was all he had to think about. He was oblivious to the volume of life admin that raising children and running a household involved. The amount of paperwork that came home from school would make Greta Thunberg weep. And Will never got woken up by the children in the

7

night when they'd had a bad dream or needed a wee, or a drink of water and then another wee. I knew all of this was part of being a parent, but Evie and Fred had two parents. Why was it all on me? Why was I the one who always had to sacrifice my career?

'You'd be brilliant in the role,' Clara said. 'You're determined and passionate and unstoppable.' I briefly wondered if this was based on how I was working my way through the champagne. 'We need more female Directors,' Clara continued. 'It's the twenty-first century, the era of #metoo, yet only ten per cent of the Directors at Ballas & Bailey are women. That needs to change.'

I sat up straight, clutching my glass. Only ten per cent? That was disgusting. Clara was right. On behalf of all women, I should take the job. What kind of role model would I be to Evie if I didn't go for it because I chose to stay at home with her and Fred? My shoulders slumped. This was a hopeless situation. If I accepted the job, taking a stand for women everywhere and championing equality, then Evie and Fred would practically be raised by childminders and babysitters. If I turned it down, then I'd be doing the right thing for them, but not for my career or for the sisterhood.

'Why not get a nanny or au pair?' Clara said. 'Works for me. They do all the housework and cooking too, so the time you have with the children is quality time, not spent doing boring jobs.'

Now, that was appealing. I hated that I couldn't give Evie my full attention when testing her spellings because I was preparing dinner at the same time, and that I'd be folding laundry while reading Fred his bedtime story. I ate my breakfast while unloading the dishwasher, did the online weekly food shop on my phone at the park and had, on one occasion, planned an entire birthday party during sex. Poor Will would be crushed if he knew. Although he might perk up if he knew he was the inspiration behind the horse-shaped piñata.

'And you're not dropped in it if one of them is ill,' Clara added.

She was good. Being at the mercy of the school secretary, Mrs Manning, was the bane of being a working mum. She could ring at any moment and insist I collect Evie or Fred *that instant* because they had a slight temperature or had sneezed. No matter what I was doing – giving a presentation, closing a deal, stealing from the stationery cupboard – I had to stop and race to the school, where I'd find them sitting forlornly in reception with the sick bucket on their knees, while Mrs Manning shot me daggers for sending an ill child to school. Within thirty seconds of getting home, they'd be racing around the living room, asking me to play because they were bored. I was convinced it was a tactic the school employed when they didn't have enough school dinners to go around. Never mind what disruption and distress it caused the parents, so long as Mrs Manning got her toad-in-the-hole. A nanny would free me from this tyranny.

'I'm very tempted,' I said. 'It's what I've always wanted, but I need to talk it through with Will. There'd be a lot to work out logistically, with the children.'

'Of course.' Clara raised her glass to mine. 'You'll make it work, I know you will.'

I leant closer to Clara. 'When's Jasper going?'

'He was told last night,' Clara said in a low voice. 'Thought it best he didn't sit in on today's conference, given that it's outlining our strategy for the next year.'

'He's gone already?'

Clara put a finger to her lips. 'It hasn't been officially announced, so don't say anything.' I nodded. 'If you go for the job,' Clara continued, 'we'd want you to start straightaway. You'd need to hand your existing clients over to someone first, but the sooner the better.'

My stomach lurched. Straightaway? I couldn't make such a massive decision that quickly. There was too much to consider. How would Evie and Fred feel about me not being around so much? How would I feel about being away from them? How could I find someone to look after the children – someone they liked, Will and I trusted, *and* who used quilted toilet paper?

My heart pounded and I grew breathless, as panic rose within me. 'Smell the flower, blow out the candle,' I told myself, employing the breathing exercises I used to help Evie and Fred calm down when they were stressing out. Clara refilled our glasses. I focused on the bubbles chasing themselves up my flute and felt my breathing regulate.

'Of course there'll be an interview process first and the partners will take a little time to reach a decision,' Clara said.

I frowned. Why did I need to be interviewed for a job she'd just offered me? I cast my mind back to the start of our conversation. Oh yes, she'd asked if I'd like to *apply* for the job. I'd forgotten the small print.

'Have many people been invited to apply?' I asked. If it turned out that everyone in the company, from me to the guy who delivered the water-cooler refills, had been asked, then the invitation lost its kudos somewhat.

'Just two of you.' Clara nodded her head to the other side of the room.

I followed her gaze to where my colleague, and now rival, Tom Page was also sitting with an HR representative, away from the throng of the party. Tom and I had worked together on several projects before, and he was hard-working and easy-going. He'd only been with the firm for a few years, but he'd won and led an impressive number of marketing projects by taking risks and giving the client something they weren't expecting. What he lacked in experience, he made up for in balls. Although, as Clara was keen to increase female representation, that might go against him.

'You're the stronger candidate,' Clara said. 'Tom's career-hopped his way here, moving companies every few years. You've demonstrated your loyalty, both to us and your clients.'

I assumed a loyal expression. Clara didn't need to know I barely had the energy to change the bedding, let alone jobs.

'The Partners know they can depend on you,' Clara continued. 'You're not going to get what you can out of the company, then run.'

I nodded. Definitely didn't have the energy to run.

'Remind me how old you are,' Clara said.

'Forty-two,' I replied.

'Five years older than Tom,' Clara said. 'That means you have five years' more experience.' She gave a satisfied nod. 'He might be dynamic, but you're dependable.' Clara clinked my glass again. 'And don't forget that you're a woman.'

'I won't,' I said solemnly, though there was a risk I might forget if I kept drinking.

Clara slid off her bar stool. 'Give it some thought over the weekend and let me know on Monday.'

I smiled. 'I will. Thank you for thinking of me.'

Clara smiled back. 'You're the obvious choice, in my eyes. It'd be a shame if you didn't apply. These opportunities don't come up very often.' She gestured to my chest. 'Don't wear that to the interview, though. Might give the wrong impression.'

I looked down and cringed to see my bra on display again. I was never wearing this wrap dress again.

Clara walked away and I looked around for Will, desperate to speak to him. To get his thoughts and see if, together, we could make it work. The room now contained an assortment of well-dressed marketing professionals in various states of drunkenness. A disco had been set up and I spotted Will throwing some shapes on the dance floor. Not even a mathematical genius could tell you what shapes they were, though. Any thoughts he might have about the Director job probably wouldn't be coherent ones. I'd talk to him about it when we got to the hotel.

I took a sip of champagne, a smile growing on my lips.

I could be a Director. This was amazing. And exciting. And what I'd worked so hard for. And, my smile faltered, impossible. We couldn't both put in such long hours. It wasn't fair on Evie and Fred. It'd never work. Would it?

Chapter 2

Will

Someone was shaking my shoulder so hard that it was making my head jerk back and forth.

'Will, wake up,' Sarah hissed in my ear.

I grunted and shrugged her off. Why was she so loud and grumpy? I was the one who should be grumpy. I'd been having a lovely sleep before she woke me.

'Will.' She was using her sternest voice. The one she used on the kids when they were being annoying. Well, I wasn't annoying, so she didn't need to use it on me. I squeezed my eyes tightly shut.

'If you don't get up, I'm leaving you. This is your last chance.'

Talk about dramatic. I wouldn't dignify that ultimatum with a response.

'Come on, mate,' a male voice said.

Tom? Urgh. Now, he *did* qualify as annoying. But what the hell was he doing here? He'd flirted with Sarah earlier, when he thought I wasn't looking, but she wouldn't have brought him to our hotel room. We'd outgrown piling into someone's room and raiding the minibar after a night out, and she wasn't into threesomes. She was so precious about her sleeping space that it was a wonder she let *me* in the bed. No way would she sacrifice any more of the mattress to someone else.

So why was Tom in our room? I couldn't remember him

coming back with us. Although, I couldn't remember getting back at all.

'Will, please.' Sarah sounded desperate now. 'The train's about to go.'

My eyes sprang open. No wonder I couldn't remember getting to the hotel. It hadn't happened yet.

'Fuck.' I launched myself out of my seat and hurtled towards the door as it started beeping, grabbing Sarah's arm on the way and hauling her off onto the platform with me.

She stumbled in her heels, recovered herself and waved goodbye to Tom through the glass door. He grinned and tapped the side of his head in a salute. Arsehole.

Sarah's smile dropped the moment his carriage passed.

'You promised you wouldn't fall asleep,' she snapped.

'I didn't mean to. Just closed my eyes for a moment.' It was all coming back to me now. The stagger to the station from the conference centre. The exhaustion that hit me as soon as I sank into a seat. The inability to keep my eyes open once the train had started moving.

'You do this all the time.' Sarah strode towards the exit.

'No, I don't.' I hurried after her. 'It hasn't happened for ages. Wouldn't have done tonight if you hadn't been there.'

'Don't blame this on me. If I hadn't woken you, you'd have ended up in the sidings again.'

'That was years ago. Before the kids,' I said. 'No, I mean if you hadn't come, I'd have left earlier and wouldn't have drunk so much.'

'Well, that'll teach me to arrange a sleepover for the children and book a nice hotel, so we can have a proper, grown-up evening.' Sarah's heel caught on the escalator. I put out a hand to steady her, but she snatched her arm away. This didn't bode well for any proper, grown-up activities when we got to the hotel.

'I'm sorry.' Showing contrition was the best way to get the evening back on track. 'Sitting down was a mistake. I wouldn't have, if I'd been on my own.'

'Next time you will be on your own.' She stared pointedly ahead as the escalator whirred upwards. She must be pissed off. Usually, she loved studying the posters as we passed them and commenting on which West End shows she wanted to see – *Moulin Rouge*, *Mamma Mia*, *Dirty Dancing*. All the crap ones, basically. Although the women didn't seem to wear much in *Moulin Rouge*, so maybe that one wasn't as crap as the others.

I was so distracted by the posters that I didn't realise I'd reached the top and almost toppled over. Sarah didn't wait as I steadied myself and I had to run to catch her up. Was it my imagination or did she walk even faster?

'Were you OK dropping the case off at the hotel?' I asked breathlessly, tapping my rail pass and following her through the turnstile.

'Course I was. I'm not a moron.' The look she gave me as she put her wallet back in her bag implied that I, however, *was* one.

She gripped the strap of her bag tightly and headed out of the station. I reached up for the strap of my man bag and instead fumbled my shoulder. The strap wasn't there. And if the strap wasn't there, then the bag wasn't either.

'My man bag,' I shrieked.

Sarah stopped and turned.

I looked over each shoulder in the vague hope my bag was somehow hanging at my side without me having noticed. It wasn't. 'It's been stolen.'

'It can't have been. No one's been near us to take it.' Sarah looked me up and down, clearly of the same mindset that it must be somewhere on my person and I was too pissed to realise. She couldn't find it either.

'Maybe I left it at the conference centre,' I said. My memory of leaving the bar and staggering to the train station was a bit hazy.

'No,' Sarah said. 'You definitely had it. It got wedged in the train door when it closed.'

Oh yes. I remembered Tom laughing as I'd lurched forward. Immature tosser.

Sarah crossed her arms. 'And the engineer had to force the doors open so you could get it out and the train could leave.'

Cue more childish cackling from Tom. None of the other passengers had found it remotely funny.

'So where is it now?' I asked, dumbfounded.

Sarah nudged up her glasses. 'You must have left it on the train.'

Fear jolted through me so intensely that I actually felt my testicles contract.

'No.' I clutched the sides of my head. 'It's got my laptop in.'

Sarah closed her eyes and let out a long, shaky breath. 'Bugger,' she murmured.

A whimper escaped me. If my level-headed, practical wife was worried, then this was bad.

'We have to go back.' I spun round and started running towards the turnstile.

'Stop,' Sarah shouted after me. 'The train's gone. You can't run after it.'

I turned back and charged towards her. 'We'll get an Uber to the end of the line. Where does it go?'

'Peterborough. We'd never get there before the train and it'd cost a fortune.' Sarah took her phone out of her bag. 'I'll call Tom.'

'Why?' I spluttered. 'He can't get to Peterborough quicker than the train.' Tom might do loads of triathlons, and he might have fixed the water cooler that I'd noticed was leaking and ignored, and he was, some might say (not me), kind of good-looking in that conventional, chiselled jaw, piercing blue eyes Henry Cavill way, but he wasn't *actually* Superman.

Sarah gave me a withering look. 'If he's still on the train, he can get your bag for you.'

'Oh, right. Yes.' My balls relaxed slightly. There was still hope.

Sarah called Tom and I heard it go to voicemail. Superman's phone wouldn't go to voicemail.

Sarah hung up. 'I'll message him.'

'He won't get it if he's not getting calls.' My heart rate quickened. If I didn't get that work laptop back, I was screwed. 'I've got to get to Peterborough.' I thrust an arm in the air to hail a cab.

'Stop,' Sarah said. 'The train might go through pockets of reception. Sometimes I get messages when I'm underground.' She tapped out a message and pressed send. 'Just give it a couple of minutes and see if he replies.'

The happy, drunken buzz that I'd had when we'd left the conference centre was long gone. The shock must have sobered me up. Sighing, I slumped against the wall, slid down it and landed heavily on my arse. Not exactly sober then.

Sarah studied her phone. 'One tick. Ooh, two ticks. It's gone through.'

I looked up at her from my new resting place on the floor. She was gripping the phone as enthusiastically as a scratch card that had revealed she only needed one more matching symbol to win a trillion pounds. Poor, deluded Sarah. Always so positive and willing to believe in the best possible outcome. She'd save herself so much wasted energy on disappointment if she accepted that life was pretty much a shitshow most of the time.

'The ticks have gone green,' she said excitedly. 'He's read it.'

I scrambled up. 'Really?' Hope was restored. Maybe I'd treat Sarah to a scratch card as a thank you.

Her phone vibrated. 'He's ringing!' She pressed the phone to her ear. 'Tom,' she said breathlessly.

What was with the breathlessness? That wasn't the voice she used when I rang her. She spoke in a resigned, weighty way when I called to say I'd be working late or had to take a client out, as though I'd engineered it deliberately to get out of putting the kids to bed. If I wanted breathless, I had to sit through a long rant about how fed up she was with doing everything, till she ran out of oxygen.

'Will left his bag on the train,' she said into the phone. 'Navy, rectangular. Shoulder strap. Just a standard bag, really.'

'*Man* bag,' I corrected. 'Tell him to check the luggage rack,' I added. 'That's where I usually put it.'

Sarah nodded. 'Can you—' She paused, then mouthed to me: 'He's looking.'

I stared at her, willing Tom to find the bag. A burning sensation grew in my chest. Oh God, I wasn't going to have a heart attack, was I? It didn't go down well at work when people were off sick. Although, it might deflect from losing a laptop. I made my hand into a fist and tapped my chest, encouraging the discomfort to manifest. A little heart attack could be just what I needed to get me out of this. The burning grew – it was working.

Sarah gasped. 'He's got it.' She grabbed my arm. 'He's got the bag.'

Relief flooded through me. Thank fuck. Or thank Tom. Same difference, really.

'Thank you so much, Tom,' Sarah said. 'You're a lifesaver. Don't know what we'd have done if you hadn't been there.'

I grimaced at her gushing. Urgh. He must be loving this. She turned to me with a wide smile on her face and I forced myself to reciprocate, despite the heartburn and the fact she was behaving as though Tom were the new Messiah. Sarah's gratitude was over the top – picking up a bag did *not* elevate him to the same status as other lifesavers, such as firefighters, police officers, surgeons or Iron Man – but he had helped me out. I opened my mouth to say thank you and an enormous belch erupted into Sarah's face.

She stepped back, disgust on her face, wafting the second-hand aroma of bar nuts and ale away with her hand. 'Sorry,' she said into the phone. 'That's Will's way of saying thanks, apparently.'

Not my finest moment, but at least she couldn't put on a sexy voice while she was gagging.

She laughed at something Tom said and I resisted the urge to wrestle the phone from Sarah – instead, I held my hand out for it. She looked at it with disdain.

'Can I thank him?' I asked politely.

She hesitated, then nodded. 'Will has something he'd like to say,' she told Tom, as though admonishing a five-year-old for pissing in his auntie's pond. At least Tom couldn't wallop me with the back of a brush the way my auntie had.

She handed the phone over and I cleared my throat by hiccupping loudly.

'Thanks, mate,' I said. 'I owe you one.'

'No worries,' Tom said. 'It's no big deal to pick up a bag.'

Exactly. Even an egotistical prick like him could see it wasn't worthy of the moniker lifesaver.

'Well, I appreciate it.' I could feel another hiccup (OK, burp) brewing, so spoke quickly to cover it up. 'I don't want to do a Jasper.'

'A what?'

'You know, Jasper Si-iii-mmons.' My burp exited halfway through his name, but I ignored it. 'Got sacked for losing his work laptop. Confidential client data and all that.'

Sarah looked at me sharply. 'How do you know that?'

I shrugged. 'Everyone knows.'

'Your laptop's in here?' Tom asked down the phone.

'All right, don't tell the whole carriage,' I whispered. 'Don't want anyone nicking it just when you've saved it. I mean, picked it up,' I corrected.

'Don't worry. It's safe. Your bag's tucked securely under my arm.'

'*Man* bag,' I mumbled.

'What?'

'You'll bring it to work on Monday?'

'Yep, no worries.'

'Great. Thanks again.'

'Can you pass me back to Sarah?' Tom asked.

I hung up and tucked the phone into Sarah's bag.

Sarah pushed her glasses up. 'Thank you?'

I must have put the phone in the correct pocket in her bag. 'You're welcome.'

Sarah closed her eyes, took a deep breath and released it slowly. I could almost hear her chanting 'smell the flower, blow out the candle' that she'd got from her mindfulness app.

She opened her eyes. '*You* should be saying thank you to me,' she said. 'For contacting Tom and getting your bag back.'

As if the situation couldn't get any worse, now I was in Tom's debt. He'd be crowing over me forever about this.

'I would have got it back,' I said defensively. 'You jumped in and took over, like always.'

Sarah took another deep breath. 'You're drunk and talking rubbish,' she said. Bet she didn't get *that* line from the mindfulness app. 'Accept that you messed up and be grateful I helped you.'

'He read your message fast enough,' I blurted out. 'Takes him hours to reply to mine.'

'You're being ridiculous,' she snapped. 'What have you got against Tom?'

'He was flirting with you all night.'

Sarah sighed. 'I spoke to him for half an hour at the end of the evening and it was about work.'

'He laughed when I got caught in the train doors.'

'You laughed when he tripped over the flip chart in the meeting room.'

'That was different.'

'Why?'

'Because he's a prick.'

Sarah clenched her fists. 'I've had enough,' she said through gritted teeth. 'I'm removing myself from this conversation. Don't even think about trying anything when we get to the room.'

She strode off in the direction of the hotel and I ambled after her. This night was screwed. And, sadly, I wouldn't be.

Chapter 3

Sarah

'I feel terrible.' Will sank down onto his knees as soon as I'd closed the front door behind us. He leant forward, as though in prayer, his shoulders and forehead on the floor and his bum up in the air. I fought the temptation to kick it and headed upstairs.

'Are you going to bed?' Will asked, a note of hope in his voice. Even in his roughest state, he could summon up the enthusiasm for a shag. I'd *issue* a summons against him if he dared try. Even if he hadn't been a complete idiot the night before, the stale alcohol infused with garlic fumes emanating from his pores wasn't exactly a turn-on.

'No.' I stomped up the stairs. 'Need to change the children's bedding before Tonya drops them home.'

'Why?'

'Because no one else is going to do it.'

'No, why do you have to do it *now*?' Will whined. 'We should make the most of the kids being out to, you know, be together.'

I almost threw the pile of bedding I'd just taken out of the airing cupboard down the stairs at him, but stopped myself. I'd only have to go and pick it up again. Instead, I took a deep breath and exhaled slowly. Smell the flower, blow out the candle.

'The whole point of last night was to be together,' I said through gritted teeth. 'But you ruined it, you … you silly man.' The mindfulness advice didn't advocate calling people dickheads, which was a serious flaw in my eyes.

'I'm sorry,' Will said quietly into the floor.

It was going to take more than that to make it up to me. Although Will didn't know it, I'd been desperate to talk to him about the Director job. Instead, I'd ended up talking to Tom. He'd sought me out to say that he looked forward to working for me in the future, as I was clearly the better candidate. It was charming nonsense, of course. He was hungry for the role; I could see it in his eyes. The only hunger Will had displayed of late was when we'd passed a kebab shop en route to the station.

He'd passed out on the floor as soon as we'd got to the hotel room. As sex was off the cards, he clearly couldn't see any point in retaining consciousness. By contrast, I'd lain awake most of the night, wondering what to do about the job. I'd alternated between thinking that it was impossible and I should forget about it, and deciding that it was worth giving the interview a shot. And giving Will a shot of something lethal if he didn't stop snoring.

I went through to Evie's room, and stripped and changed the bed, shaking out the duvet and pillows vigorously. I did the same with Fred's bedding, then ours, sneaking a quick right hook into Will's pillow. Not very mindfulness-friendly, but sod it.

Will was still kneeling, face first, in the hall when I came down the stairs with the laundry basket. A snore that sounded like a warthog devouring a carbonara vibrated against the floor. I grimaced. Could he be any more disgusting? He farted loudly. That answered that question.

Muttering obscenities to myself – I wasn't going to open my mouth to mutter them, with Will's toxic gases in the air – I fed the first lot of bedding into the machine. This was so typical. We'd both worked all week. We'd both been at the conference until late and got up early to be back for the children. We were both hungover. But he got to sleep his hangover off, while I had to revert straight back to the mum/cleaner/cook role the second I walked through the door. Speaking of which, Evie and Fred would want lunch when Tonya dropped them back from their swimming lesson. As I switched the washing machine on, a beeping outside signalled the Tesco van reversing into our drive.

I nudged Will with my foot. 'Get up. The food delivery's here.'

Will didn't move.

The doorbell rang and I answered it, an apologetic smile on my face in readiness for explaining why my husband was lying comatose on the floor. As well as the delivery driver, Evie, Fred and Tonya stood on the doorstep.

'Mummy,' the children cried, throwing their arms around me. I knelt down and hugged them back.

'I got my twenty-five metres certificate!' Fred waved a piece of paper in my face.

'I'm starving.' Evie rubbed her stomach dramatically.

'Where shall I put these?' Tonya asked, juggling about fourteen bags.

'Have you checked your substitutions?' the delivery man asked.

I shook my head. 'I'm sure they're fine. Just bring it through.'

I took a couple of bags from Tonya. 'You can dump the rest on top of your brother.'

'Ow,' Will shrieked a moment later. I had no idea if this was caused by Evie and Fred jumping on his back, Tonya taking me literally and dropping their bags on him, or the delivery man walking over him on his way to the kitchen. And I didn't care.

Half an hour later, Tonya and I sat at the breakfast bar with coffee and freshly delivered pastries. Will had retreated to the sofa, but instead of having a nap, as he'd clearly intended, Evie and Fred were talking him through whatever they were watching on CBeebies, while spraying him with ham-and-cheese sandwiches.

Tonya tapped her nails against her mug. 'Aside from my brother ruining the end of the night, was the rest of the conference good?'

I nodded. 'Thanks again for having the kids so we could go.'

'Pleasure,' Tonya said. 'They're growing up fast. Unlike my brother.' She rolled her eyes in the direction of the living room. 'He won't stay a Director if he gets that wasted at work events.'

'In fairness, everyone was wasted. He let himself go because he didn't need to worry about getting home. If I hadn't booked the hotel, we'd have left earlier.' I felt slightly guilty at having had such a go at him the night before. He'd had a tough time lately. All the Directors had. Speaking of which …

I leant closer to Tonya. She raised her eyebrows and leant in, too.

'Clara, the HR Director, approached me about applying for a Director's position,' I whispered.

Tonya widened her eyes. 'About time! You've been there longer than Will has.'

'I know, but he hasn't had to take two lots of maternity leave.'

'So unfair.' Tonya tutted. 'It's bad enough that our fannies get a battering, without our careers getting one too.' I giggled into my coffee. Tonya rubbed her hands together. 'Tell me about the job.'

'One of the Directors has been sacked for losing his work laptop and stealing envelopes.'

Tonya frowned. 'Envelopes?'

'More to do with the laptop, to be honest.' I glanced through the kitchen door to the living room to check that Will couldn't hear. He was lying on the sofa with a cushion over his head. I wondered if he'd managed to fall asleep despite the blaring TV. As Fred was sitting on the cushion, it was unlikely. 'Clara thinks I'd be perfect for it. I've got the experience and have been loyal to the company, and they want more women in senior positions.'

Tonya whooped. 'This is so great.'

I put a finger to my lips. 'I haven't told Will. Don't know if there's any point. I couldn't take it if I got it.'

'What?' Tonya shrieked in the same way Will had when he thought he'd lost his bag, but less high-pitched. 'You have to. This is why you've stuck with that company for so long, working crazy hours.'

I nudged my glasses up. 'It wouldn't be fair on the children. They already have to go to breakfast club before school and the childminder afterwards three days a week. It's always rush, rush, rush, and such a long day, especially for Fred. He's still getting used to starting school and is exhausted. So am I,' I added. 'I love it, but it's taking everything out of me.'

'How different would it be if you were a Director?' Tonya asked. 'Doesn't sound like you could work harder than you already are. You may as well get more dosh and the title.'

'That's what Clara said. But I couldn't work flexibly anymore, and I'd have to travel and take clients out. You know what it's like for Will. Some weeks I barely see him outside the office. Who'd look after the children if we both worked such long hours?'

Tonya shook her head. 'You've taken a back seat for years, and not complained when Will's career took off and yours stagnated. It's not right that you miss out again.'

'It's not right that the children are abandoned either.'

'Stop thinking about what's right for everyone else and think about what's right for you.' Tonya reached over and squeezed my hand. 'What do you want?' She splayed her free palm over her heart. 'What drives you? What motivates you? Search deep within yourself. What do you *really* want?'

'A night with Regé-Jean Page,' I sighed.

'Not that kind of deep within yourself.' Tonya tutted. She gave my hand a firm shake. 'Take it seriously this time.

What do you want *professionally*?' She emphasised the last word to ensure I didn't go off on any more lustful tangents.

'To be a Director,' I said.

She smiled. 'There you go then.'

'But I want to be a good mum too.' I put my head in my hands. 'I've been through every scenario of how to make it work. The only way is with a nanny or an au pair, which I really don't want.'

'But if you got someone the kids loved and you trusted? It might not be as bad as you think, and you wouldn't be disappearing from their lives if you took the job. It's not like they never see Will or don't know that he's their dad.'

'I know it works for lots of families and that's great, but it doesn't feel right for me. For us.' I looked through to where Evie and Fred were still tormenting Will on the sofa. 'Also, it's pretty much mandatory for the nanny and husband to have an affair, and I haven't got time for all the paperwork that comes with a divorce.'

Tonya snorted. 'He'd never cheat on you.'

I grinned. 'I know.' Will might be an idiot at times – when he fell asleep on the train, for example – but he was loving and loyal, and I knew our marriage was solid and secure. I sat up straight and adjusted my glasses. 'The job would be great, but it's not the right time. There'll be other opportunities when the children are older.'

Evie wandered into the kitchen. 'I'm starving,' she said, pointedly staring at Tonya's pastry. I was beginning to wonder if Evie had any other vocabulary. She must be on the verge of a growth spurt. Or on the verge of exploding. It could go either way.

'Have it, sweetness.' Tonya handed the croissant over and Evie was out the door before I could take it away and give her an apple instead.

'Aren't you hungry?' I asked Tonya.

She stood up and patted her hips through her jeans. 'I need to keep this figure tight.'

'You look amazing,' I said, admiring her toned arms. She'd helped the Tesco man carry in the food crates and had managed much more ably than he had. Although, admittedly, he'd had the one with all the wine. I couldn't resist stocking up when there was a twenty-five per cent discount on purchases of six bottles or more. Not that there had been one of those offers on, but no one needed to know that. 'Those PT sessions have paid off.'

'Come with me,' Tonya said. 'It's tough, but you feel amazing afterwards.'

'Will's never back from work in time. Running for the train or to school will have to be my exercise for now.'

'You could afford your own personal trainer if you got the Director job.' Tonya wound a coil of her long, black hair around one finger.

I laughed. 'Not going to happen.' I stood up and put the rest of the pastries in the bread bin before Evie polished them off. 'No guarantee I'd get the job anyway,' I added. 'This other guy, Tom Page, is in the running and he's a real high-flyer. Moving his way up the firm quickly and impressing everyone.'

Tonya's eyes widened. 'Page? As in—'

'No relation.'

'Shame.' She raised an eyebrow. 'Does he at least look like Regé-Jean?'

I shook my head. 'More like Henry Cavill.'

'Not exactly ugly then.'

'No, but not my type.'

'I hate kids' TV.' Will walked into the kitchen, took two croissants from the bread bin and stuffed one in his mouth. 'Those chirpy, loud presenters shouldn't be allowed.'

'*You* shouldn't be allowed,' Tonya said. 'You're a disgrace. Getting so drunk you fall asleep on the train and your poor wife has to drag you off the carriage. Then lazing about the next day, letting her do all the work.'

Will looked over to where I sat at the breakfast bar with a

mug and plate in front of me. He opened his mouth, probably about to point out that he'd seen more industrious sloths, but Tonya lightly slapped the back of his head before he could speak.

'Where were you when the shopping needed unpacking, hmm?' she asked. 'On the hall floor, that's where, you fool.'

Will rubbed the spot Tonya had slapped. It hadn't been hard enough to hurt him, but he was so hungover, the brush of a butterfly's wing would probably cause him to wince.

'Yeah, sorry.' He looked down at the floor. 'Not my finest hour.'

Tonya crossed her arms. 'Sarah's the one you should be apologising to. Not quite the romantic night she'd had planned.'

Will grimaced. Most of the time he loved that his wife and sister were best friends, but not when it came to discussing his love life.

Tonya grimaced too, clearly of the same mindset. She picked up her bag. 'I'm off.'

'Thanks for having the kids, sis.' Will went to hug Tonya, but she held up a hand.

'For the love of God, have a shower. You stink.' She rolled her eyes at him, then walked across the kitchen to kiss me goodbye. 'Please think about the Director's job,' she whispered. 'I'm sure there's a way to make it work.'

After she'd gone, Will and I looked at each other warily. I was still annoyed with him, but wasn't sure I had the energy required to sustain it.

'What was Tonya whispering about?' he asked.

'That you're not too old for a hiding and I shouldn't let you get away with any rubbish,' I said. He didn't question my lie. It wasn't anything he hadn't heard before.

'She's right.' He sat opposite me at the breakfast bar and took my hand. 'Sorry about last night. I messed up.' He looked directly at me.

I sighed. There was no way I could stay cross now. I

couldn't resist those deep brown eyes. Even if they were bloodshot, and with creases from the cushion around them.

'Thank you for saying that.' I leant forward to give him a kiss, got a whiff and backed off sharpish.

Will winced. 'Sorry. I'll go shower. Then I'll take the kids to the park to give you some space.'

'No, I'll come too. Be nice to spend some time together.'

Will grinned, attempted to jog out into the hall, realised this was beyond his hungover capabilities and reduced his efforts to a shuffle.

I smiled back, but my face fell as soon as he'd left the room. There was no point telling him about the promotion. I couldn't go for it and he'd then feel bad, which wouldn't do our relationship any good. Simmering resentment was a much healthier approach.

I shook myself. There was no need to be resentful. I just had to accept that I couldn't have my cake and eat it too. But I could have a croissant. I went to the bread bin and realised that Will had eaten the last one. Simmering resentment, here I came.

Chapter 4

Will

I paced up and down the meeting room, constantly checking the time. It was 8.25 a.m. and I'd arranged to meet Tom at eight thirty to get my man bag back. I was early – I hadn't sprung out of bed so eagerly since the day Kylie Minogue's advert for Agent Provocateur was released – and wouldn't be able to relax till the laptop was in my hands.

I needed to find a way to thank Tom. He might not be my favourite person – and that was with David Cameron on the list – but he'd helped me, and I should show my appreciation. Sarah had suggested buying tickets to see his favourite football team play. As I was a Spurs fan and he was Arsenal, I'd rather gift him one of my kidneys. I paused the pacing. Was that why I didn't like him? The old Spurs-versus-Arsenal rivalry? How could I be so shallow? He was friendly, helpful, a team player, and he didn't frown and pointedly open a window if someone let one go during a meeting, as some of the other bods did. I had to get over this pathetic hostility and embrace him as a trusted colleague.

The door opened and Tom walked in. My heart soared, and I fought the urge to run across the room and actually embrace him.

'Good to see you, mate.' I shook his hand energetically. 'Thanks for coming in early with my bag and, you know, finding it and looking after it.'

'No worries.' Tom looked flustered, as though he'd overslept and run to work. Or was on the receiving end of an overly enthusiastic handshake. I released him and stepped back.

'Can't thank you enough,' I babbled. 'I'd have been screwed if you hadn't been on the train. Can't believe I was so stupid. Especially after Jasper getting sacked.' Relief caused my words to spill out of me. I hadn't realised just how scared I'd been until I saw Tom. My whole career could have been over if it wasn't for him. If he needed a kidney, mine was his for the asking. He still wasn't getting those Arsenal tickets, though. I had to maintain some standards.

'It's OK.' Tom gave a nervous laugh and looked away. I hadn't realised I'd been staring manically at him, as though he were a demigod. Or Glenn Hoddle in his glory years. I needed to calm down. I was scaring the poor bloke. Tom cleared his throat. 'It was a mistake anyone could make.'

I nodded enthusiastically, wishing Sarah could hear this. *It was a mistake anyone could make.* Not one only made by 'total fuckwits', as she'd unkindly claimed.

We stood awkwardly in the middle of the room for a few moments. Tom was still avoiding my gaze. Couldn't blame him, really. I'd been gushing so much that he probably thought I was on the verge of proposing.

I clapped my hands together. 'If I could just get my bag …'

'Course, sorry.' Tom slid his own bag from his shoulder.

'Thanks again for this, mate,' I said. 'I owe you one.'

'It's no big deal.' Tom held out his bag. 'You don't owe me anything.'

I looked at him blankly. 'Why are you giving me your bag?'

Tom frowned. 'It's not mine. It's yours.' He pushed it towards me and I stepped back, eyeing it in horror.

The pristine, so-blue-it-was-almost-black, clearly brand-new bag looked nothing like the worn, faded man bag I lugged around. My stomach hit the floor, as realisation dawned. Tom hadn't picked up my bag on Friday night. He'd picked up someone else's. And that someone else now had my bag and, more importantly, my work laptop.

When people claimed that they felt all the blood drain from their body, I'd always thought they were talking bullshit. And it turned out they were. Instead of draining away, my blood was coursing through my veins at high speed. If anything wanted to drain away, it was the contents of my bladder, with some urgency.

'It is yours … isn't it?' The uncertainty in Tom's voice showed he already knew the answer to that question.

I stared at him, my new-found respect vanishing. To think I'd considered donating an organ to him. His Adam's apple bobbed up and down as he swallowed. I imagined pulling my arm back and punching his stupid, handsome face, so that his head wobbled like the nodding Elvis toy that Sarah had stuck to the dashboard because she thought it was fun, which it wasn't.

I looked away. This wasn't Tom's fault. Punching him wouldn't help the situation. Plus, who was I kidding? Aside from the fact I didn't advocate violence, Tom was fitter than me, not to mention several years younger. If I attempted to hit him, he could block me and fire a punch straight back without batting an eye. And I definitely didn't advocate violence when it was directed at me.

Reluctantly, I took the bag from Tom. Hope glimmered as I felt a laptop through the bag's fabric. Please let it somehow be mine. I put my hand inside and pulled out an A4 hardback book, roughly the size and weight of a laptop. The glimmer of hope I'd entertained gave the book one look and buggered off out of the door without a backward glance. If Tom hadn't been standing in front on me, a look of sheer panic on his face, I'd have cried.

'See if there's any ID in there,' Tom said. 'Maybe the person who left this bag picked up yours. You can contact them and swap back.'

It seemed unlikely that whoever now had the latest MacBook Air in their possession would want to trade it in for – I checked the cover – a *Beano* annual, but I tipped the bag upside down anyway. Some gel packs fell onto the floor.

'There must be something else.' I shook the bag manically, then wrenched it wide open, ripping the zip fastening. Nothing. 'What sort of freak uses a bag if all they've got is a book? They could just carry it.' Tossing the bag on the floor, I clamped my hands to my head.

'Don't panic.' Tom held his hands up, as though trying to pacify an armed gunman. 'Your bag's probably been handed in. Call the station's lost property.' He took his phone from his pocket. 'I'll google the number and Airdrop it to you.'

I nodded numbly and stood there helplessly as he sprang into action. Sarah was right – Tom was a decent guy. Yes, he'd ballsed up by picking up the wrong bag, but he clearly felt wretched about it and was doing everything he could to help me out.

'Got it,' Tom said.

My phone beeped with the Airdrop contact. 'Thanks, mate.' I rang it immediately, but the line was engaged.

Tom gave me a sympathetic smile. 'Sorry, but I'd better go. Got a meeting at nine.'

'Yes, go,' I said firmly, determined to act like a professional. As a Director, I was his superior and needed to maintain a mature, dignified stance, even though in reality I wanted to piss my pants and run home to my mum. 'Thanks for all your help. Means a lot.'

'I wish there was something else I could do.' Tom shuffled uncertainly from foot to foot, a different man to the smiley, self-assured one who usually annoyed the arse off me.

'OK.' I threw the poor guy a bone. 'You can tell Nancy I've been held up and to postpone my team's briefing. I'll update her when I can.'

Tom nodded eagerly. Perhaps out of relief that he'd been given a job to do. Or perhaps there was truth to the rumour that my PA, Nancy, had comforted him through his recent marriage break-up and he welcomed any excuse to talk to her. Whatever the reason, I was grateful.

I gave him a grim smile. 'Do me a favour – don't mention this to anyone.'

'Course not.' Tom put his hands up. 'You don't need to—'

'Thanks.' I pressed redial on my phone and it actually rang this time. I gave Tom a thumbs up as he left the room, and my call was picked up. 'Hello,' I said firmly. 'I need to—'

'Please choose one of the following options,' said the automated message.

I sank down onto the sofa at the end of the meeting room and hoped that one of the options involved punching something. In a non-violent way, of course.

Sarah answered my call instantly. It sounded as though she was running. 'Everything OK?'

'No.' I swallowed hard. 'Tom picked up the wrong bag.'

She came to an abrupt halt. 'He hasn't got your laptop?'

'No.' The word came out in a squeak.

'Bugger, bugger, bugger.'

I dumbly nodded my agreement.

'Right, OK.' Sarah sprang into problem-solving mode. 'The first thing to do is call the train helpline. Hopefully, someone's handed it in.'

'Already did.' My voice cracked. 'Couldn't speak to anyone. Had to leave an answerphone message. They'll only call back if they locate my property.' I ran a hand back and forth across my cropped hair. 'What's the second thing to do?'

'The second thing is …' Sarah paused. 'Not to panic.'

'That's it?' Heat raced up my neck to my face. 'My job's on the line and all you can say is don't panic?' Beads of sweat popped up on my forehead. 'What am I supposed to do? Have a herbal tea, do a yoga pose and then everything'll be all right?' I spied the air-con controls on the opposite wall and hurried over.

'No,' Sarah said calmly. 'It's just not going to help if you're running around like a headless chicken.'

'I am not running around,' I snapped, slowing to a fast walk. Flipping the control panel open, I jabbed at the buttons, desperate to get some cool air in the room. 'Why are *you* running? Shouldn't you be at your desk?'

'Yes.' Sarah's pace started up again. 'Forgot Evie's guitar this morning, so had to go back home for it, then drop it into the office. Mrs Manning wasn't impressed. Said that Evie should be taking responsibility, not relying on me to save the day.' Her voice juddered as she ran. 'Silly cow. She's only seven.'

Mrs Manning was a silly cow, but in this case, she was right. Sarah shouldn't be saving Evie. She should be saving *me*.

'What should I do?' Sweat was coating my face. If this carried on, I'd look as though I'd been on a log flume ride.

Sarah slowed down, and I heard our front door open and close. 'I think you're going to have to—'

Don't say it, I silently begged.

'Tell Andy.'

A bead of sweat trickled down my back. I didn't want to tell Andy. Andy was my boss. One of the big Partners who pretty much ran the company. Telling him would be a last resort. I needed to try to fix it, or at least present him with a solution, not a problem. I paced the room, re-energised now that I had a plan. Well, not a plan exactly, but a plan to formulate a plan.

'Tell Andy now. Get it out of the way. He'll probably take it better than you think he will.' She paused. 'You haven't stolen any stationery from work, have you?'

'What?' I said irritably. 'Why would I steal stationery? The house is full of it.'

There was a clink down the phone that had mystified me for years, but that I now identified as Sarah pushing her glasses up. 'Probably best not to mention that.'

'I'm not mentioning anything to anyone.' I took an extra-large stride forward and somehow whacked my head on the ultra-trendy, ultra-pretentious arched floor lamp that some ultra-expensive designer had installed. Instead of being ultra-annoyed, though, I had a lightbulb moment. Caused by an actual lightbulb! I wasn't going to wait around for someone from the lost property department to get back to me, like one of the poor saps on the subs bench. No. I'd go to the lost property office. They couldn't fob me off if I was standing right in front of them. They'd have to get off their arses and get it for me. Genius.

'I'm going to go and pick it up,' I said to Sarah.

'How—' she started, but I hung up. There wasn't time to chat. I was on a mission. I was going to get my laptop back.

Chapter 5

Sarah

Mondays I worked from home. In theory I could be more productive without the distractions of the commute and other people around, but after my conversation with Will, I struggled to focus. There was a constant churning in my stomach, which I got whenever something wasn't quite right. Such as if I'd argued with Evie or Fred before school, then spent all day fretting that it'd damage their education or our relationship. Or if I'd had to jump in on a pitch when a member of my team floundered and I was worried it'd knock their confidence. Or when I'd polished off the chocolate Hobnobs and was waiting for Will to discover that I hadn't shared them with him.

Today's worry was how Will was getting on. Every time my phone went, I grabbed it as eagerly as if it were Giovanni Pernice asking if I'd be his partner on *Strictly Come Dancing*. But Will hadn't rung, so I'd had no choice but to carry on with my work as best I could and wait to hear.

Inevitably, the call came when I was on the loo. I answered it immediately, thankful it wasn't Giovanni, as I'd have had to risk a water infection by stopping mid-flow. Will had heard me peeing plenty of times, so didn't warrant such formalities.

'How did you get on?' I asked.

'More chance of the Holy Grail being handed in on a Friday night than a bag, apparently.' His voice was full of despair. He must be low not to realise he wasn't calling it a man bag. I wished I was with him and could give him a hug. 'I've registered it with the lost property manager at the train station and the police station,' he continued. 'They'll let me know if anything comes in, but said not to hold my breath. Bags that turn up have usually been emptied and chucked in bushes. Not many get handed in two days after they've been found.'

My stomach tightened. This didn't sound hopeful. But Will didn't need me to confirm what was obvious. He needed bolstering. 'They said *not many* get handed in. That means some do,' I said, more optimistically than I felt. 'Whoever found it might not have had time to take it in yet. Or no one was on duty when they went to the station. Or it was closed.'

Will didn't say anything, which was a worrying sign. Usually, he wouldn't hesitate in teasing me when I was desperately trying to come up with a positive slant in a dire situation. 'You can't polish a turd,' was one of his classic lines. Eventually, I banned him from saying it, so he switched to: 'You can't shine a shit,' which was worse, but it didn't stop me trying.

'Are you still there?' I asked softly.

'Yes.' His voice wobbled and my eyes welled up at his obvious distress.

'I'm going to have to tell Andy,' Will whispered.

I blinked back my tears and forced myself to sound upbeat. 'Yes, you are. But it'll be OK.' I recalled the list of positivity bullet points I'd made. 'You've won the company a lot of money over the years. You're professional, and have mentored and nurtured your team, bringing new talent into the company. You've got a good relationship with Andy, and he knows how hard you work and how dedicated you are to the company. Make sure you get that across.' I paused. 'Just don't mention stationery in any way.'

Will exhaled loudly. 'Wish I was at home, with my head on your lap and you stroking my hair.'

I shifted uncomfortably on the toilet seat. No need to

mention my exact location and spoil his illusion. 'Me too,' I said softly. 'Get back as quickly as you can so I can give you a huge hug.'

'Can't,' he sighed. 'I'll have to work late. Make up the time I missed this morning.'

'Well, go and get yourself a coffee, gather your thoughts, and then tell Andy. It'll all be OK.'

'You really think it will be?' Will said quietly.

'Yes.' I plastered a smile on my face so that he'd hear it in my voice. 'I really do.'

We said our goodbyes and I hung up, feeling as nervous and useless as I had on the children's first days at school. Because as much as I hoped it would be OK, I didn't know for sure it would be. And for all my optimism, one phrase kept burrowing through my façade of confidence. You can't shine a shit.

Chapter 6

Will

Sarah's reassuring words had their desired effect of calming me down while we were on the phone. But the moment she hung up, my fears and anxieties flooded back. I couldn't face a coffee, but took her advice of gathering my thoughts as I walked back to the office.

Blood pounded in my ears as I agonised over how best to tell Andy. What would his reaction be? He'd be pissed off with me, that was a given. With good cause. After all, it was me who'd left the bag on the train. Couldn't blame anyone but myself for that incompetence. Could I? I searched my mind, frantically trying to think if anyone else had been involved. No. It was definitely me.

When I reached the office, I considered going around the block a few times to delay the inevitable, but forced myself to man up and go in. The sooner I told Andy, the better. He wouldn't thank me for withholding this information. Not that I expected much of a thank you for delivering the news. A gift-wrapped hamper was definitely off the cards.

Nancy looked up when I approached her desk. 'You're back then,' she said, stifling a yawn. 'Do you want your messages?'

'Not yet.' I ran a hand back and forth over my head. 'Can you get me a meeting with Andy? It's kind of urgent.'

She looked mildly interested. 'Everything OK?'

'Couldn't be better.'

Nancy gave me a pitying look as she spoke to Andy's PA. If things 'couldn't be better' than a Monday morning at work then I was clearly a total loser. Which I was. A loser of laptops. My heart pounded.

Nancy put one hand over the receiver. 'Andy's got five minutes if you want to go in now.'

I nodded. Five minutes was enough. More than enough. Ideally, I'd stick my head around the door, blurt it out and leave. The verbal equivalent of sliding a note under the door. I walked slowly through the room, towards Andy's office, hoping to eat into as much of the time as possible, but still got there far too quickly.

Andy waved me in. 'Only got a few minutes, I'm afraid.' He tapped on his keyboard. 'What can I do for you?' I closed the door behind me and Andy stopped typing. 'What's up?'

I cringed. 'I've done something stupid.'

'O-K.' Andy sat back in his chair. 'Spill your guts.'

My stomach tightened, and for a moment I worried I was going to take him up on his kind offer and spill them all over his desk, but I managed to rein the nausea in.

'I left my bag on the train on Friday night after the conference,' I said quickly, as though the words wouldn't have as much significance if spoken at speed. 'And my work laptop was in the bag.' Andy's eyes widened. 'I've reported it to the police and the train station, and they'll let me know if it gets handed in. I suggest we disable it for now, and I'll work from a desktop until it turns up or I get a replacement.' I hoped that presenting a solution would soften the news, but Andy looked as softened as a door made from reinforced steel.

'You lost it on Friday? And it's taken until …' he checked his watch '… eleven o'clock on Monday for you to report it?'

I swallowed hard and nodded.

'Confidential client data has, potentially, been in someone else's hands for over forty-eight hours?'

'I thought Tom had it, but he'd got someone else's bag.' I shifted my weight from foot to foot, well aware of how

41

stupid and irresponsible I sounded. As though I was trying to pass the buck when the buck very much stopped with me.

Andy picked up a ballpoint pen and clicked it on and off a few times. 'You don't need me to tell you that this isn't good, Will.'

'No,' I mumbled.

'Not good at all.'

If he didn't need to tell me, why was he insisting on doing it twice?

Andy reached for his phone. 'Get me the Business Security Team,' he said to his PA.

I went cold. The Security Team were the equivalent of *Star Wars*' cohort of Sith Lords. It was very probably where Darth Vader et al. went to get trained up, before graduating to do the Dark Side's work of torturing, maiming and murdering anyone who mislaid their laptop.

'We need to assume that it's gone, potentially stolen,' Andy said while he waited to be connected. 'Not sure what the protocol is. Possibly inform our clients that there's been a breach of confidentiality. Formulate a plan as to how to compensate … What?' he snapped into the phone. 'Keep trying.' He tutted and hung up. 'Engaged.' Flopping back in his chair, he shook his head. 'I'll be honest, Will. This isn't—'

'It could still get handed in,' I interrupted, before he could tell me yet again that the situation wasn't good. I was well aware of that fact. If it were good, then I wouldn't be stood here, clenching my arse cheeks so tightly that not only could they crack nuts, they could reduce them to flour.

Andy gave a hollow laugh. 'Get real. No one's going to hand in a top-of-the-range laptop. Christmas has come early for them. More chance of one of Beckham's golden balls turning up in lost property.'

From the Holy Grail to David Beckham's nutsack. Nothing, it seemed, was as sacred as this laptop.

Andy must have noticed the look of despair on my face,

because he gestured to the seat opposite me. 'Will …' he started.

I nodded vigorously and sat down, desperately hoping he was about to say: 'These things always seem worse than they are,' or, 'Let's pretend this never happened,' or, 'Look what I've just found,' before pulling my laptop out of his top drawer. He didn't say anything else, though. Instead, he gave a tight smile and clicked his pen on and off repeatedly. I continued to nod, my vigour subsiding, until my head was bobbing gently in time to Andy's clicking. All we needed was an air guitar and we'd have a full-blown band.

We both jumped when Andy's phone rang. He grabbed the receiver so fast it almost slipped out of his hand.

'Thanks,' he said, then paused while waiting to be put through, studiously avoiding my gaze.

I put my head down and listened as he explained to Darth Sidious, or whoever he'd got through to in the Security Team, what had happened. There was a small hole in my suit trousers above the knee. It must have happened when I'd fallen over on the train on Friday night. Heat flooded my cheeks. I'd give anything to be back on that train now. Instead of tossing my bag onto the luggage rack, slumping into a seat and falling asleep, I'd stand the whole way and hold on to my bag so tightly it would have to be surgically removed on my deathbed.

'Will you inform HR or should I?' I heard Andy say.

My heart sank even further. HR's involvement took this to a whole other level. The HR Director, Clara, didn't suffer fools gladly. Sarah got on with her, but she always saw the best in everyone. 'You can't dislike someone called Clara,' she'd said once when I'd been having a moan. 'Think of *The Nutcracker*.' As if that would make me less wary. It was all right for Sarah. She didn't have any nuts that Clara could crack.

Andy hung up. I couldn't read his expression. Was it a sympathetic smile or a 'you're screwed' grimace?

'I need to tell HR.' He fiddled with his tie. 'I'll call Clara. Wait in your office till you hear from her.'

Definitely a 'you're screwed' grimace.

I nodded and stood up to leave.

'Will,' Andy called after me. I hesitated at the door. 'Don't use your desktop computer.'

'But I won't be able to work.'

Andy flushed and I realised that that was the point. They didn't want me anywhere near client data in case I sabotaged or copied it. I nodded and held a hand up to convey that I understood this was standard procedure and nothing personal. Andy smiled his appreciation and I took comfort from this. What a professional I was. Well, apart from compromising confidential client details, risking losing the trust of our customers and possibly being fined by the ICO for breach of data protection. Yep. A true pro.

When I reached my office, I asked Nancy to hold any calls and tell everyone I couldn't be disturbed for the rest of the morning. She didn't ask why. Either she respected me enough to accept my instructions without questioning them, or she just didn't give a toss.

In my office, I shut the door, slumped down in my chair and waited. So many times I'd sat at this desk, wishing I could pause time. That the phone would stop ringing or people would stop coming in, so I could tackle the mountain of emails that needed answering and get on with my work. Now that I had the silence I often craved, I missed being busy and overworked. I found a stray paperclip on my desk, bent it out of shape, felt guilty for rendering a perfectly useable paperclip useless, and tried to manipulate it back into shape, failing miserably. I tossed it into the wastepaper basket with a sigh and looked at the clock. Three minutes? Was that really all the time that had passed? How long was I going to have to wait to find out my fate?

Forty-eight minutes, it turned out. By which time I'd destroyed and failed to repair many more innocent paperclips. Just as I'd been reaching for the last one, the one that I was convinced I could restore to its former glory, Clara rang and asked me to come up and see her. Not in a seductive Mae West–type way. More a clipped, formal, I-have-a-nutcracker-and-I'm-not-afraid-to-use-it way.

Sweeping the paperclips into the bin, I smoothed my jacket down and made my way purposefully to the lift and up to the HR department. As purposefully as a man can when his testicles are quivering in fear.

'Hi Will.' Clara was sat at her desk. An A4 notepad and a row of coloured pens were lined up so neatly that they must have been arranged with a set square. 'Shut the door and take a seat.'

'Thanks.' I sat opposite her and crossed my legs to avoid any manspreading, which Sarah had told me could be viewed as a predatory sign of dominance. Although, I suspect she just wanted somewhere to put her coat on the train. My gonads squirmed in discomfort.

'You know why you're here.' Clara laced her fingers together and placed her hands on top of the notepad. 'By losing your laptop, you've compromised client data. The IT team have used cyber security to lock down the data. They've also done a search to find out what network the laptop's being used on. It doesn't look as though anyone's accessed it since Friday morning at the conference centre. Presumably that was you?'

I nodded. This was good news. Second best to the laptop being recovered was the knowledge that the client data was safe. It hadn't fallen into a competitor's hands or been shared with criminal organisations who would use it to do whatever it is that criminal organisations do with data – fraud, hacking, TV licence fee avoidance. And if these dastardly deeds had been thwarted, then this wasn't as bad as it could have been. Relief flooded through me. If I could just get some circulation back to my balls, I'd be laughing. I went to uncross my legs, but my knee nudged the desk and one of the pens rolled into its neighbour. Clara frowned and put it back into position. I recrossed my legs.

'So,' I said slowly. 'Does that mean everything's OK?'

Clara's frown didn't budge as her eyes travelled from the row of pens to me.

'Not OK,' I amended. 'I'm not trying to downplay losing the laptop. But if the data's not been compromised and the laptop's locked down ...' I trailed off, giving Clara the opportunity to jump in and confirm that this was no longer a Code Red situation. If indeed this had ever been a Code Red situation. The only time I'd come across one before was when the canteen had replaced the triple-chocolate brownies with apple turnovers in a bid to promote healthier eating.

Clara shook her head. 'It's not as simple as that. Just recently we explained to all employees, from Partners and Directors to junior-level staff, the importance of protecting our clients' confidential data. A Director was fired for breaching a number of protocols, including losing his laptop. All staff were informed that this behaviour would not be tolerated.'

A number of protocols? What else had Jasper been up to? Downloading porn maybe? Thankfully, my conscience was clear there. I'd never done that and never would. Not on the work laptop anyway.

Clara tapped her notepad. 'The main problem is that you didn't report the incident for forty-eight hours. If you'd called it in that night, or first thing Saturday morning, then you'd have done everything possible to limit the risk. The fact that you ignored it for two days goes against you.'

I nodded. Never mind that I'd thought Tom had it, the onus was on me to have checked. I deserved this bollocking. Speaking of which, my own were almost in a Code Red situation. Carefully, I unfolded my legs and resisted the urge to moan out loud with relief.

Clara's eyes flitted to the line of pens, which I hadn't disturbed this time, before carrying on. 'Your years of loyalty, knowledge and experience stand you in good stead, but we can't just ignore what's happened. What kind of example would that set?'

One of forgiveness and understanding, I wanted to say, but I let Clara finish without interrupting, determined to present myself as a model employee. Apart from the losing the laptop bit.

Clara cleared her throat. 'The usual course of action would be to suspend you on full pay pending an investigation.'

I jolted forward in the chair as though I'd just received an electric shock.

'Suspended?' My head spun. 'But it was a mistake.'

'Suspension is not a punishment.' Clara's voice sounded faint and tinny. 'Your pay and employment rights will still be in place. It's best if you're away from the office to avoid any compromise to the process. You'll be interviewed and may be invited to a formal hearing, once the investigation procedure's complete, to respond to the allegations.'

I gripped the arms of the chair to steady myself. This was scarily serious.

'You're welcome to bring a colleague or union representative to the hearing with you,' Clara added. 'Not Sarah, as she was with you on the train, so is technically a witness.'

Sarah was the only person I'd want in with me. Her or my mum, so they could hold my hand and tell me they loved me no matter what. Probably not what Clara had in mind.

'The investigation should only take a few days,' Clara continued. 'We won't make it any longer than is necessary.'

'And then I can come back to work?' I asked quietly.

'It depends on the outcome of the hearing. If it goes to a more formal disciplinary hearing—'

'A disciplinary?' I barked, my vocal cords restored to full volume.

'I appreciate that this is a lot to process.' Clara laced her fingers together. 'Is there anything you'd like to ask?'

'Why are you behaving like a monumental arsehole?' was on the tip of my tongue, but I doubted it'd help my case, so I used what Sarah had advised me to say instead.

'I've brought in a lot of business and made a lot of money for the firm,' I recited. 'Feels as though that counts for nothing after one mistake that's being dealt with.'

'We're down a top-of-the-range laptop,' Clara reminded me.

I held my hands up. 'Yes, but the client data protection side of things is safe and that's more important. And I'm very loyal. I've been headhunted and never followed it up.'

'That will be taken into consideration.' Clara stared at her notebook, then her eyes flitted up to mine. 'One of my concerns is how this could reflect on Sarah,' she said. 'Can't risk it jeopardising her career trajectory.'

I frowned. What was she talking about?

Clara smoothed her hair behind her ear. 'There is another way we could handle this matter.' She gave me a long, hard look. 'Are you willing to enter into a "without prejudice" conversation? That means that what we say is legally protected. Neither party can disclose what's been discussed.'

'I know what it means,' I snapped. I'd had no idea what it meant.

Clara raised her eyebrows, reminding me that I was not in a position to be arsey. 'And are you willing?'

I nodded. 'Yes. Sorry for being defensive.'

Clara relaxed her eyebrows. 'It's understandable. This is a lot to take in.' She looked me straight in the eyes. 'You should know that there's a strong possibility this will be viewed as gross misconduct and you will be dismissed.'

I gasped audibly. Dismissed? The word ricocheted around my head. I couldn't be dismissed. I just couldn't. We needed my salary. I needed my job. This wasn't in the career plan. It wasn't in any plan. Sarah organised our lives meticulously. If it wasn't on the calendar, it wasn't happening and she definitely hadn't scheduled this in. I wanted to object, but it was as though Clara's eyes were pinning me to the chair and I was unable to move.

'The process could take a long time and would be

humiliating for you, and for Sarah,' Clara continued. I shrank into my seat under her gaze. 'We could do it the long way with an investigation, possible disciplinary hearing, then a tribunal. Or we could take an alternative approach.'

I remained silent, still unable to move. Undeterred by my lack of participation, or perhaps thankful for it – the last time I'd objected with any severity about anything had been the apple turnovers, after all – Clara carried on.

'You're on a six months' notice period. If you agree to leave without objection, we could pay you half of that now and the balance in three months. Your Christmas bonus would be included as part of the package.'

I managed to break her gaze and put a hand to my head. This couldn't be happening. We'd gone from 'suspension isn't a punishment' to 'go quietly now and you'll get a goodie bag'.

'If you agree, you'll need to appoint yourself a solicitor, whom I'll liaise with,' Clara continued. 'We'll come up with a legally binding agreement, and buy you out of your employment and contractual terms. There'd be no future claims on either party.'

I blinked furiously. Her words kept flowing, but I couldn't compute them. They were coming at me too fast and were so alien to anything I'd expected to hear. But still she spoke.

'As part of the agreement, we'll draft up a reference that you're completely happy with. That reference will be legally binding.'

And there was the final sweetener. The assurance that I'd get a decent reference and could, therefore, get a decent job in the future. Provided I left now without a fuss.

But defending my position wasn't making a fuss. It was the natural thing to do. I gripped my knees. I would take it to a tribunal. Any judge would see it for what it was – a silly mistake. I hadn't thrown the laptop away or put it on a table in the middle of Trafalgar Square with a sign saying: HELP YOURSELF. I'd fight for justice. Hang the wankers out to dry and then … My thought process stumbled. And then what? Come back to work for a company that hadn't fought my corner or given me any support? Work alongside people who knew what had happened and would always have that in the back of their minds? Accept that I'd always be viewed as unreliable and never be offered the bigger, more exciting projects, and would always be passed over for promotion? What kind of an existence would that be? I'd be miserable.

'What are your initial thoughts?' Clara asked gently.

My shoulders slumped. I suddenly felt exhausted. 'Doesn't sound as though I have much choice,' I muttered.

'You definitely have a choice.' Clara smoothed her hair. 'I'm not trying to pressure you; I'm giving you the options.'

The options seemed to be fight or flight. Flight had always seemed like the wimp's way out. Much better to fight. Except that I was one man going up against a corporation. I didn't have the money or the belly for it. I was more of a lover than a fighter. A lover of pies, judging by said belly.

'You don't have to decide now,' Clara said. 'Go home, talk it over with Sarah. You two have even more to consider now. It should be a joint decision.'

Should it? Why? Yes, we made most decisions together, but the 'What takeaway shall we have tonight?' and 'Which TV series shall we fall asleep in front of tonight?' type. Not this. This was *my* decision and I'd sodding well make it myself.

'I'll do it.' I sat up tall and returned Clara's gaze. 'I'll take the package.'

Clara nodded. 'Forward me your solicitor's details and we'll go from there.' She gave me a small smile. 'I'm sorry it's come to this. I'm not unsympathetic to your situation but, ultimately, I'm here for the company.' She paused. 'It'll make the transition smoother for Sarah this way.'

Why did she keep going on about Sarah? Clara seemed more interested in talking about her than about me. Before I could question it, Clara hit me where it really hurt.

'I'm going to have to ask you to leave your work phone with me.'

I winced and my hand instinctively went to my trouser pocket where I kept it. Now I knew how Axel Foley felt in *Beverly Hills Cop* when told to hand in his badge and firearm. Hurt, misunderstood and humiliated. But I didn't have Eddie Murphy's balls, wit or scriptwriting team to get out of this with my head held high. After keeping my legs crossed for so long, I barely had any balls.

'Your calls will be redirected,' Clara added.

'Who to?' I clutched my phone through my pocket. I didn't know why this mattered, but somehow it did.

Clara shook her head. 'Don't know. That's Andy's decision. We'll let people know that you've had to take some time off for personal reasons. A family emergency perhaps.' She picked up one of her pens and tapped it against the notepad. 'Although that wouldn't explain why Sarah's still working. I'll ask her what she thinks is best.'

Never mind Sarah. What about what I thought was best? I wanted to grab Clara's precious pens and throw them across the room.

Clara held out her hand. 'Your phone. Sorry.'

Reluctantly, I slid it from my trouser pocket. It was warm from where it had been wedged against my groin and I took some small satisfaction from Clara's grimace, as I pressed it into her palm.

She put the phone in her top drawer, probably planning to disinfect it as soon as I left.

'I won't call someone to see you out. Leave by the back to avoid having to engage with anyone.' She stood and walked me to the door. 'Do you have any personal items in your office that you need?' Did my dignity count? 'I could get them sent to you, or Sarah can bring them home.' She mistook the tightening of my jaw as discomfort about the subject matter rather than the fact I was royally pissed off about Sarah getting more airtime than me, in my own sodding firing. 'I'll tell Nancy you've gone home because you're unwell,' Clara continued. 'We'll keep it as confidential as we can.' She shook my hand as I passed. 'I'll be in touch. Bye, Will.'

I walked numbly along the corridor towards the fire exit, my feet dragging along the carpet as I moved. This was bad. *Really* bad. It certainly put the apple turnovers into perspective. I reached the fire exit and leant my head against the door. I'd lost my job. I was unemployed. We'd be OK for six months, but then what? Sarah's salary wasn't enough for us to live on. My throat tightened and I fought back tears. I'd let my family down. I pushed the door open and hurried down the stairs, desperate to get out of the building. Once in the fresh air, I bent over, rested my hands on my knees and breathed deeply. How the hell was I going to tell Sarah?

Chapter 7

Sarah

On my way home. I'll explain when I see you.

I read Will's text message several times. Why was he coming home in the middle of the day? Had Andy suggested he came back to have a more thorough look for the laptop? It'd be futile, but perhaps Andy was letting Will buy himself some time until someone handed it in. Or perhaps Will hadn't told Andy, and was pulling a sickie until the laptop turned up. *If* it turned up. If I found a bag on the train, I'd take it straight to the station office, but not everyone was like me, as Will frequently told me. Not always as a compliment.

I rang him, but his phone went straight to voicemail, telling me he'd call back as soon as he could, without giving any hint of what was going on. I read his message again. That wasn't exactly dripping with clues either. Although, I realised – with a deduction usually reserved for guessing the killer in murder mysteries or the person responsible for not refilling the photocopier – Will had sent this message from his personal phone, not his work one.

I called his personal phone, but that too went to voicemail. Which it would if he was on the train, I told myself rationally. There was nothing to worry about. If it was bad, he'd have rung me. I needed to focus on my work until he got home and told me what was going on.

The Zoom ringtone came through on my computer.

Clara's name appeared on the screen and I eyed it warily as the ringtone pulsed in my ears. It'd be about the Director position. She'd probably have another go at persuading me to go for it, and I wasn't very good at saying no. It felt as though I was letting down the person who was asking. But, I reminded myself, I'd be letting Evie and Fred down if I took the job. Much as I liked and admired Clara, I liked my children more. Except when they had nits. On those occasions I'd choose Clara over them without hesitation.

I clicked Join and Clara's face appeared on my screen, her bob smoothed to perfection. My ponytail, I noticed in the tiny window on the side, was dishevelled after my unscheduled run to and from school with Evie's guitar.

'Hi Clara,' I said brightly, coiling my ponytail into a topknot to neaten it up. I could do this. Explain calmly why I couldn't apply, but that I was very flattered to have been asked.

'Hi.' The way Clara said it sounded like a question. As though we were on a game show and I'd asked if she wanted to bid high or low, and she wasn't confident about her decision. Perhaps she wasn't ringing to persuade me to apply for the job at all. I put my 'thanks, but no thanks' speech on hold in case the Partners had changed their minds.

'Have you spoken to Will?' she asked.

I hesitated, unsure whether to pretend I had or not. Clara might mention the job to Will in passing at some point and would know I'd lied if it was the first he'd heard of it. But I didn't want to admit that I was rejecting the offer without discussing it with my husband.

I nudged my glasses up. 'We have talked,' I said. It was true; we had. But probably not about what Clara thought. Sending the children to school in swim caps to prevent nits, yes. Applying for the Director position, no.

'We need to give a reason for his departure,' Clara said. 'I've told Nancy that he's gone home ill today, but obviously that's a very temporary excuse.'

My hair sprang out of its topknot.

'When someone leaves suddenly, I usually cite a family emergency,' Clara continued. 'But people will wonder why you're working, if that's the case.'

I went cold. Was Clara telling me that Will had been sacked? My throat tightened. That's why he was on his way home and why he hadn't used his work phone. He didn't have one anymore. He didn't work anymore.

'Or,' Clara said, as nonchalantly as if she were deliberating between rice or pasta for dinner, 'we could simply tell everyone that he's left. To spend time with his family perhaps.'

I gripped the edge of the desk. This couldn't be happening. Just because the company had said there'd be a zero-tolerance policy on work devices being mislaid didn't mean they had to go through with it. I told the children all the time that there would be zero tolerance for various misdemeanours, usually involving flatulence, but I forgave them if they promised not to do it again. The desk dug into my palm. Will wasn't a child, though. Promising he'd never, ever do it again, on his goldfish's life, wasn't enough to get him out of trouble. Especially as his superiors would be aware that goldfish only lived for about three weeks. I'd had to replace Ant and Dec so many times, I was single-handedly keeping the local pet shop in business.

'Sarah?' Clara asked.

I needed to pull myself together and present a professional front. I couldn't be seen as flaky. Not when we needed my job more than ever. I let go of the desk and released a shaky breath.

'Spending time with his family could work,' I said, hoping the quiver in my voice wasn't detectable.

Clara shook her head. 'Forgive me. I'm rushing this. We'll fob people off with a sickness bug for now and make a formal announcement next week, when you've given it some proper thought.' She gave me a sympathetic smile. 'How's Will? He looked quite shell-shocked earlier.'

Oh God, poor Will. He was going through this on his own. He'd had to leave the office, knowing he wouldn't be going back. Would he have been allowed to walk out, or would he have been escorted off the premises? So degrading.

'He's on his way home.' My throat was dry and I reached for a glass of water, but my hand was shaking too much to pick it up.

Clara nodded. 'What have you decided about the Director role?'

My mind went blank, which was ridiculous considering I'd thought about nothing else since Friday night. I'd even crafted a list of pros and cons for the job in my organiser.

'Sorry if this seems insensitive,' Clara said. 'But of course there are two positions available now. You wouldn't need to compete with Tom for the role. Not that it would have been much of a competition, as far as I'm concerned. You're far more experienced.'

I flinched. Two positions. Jasper's and Will's. Two Directors who were in secure, rewarding careers one minute, and unemployed the next, all because of one stupid, stupid mistake.

'I appreciate that it may put you in an awkward situation,' Clara continued. 'As you'd effectively be taking over Will's job.'

My hand flew to my mouth. Talk about rubbing salt into the wound. I'd be piling yet more humiliation on top of Will. And the gossips at work would have a field day. Will leaves work to spend time with his family, while his power-hungry wife throws herself into her career. That's if anyone bought the lie. Chances were everyone already knew he'd been sacked, even if they didn't know why. For all they knew, it could be because he'd launched a petition against the apple turnovers.

'Please seriously consider it,' Clara said. She began reiterating the merits of the job and why she thought I was perfect for the role.

I scanned my list as she spoke, ticking the pro points: job fulfilment; recognition; new challenges; no longer feeling resentful that my career was stagnating; more money. I drew a big star by the last point. If we were down to one salary, it needed to be a good one. Then I looked at the cons. School runs; school events; kids' clubs; the need for a cleaner and possibly a nanny; the ability to time-travel, be in two places at once or survive without sleep. I drew a line through each point. With Will at home, they were null and void. He'd be around for Evie and Fred, and would do the jobs involved with looking after them and running a household.

I reached the next point. More stress and longer hours. I already worked ridiculously long hours so that I could juggle work around time with Evie and Fred. I wouldn't need to do that if Will was taking care of that side of things. I could enjoy being a mum when I was with them, instead of nagging them to get dressed/undressed/at least put some pants on or conjuring up a healthy, nutritious meal that they'd actually eat. Nothing was more stressful than that. I crossed it off.

'The Partners want to move quickly on this,' Clara said. 'I don't want to pressure you, but I need a decision. How much time do you need to think about it?'

The wonky star I'd drawn by 'more money' stood out on the page. Above it was a row of ticks. Below, everything was crossed out. Seeing it in black and white like that, it was obvious. There was only one con that hadn't been addressed – 'less time with Evie and Fred'. I closed my organiser. I couldn't afford to be sentimental. I had no choice.

'I don't need any time,' I said firmly. 'I'll take it.'

Chapter 8

Will

I reached my front door and, in what was fast becoming a habit with doors, faced it with a sense of dread. Usually, I felt relieved or comforted when I got home. I could forget about the stresses of work for the evening or, better still, the weekend. This was my place of solace. My safe space. My calm port in a storm.

Actually, that was bollocks. There was nothing calm, solace-like or even safe about my house when Evie and Fred were overtired or had been at the Smarties. Even so, I was always glad to be home. Apart from today. Today I had to tell Sarah that I'd lost my job. That I'd failed in my role as provider for the family. That I was officially crap.

I stared at the key in my hand but couldn't bring myself to put it in the lock. I'd had the entire journey to work out how I was going to word it, but hadn't come up with anything that would explain or excuse what had happened. I toyed with the idea of doing what Tom Wilkinson's character in *The Full Monty* had done – pretend to go to work every day and sneak down the Jobcentre instead. As Sarah worked with me, keeping a veil over any sort of double life would be tricky. Trickier still would be the dancing-naked-on-stage part of the story. I'd want more than a veil there.

The front door opened. Sarah stood with her phone in her hand, no doubt open on the Find My Friends app. I hated that she could track my whereabouts at all times. It was too

Big Brother for me, or Watchful Wife, but I couldn't delete the app, as it'd seem like I was covering up an affair. And it *had* come in handy the time I'd fallen asleep on the train and woken up in the sidings at Peterborough station. I cringed at the memory. Why hadn't I learnt my lesson? I wouldn't be out of a job if I'd used that experience as a wake-up call and actually stayed awake. I was such a monumental dick. And now my whole family was going to suffer because of it.

'Come in,' Sarah said, taking my hand.

As soon as she closed the door, she wrapped her arms tightly around me. She gave the best hugs. All enveloping and full of love. Tears filled my eyes. I willed them to sod off. I needed to tell Sarah what had happened and couldn't do that if I was bawling like a baby.

'Clara called,' Sarah said softly. 'I'm so sorry.'

My body sagged and I held on to her tightly. She knew. And she wasn't shouting or smashing plates or kicking me out. Relief flooded through me and a muffled wail/snort/random-noise-that-I-hoped-we'd-never-speak-of escaped me. I buried my head into her shoulder and openly sobbed.

'It's OK, baby,' Sarah murmured, in the same way she comforted the children when they'd hurt themselves or had a bad dream or wandered into the bathroom when I was towelling myself dry. 'It's OK.'

I shook my head. 'It's not,' I croaked into her shoulder. 'I've lost my job and it's all my fault.'

'It's not—' Sarah paused, presumably wanting to be supportive, but unable to avoid the glaring truth that, yes, it was totally my fault. 'The end of the world,' she said kindly instead. 'It's only a job. Plenty more of them out there.' She gave me another tight squeeze, then relaxed her grip. Disappointment coursed through me. I didn't want the hug to end. Didn't want her to scurry back to the study and resume her work, because where would that leave me? I couldn't lie on the sofa, crying and watching TV all day. There was never anything decent on in the daytime. Not even *Neighbours* anymore, although that hadn't been the same since Kylie left. I fought back more tears.

Sarah placed a palm on each side of my face. 'Don't worry,' she whispered. 'We and the children are OK. That's what matters; not stupid work.' She kissed my cheeks, wiping away the tears, before placing her lips on mine. I was too stunned to respond straightaway. I'd expected her to be angry or disappointed or worried. Not randy. Sarah kissed me more firmly and this time I acted on it, pulling her close and kissing her back.

'Shall we go upstairs?' Sarah murmured.

Nodding, I reached down to scoop her up and carry her up the stairs, felt a twinge in my lower back, and took her hand instead. Not as grand a gesture, but the last thing I needed was an injury. Clara hadn't mentioned my health insurance, but that was bound to be cancelled with immediate effect.

My back held out during what ended up being a rather passionate shag. The pent-up fear, followed by a swelling of love for Sarah's understanding and compassion, channelled themselves into a mutually satisfying performance.

Afterwards, I smiled down at my beautiful, loving, caring wife. 'How did I get so lucky to land you?' I murmured into her hair.

'Beats me.' She giggled and snuggled closer.

I kissed the top of her head. 'Maybe six months' gardening leave won't be so bad after all. Not if we get to do this on a regular basis. Can't beat a bit of *afternoon delight*.' I sang the last two words and chuckled to myself at the memory of Will Ferrell's rendition of the song in *Anchorman*, one of the finest films of all time.

'They've given you six months' gardening leave?' Sarah asked.

'On full pay. And I get my Christmas bonus. That'll take the pressure off while I put my CV together and see what's out there. Although I can't work for those six months.' I hummed the song 'Afternoon Delight', trying to remember the lyrics. I clearly needed to watch the film again. I had time now, I supposed.

'That's amazing.' Sarah propped herself up onto one elbow. 'I assumed your salary would stop straightaway.'

And still she'd been more concerned with how I was. She was an incredible woman.

I nodded. 'I get to approve the reference, too. It was all part of the deal.'

Sarah frowned. 'What deal?'

OK, Clara hadn't told her the full story, just that I was no longer with the company.

'We had an "off the record" chat,' I explained. 'They were going to suspend me while they investigated it. Clara said I'd probably be dismissed, which I could dispute but would take ages, or agree to leave quietly. I thought that was the best thing to do.'

Sarah's mouth dropped open.

'I know I should have discussed it with you,' I said quickly. 'It all happened so fast and—'

'No, no, I understand,' Sarah said, equally quickly. 'Sometimes you have to make a snap decision.'

I smiled at her, blown away with love. Even in the face of adversity, she was calm, kind, understanding and up for a shag. I really had lucked out with her. 'Clara said it'd be better for you too,' I added. 'An investigation could reflect badly on you.'

Sarah nudged the side of her glasses up, but wasn't wearing any and almost poked herself in the eye. She really was adorable.

'Did Clara say anything else about me?'

'No.' I began singing the chorus of 'Afternoon Delight'.

'The thing is …' Sarah placed a hand on mine.

What were the other words?

'I wasn't going to say anything. There didn't seem to be any point when I didn't think I could do it.'

I picked up Sarah's hand and extended her arm, holding it

across my chest and strumming it as though it were a guitar. She was saying something about Two Direction. I stifled a laugh. The band was *One* Direction and, as far as I knew, they'd never covered 'Afternoon Delight'.

'It's like what happened with you,' she continued. 'I had to make a snap decision. So, I said yes.' Sarah took a deep breath. 'I hope that's OK.'

'Course,' I said with a smile, giving her her arm back. Whatever she did was OK with me.

'Thank you.' Sarah put her hand to her chest. 'That's such a relief. Some men would think it emasculated them somehow, when of course it doesn't. It's the logical thing to do.'

Shit, what had I agreed to? Please don't say she'd bought tickets to a One Direction reunion and expected me to go.

'I know it'll take a bit of getting used to for all of us, but that happens in life, doesn't it? We take on new challenges and adapt to them.' Sarah snuggled into me. 'The important thing is we still have a good salary coming into the house, and one of us is around for Evie and Fred. I'll miss being so involved, but they'll love having you around.'

OK, seriously, what was she talking about?

'In fact, we'll have two good salaries for the first six months, thanks to your clever negotiations.'

Sarah's cheeks were flushed and her eyes bright. She didn't look like someone who'd just learnt that her husband had lost his job. She looked like someone who'd just won the lottery.

'What do you mean two good salaries?' I asked.

'Two Director-level salaries.' Sarah's smile widened. 'That's what I've been saying. I'm a Director now.'

Chapter 9

Sarah

Will couldn't have looked more horrified if I'd told him that Evie and Fred weren't his.

'You're a Director?' He pushed me away, jumped out of bed and pulled on his boxers with a speed usually reserved for doing the same three actions in reverse. 'Since when?'

'Since about an hour ago.' I pulled the duvet up and reached for my glasses on the bedside table. 'That's why Clara rang.'

'She rang and offered you the job out of the blue?'

I instantly regretted putting my glasses on, as Will looked even more annoyed in sharp focus. 'No. She asked me to apply for the role on Friday, at the conference.'

Will picked up his suit trousers from the floor. 'Why didn't you tell me then?'

It felt churlish to remind him that we hadn't been talking after the conference. 'I told her I couldn't do it,' I said instead. 'There's no way we could both work those hours. But now …' I winced, feeling horrible for voicing it out loud. 'Now I can, as you'll be at home.'

'No, I won't. I'll be job-hunting.'

'Yes, but you'll be doing that from home,' I said. 'Online and through recruitment firms. You won't be out, physically hunting.'

Will looked momentarily disappointed, as though he'd genuinely thought he'd be embracing his inner caveman and heading off each morning with a spear in his hand. I knelt up, making sure the duvet was securely tucked around me. After twelve years together, I was more than comfortable being naked in front of Will, but having a conversation of this magnitude while topless – and bottomless, for that matter – didn't feel appropriate.

'What happens in six months when I'm able to work again?' Will glared at me. 'How will you do the Director job then?'

'I don't know. It's just happened. I haven't planned—'

'Bullshit,' Will snapped. 'There's always a plan.'

It was usually true. Planning everything meticulously was the only way to keep on top of my hectic life and retain some sanity. I even factored in an extra five minutes for every activity involving the children, as you could guarantee someone would need a poo at the exact moment we were due to leave. Sometimes that someone was Will.

I nudged my glasses up. 'I honestly haven't thought that far ahead. But it makes sense for me to take the role and have a guaranteed wage coming in. Who knows what the future holds. We need that security.'

'Thanks for the vote of confidence.' Will scrunched up the trousers in his hands.

I shook my head. 'I don't mean you won't get a good job, but there's no guarantee it'll happen straightaway. Or you might decide to do something different and retrain.'

'Retrain?' Will gave a hollow laugh. 'I'm forty-six. I can't go back to college. I'd be older than the teacher.'

'That's just an example.' I looked desperately around the room, searching for something I could use to soften the blow of my new role. A photo of the four of us sat on my bedside table. 'You might enjoy being at home with Evie and Fred so much that you want longer off. My Director's salary would give you the freedom to do that.'

'Great. I'll be a stay-at-home dad while you're out living the high life.' He threw his trousers across the room. They landed on the chest of drawers, then slid down the back. 'Won't be needing those anymore.' He strode across the room and yanked open the door to my half of the wardrobe. 'Got an apron I can wear?'

My patience dissolved. 'Stop being such a sexist pig. What's wrong with the man being at home with the children while the woman works? Lots of couples do it now.'

Will slammed the wardrobe door. 'There's nothing wrong with it. It's just not me.'

'Grow up,' I snapped. 'We're lucky we still have money coming in. What would we do if we had nothing to live on?' I climbed out of bed to face him. Not an easy task while dragging a king-size duvet with me. 'We all have to do things we don't want to sometimes. I didn't particularly want to put my career on hold while I raised our children, but I did it for the good of the family and because I knew we were lucky to have them.' The duvet slipped down, revealing my breasts. Will didn't even glance at them, so I knew he was angry. But so was I. So much so that I'd have slapped him if he'd taken a sneaky peek. I couldn't believe he was being so condescending and bigoted. I thought I'd married a modern man. Although he never had warmed to sourdough bread, so that should have been a warning.

I gave up on the duvet and grabbed my dressing gown from the back of the door. 'It was OK for you to do the job you wanted, while I sorted everything out at home and with the children.' I watched Will's expression, as I fumbled with the belt. He was staring stony-faced out of the window, as though being told off by his mum. 'In fact, I'm still doing everything, even though I work full-time. It's about time you helped out. It's only for six months, until your gardening leave ends and you get another job.'

'You took it without asking me,' he said sulkily.

'Yes.' I pulled the dressing gown so tightly around me, it was a wonder I didn't perforate an internal organ. 'Just like you didn't ask me when you accepted your promotion to Director. You've never acknowledged that I'd probably have got that promotion if I hadn't gone part-time after maternity leave.'

'Thought you wanted to be with them. You've always made a big deal about how important it is to have a parent around.' He looked triumphant, as though this point nullified everything I'd said. It was certainly on the verge of nullifying my wedding vows.

I clenched my fists. 'It *is* important.' My words came out in short, sharp breaths. 'That's why I told Clara I couldn't apply for the job when she asked me on Friday. And that's why I told her today that I could take it. Because you're going to be at home now. Ergo, they still have a parent around for them.' I'd never used the word ergo before in my life. But I'd also never before wanted to stamp my feet and scream at Will that he had no right to complain, as this was all his own stupid fault for losing his laptop and, ergo, his job.

Will's eyes narrowed. 'Wait – Clara asked you to apply on Friday, but offered it to you today? Why don't you have to apply now?'

'Because there was only Jasper's Director job going on Friday, but two of us were eligible,' I snapped. 'Now there's—' I stopped short.

Will's jaw clenched. 'Now there's …'

I shook my head. I couldn't say it. I was furious, but I didn't want to be cruel.

'Now there's my job going, too,' Will said quietly. 'You've got *my* job.' This discovery was possibly worse than finding out Evie and Fred weren't his. This was akin to me telling him they'd been sired by Arsène Wenger.

'No.' I took a step towards him. 'Clara said Jasper's was probably mine, if I'd gone for it.'

Will opened his side of the wardrobe and pulled out jeans and a sweatshirt. 'It's my job and you know it.' His voice was cold, as he pulled his clothes on.

'It's not like that,' I said.

'It's exactly like that.' Will strode out of the room. His feet hammered down the stairs, then the front door slammed shut. I sank down onto the edge of the bed. I didn't know where he'd gone, when he'd be back or what he was going to say. And I had no idea what I was going to say either.

Chapter 10

Will

'Pint of Black Sheep, please.'

I fumed silently as I waited for my drink. Sarah had taken my job. *My* job. And she expected me to look after the kids and clean the house and do all the crappy jobs that she made endless lists of – check the washing-machine filter, descale the kettle, deadhead the flowers in the window box. She could fuck off if she thought I was doing any of that shit.

I took a seat at the end of the bar. The pub was practically empty. Not surprising, considering it was early afternoon on a Monday. I stared into my pint. How could Sarah do this? My getting fired was bad enough, but for her to step straight into my office, before my seat was even cold, was brutal. She must know how humiliating this was for me. What would everyone think? I was a Director. I wouldn't just disappear. No one would buy the story that I was taking some time out to be with my family, without a handover period and a leaving do. I'd be a laughing stock, especially with my wife now doing my job. They wouldn't even need to change the surname on the door.

I downed half my beer, put it down, then picked it up again and downed the other half. Fuck it. I had nothing else to do. Might as well get pissed.

I was well into another beer when Howard, the landlord, leant over the bar. 'You're not usually in at this time ...' He faltered, searching for my name.

'Will,' I said. I'd told him numerous times over the years, but he never remembered.

'Will, that's it.' Howard tugged his beard. 'None of my business, and you can tell me to get lost if you want, but are you all right?'

I took a long sip of my beer while I contemplated how to tell him to get lost without the risk he'd spit in my next drink.

'A problem shared is a problem halved, mate.' He'd forgotten my name already.

I stiffened. 'What makes you think I've got a problem?'

'You're on your third pint and you've only been here ten minutes.'

I put my glass down. Had it really only been ten minutes? How was I going to get through each day if they lasted this long? Sod it, I thought, and told him. A tailored version obviously, so he didn't write me off as a complete laptop-losing twat, then sat back to receive his condolences or, ideally, a free pint.

Howard grinned. 'You lucky sod.'

I would have spat my beer out, but that might have lessened the chances of a free pint. 'Lucky?' I spluttered. 'In what way?'

'Six months' paid leave. Six months with no pressure to find another job. Hell, you're not *allowed* to get a job for six months.' Howard slapped the bar. 'People would kill to be in your shoes. So what if you have to take the kids to school and pick them up? They're there all day, every day. You have all that time to do whatever you want. It's a gift.'

I still wasn't convinced. 'Everyone at work's going to think I'm a loser.'

'So? You're not going to see them again.'

'My wife will.'

Howard shrugged. 'They're not going to say it to her face, even if they think it.' He batted the air with his hand. 'Forget them. They're in the past. Think about the now. The now that is yours to seize and do with what you will.'

I ran a hand across my head. The way Howard described

it, I'd not only won the lottery, but each crisp banknote was going to be personally signed by the monarch and hand-delivered by The Pussycat Dolls.

'Know what I'd do if I had all that time?' Howard asked.

As Howard had a copy of *Playboy* tucked behind the bar, I wasn't sure I wanted to know.

'Go on,' I said, with trepidation.

'Rewatch all eighty-six episodes of *The Sopranos* back to back.'

That wasn't a bad idea.

Someone shuffled to the other end of the bar. Howard nodded to him and slapped me on the arm. 'Stay positive, mate. Catch up with you later.'

'Thanks, mate,' I said. 'Appreciate it.'

Howard wandered off to chat to the other saddo and I stared into my half-empty pint. Or was it half-full? Howard certainly thought so. Although, by the sound of the conversation he was now having, he also thought squirrels could be trained to drive a tractor.

Maybe I'd been looking at this all wrong and it was a great opportunity. It wasn't as if I loved my job. I liked the projects and the people, but the company wasn't the kind I dreamt of working for. Every tiny step of the process had to be approved and signed off. We were even interviewed by HR if we were off ill. I understood that they didn't want people throwing a sickie every time they were hungover or wanted to watch the Test cricket, but it had been rather humiliating to be asked by Clara for a detailed description of my ailments the time I was off with the squits.

A fresh start with a new company could be what I needed. But I didn't have to think about that yet. For the first time since I was a student, I'd have time for myself. And time for Evie and Fred. I pictured their faces lighting up when they saw me at the school gates. Their eager smiles as they ran across the playground. Their excited squeals as I picked them up and spun them around. They'd tell me about their day while we walked home, then we'd sit in front of a roaring fire and recreate the Spurs Stadium in Lego bricks.

This would be OK. Abandoning my half-full pint, I got up, eager to get back to Sarah and apologise for losing my temper. None of this was her fault. She hadn't engineered my downfall to seize my job. I could see now that she'd had no option but to accept it. The new arrangement would take some getting used to, but we'd make it work. After all, how hard could it be?

Chapter 11

Sarah

I checked my makeup in the hall mirror. Too much eyeliner? My hands were so shaky, I couldn't control the brush, and the discreet upper-lid line I'd tried to apply had morphed from a subtle feline flick into a shape that wouldn't look out of place onstage in *The Lion King*.

I didn't have time to take it off and start again, though.

In the kitchen, Evie and Fred were decimating bowls of cereal while Will scrolled through his phone, an espresso in his hand. How had he found time to make himself an espresso? If I wanted a drink in the morning, I had to slurp the leftover milk from the children's breakfast bowls. I was always unloading the dishwasher, or transferring washing from the machine to the dryer, or emptying bins, or filling water bottles – all while getting myself ready for work. I'd done the school run in my slippers so often that the other mums must have thought it was a fashion statement and once, when Fred was a toddler, had accidentally put a soiled nappy in Evie's PE bag. Apparently, the teacher, Miss Boast, discovered it when plunging her hand into the bag to find Evie's trainers, which were of course in the wastepaper basket in the bathroom. Miss Boast hadn't spoken to me since.

I smelt the flower and blew out the candle. I had no right to be resentful of Will's espresso. Not when he was being so understanding and lovely about my job. I hadn't expected him to come around so quickly – if at all. After he'd walked out the day before, I'd come up with a list of fun projects to make his gardening leave more appealing: training for a half-marathon; learning a language; inventing an app; taking guitar lessons. He took umbrage to this last one, as he could already play the guitar. True, but in the same way I could poach an egg – you can kind of tell what it's meant to be, but you wouldn't necessarily want to be in the same room. It turned out he already had a project, though. To watch all eighty-six episodes of *The Sopranos*. I'd have preferred a show that wasn't shot in a lap-dancing bar, but if it got us through this transition period, then so be it.

Will glanced up from his phone. 'You look nice.'

'Thanks.' Could I admit how nervous I felt or would that be rubbing salt into the wound?

'Have you got a new job?' Evie asked.

'Not really. It's no big deal.' I shot a furtive look at Will, but his attention was back on his phone.

Evie looked at me thoughtfully. 'You look like a model.'

I eyed her sceptically, but she gave me such a genuine smile that I felt a swell of love for her. I smoothed my dress. 'A model?'

Evie nodded. 'An old lady one, obviously.'

Obviously.

I looked at my watch. 'Right, teeth clean, then let's go.' I was going to school with them today to show Will the ropes, but as of tomorrow, I'd be on a train or at work by now. I'd miss this, I thought sadly.

I helped Fred do his teeth. As always, I had to pin him down to do them, while he wriggled away. Evie did her own, but managed to spit toothpaste down both her uniform and my dress. There were elements I wouldn't miss.

Evie and Fred clearly loved having Will on the walk to school, both insisting on holding his hand. The pavement wasn't wide enough for all four of us, so I was forced to

73

walk behind, lugging the bags, like the hired help, while they skipped along. Even Will skipped. Must have been a double espresso.

A lump formed in my throat when we got to the playground. This was the last time I'd be taking them to school. I'd been hoping for a loving and meaningful farewell, one that I could store in my memory bank to fondly reflect on. But they must have sensed I was going to embarrass them by showing some affection and were off without a backward glance as soon as they saw their friends.

Blinking hard, I turned to Will. 'Let me introduce you to their teachers properly. Just to warn you, Miss Boast comes across as nice at parents' evening and sports day, but she's a right cow.'

Will shoved his hands in his coat pockets. 'Do I have to?'

'Yes. You're the first point of contact now.'

Sighing, he followed me across the playground, weaving his way through children charging around as though they'd had double espressos for breakfast, too.

Miss Boast was talking to a group of Reception children, including Fred.

He jumped up and down with excitement when he saw Will. 'Miss Boast, this is my daddy.'

Miss Boast, who had given me the evil eye for the past two years, since the soiled-nappy incident, tossed back her long, chestnut hair and gave Will a radiant smile. He perked up immediately.

'Of course, I remember from when Evie was in my class. Lovely to see you again,' she said, turning and blocking me out.

'And you. Please, call me Will.' Will extended his hand and Miss Boast grasped it with her own.

'I will, Will,' Miss Boast giggled. Will laughed heartily, as though it were the first time this hilarious play on words had ever been used. In reality, he'd heard it so often, he had to physically stop himself punching the person who'd said it. On occasion, I'd had to stop him. 'Call me Fran,' she simpered. Simpered! 'Not in front of the kids, though,' she added, with a wink. A wink! And what did she mean, 'not in front of the kids'? When else would they be having a conversation?

Coughing loudly, I stepped around Miss Boast (I would not be calling her Fran – and not because I hadn't been invited to, although that detail hadn't passed by unnoticed) and slipped my arm through Will's.

'Fred's dad's going to be doing the school drop-offs and pick-ups from now on,' I said.

Miss Boast beamed at Will. Beamed! 'Fantastic. It's great to see dads involved with their children.'

My jaw tightened. I'd been involved with my children since they were born and never got a 'fantastic'.

'Parents are invited to read with their children for the first twenty minutes of each day, if you'd like to join us?' Miss Boast said. 'Fred's mum rarely stays, and I worry he's missing out. Research proves that it furthers their development and mental health.'

Fred's mum – aka me, the woman standing right there – bristled at the insinuation that Fred's educational and emotional growth would be stunted because I selfishly worked. 'I come in twice a week,' I interjected.

'I'm sure Fred would love it if you could,' Miss Boast said to Will, completely ignoring me.

'Count me in.' Will smiled.

He wouldn't be for long. Sitting cross-legged on a carpet that had been weed and thrown up on more times than a stag party's shared bathroom, phonetically reading a book about a dog and a ball every single day would wipe that smile straight off.

'And there's the PTA,' Miss Boast said. 'It'd be great to get some testosterone in the committee.' She smiled innocently, but I was pretty sure 'the committee' was code for her fanny.

'I'd better introduce you to Evie's teacher, Mrs Fisher,' I said, tugging Will's arm.

Mrs Fisher was a level-headed, middle-aged woman, whom I was confident wouldn't flirt outrageously with my husband. Not only because it was unprofessional, but because she'd never been elbow-high in a shitty nappy as a result of my mistake.

Before I could drag Will away, the bell rang and all the children swarmed towards us, ready to stand in line to go into school.

'You may as well come in with me.' Miss Boast slipped her own arm through Will's and led him away from me. How brazen could someone be? I half expected her to give me a side-eye, but that would have meant acknowledging me, which was clearly beneath her.

'Bye, then,' I called after them.

Will mouthed, 'Back in a sec,' to Miss Boast and jogged over to me. 'Hope today goes well.'

'Thanks.' I looked around for Evie and Fred, but they were far too occupied with their friends to notice me. A lump formed in my throat. This was it. The last day I'd be taking them to school. And they didn't care. I turned back to Will. 'Don't forget to pick them up at three thirty. Evie's got ballet at five. Tonya's taking her tonight, so you don't need to worry about that, but she needs help with her leotard.'

'We're going in, Will,' Miss Boast called.

'There's some leftover macaroni cheese in the fridge for their tea,' I babbled. 'Put Fred's veg on a separate plate or he won't eat it.'

'Come on, Daddy,' Fred called. Miss Boast probably put him up to it.

Will gave me a quick kiss. 'Got it. See you later.' He hurried back to join Fred and bloody Miss Boast, and they walked into school without a backward glance.

Tears pricked my eyes, as I walked towards the station. I blinked hard. I would not cry. Career-driven Directors didn't cry. Nor did anyone wearing this amount of eyeliner, unless they wanted to resemble an Alice Cooper tribute act. But it was hard, so much harder than I thought it'd be, handing over all responsibility to Will and turning off that primitive, protective, only-I-can-do-this-properly maternal drive. Had Will even listened when I told him about pick-up time and ballet and Fred's vegetable OCD? At least Tonya would be coming over. She'd help if he was struggling. But she wouldn't be coming over most evenings. It was lucky timing that she had a night off. What would happen to the children on the days she wasn't around?

I stopped walking and sank down onto a bench. What was I doing? I'd had the perfect balance before. Why was I messing it all up for my career, when my children were so much more important?

I smelt the flower and blew out the candle, but it didn't help, and I didn't have the time or inclination to do it another nineteen times until it did. I FaceTimed Tonya instead.

'I've made a mistake,' I said when she picked up. 'I shouldn't be abandoning the children for a stupid job.'

Tonya shook her head. 'Leaving them with their dad is not abandoning them. And it's not a stupid job. It's the job you deserve and should be doing.'

I nodded. The rational part of me knew they wouldn't have offered me the job if they didn't think I could do it and, although nervous, I was excited about the role. I was more nervous about how Will and the children would get on.

I nudged my glasses up. 'Will's never had to do the day-to-day minutiae before. Suppose he forgets to pick them up?'

'The school will ring him.'

I gulped. That prospect was far more terrifying than anything the Director role could throw at me. Mrs Manning would probably throw the children.

Tonya indulged me. 'Want me to go with him to pick them up?'

'Yes, please.'

'OK.' Tonya pointed at me, then to the side of the screen. 'Now go. You've got this. Girl power!'

'Thank you. You're the best.' I blew her a kiss, feeling much better. Tonya was right. I had this. And now that I didn't have to worry about Will forgetting to pick Evie and Fred up, I could focus on work today. I'd worry about all the other days tomorrow.

Chapter 12

Will

'Did you know that reading for twenty minutes a day improves a child's vocabulary by two million words a year?' I asked Tonya, as we walked to school. 'Developed vocabulary leads to better job opportunities, better reasoning skills and improved mental health.'

'Thought you were taking the kids to school, not going there yourself,' Tonya said.

'Ha ha.' I'd learnt more that morning from Fran – Miss Boast – than I had in years. 'I just think it's cool that a little commitment from a parent can make such an impact.'

I pushed my hands deep into my pockets. It was only early November, but it was already cold. I didn't pay much attention to the weather in London. Probably because I usually had a coffee to keep my hands warm, or I was thinking about work or enjoying the buzz of the city. I didn't have those distractions in our home town of Huntonbrook, in Hertfordshire. Not only was there no work for me to think about, but the little buzz that the town had once enjoyed was now virtually non-existent due to the unfortunate decline of the bumblebee. As for a warming coffee, carrying the PE kits, school bags, musical instruments and water bottles was hazardous enough without adding a scalding beverage to the mix.

Tonya nudged me with her shoulder. 'I'm only teasing. Well done for getting involved. I'm proud of you, bro.'

I nudged her back. 'Thanks.' I thought back to the joy on Fred's face when I'd perched on the tiny seat next to him. Admittedly, there hadn't been much joy on my face after twenty minutes of having the edge of a hard plastic chair wedged up my arse crack, but it was worth it to make him happy and get him up to two million words a year. 'I'm a bit pissed off with Sarah, to be honest,' I said.

'What? Because she's taken the Director's job?' Tonya's eyes narrowed.

I held my hands up. 'No. Because she didn't do the reading every day. It's so important for their development.' I thrust my hands back in my pockets. It really was cold.

'Sarah had to get to work,' Tonya snapped. 'She didn't have the luxury of a day with nothing to do, like you do. Don't go getting all sanctimonious and judgey after one reading session.'

That was the trouble with my sister being my wife's best friend. She was always going to take her side. There was no point arguing, even though I thought Sarah should have found a way around it.

'Don't forget that Sarah's done everything for the kids while working,' Tonya added, as though reading my mind. 'She takes parenting very seriously. If she could have read every day, she would have. You know how thoughtful she is.'

It was true. Sarah was unbelievably thoughtful. Not just with the kids, but with me too. All those little gestures she did to make me feel special. The notes hidden in my case when I went away. The cinnamon swirls bought from my favourite bakery, even though it was the other side of town. Asking how she could help, when I was busy or stressed or tired. Pretending to recognise the tune I played on my guitar. She really was a keeper.

We reached the school and waited in the playground with the other adults. They were almost all women, huddled together in groups, chatting away. So much for Sarah's claim that stay-at-home dads weren't that unusual. As I scanned the playground, my eyes met those of a woman. I'd noticed her that morning in Fred's class, reading with her own son. Petite and willowy, with a sheet of poker-straight, glossy, black hair and beautiful dark eyes, she was hard not to notice. Two million words weren't needed to describe her. One would do: Fit. With a capital F.

Fit Woman waved. I gasped. Was she waving at me? I considered waving back, but then had a swift reality check. I was happily married, and even if I wasn't, the likelihood of a woman like that waving at me was zero. Which was fine, because I was, as I had just reminded myself, married.

'Fred's teacher doesn't know what she's talking about.' Tonya held her phone up, oblivious to the waving. 'According to Google, there are a total of three-quarters of a million words in the English language.'

'What?' I pretended to look at Tonya's phone, rather than across the playground to see if Fit Woman was still not waving at me.

'So it's not possible to learn two million new words a year. They don't exist.' Tonya studied my face. 'Are you OK? You look a bit, I don't know, dewy.'

I shrugged. 'Bit warm, that's all.'

Before Tonya could point out that it was freezing, the school doors opened. Within seconds, the playground was filled with children, charging about as though they'd just been released after years of captivity. Somehow Evie and Fred found us among the mayhem.

'You're here,' they cried, throwing their arms around me.

'Said I would be.' I hugged them back. Why did parents moan about the school run? This was magical.

Evie and Fred chatted all the way home about what they'd eaten and who they'd played with. What they'd been taught didn't feature. Who could blame them? They had a lifetime ahead of them, before their working day would absorb their every waking moment. Unless they took after their dad, lost their jobs and then didn't have to think about work for six months. Always good to aim high.

Back home, once the kids were settled in front of CBeebies with a bowl of carrot and cucumber batons that Sarah had left in the fridge for them, Tonya and I sat at the kitchen table with a coffee.

'How's your first day been?' Tonya asked.

'Surprisingly good.' I ran a hand over my head. 'Yesterday it seemed like the worst thing that could ever have happened. Worse even than when Sol Campbell moved to Arsenal.' I ignored Tonya's eye roll. She had no idea how much that had hurt. 'But I've enjoyed it. It's nice to be a part of the kids' everyday lives.'

'Good for you.' Tonya took a sip of her coffee. 'What have you done all day?'

I was rather proud of what I'd accomplished. 'Managed to get through most of *The World's Strongest Man*. Been wanting to watch it for months, but never had time.'

Tonya's eyes flickered. Either she had something stuck in them or she was stifling another eye roll. 'Productive as that is,' she said, 'shouldn't you be looking for a job?'

I shrugged. 'No point yet. I'm not allowed to work anywhere else for six months.'

'But you could be putting out feelers. Talking to your contacts, see what's out there. Get your CV together.'

'All right, Mum.' I tutted. 'Got loads of time for that. Let me have one week off.'

Tonya tapped her nails against the side of her mug. 'Have you spoken to Sarah?'

Why was Tonya asking about Sarah? It was me who was adjusting to a completely new way of life. 'She rang to remind me to pick up the kids.' I tutted. 'As if I'd forget.'

'You left Fred asleep in his pram in the park once.'

'Yes, but he was new then. I was still getting used to having him, and Evie was distracting me. It was only for a couple of minutes.'

Tonya couldn't resist another eye roll. 'How's Sarah getting on?'

I hadn't actually asked. She'd rung at a crucial stage of the Stone Carry event. 'She'd have said if something was wrong. No news is good news.'

'Or no news is what you get when you don't ask someone.' Tonya's eyes were off again. 'She was nervous this morning. Worrying whether she'd done the right thing.'

'Bit late for that.' A spark of indignation flared up within me. 'She'd already accepted the job.'

Tonya glared at me. 'Because you'd lost yours.'

I slunk down in my chair. Sarah still should have discussed it with me, given that it was *my* job she'd taken.

Tonya sat forward. 'You've got a degree and, until yesterday, had a very good job, so I'm assuming you're an intelligent man, despite all the contradictory evidence.'

I flicked her the V-sign, which didn't help to disprove her argument, but felt good.

'Sarah needs your support. I get that this role reversal is hard for you, but don't blame Sarah for what's happened. She's taken the job for the good of the family.'

I chewed on my lip. Yes, the family would benefit from the salary, but what about for the good of me? Did either of them appreciate how humiliating this was?

'Don't let your pride turn you into a dick.' Tonya gave me a hard stare. 'Try to be happy for her.'

I picked up my mug to avoid her gaze. Yes, I'd support Sarah. She was bloody good at her job, and I was proud of her and what she had achieved. But be happy about being stuck at home while she scampered up the career ladder at work? That was asking too much.

Chapter 13

Sarah

It was Friday already. The four days since Will had lost his job and I'd been appointed Director had been a combination of nerves, adrenalin, guilt, excitement and the realisation that I didn't have enough tights to get me through a full week of work without doing some laundry.

I hadn't actually started the Director's role yet. Clara felt we should begin afresh the following Monday, which suited me. I'd been able to leave work each day at five, as though going to collect Evie and Fred from the childminder, so had been home in time for dinner with them. I wasn't ready to go from being the primary carer to a mostly absent one. My stomach scissor-kicked at the thought. I'd make up for it at weekends. I'd be the most present parent it was possible to be.

Clara had called a meeting and when I arrived at her office, Andy was sitting next to her, with Tom opposite. Both men stood when they saw me. In the last few days, Will had also taken to standing when I entered a room. And promptly exiting it. I was trying not to let it upset me. His pride had taken a knock and it would take time to adjust. I hoped he'd adjust before tonight. It was traditional to get an Indian takeaway on a Friday and I couldn't justify ordering as many sides if he wasn't going to split them with me.

'How's it going?' Clara asked.

I took the chair next to Tom. 'Great, thanks.' I smiled brightly to mask my concern that my husband was avoiding me and, if things didn't change soon, I'd have to choose between rice and a naan. 'Looking forward to starting the new role next week.'

'Me too.' Tom grinned at me.

'Great stuff.' Andy clicked the end of his ballpoint pen on and off. 'We need to decide how to allocate Jasper's and Will's clients fairly. Usually, it'd be a direct handover, but there are some particularly important clients in both portfolios that need extra TLC.' He clicked his pen in my direction. 'You're more experienced, Sarah, so you should get the lion's share of these.'

Adrenalin coursed through me. The clients he was talking about had mega budget accounts, which meant that there were no restrictions when planning their marketing campaigns. I'd once hired an Elvis impersonator for a promotion. With these clients' expense accounts at my disposal, I could get the actual Elvis resurrected.

'It means you'll do more of the travel,' Andy said. 'At least one week each month.'

My excitement subsided. Having less time with Evie and Fred day-to-day was painful enough. Week-to-week was unthinkable. It was only day four and I already missed their sleepy faces in the morning and their wide smiles when I picked them up from school or the childminder. I knew I was viewing the situation through rose-tinted glasses. Mostly, the drop-offs and pick-ups were a frantic, nerve-jangling, will we/won't we make it, chaotic mess. The slice of life that has therapists, Prozac manufacturers and mindfulness app shareholders rubbing their hands with glee. Despite knowing this, I still didn't want to go away and leave them.

My silence must have spoken volumes, because Clara asked if I was all right.

I opened my mouth to say, 'Yes, great!' but then realised that I had to be upfront and honest if I intended this job to be long-term.

'Thank you for entrusting me with these clients,' I started.

'I know I can do a good job for them.' My hand shook as I nudged my glasses up. 'But I can't be away from my children that much. Not to start with, anyway.'

Clara and Andy exchanged looks. Andy's pen-clicking went into overdrive. I could feel the Director's job slipping away from me, unless I convinced them that the travel wasn't essential.

I sat forward. 'The meetings and pitches can be done via Zoom. It doesn't need to be face-to-face. It's more economical, financially and timewise, and better for the environment this way.' I hoped my argument was strong enough. Saving the company money was in their interest, and saving the planet should be in everyone's interest.

Clara nodded, but Andy didn't look convinced. I'd witnessed him tossing a cardboard sandwich wrapper into the general bin rather than the recycling one, so it wasn't a huge surprise.

'We don't want our clients to feel as though we only make the effort when it suits us,' he said. 'They need to feel valued. I know you've won pitches on Zoom, but you can't beat human interaction. You can't bond in a virtual meeting.' He punctuated each point with a click of his pen. It wasn't irritating in any way. He shook his head. 'Such a shame about Will.' Click, click, click. 'We lost a good man there.' The company was at risk of losing another good man if he didn't stop clicking that bloody pen.

Clara smoothed her hair. 'There must be a compromise. Sarah's a valuable asset. She's proved how capable she is and is prepared to do some travel.' She tweaked the position of her folder, so that it sat perfectly lined up to the edge of the desk. If I ever found time to redecorate our stairwell, Clara would be top of my list to do the cutting in. 'It's a lot to expect anyone to do both Will's and Jasper's combined travel,' she continued. 'Much better to share it out.'

Andy tapped his pen against his teeth. Marginally better than the clicking, but only because it would be easier to ram it down his throat at such close proximity. 'Tom's not quite ready for the bigger clients yet, though.' He nodded to Tom. 'You need a bit more experience below your belt first.'

'The travel isn't an issue for me and I'd love the chance to prove myself,' Tom said.

I stiffened. Was he trying to take the big clients for himself? Maybe he wasn't as nice a guy as I'd thought he was.

'I appreciate what you're saying about Sarah's experience, though,' Tom continued. 'So, how about we combine the two portfolios and work on them together?' He gestured to me. 'Sarah would have control over the major projects and I'd do the travel needed to maintain the relationships.'

I could have kissed him. This was the perfect solution. I'd get to work on the big projects without having to sacrifice time away from Evie and Fred.

'Brilliant idea.' I grinned at Tom. His nice-guy status had just gone up a notch. No, two notches!

Clara nodded. 'Works for me.' She looked at Andy. 'Tom will benefit from Sarah's experience and expertise, and can do the wining and dining that Sarah isn't able to do just yet.'

'I can do a little bit of travel,' I said quickly. Evie and Fred would be OK without me for the odd night, and I didn't want to miss out on *all* the wining and dining. 'To the Netherlands, for example.' The flight to Amsterdam was so short that my coffee hadn't cooled enough for me to drink it the last time I'd been.

'*Ik spreeken Nederlands,*' Tom said.

Clara nodded. 'I remember now from your interview. Your uncle's Dutch, isn't he?'

Tom nodded. '*Ja.*'

'OK, great.' Andy put his pen down, which I was very thankful for. 'You'll both do the European trips and Tom will do the long-haul ones for now.' Andy looked at me. 'I assume your reluctance to travel is a short-term issue and you'll do more as your children get older?'

'Definitely.' No need to point out that our reference points of when the children were older probably differed by a decade.

'Good.' Andy reached for his pen, but Clara whipped it away. The clicking must have been driving her mad too. 'Well done, Tom,' Andy said. 'Good solution.'

'Thank you.' Tom held out his hand to me and gave me a sheepish smile. 'Look forward to working with you.'

'You too.' I shook his hand and gave him a grateful smile.

'Perfect,' Clara said. She opened a ring binder, unclipped a page and smoothed it through its protective plastic wallet. 'We need to make a statement about why Will's left the company. People think he's off sick at the moment.'

My smile dropped.

'We need a reason that doesn't show him in a bad light, for Sarah's sake.'

Everyone nodded, me most enthusiastically. Will may have done something stupid, but I loved him and didn't want his former colleagues bad-mouthing him. That was my prerogative.

'The four of us are the only ones who know what happened,' Clara said. Tonya knew too, but I was confident we could rely on her discretion. 'Can we agree that it'll go no further?' Again, we all nodded. 'And that we'll stand by the statement released concerning Will's departure?' More nodding, this time with a few muttered affirmatives. If one of us dozed off, it'd be an exact reproduction of Prime Minister's Question Time.

'Sarah and I have discussed telling everyone that Will's taking time out to spend with his family.'

I nudged my glasses up. 'I'm worried this doesn't ring true. He'd have told people; he wouldn't just have left without saying goodbye.'

Andy nodded. 'Jasper's sudden departure had everyone speculating within minutes. That's why we admitted what had happened and warned of the risks involved with losing a company device.'

Tom tugged at his cuffs. 'Could you pretend you'd always planned this? That Will would be Director for a few years, then it'd be your turn. Like when Gordon Brown took over from Tony Blair mid-term.'

I fought the urge to scrunch up my face. I wasn't comfortable with a role-play scenario in which Will and I were Tony Blair and Gordon Brown.

'OK, bad example,' Tom said. I clearly hadn't fought the urge very well. 'Think of it like a different actor taking over a well-known role. Such as Henry Cavill becoming Superman after Christopher Reeve.'

Although this scenario was more aesthetically pleasing, it was still a terrible idea. I didn't want to shoot Tom down, though. He was trying his best and I hadn't come up with anything.

'Possibly,' I said diplomatically, arranging my features into what I hoped was a thoughtful expression.

Tom grimaced. 'You're right. It's a stupid suggestion.'

I really needed to work on my poker face.

'You look a bit like Henry Cavill, actually,' Clara said.

'Oh, I don't know about that.' Tom inclined his head. 'But thank you.'

'Let's get back on track,' Andy – who did not look like Henry Cavill – said sharply. 'What reason shall we give for Will leaving?'

I fiddled with the arm of my glasses. 'Let's stick with the story that he's taking some time off to be with his children. It's the closest to the truth we can get.'

'Great.' Clara made a note on her piece of paper, before slipping it back into its plastic wallet and returning it to the folder. Bet she rinsed her dishes before putting them in the dishwasher.

I exhaled loudly. 'I've got six months to work out what I tell everyone when Will gets another job.'

'Wouldn't worry about that,' Andy said, standing up. 'It's unlikely anyone will hear about it.'

I stood up too. 'They will if he ends up with one of our competitors.'

Andy frowned and looked sharply at Clara.

'Will can't work for one of our competitors,' Clara said.

'But he's got a good reference from you.' I looked from Andy, to Clara, to Tom. 'We've all sworn not to tell anyone what happened, so that can't go against him.'

'That's not the reason,' Clara said gently. 'As long as you work here, there'll be a conflict of interest. We wouldn't want your spouse working with a rival, able to find out about our pitches and marketing campaigns – and they wouldn't want it either.'

Tom shuffled awkwardly from one foot to the other. Andy looked around desperately for his pen.

I sank back into my chair as the reality of what Clara was telling me hit home. 'So, Will can't get another job in this industry because …' I trailed off, unwilling to say the words out loud.

'That's right.' Clara nodded and gave me an apologetic smile. 'Because of you.'

Chapter 14

Will

There was a definite sense of excitement in the playground at pick-up. That Friday feeling was evident in the hyped-up kids, the exhausted teachers and the gritty 'two days to get through before I can offload them again' determination of the parents.

Fred ran over, but ignored my open arms. My hugs were old news already.

'Can I go to Max's?' he asked, jumping up and down on the spot.

I thought quickly. If Fred went to Max's, I'd have to engage in small talk with his mum – and I tried to avoid all communication with other parents by arriving the exact moment the bell rang after school and adopting a drop-and-run tactic when it wasn't reading time in the morning. Some mums chatted long after the kids had gone in. For all I knew, they made a day of it, with sandwiches and a flask. I'd *have* to talk to Max's mum, though, to find out where they lived, make sure she wasn't an axe murderer, and subtly deduce if the play date included dinner. I'd then have to collect Fred, which would involve more small talk. Worst of all, I'd have to return the favour.

'Not tonight,' I said.

Fred stopped jumping. 'Why?'

Hmm. Why? 'I can't be arsed' wasn't a reason that Fred would respond well to.

I was saved from answering by Evie skipping up.

'Can I go to Jacob's for a play date?' she asked.

Another play date? What was with all the spontaneity? Shouldn't these things be organised well in advance, thereby giving me ample time to think of an excuse to get out of them?

They both looked up at me eagerly.

'Sorry, kids, not tonight.' Their faces fell. 'You were at the childminder's the last two days. It's my turn to be with you.'

'You've got all weekend with us,' Evie said. She was quick, this one. Some mindless TV should cure that.

'Yes, but I've got something planned for tonight.'

'What?' Evie asked.

'Building the Spurs Stadium out of Lego.' I grinned, delighted that I'd thought of something. 'It'll be awesome.' I offered them both a hand. 'Come on. Let's go.'

Fred stuck out his lower lip. 'Home's boring.'

Had he not heard me say Lego Spurs Stadium?

'Want to go to Jacob's,' Evie said quietly.

'I want to go to Max's,' Fred said very, very loudly.

Mrs Manning, who was patrolling the grounds to make sure everyone left, did an abrupt U-turn and headed our way.

'Come on, guys,' I said. Just four days ago, having me at home was The Best Thing that had happened to them in their entire lives. Now that Max and Jacob – whom I'd never heard of before – were on the scene, Evie and Fred couldn't get away from me fast enough. I tried to take their hands, eager to escape before Mrs Manning reached us, but they ran off. Mrs Manning's Scholl-clad feet neared. If we didn't get out of there fast, she'd probably put me on community service.

'Mr Campbell?' said a soft voice behind me.

I turned and faced the Fit woman I'd seen in the playground not waving at me. She was even more stunning close up, with deep brown eyes, delicate features, a shy smile and a shiny sheet of black hair that flowed to boob level. Not that I was looking at her boobs.

I nodded, lost for words. Even the simple ones like 'yes' and 'hello'.

'I'm Lauren,' she said. 'Max and Jacob's mum.'

I nodded again, devoid of all other communication skills. I really needed to work on my small talk.

'A few of us get together after school on Fridays. The children play; we drink, unwind, catch up. We call it the Friday Fizz Club.' Lauren laughed. A small, tinkly laugh that couldn't be more different to Sarah's, where she threw her head back and gave a full-on belly-laugh. I realised I hadn't seen her laugh like that for a while. Not even at my expense. 'I'm hosting tonight and wondered if you'd all like to come,' Lauren said.

'Thank you.' At last – some words. 'Hadn't realised the invitation was for me, too.'

'We pretend the Friday Fizz Club's for the children, but it's for us, really.' Lauren laughed again. 'Gives us a couple of hours off from entertaining them while they play. Hi Mrs Manning,' she added, as the school's equivalent to Goebbels reached us. 'I'm trying to persuade Mr Campbell to sign up for the PTA.'

Mrs Manning sniffed. 'Can you take it outside the school grounds, please? The caretaker's waiting to lock up.'

'Of course, Mrs Manning,' Lauren said sweetly. 'Have a good weekend.'

Mrs Manning escorted us to the gate and nodded curtly. 'Mrs Lo. Mr Campbell. Children.' She managed to make all three addresses sound like insults.

The gate slammed shut behind us. Lauren giggled. 'My house is down there, if you'd like to come.'

I wasn't sure what to do. I'd said no to the play date. Would going back on my decision diminish my parental authority? Would Fred and Evie assume that I didn't really mean it whenever I said no? And what about the Lego Spurs Stadium? It wasn't going to build itself.

Evie and Fred stood with Max and Jacob. They had

Lauren's eyes and neat, jet-black, shiny hair. It made me realise what a state Evie's hair was. Her ponytail was at a right angle and on the verge of falling out. She'd inherited Sarah's hair, so it'd never be neat and shiny. Sarah claimed her waves were pre-Raphaelite, but prehistoric seemed a more accurate description.

'Can we go, Daddy?' Evie asked. 'Pleeeeeeease.' The word seemed to last for forty-five minutes. I hesitated, still concerned that going back on my initial decision would come back and give me a monumental kick up the arse at some point. Plus, Lauren was a woman and I was a man. I wouldn't like it if Sarah went round some bloke's house.

'There'll be quite a few of us,' Lauren said, as though reading my mind. Although her hint that nothing untoward would be happening was probably more a statement than an assurance.

Evie opened her mouth and took a deep breath. 'Pleeee—'

'OK,' I said. 'For a little while.'

All four children squealed with excitement, then sped off down the road.

Lauren laughed and ran after them. I had no choice but to follow.

Half an hour later I was sitting in Lauren's summer house, a drink in my hand, a bowl of Kettle Chips within reaching distance, and a view of Evie and Fred playing with a group of children in the garden. Why had I been so anti-play dates? This was bliss. My children were happy and entertained; they were getting exercise and fresh air, which hopefully meant they'd conk out at bedtime; and I had carte blanche to drink in the middle of the afternoon.

I'd briefly considered declining the flute of prosecco that Lauren handed me when we arrived. It wasn't my first choice of beverage, but it seemed churlish, and frankly rude, to decline. I wasn't driving and this was the Friday Fizz Club. What was the point in coming if not to partake in fizz?

While Lauren sorted drinks and snacks for the kids, I settled back on the sofa. The other parents hadn't arrived yet. Either they'd popped home first or Mrs Manning had had them executed for loitering in the playground. The sun streamed through the open doors, warming me against the chill of the November afternoon. I'd always thought 'summer house' was a posh description for 'shed', in the same way that 'glass technician' really meant 'window cleaner', and 'influencer' was a polite substitute for 'freeloader'. But this – with its furniture, pictures and lighting – couldn't be more different to a shed.

Lauren came in, carrying an ice bucket.

'This is an amazing space,' I said.

Lauren smiled. 'Thanks. It was fun to build.' My mouth dropped open and she giggled. 'It's not that big a deal. Came in a flat-pack kit. Kind of like a giant jigsaw. I just followed the instructions.'

'It's very impressive.' I sometimes struggled to complete a standard-sized jigsaw. I looked around, taking in the skilfully crafted, robust building with renewed wonder. How did someone so petite manage? Surely putting together something of this scale needed some serious muscle? I had to ask. 'How did you physically erect it?'

'Said the actress to the bishop,' a voice said behind us. Three women stood in the doorway; two of whom were identical. 'What's this about erections?' asked the non-identical one.

I wished the ground would open up and swallow me, but Lauren's insulated floor panels were far too securely constructed for that.

Lauren burst out laughing. 'Will was asking me how I built the summer house.'

The woman sighed. 'That's not very exciting. Thought we were going to get some juicy gossip.'

'Sorry to disappoint you.' Laughing, Lauren poured each of them a glass and invited them to sit down. 'Will, this is Vicky, Lizzie and Lisa. Lizzie and Lisa are twins, as you probably gathered. And in answer to your question, I had help with the heavy lifting.'

The three women raised their glasses and said hello. I returned their 'nice to meet yous', but inwardly sighed. Conversing with strangers, when the only common link was your kids, was not my ideal way to spend a Friday evening. I'd finish my glass, then leave. Tipping my head back, I downed the contents.

'Mrs Manning and Mr Owen were shagging in the stockroom again,' Vicky said.

Prosecco sprayed out of my mouth with such force that the fact I didn't take the roof off was further testament to the durability of Lauren's summer house.

Vicky grinned at me. 'Apparently, it's been going on for thirty years. Can you believe it?'

'No,' I croaked, mopping up prosecco with a napkin. 'Who's Mr Owen?'

'The caretaker.' Lauren knelt next to me and helped me clean up. 'Don't worry,' she said, when I apologised. 'I've got two boys. This floor has seen a lot worse.'

'So has the floor in the stockroom, by the sound of it,' I said.

All four women roared with laughter. My chest puffed with pride. It wasn't often I reduced anyone to hysterics. Sarah had been rather hysterical the time I'd put a bag of clothes out for recycling when they were intended for the dry-cleaner's, but that hadn't been such a positive experience.

'I'm embellishing a bit,' Vicky said, wiping her eyes. 'Don't know for sure that they were actually shagging today. After thirty years, it may have downgraded to something less taxing, like a foot rub.'

'Through her Scholl's?' Lizzie or Lisa said. I had no idea which was which.

More laughter, but nowhere near as much as I'd got. Not that it was a competition. But if it were, I'd have won.

Lauren refilled my glass. 'Vicky's a dinner lady at the

school. That's how she gets all the gossip.' I did a double take. At my school, the dinner ladies had been old, warty women who looked as though they ate the entire contents of the giant metal serving trays as a starter. Vicky, with her cropped, blonde hair and skinny jeans, was as far removed from those women as Mrs Trunchbull was from Holly Willoughby.

'Vicky, did you find out what happened to Miss Lowe?' Lauren looked at me. 'She was a supply teacher. Very young. It was her first job and she seemed to be doing well, but then disappeared.'

'Yes!' Vicky clapped her hands. 'She was showing some of the kids photos of cute kittens on her phone and a dick pic came up on the screen!'

We all inhaled sharply. I was really getting into this.

'The kids told their parents, who reported it, and Miss Lowe's supply work ended abruptly.'

'Why would a dick pic come up on her phone?' Lizzie or Lisa asked.

Vicky pursued her lips. 'She was on some dating website. Apparently, that's what guys do now. Send photos of their dicks.'

All four heads swivelled to look at me. I shrank back in my chair. 'I've never sent one,' I said, truthfully. If I sent a photo of my privates to Sarah, she'd probably think we had a dead hedgehog in the garden. Thankfully, phones had been in their infancy when I'd started dating. They were, ridiculous as it now seemed, used solely for making and receiving calls. Messaging had been introduced by the time Sarah and I got together, but not cameras, thank God. The 'should I ask her out or shouldn't I?' dilemma was nerve-racking enough, without the conundrum of whether to end the text with a smiley face, a winking emoji, a heart-shaped GIF or a snapshot of your cock and balls.

'It's disrespectful and degrading,' I added. 'Whoever sends those kinds of photos is only after one thing.'

They nodded approvingly and I relaxed back in my chair, feeling as though I'd passed a test. Lauren refilled my glass, which I hadn't realised I'd finished already. This really had to be the last one.

'Poor Miss Lowe,' said Lizzie or Lisa. 'She was a victim, really.'

'Yes.' Vicky held up her glass so that Lauren could top it up. 'Unlike Mr Cole. He deserved everything he got.'

'What did Mr Cole do?' I asked, desperately hoping it wasn't something that would reflect badly on men and, more importantly, me.

'Lost all the SATs papers.' Vicky shook her head. 'How could you lose something so important?'

I froze. I wouldn't be sitting here if I hadn't lost something very important. My instinct was to defend Mr Cole, explain that these things happened. But then I'd have to reveal how I knew this, and I didn't want my new friends finding out I was an idiot.

'I'd better go,' I said, struggling out of my chair.

'Not yet,' Lauren said. 'I'm about to make pizzas.'

'You can't miss Lauren's pizzas,' Vicky said. 'They're legendary. And gluten-free.'

Lizzie or Lisa nodded. 'Vicky can't eat gluten.'

'It makes her sick,' Lisa or Lizzie added.

Lauren turned to me. 'You can help with the pizza oven if you like?'

As Lauren had built a summer house single-handedly, I doubted she needed help making pizzas, but it seemed rude to say no after she'd been so accommodating. So, twenty minutes later, with another glass of fizz on the go, I was shovelling freshly made pizzas in and out of a million-degree pizza oven in the garden. Lauren and her friends formed a production line: Lizzie (or Lisa) overseeing the kids putting on their own toppings, Lisa (or Lizzie) carrying them out to me and taking the cooked ones back, Vicky distributing them to the children, and Lauren making sure I was OK and everyone had a drink. When all the kids had been served, the adults had their pizzas, which were, as Vicky had testified, legendary. I didn't know if it was down to the fizz, the lack of gluten or the manliness of having cooked my own food outside, as cavemen would have done (admittedly, without the oven, utensils and heat-resistant glove), but it was the best pizza I'd had in my life.

Sarah rang while we were eating, but I let it go to voicemail. It would have been rude to answer mid-meal and she was probably only calling to make sure I'd picked the kids up, or fed them, or not accidentally taken them on an evening stroll down a live train track. She underestimated my capabilities and it was starting to grate. I'd successfully managed megabuck projects for years, and now I was successfully parenting. I'd overcome my fear of play dates for Evie and Fred's benefit. I deserved some credit for going outside my comfort zone I thought, accepting another slice of pizza and a top-up of prosecco.

Over dinner, I learnt that Lizzie and Lisa were a medical insurance advisor and a doctor's receptionist. Still wasn't sure who was who, but I knew where to go if I ever needed a second opinion. Lauren was doing an online psychology course, which sparked my interest. I'd touched on it as part of my marketing degree and always thought it'd be good to learn more. Now could be my chance.

Inevitably, they asked me what I did workwise and why I was suddenly around. I'd been pondering what explanation to give since accepting Lauren's invitation and certainly didn't want to admit to the truth.

'I'm taking a six-month sabbatical,' I said. 'To spend time with Evie and Fred.' This earned a round of aaaahs, which fessing up to doing a Mr Cole would not have done.

'What about your wife?' Lauren asked. 'I tried to catch her a few times in the playground, but she was always rushing off. Does she do something high-powered?'

'Yes,' I said simply. No need to elaborate. I didn't want

them to think badly of Sarah for taking my job. Plus, after the amount of alcohol I'd consumed, I wasn't physically capable of elaborating. 'She's got a very good job in the City.' I pushed myself up to standing, hoping none of them saw me wobble. 'Thank you, Lauren, for a wonderful time. I owe you several bottles of fizz.'

'Don't worry about that.' Lauren stood, too. 'You can pay me back when you host. That's how the Friday Fizz Club works.'

'My turn next week,' Vicky said. 'I'm going Mexican, with margaritas and fajitas.'

'Wouldn't miss it,' I said. And I meant it. I'd had a great time and so had the kids. I was going to get some serious dad points for this.

Chapter 15

Sarah

Where were they? It was six o'clock and they clearly hadn't been home after school. I'd been able to open the door without having to push against school bags and coats, which they dumped on the mat, and I hadn't tripped over three pairs of shoes in the hall.

Disappointment coursed through me as I walked into the empty kitchen. Having missed them all week, I'd been excited about seeing them when I got in. I wasn't expecting the three of them to be lined up in their Sunday best waiting for me, but I had thought they'd be here. Will hadn't read, let alone responded to, my text telling him I was on my way back, or answered when I'd rung from the train. I tried again, but it went to voicemail. Where were they? There weren't any clubs on a Friday and Tonya was working, so they hadn't gone to hers. I went cold. Suppose they'd been in an accident on the way home? A bus could have veered out of control, mounted the pavement and knocked all three of them over. Or Mrs Manning could have come good on her threat of stun gunning anyone who wasn't off the school grounds within five minutes of the bell ringing.

I took a deep breath. Smell the flower, blow out the candle. If something bad had happened, Will would have rung. Worst-case scenario, the police would have rung. I needed to stay calm and think rationally.

With slightly shaky hands, I opened my Find My Friends

app. Will was on Brecon Avenue, which was only a few streets away. I frowned. We didn't know anyone who lived there and it didn't have any shops. I rang again, but again got his voicemail. Slipping my coat back on, I picked up my keys and went out to find them.

I was on Brecon Avenue in minutes. I walked towards the house highlighted on my app, wondering which would be less stalkerish – knocking on the door and asking if my husband and children were there, or peering through the windows. I didn't need to do either, as halfway down the road, Will emerged from a driveway with Fred on his back and Evie clutching his hand. I waved, but Will didn't see me. He was too busy toppling into a wheelie bin. I hurried towards them, but Will turned and walked away in the opposite direction.

'Will,' I called. 'Evie, Fred.'

Evie stopped and turned. 'It's Mummy.' She let go of Will's hand and ran towards me. I crouched down and scooped her up into a big hug. 'We had pizza at Jacob's house.'

'That's nice,' I said, wondering who Jacob was.

Will gave me a broad smile. 'Hi.' He stumbled and Fred almost fell to the ground.

'Are you all right?' I lifted Fred off Will's back. 'You seem disorientated.'

'I'm fine.' Will staggered to the side and ricocheted off a bush.

He wasn't fine. He was pissed.

'You're drunk,' I said, remembering to curb my language for the sake of Fred and Evie. 'It's not even six thirty. What have you been doing?'

That was a stupid question. It was obvious what he'd been doing.

'Friday Fizz Club,' Will said. He was slurring so much that I could barely make out the words. 'Lauren's house.'

'Who?'

'Need to get home. Desperate for the toilet.' Will stumbled off.

'You're going the wrong way.'

Will turned and walked purposefully in the right direction. As purposefully as someone can when they're swaying from side to side and attempting to move with their legs crossed.

'Is Daddy all right?' Fred asked.

'Of course.' I squeezed his and Evie's hands. Yes, Daddy was all right. For now.

Two hours later, after I'd bathed the children and put them to bed, I found Will stretched out on the sofa, one hand behind his head, the other resting on the floor. I deliberately trod on it as I walked past.

He yelped. 'Careful.'

I gritted my teeth. 'Careful? You almost dropped Fred earlier. He could have been hurt.' I sat down in the armchair across from Will.

Will massaged the palm I'd just trodden on. 'Don't be so dramatic. Had it all under control.'

'Are you joking?' My fists clenched. 'You weren't even in control of your bodily functions.' Will had stopped to wee behind a tree on the way home, as he couldn't hold it in any longer. Fred thought this was brilliant. He'd probably start doing it in the playground now. I doubted that'd earn him Achiever of the Week from Miss Boast. 'You're supposed to be looking after the kids, not getting inebriated.'

'I was not in … in … pissed.'

He'd fallen into my trap. Will glowered, possibly wishing he could set a trap for me. One that was used to catch bears.

'How did it happen?' I asked. 'Who's Lauren?'

'Max and Jacob's mum,' Will said, as though this would explain everything.

'Who?'

He sighed. 'Max is in Fred's class. Jacob's in Evie's. They invited them for a play date. Parents go too. It's called the Friday Fizz Club. The kids played. We ate pizza.' He spoke in a monotone, as though every word was an unnecessary

103

exertion. If he carried on like this, our sex life would also become an unnecessary exertion. 'Yes, I had a few glasses of fizz,' he continued flatly. 'That's the whole point. It's not the Friday Water Club.' He folded his arms over his chest. 'The kids played outside with other kids. Surely that's better than sitting in front of the TV at home.'

I took my glasses off and rubbed my eyes. Yes, it was good for them. I'd always felt guilty that I had to whisk Evie and Fred home so that I could work. I never accepted invitations to play dates because I couldn't reciprocate. I'd tried it once, and Evie and her friend made so much noise that the client I was on a Zoom call with asked if I lived on a farm. I'd asked myself the same question. Little girls who've consumed a family-pack of cocktail sausages and a litre of orange juice with bits do not smell as though they're made of sugar and spice and all things nice. That was the death knell for play dates for me. But if Will was prepared to take them and return the favour, then that was a good thing. It showed he was taking his new role seriously, which was to be encouraged.

'You're right,' I said. 'It's more that I was worried when you weren't here. Why didn't you answer my calls?'

'Phone was on silent.' Will twisted his head to look at me. 'Why were you near her house? Were you checking up on me?'

'No! I told you, I was worried. Mrs Manning could have held you hostage.'

Will grinned. 'Did you know she's been knocking off the caretaker for thirty years? That's why they're so keen to get everyone out.'

I scraped my hair up into a topknot. 'That's ridiculous.'

'It's true. Vicky said so.'

First Lauren, now Vicky. Who were these women spending time with my husband? I wasn't possessive, but I'd heard enough country-and-western tracks in my time to know it's best to keep a check on your man.

'Vicky is ...'

'Another mum. And Lizzie and Lisa. Don't ask me to introduce you. I don't know who's who.'

That was some comfort. He can't have been too enamoured if he hadn't paid much attention to what they looked like. Unless he'd just been ogling their chests, of course.

'Lauren's got a pizza oven,' Will said. 'It's really cool. We should get one.' He ran a hand over his head. 'We hung out in her summer house. She built it from a flat-pack. Might make that my sabbatical project. That's what I told them, by the way.' He looked over. 'That I'd taken six months off to spend with the kids.'

My stomach tightened. Worrying about where he was, and then being annoyed about where he was, had made me forget the revelation that Will couldn't work for a rival firm. I nudged the side of my glasses up. I had to tell him. Get it out of the way.

'That's what we'll tell people at work,' I said casually. 'That you wanted time with Evie and Fred. It was that or a career change.'

'Don't know about career change, but I might do some studying.' Will yawned. 'Lauren's doing an online psychology course. Sounds interesting.'

Was there anything Lauren didn't do? I fought back the urge to make a derisive comment – projects that excited Will needed to be encouraged – and instead channelled any uncharitable thoughts into hoping she was ugly.

'Thought I'd look into it,' Will said. 'Loved the module I did at uni. Wouldn't need to worry about being older than everyone, as it's online.'

'That's a great idea!' I went over and kissed him. Anything that distracted Will from thinking about his career in marketing got my full support. Because if he didn't want to work in that field anymore, then he'd never need to know that he couldn't. I just had to make sure he never found out.

Chapter 16

Sarah

'Have a great day at school, guys. Love you.'

'Love you, Mummy.' Evie and Fred waved at the screen. I hated leaving home before they woke up, but the earlier I got into the office, the earlier I got to leave. I was a week-and-a-half into the job and had so far managed to make it home each evening in time to bath them and read their bedtime stories.

'Will,' I said. 'Do you think you could—' The screen went blank. I'd have to message him about that evening's dinner. The meals I'd bulk cooked and frozen had all been eaten and I'd spent last night prepping for today's meeting, so hadn't had time to cook any more. Will's new pizza oven had arrived. Perhaps he could trial it tonight. The amount it had cost, we'd need to eat pizza every day for a year to justify the price. And then I'd need to get liposuction to remove the weight I'd gained, and employ a nutritionist to cure the IBS brought on by all the dough. The cost per pizza was going to be in the hundreds.

I put my phone down and ran through the checklist I'd made of everything Tom and I needed to have ready for our Zoom meeting with a big Dutch client, Dekker. This was an important pitch. Their contract was up for renewal, so we needed to wow them with our presentation, and assure them that Tom and I knew what we were doing and could look after them as well as Will had. Hopefully, my passion and vision, combined with Tom's ability to speak Dutch, would win them over.

Another reason I liked coming in early was to have the office to myself. Tom was so eager to learn that he asked me questions incessantly. Which was fine – the deal had been that he'd do the long-haul travel and I'd train him up on the areas he was less experienced in. But I hadn't expected so many questions. He wanted to know every microscopic detail. I should applaud his dedication, but it was hard to work when I was having to explain everything, as I did it. Trainee brain surgeons probably took fewer notes. To make it worse, as Tom and I were sharing clients, Andy felt it made sense for us to share an office. All well and good in theory, but the constant chatter was rather wearing. Even a Samaritan would be tempted to ask him to put a sock in it.

I yawned. I'd worked until midnight, then got up at five thirty so was, unsurprisingly, shattered. I needed coffee. As I left my office, I snuck a look at the plate on the door that said 'Sarah Campbell' and smiled. Clara had requested that the names be hung alphabetically, so mine was above Tom's. Not that it mattered whose came first. Said no one.

I walked along the corridor towards the shared kitchen. Voices drifted out and I heard Will's name. I slowed down and strained to hear.

'Only, he didn't leave to spend time with his family.' That was Nancy's voice, the PA. 'That's just what they're saying.'

'Why did he go then?' a man I didn't recognise asked.

'Because of Sarah.'

I froze.

'She said she was fed up with taking a back seat to his career and if he didn't leave to look after the kids, then she'd leave him.'

I put a hand to my mouth. Where had this come from?

'Will's a decent guy,' Nancy continued. 'What choice did he have?'

'He should have refused,' the man said. 'I wouldn't do it.'

'She might have told him he couldn't see the kids.'

'That's outrageous. What sort of a woman tells her husband he can't see his own kids?' The man released a long breath. 'Thought she was nice. Everyone likes her.'

I am nice! I wanted to shout. I'd never say that.

'Just goes to show,' Nancy said. 'You never know what goes on behind closed doors.'

'What about Jasper?' the man asked. 'Did she have anything to do with him leaving?'

Nancy inhaled dramatically. 'Ooh, maybe. Some people don't care who they tread on to get a leg up.'

My throat tightened. Should I tell them it wasn't true? That I hadn't told Will to leave work? No one had questioned the announcement that he'd left to spend time with his family. Was that because no one believed it, preferring to make up their own version of events? Confronting Nancy ran the risk that the more I protested, the less likely she was to believe me. And, of course, it wasn't actually true. If I wasn't careful, acquitting myself would expose Will, which I'd never do.

No, now wasn't the time to steam in and try to sort it out. I wasn't prepared and there was too great a risk I'd do more damage than good. I needed to plan how to deal with this situation properly. I hurried back to my office, shut the door and leant against it. Closing my eyes, I inhaled deeply and released a long, slow breath.

'Sarah?'

I almost shot through the polystyrene-tiled ceiling at the sound of Tom's voice. I'd been so distracted that I hadn't noticed him at his desk.

'Something wrong?' he asked.

'No,' I said shortly, crossing the room and sitting down. A fresh coffee and an almond croissant sat on my desk. I softened. Perhaps not all of the notes he made were excessive.

'Thank you.' I glanced across at him. 'Sorry about snapping.'

'No worries.' He smiled. 'You can talk to me if you want to, though.'

I hesitated. If it were a personal issue – an argument with Will, something involving the children, the devastating news that Regé-Jean Page wouldn't be returning to *Bridgerton* – I wouldn't have discussed it. But this was work.

I nibbled at a flaked almond. 'I just overheard Nancy tell someone that I made Will leave so I could have his job.'

'What?' A muscle pounded in Tom's cheek. 'Can't believe that. Shall I talk to her? Put her straight?'

I shook my head. 'Thanks, but I'll talk to Clara. Ask her advice.'

Tom tugged at his cuffs. 'She's had to speak to Nancy about gossiping before. This could be her final warning.'

'I don't want her to get sacked over it,' I said. Enough people had lost their jobs. 'I'll talk to her myself.'

Tom smiled. 'You're very kind. That's one of the things I like about you.'

I picked up my coffee and croissant. 'This is the thing I like about you.' I needed to remember how sweet he was and not get irritated when he asked questions. 'All set for the presentation?' I asked.

'*Ja.*' Tom grinned. 'You?'

I smiled back. '*Ja.*'

After the presentation, I was smiling even more. We'd well and truly nailed it. It hadn't got off to the best start, as Tom had attempted to converse in Dutch with our clients. I hadn't been able to understand a word he was saying and, judging by the puzzled expressions on their faces, neither had they. After several excruciating minutes, by the end of which Tom was visibly sweating, the woman leading the meeting, Dieuwke Hillenaar, had put him out of his misery.

'It is easier to speak in English, I think,' she'd said.

I'd taken this as my cue and had, as they say, smashed it out of the park. It'd be good to celebrate by getting smashed, but preferably not in a park, as it was November and flipping cold.

I practically ran back to my desk from the conference room, eager to email Dieuwke the contract and get her signature on it before any competitors tried to woo her away. I was already typing into my computer when Tom got back to our office. He sat down heavily at his desk.

'What's wrong?' I asked, pressing send. 'We got the business.'

Tom sighed. 'No. *You* got the business. I was an embarrassment. Thinking I could speak Dutch.' He loosened his tie and undid the top button of his shirt. 'I didn't dare say anything after that. Not that I needed to. You had it covered.'

I hesitated. Perhaps I'd had it too covered. I'd been so concerned with winning the contract that I'd taken over after Tom's disastrous introduction in Dutch. In future I'd let him speak more. That was the best way for him to learn.

'We'll pitch the next one together,' I said. 'Don't be so hard on yourself about your Dutch. They'll appreciate that you made the effort.' I nudged my glasses up. 'It's probably not every day that someone compliments their badger.'

Tom clamped his hands to his head. 'I thought *das* meant tie. I was trying to say I liked his tie.'

A giggle escaped me. 'Why would you mention his tie?'

'It seemed as good an icebreaker as any.'

'It wasn't even a nice tie!' I was laughing openly now. 'It was plain brown. It couldn't have been more boring.'

Tom grinned. 'Well, I couldn't tell him that.'

'Because it'd be rude or because you don't know how?'

Tom tore a sheet of paper from a notepad on his desk, scrunched it up and threw it at me.

It landed in my empty coffee cup.

'Bullseye!' He thrust his arms in the air.

My mobile rang. Still laughing, I answered it.

'Are you at work?' Will asked.

'Yes … Where else would I be?'

'What are you laughing about?' His accusatory tone caused my high spirits to deflate quicker than Will's ardour had the time Fred ran into the bedroom announcing he'd found a worm in his poo.

'Nothing, really.' I took my glasses off and dabbed under my eyes with a tissue. 'Everything OK with you?'

'What are the kids having for dinner?'

'Whatever you want to give them,' I said lightly, although inside I was furious. If I'd phoned Will at work and asked him the same question, he'd have told me where to go and then got Nancy to block my calls. My stomach tightened at the thought of Nancy. With all the excitement of the presentation, I'd forgotten about her rumour-mongering.

'You usually leave their dinner in the fridge,' Will said.

I heard the fridge door open. Did he think I was going to magic it into existence?

'I didn't have time last night. I was working.' While Will watched *The Sopranos* and slept. I didn't begrudge him either of those things – it was my choice to put in the extra hours – but I didn't expect to be criticised for not providing a meal that he had ample time to make.

The fridge door closed. 'What did you eat? Were there any leftovers?'

'Cereal. Should I have left the bowl out so you could scrape it clean?'

Tom glanced over. I pretended not to notice.

'No need to get arsey,' Will said in an arsey tone. 'I was only asking.'

Smell the flower, blow out the candle.

I forced a jovial note into my voice. 'You could make pizzas.'

A scoffing noise came down the phone. 'I can't just make pizzas. Sourdough takes a week to prep. It needs a special starter that you feed every day.'

Will was making less sense than Tom had been when

111

speaking Dutch. I remembered again the look of alarm on Dieuwke's and Lars's faces when Tom had started waving his tie in the air to get himself understood. A giggle bubbled out of me. Out of the corner of my eye I saw Tom smirk.

'It's not funny,' Will huffed. 'No point going to all the effort if it's not done properly.'

'Fine,' I said. 'There are fish fingers and potato waffles in the freezer. That'll do for tonight. Make sure you do some veg, too.'

'Where's the veg?'

'In the vegetable rack.' Christ, next he'd be asking me how to peel the carrots.

'How do I—'

'Sorry, got to go,' I said quickly. 'I'll let you know when I'm on my way home.' I hung up, feeling a stab of guilt. I hadn't been very nice, but seriously? Will was more than capable of making his children some dinner without step-by-step instructions from me.

'Everything all right?' Tom asked.

'Yes, thanks.' Annoying as Will was, it would be disloyal to moan about him to Tom. I'd save that for Tonya.

As though sensing I'd been thinking about her, Tonya messaged me an hour later.

I'm in the City! Fancy a cocktail? her text read.

I felt a flush of excitement. Cocktails in the City? I hadn't done that for so long and it'd be the perfect way to celebrate closing the deal with Dekker. I hesitated. I hadn't seen Evie and Fred that morning because I'd left early. I couldn't miss seeing them tonight too. I typed back a message to that effect. Tonya rang immediately.

'You know how much I love my niece and nephew,' she said. 'But missing Mummy's kiss and cuddle for one night isn't going to cause lasting damage.' I opened my mouth, but she continued. 'They need to get used to you being away sometimes. This is the ideal opportunity to ease them into it.'

'Not seeing them because I'm working is one thing,' I said. 'Not seeing them because I'm in the pub with their auntie is another thing entirely. It wouldn't be fair on them or Will.'

'I don't remember him rushing home for bedtime story very often.'

'Sorry, Tonya. I can't.' I already felt guilty for not having been around much. I didn't want to add to it. Plus, if I was going to spend time with anyone, it should be Will. We were bickering too much at the moment and needed to get back on track with a nice evening together. One that didn't involve me teaching him how to peel carrots.

'But I'm hardly ever in London and I haven't seen you for ages. Just one drink. I miss you.'

'I miss you, too.' We hadn't actually spoken since I'd started the job, which was unheard of.

'If we meet in King's Cross, we're already halfway home,' Tonya added.

I fiddled with the arm of my glasses. If I just had one drink, I'd be home by seven, before the children went to sleep, and I could still spend some time with Will. It'd be great to see Tonya and I could ask her advice about Nancy. I couldn't ask Will. He'd be humiliated.

I was about to tell Tonya that I would come, but then realised I wouldn't have time to go to the supermarket and buy food for tomorrow night's dinner if I went out.

'Go for it,' Tom whispered. 'You've earned it.'

I looked across. 'Can you hear her?' I mouthed.

He grinned and nodded.

I smiled. Sod tomorrow night's dinner. Will would have to speed up his pizza-making skills or go to the shop himself. 'OK,' I said to Tonya. 'I'll meet you at six in Caravan. Just one drink, though. No more.'

I hung up, opened my WhatsApp and started typing a message, letting Will know I was going for a drink. Halfway through, I stopped. He never used to tell me when he went for a drink after work. He hadn't even told me the other

Friday when he went to the Fizzy Whizzy Club or whatever it was called. I shouldn't feel obliged to tell him my every move. If we were doing this role reversal, then I needed to do it properly. He'd understand. Wouldn't he?

Chapter 17

Will

I stared at the bank balance on my laptop. Aside from the time our mortgage loan had been paid into my account, and been transferred out again three seconds later, this was the most money I'd ever had. Clara had, as promised, secured my Christmas bonus and put it through with the first three months of my gardening leave. I was officially rich.

Obviously, I wouldn't spend any of it. This had to last until I got a new job or, better still, be used for something that'd benefit the family or home. Knocking a bit off the mortgage. Replacing all the windows. Upgrading the boiler. Taking the kids to Disneyland or – I inhaled sharply with excitement – into space. Sensible shit like that. I googled how much Jeff Bezos's space flights cost: several million dollars. OK, scrap that one. Sarah wouldn't want to go anyway if she couldn't take her straighteners.

I went to transfer the balance into our high-interest savings account and hesitated. I could spend a little bit, couldn't I? Just get a few essentials. First up were some trainers with a sponge heel for extra support. Lauren had recommended them when I mentioned my bad back. My eyes bulged at the eye-watering cost, but you couldn't put a price on health. I put them in my basket, then added a wind-resistant waterproof jacket. Another health necessity. Didn't want to catch a nasty chill on the school run.

I had the bug now. Trawling round shops was a ball-ache,

but sitting in the comfort of my own home, with the retail world at my fingertips – and beyond, if I happened to have several million dollars to spare – was fun.

My phone beeped with a sports news update. I noticed that it only had fourteen per cent charge left, although I hadn't made any calls that day. It had reached the stage of its life where the battery ran down every couple of hours. Now I was the school's primary contact, having a reliable phone was crucial. I looked at the latest models. They weren't cheap. Sod it. I wasn't being frivolous; this was an essential purchase. A flat-pack summer house was next in my basket. The kids could make as much noise and mess as they liked down the bottom of the garden, and it'd be fun to build. So what if it cost two grand? It was worth it.

Feeling slightly guilty that I'd just spent several mortgage payments in ten minutes, I decided to buy a present for Sarah. I'd noticed her eyes light up at an advert for a state-of-the-art hairdryer brush that promised to de-frizz curls. In case I'd missed her eyes light up, she'd pointed at the TV and said she'd like that for Christmas. No need to wait till Christmas, my sweet. I'd get it for her now.

I scrolled the internet until I found the one she'd been drooling over ... £500? Fuck me. That was more than the pizza oven had cost. This wasn't the time for penny-pinching, though. This was my way of showing her I loved her. Even though I'd never have left my laptop on the train if she hadn't been there, and even though she should never have accepted the Director job without discussing it with me first, and even though she didn't bother telling me when she went out with my sister, I still loved her. I gritted my teeth and punched my card details into the laptop. Yep, still loved her.

My phone beeped and a message from Sarah appeared on the screen.

Hi. When you do the Tesco order, please can you add satsumas. Thanks. X

No *How are you?* or *Hope all's well*. I considered cancelling the order for her £500 hairdryer, but wasn't entirely sure how to.

Begrudgingly, I logged onto the Tesco website, booked the first available slot and added satsumas to the basket. The site had a £40 minimum spend on it. The satsumas only cost £1.25. I couldn't be bothered to scroll through the entirety of Tesco's online store, so increased the number of satsumas till I got to £20 and then added a £50 bottle of whisky. Not something I usually drank, but it'd do as a placeholder.

I confirmed the order, checked out and closed the laptop. All the fun of online shopping had gone now. Sighing heavily, I looked around the room, wondering how to fill the hour till I picked the kids up. I could pop into the Radcliffe for a quick pint and a bolstering from my mate Howard, who still revered me for living the dream, even if he couldn't remember my name. I didn't like to spoil the illusion by telling him he was talking shite. If I were living my dream, I'd be a billionaire, James Bond would call me for help when he was in a spot of bother, and Halle Berry would have taken up pole dancing and asked me to be the pole. Tesco orders and school pick-ups would not feature heavily.

My gaze landed on a psychology textbook that Lauren had lent me. I should read it, in case she needed it back. She'd offered to come round and discuss it, which was very kind of her, but I wasn't entirely comfortable about just the two of us getting together. It felt a bit, I don't know, disloyal to Sarah. Silly really, because Lauren was just a friend.

I ran a hand over my head. Deep down I knew why I wasn't comfortable about it. Lauren was hot. And single. Vicky had filled me in. Max and Jacob's dad worked on an oil rig and was away for six months at a time. They'd tried to keep the relationship going but had grown apart and the last time he came back, they'd agreed it wasn't working. It had been an amicable break-up: they still cared for one another, and the sex was phenomenal – Vicky believed in painting a full picture – but they couldn't keep going as they were.

No wonder Lauren was so independent and capable. After bringing up two kids on her own, knocking up a summer house was a breeze. Of course, just because Lauren was single, didn't mean she fancied me. And just because she was single, didn't mean I fancied her.

The trouble was, I did a bit. A tiny bit. What straight man wouldn't? She was beautiful, fun, intelligent, resourceful and very nice. But this tiny crush didn't come close to the love I felt for Sarah (see earlier £500 hairdryer purchase for proof). I'd never do anything to jeopardise our marriage. I didn't want to have an affair with Lauren. I genuinely did think of her as a friend. But my stupid, primitive male instincts couldn't help but notice her attributes. Particularly the ones in the tits and arse area. Consequently, there wouldn't be any one-to-one get-togethers. The more people around us, the merrier. Provided none of them were on leave from an oil rig.

I picked up Lauren's psychology book. Perhaps there'd be something in here that'd tell me how to switch off the testosterone-fuelled part of my brain when I was around her. I flicked through the boring science bits and went straight to the chapter on understanding body language fundamentals. This was the real reason people studied psychology, after all. They might say it's to pursue a career in counselling, healthcare, education, blah, blah, blah, but really it was so that they could work out what others thought of them.

My eyes grew heavy as I read. I was on the verge of falling asleep when my phone beeped and I jerked awake. Shit, that was a close one. I had to get the kids in an hour. Mrs Manning would call me in to have a word if I was late. I didn't know what that word would be, but it would be insulting.

The message was from Lauren.

I've made you some sourdough starter! Shall I bring it
to school or come over tomorrow with it?

Shit. School, definitely. She couldn't come over till I'd
memorised the whole body-language chapter to ensure I'd
never give away any signals.

I fired a quick message back and started reading in earnest.

Chapter 18

Sarah

'Lin – great start to your presentation,' I said with a smile. 'I've a few thoughts on how we can develop it. Do you want to run through them now or later?'

Lin looked nervously around the table at the rest of her colleagues.

'Tell you what, let's do it after this.' I made the decision for her. She was clearly a bit shy and I didn't want to knock her confidence by putting her work under a microscope in front of everyone else.

'Jed.' I swivelled to face the other side of the table. 'About your pitch.' His pitch had been poor. It looked as though he'd cobbled it together five minutes before emailing it to me. Fred could have put together a more persuasive marketing strategy. Obviously, I wasn't going to say any of this and embarrass Jed, but he needed to know that he couldn't get away with it, and that I was here to help him learn and improve.

Jed nodded. 'Tom's already talked to me about it.'

This was news to me. Why hadn't Tom told me? He told me everything else. I liked him, but it was exhausting, having him constantly there. I'd go to make a note and he'd hand me a pen. I'd reach for my water and he'd give me the glass. I'd stand up and he'd open the office door. Next time I went to the toilet he'd probably slide a tampon under the cubicle.

I wouldn't question Tom about this now. Having just lost

their bosses, the team needed to see us as a united front. I'd said those exact words to Tom earlier. I checked my notes. 'That's everything I need to cover. Over to Tom.'

Tom walked to the front of the table, a broad smile on his face. 'Thanks everyone for pulling together and for all the great work you're doing. Remember, Sarah and I are a united front. Any time you want to talk about anything, you can come to either of us. We're a team.' He really did take note of everything I said.

'Felix, let's start with you,' Tom continued. 'What ideas have you had for—'

My phone rang loudly in my bag. Not my work phone, with its professional, standard ringtone. My personal phone with its *Star Wars* theme tune that Will had downloaded for us both. Horrified, I stared at my bag. That phone was always on silent at work. How had I knocked the ringer?

'Great tune.' Tom smiled.

I gave him a grateful look, as I scrabbled in my bag for the phone. It wasn't in the inside pocket where I kept it, but hidden in the depths, underneath tissues, hand gel, makeup and some unidentifiable objects. 'Sorry,' I said, rooting through the contents. Where was it? It hadn't taken Harry Potter this long to find the Horcruxes, and that film went on for hours. The ringing seemed to be getting louder. This was so unprofessional. 'Sorry,' I said again. I picked up my bag, which was still blasting away. 'I'll take it outside.' My face flaming, I left the meeting room, closed the door and emptied the contents of my bag onto the floor. The phone tumbled out, along with everything else, and stopped ringing immediately. Typical.

I turned it to silent, which it should have been on already, and glanced at the screen. The missed call was from the school. With my heart in my throat, I returned the call. It was 3.45 p.m. Was one of the children injured? Had something happened to Will?

'It's Sarah Campbell. Evie and Fred's mum,' I said breathlessly when it was picked up. 'You just rang?'

'Yes, I did.' Mrs Manning sniffed. 'We have a situation.'

My stomach plummeted. My poor babies. What had happened to them? Why wasn't I there when they needed me? Why had I taken this stupid job?

'They've been abandoned,' Mrs Manning said.

'Abandoned?' I spluttered. 'What do you mean?'

'I mean no one's collected them. They're sitting here in reception without a responsible adult.'

Bit worrying that Mrs Manning didn't consider herself to be a responsible adult, but this wasn't the time to question it.

'Have you called Will? He's their primary contact now.'

'Obviously, we rang the primary contact first.' Mrs Manning's clipped tone would send a chill down Dracula's spine. 'He's not answering.'

My stomach tightened. Why wasn't he? He always had his phone with him. A vision of Will on the kitchen floor, clutching his heart, flashed through my mind. I forced it away. He'd probably just got muddled with the days and thought the childminder was collecting them.

'Let me try him,' I said. 'If I can't get through either, I'll get someone else to come and collect them.'

'You are aware that school closes at three thirty?'

Yes, I was aware. 'I'm worried about Will,' I said. 'He's usually very reliable.' Clara and Andy might beg to differ.

Mrs Manning sniffed again. 'Mr Owen's waiting to lock up and I have things to be getting on with.'

Mr Owen being one of them, according to Will's source.

'I really appreciate your patience and understanding, Mrs Manning.' That should buy me some time while she went and looked them up in the dictionary. 'I'll call you back in a few minutes.'

I hung up and rang Will. The call was rejected immediately. I opened the Find My Friends app. He'd been at home an hour ago. I refreshed it, but it didn't update. What did that mean? That his phone was no longer functioning? Because it had been crushed under the wheels of a bus, along with

Will? My legs gave way, and I slid down the wall and landed in a heap on the ground. 'Please let him be OK,' I whispered, redialling his number. Again, it was rejected. And again, and again, and again.

I thrust my hands into my hair. What was I going to do? It'd take at least an hour to get back. The children needed picking up immediately, before Mrs Manning handed them over to social services, and I had to find out where Will was and – a stabbing pain formed in my chest – whether he was all right. My throat tightened. It had been a mistake to take the job. I should be with Evie and Fred. If I hadn't put my career first, I'd be the one picking them up. Everyone would be safe. Instead, I'd thrown my family's well-being away for a few extra quid and my name on a door. Pathetic. I was ashamed of myself.

A sob escaped me. I took my glasses off and wiped the tears away. I had to pull myself together. Taking a deep breath and releasing it slowly, I focused my mind. First things first: get someone to collect the children. Tonya would be at the restaurant by now. I'd try Sinéad. It wasn't her day to have them, but this was an emergency. Replacing my glasses, I dialled her number.

'Hi Sarah,' she said. I could hear happy squeals from children in the background. 'Everything OK?'

I explained the situation as succinctly as I could, my voice juddering as I tried not to cry.

'No problem,' Sinéad said. 'I'm at the park opposite the school. We'll go get them and I'll look after them till you or Will collect them.'

'Thank you,' I whispered, tears threatening to spill again. What if Will physically couldn't collect them? 'Really appreciate it. I'll be there in about an hour.'

'No rush. See you soon.'

She hung up and I clasped the phone to my chest. That would get Mrs Manning off my back. But what about Will? Where was he? I had to get home and find out. I shoved everything back in my bag, scrambled to my feet and went back into the meeting room. All heads turned towards me. I must have looked a state, with wild hair and smudged mascara, but I didn't care. Will was all that mattered.

'Everything OK?' Tom asked.

'I have to go,' I said abruptly.

'But we're in the mid—'

'I know. Sorry, everyone, but this is an emergency. I'll explain later.'

Tom stepped forward, concern etched on his face. 'Is there anything I can—'

'No.' My determination not to cry made my voice sharp.

He took a step back, looking as though I'd slapped him. I opened my mouth to apologise, but before I could speak, the *Star Wars* theme tune started up again and the school number came up on my phone. Bloody Mrs Manning. If she could just hang on two minutes, Sinéad would be there.

'I have to take this.' I backed out of the door. 'Speak to you later.' The door slammed behind me. 'The childminder will be there any minute,' I barked into the phone, running towards my office to get my coat.

'Why is Sinéad coming?' said a familiar voice that was marginally lower than Mrs Manning's, but not as gravelly. 'It's my day to get them.'

'Will?' I made it inside my office and dropped my bag on the floor. 'You're OK.' I leant against the desk. 'Thank God. I've been so worried. I thought something had happened to you.'

'School's closed,' Mrs Manning bellowed in the background. 'No one is permitted on these premises after three thirty.'

'It's OK, Mrs Manning,' Will said. 'She came to collect Evie and Fred, but I'm here now.'

'Why did Sarah ask me to get them if you're here?' I heard Sinéad ask. 'I've just had to get four kids off the climbing frame and over that road for nothing.'

I cringed. Poor Sinéad. I knew from experience that coercing children out of a park was not an easy task. Whoever coined the phrase 'it's a walk in the park' had not attempted said stroll with children in tow who would rather have their toenails removed than get off the monkey bars.

'Bit of a mix-up,' Will said. 'I'll get Sarah to call and explain.'

Cheers for that, Will. I instantly chastised myself. He was alive and well. Cheers for *that*.

'Control these children,' Mrs Manning yelled in the background. 'They should not be in here.' I'd have to give Sinéad some extra money for this.

'Why didn't you pick them up?' I asked when Will came back on the phone. 'I thought you'd had a heart attack or been in an accident.'

'Fortunately not,' Will said. 'The only thing that died was my phone battery.'

I waited for him to elaborate, but if I wanted more of an explanation I was going to have to ask. 'Why did your phone dying make you so late? Were you giving it a funeral?'

Will laughed. 'No, but you'll be pleased to know I've ordered a replacement, so it'll never happen again.'

I'd received more pleasing news in my time. Trump not being re-elected. Single-use plastic being phased out. The local salon doing a two-for-one offer on a brow tint and tidy. That kind of thing. But that didn't matter. All that mattered was that Will was OK.

'So, where were you?' I asked, genuinely baffled.

'At home.' Footsteps thudded down the phone and Will chuckled. 'It's like a Benny Hill sketch here. Six kids running around, and Mrs Manning, Mr Owen and Sinéad trying to catch them.'

I pushed my glasses up. 'Why were you at home when you were supposed to be at school?'

'Oh, I fell asleep.' Will laughed again. 'Wish you were here to see this. It's hilarious.'

125

I wished I were there, too. So I could give him a short, sharp kick in the goolies.

'I've been worried sick,' I hissed. 'And you were asleep.'

Will stopped laughing. 'It was an accident. If my phone hadn't died, I'd have got Mrs Manning's call and gone straight to pick them up.'

'You'd have still been late.'

'I told you, I've ordered a new phone. It won't ever happen again.'

My face burnt. 'I left a meeting to sort this out. You never had to deal with any of this when you were working. I sorted it, even though I was working too.'

'Sorry,' Will said quietly. 'I ordered you a hairdryer.'

I shook my head. 'How is that going to help?'

'Your hair won't be as frizzy.'

My desire to give Will a short, sharp kick in the goolies was growing into a desire to remove them completely.

'I have no idea what you're talking about and I don't care.' I scooped my bag up off the floor. 'I have a meeting to get back to and you have two children to look after. Do your job so I can do mine.' I hung up and hurled the phone into my bag.

Did he think this was a game? He'd play at being Daddy Daycare when it suited him, but as soon as he fancied some time out for something more interesting, such as a nap, then he'd switch off and let the missus take over. Well, bugger that. I was the breadwinner now. My career came first and it was about time he respected that.

I strode out of the office and into the ladies to splash some water on my face. I did a double take at my reflection. My eyes were blazing, my cheeks flushed, and my hair practically standing on end. Tom Hanks's character in *Cast Away* was better groomed than this. I scraped my curls into a topknot and brushed some powder on my dayglo face. It was the makeover equivalent of placing a damp tea towel on an erupting volcano and hoping it would extinguish the flames.

I walked to the meeting room, blood pumping. I was so angry with Will. So, so angry. I placed my hand on the door handle. Smell the flower, blow out the candle. Smell the flower, blow out the … Bang! The meeting-room door thudded against the wall as I pushed it open. Everyone inside jumped. I hadn't mindfulnessed myself enough, judging by the force with which I'd opened the door.

'Sorry about that. Guess I don't know my own strength.' I attempted a laugh, but it sounded more like a snarl.

'You're back.' Tom stood up. 'Everything OK?'

I nodded. 'False alarm. Sorry, everyone.' I forced a smile. The woman sitting closest to me looked genuinely frightened. I walked round to where I'd been sitting, but my chair was gone. It must have been taken away so that everyone could spread out around the table more comfortably. Made sense, but it did feel a little as though they couldn't wait to get rid of me. Would they jump in my grave that quickly? If Will didn't get his act together, he'd have a grave of his own in the near future that they could jump into instead.

'Here, have mine.' Tom sprang up and offered me his own chair.

To my alarm, tears sprang to my eyes. After the frantic combination of worry, relief and fury, Tom's kindness was the catalyst for all my emotions to come tumbling out. I couldn't cry in a meeting, though. I was supposed to be in charge, not bawling with my head on the table. I didn't dare thank Tom in case speaking triggered the waterworks. Instead, I plonked myself down in the chair, crossed my arms and put my head down, trying to make myself as small and inconspicuous as possible until I was sure I wasn't going to burst into tears.

Tom wrapped the meeting up, neatly summarising the points raised and areas that needed working on. I let the familiar words wash over me, glad he listened so intently that he could parrot what I'd rehearsed word for word.

127

'You're all doing a great job and we're very pleased with how well you've adapted to the situation,' Tom said. I was pleased he'd included that. 'Drinks on us in The Tavern after work,' he added. 'A small token of our appreciation.' A cheer went up. That had been my idea. An opportunity to get to know everyone in a relaxed environment and make them feel valued. 'Thanks for your time, everyone.'

Chairs were pushed back around me and they all filed out. I could hear Tom patting people on the back and muttering more messages of thanks. Once the last person had left, he closed the door, came over and sat next to me.

I took my glasses off and rubbed my eyes. 'That was awful. I'm so embarrassed.' My breath caught in my throat. 'What must everyone think of me?'

'Don't worry about that. What happened? You look dreadful. As in upset,' he added quickly. 'Dreadfully upset, not ...' He trailed off. Even Tom, with an outlook so life-affirming and cheerful it could rival that of a Christmas elf, couldn't put a positive spin on the fact I looked horrendous.

I flopped back in the chair. 'It's boring domestic rubbish.'

'So, bore me.' Tom smiled. 'We're partners, remember? You can tell me anything.'

I sighed. 'I suppose it would be nice to get it off my chest.'

Was it my imagination or did Tom's eyes flicker to my chest? I slid my glasses back on and surreptitiously glanced down. Bugger, a couple of buttons on my shirt had come undone, revealing a hot-pink bra. Getting ready at six, as I had done this morning, meant I didn't have time to root through my underwear drawer for a muted-coloured bra. Whatever was at the top had to do.

'I, er ...' I pointed at the whiteboard in the corner of the room. 'Are those your notes?'

Tom looked round and I quickly did up the buttons.

'Yes. I'll wipe them off before we go.' He studied my face intently. Waiting for me to speak, or studiously avoiding my cleavage? 'Go on,' he said.

I relayed the story in brief. 'I was so worried, then so angry.' I threw my hands in the air. 'When I got back in here, it was all suddenly too much and I was worried I'd cry if I said anything.' I shook my head. 'I was so unprofessional.'

Tom squeezed my shoulder. 'Don't be ridiculous. It was obvious something was wrong. You'd done a great job before the call.'

'Apart from Jed's pitch. I didn't realise you'd gone through it with him. He must have thought it odd I didn't know.'

Tom winced. 'My bad. I happened to be walking past his desk and he asked me about it, so I told him where it needs improving. Completely slipped my mind when I got back to the office and we started talking about something else. Think it was the latest episode of *Succession*.'

I inhaled sharply. 'Don't say a word. I'm massively behind.'

Tom winked. 'My lips are sealed.'

'I'll have a chat with Jed in the pub,' I said. 'Make sure he understands where I was coming from with the changes I asked for.'

'Good idea.' Tom hesitated before getting up. 'If you want to give tonight a miss, I understand.'

I shook my head. 'This is the first time we've been out as a team. It'd look terrible if I didn't show up.'

'There's no guarantee any of them will show up,' Tom said. 'We've only just mentioned it. They might already have plans.'

'I'm sure most of them will, even if just for one.' I nudged my glasses up. 'After the way I behaved today, I have to go. Show them I'm not like this usually.'

Tom placed his hands lightly on my upper arms. 'After the day you've had, the last thing you need is to force yourself to go out. It was obvious you were upset and something distressing had happened. No one will think badly of you for going home to sort it out.'

I hesitated. 'Really?'

'Definitely.' Tom gave me a warm smile. 'Go home, spend

some time with your children and then do something for yourself. Have a bath, read a book … no, I know, catch up on *Succession*.'

Tom had just described my perfect evening. 'That does sound tempting,' I murmured.

'Do it,' Tom said firmly. 'I'll tell anyone who comes that you had to get home, but that you'll be there next time.' He squeezed my arms. 'Come back refreshed tomorrow, ready to face the day, and tell me what you think about Logan's latest antics.'

'Thank you,' I said. 'For everything.'

'No worries.' Tom held my gaze.

My cheeks grew warm and I pulled away. 'Right,' I said briskly. 'See you tomorrow.'

'Tomorrow.' Tom smiled. 'Looking forward to it.'

I hurried out the door. The worrying thing was, I was looking forward to it too.

Chapter 19

Sarah

'Don't forget they've both got football club after school.' I flipped the sun visor down and checked my makeup in the mirror. I'd sobbed at the school gate when saying goodbye to Evie and Fred, even though I was only going away for one night. It hadn't stopped Miss Boast giving me a dirty look. She was never going to forget that soiled-nappy incident.

'You'll have to wash the football kit tonight, so that it's dry in time for Evie's match on Thursday. Don't tumble-dry it, though, or it'll shrink.' I paused. 'Bugger, I forgot to take the lasagne out of the freezer. Can you put it in the fridge when you get back, so it's defrosted for tomorrow?' What else was going on during the twenty-four hours I was away? 'Evie's got ballet tonight.'

Will exhaled loudly. 'Why bother writing on the calendar if you're going to say it all anyway?'

I closed the visor with a sharp click. 'Because you don't always look at the calendar.' By always, I meant never. I wasn't sure he read the notes I left either. Although he couldn't have missed the one where I'd written STAY AWAKE in massive, red letters.

'This is a fun journey,' Will muttered. 'Glad I volunteered to take you to the airport.'

It wasn't as though he had anything else to do. I didn't say this, in case he did a swift U-turn and bombed down the hard shoulder in the opposite direction. Things had been

131

fractious between us since he missed school pick-up. He thought I was overreacting. I thought he was an idiot. I sighed and crossed my arms.

'That's classic negative body language,' Will said. 'Defensive blocking – signalling that you don't want to engage or listen.'

He was spot on, but acknowledging this would involve engaging with him, which, as he'd correctly identified, I didn't want to do.

'I'm really enjoying the psychology book,' he continued. 'It's a fascinating subject.'

'If it's so fascinating, why did you fall asleep?'

Will gripped the steering wheel. 'That was two weeks ago and it hasn't happened since. I've programmed an alarm into my new phone to remind me to pick them up.'

MI5 should get him on their task force. His precision skills were wasted on the school run.

His mention of the new phone reminded me that I was also cross about the number of new parcels that kept arriving. It was like living in an Amazon warehouse.

'You've got to stop buying stuff,' I said. 'That money has to last.'

'Shouldn't I have bought you that new hairdryer then?'

'No,' I snapped. 'It was an unnecessary extravagance at a time when we should be being careful.' Without thinking, I smoothed the side of my hair. My new hairdryer was not unnecessary. I wasn't sure how I'd got to this stage of my life without it. If the house burnt down and we could only salvage what we could carry, it was touch-and-go if it'd be the children or the hairdryer.

Will chuckled beside me, and I whipped my hand down and folded my arms even more tightly.

Will opened his mouth to speak, but I jumped in quickly. 'I'm cold. My arms are crossed to warm me up. Nothing to do with being annoyed with you. But don't spend any more money,' I added.

'Most of it's been on the kids' Christmas presents,' Will said. 'Have you seen how long their lists are?'

'They're wish lists, not order forms.' I threw my hands up in the air. 'You're not supposed to buy everything they ask for. They'll be spoilt. They just need a main present from Santa and a few bits from us.'

A wave of sadness swept over me. I loved Christmas shopping. Seeking out little gifts that would make their faces light up with joy. For about three seconds, until they tossed it all aside in search of the next present. I'd still do their stockings, I decided. I'd somehow find the time. There might be a few things at the airport, and Amsterdam would be a treasure trove of stocking fillers. Spliff-flavoured lollipops and magic mushrooms would make an original alternative to chocolate coins and satsumas. Which reminded me …

'What happened to the satsumas I asked you to order? Fred was supposed to take one into school to decorate for Christingle.'

Will looked sheepish. 'They didn't come. Sorry. I must have messed up the order. It was OK, though,' he added. 'Miss Boast had a few spares, so he didn't miss out.'

I tutted. 'She's going to hate me even more now.'

'You're imagining it.' Will drummed his fingertips on the steering wheel. 'She's nice to everyone. You can tell from her use of body language that it's genuine. And she's great with the kids. Very understanding and flexible.'

I stiffened. I didn't want Miss Boast using her flexible body language anywhere near my husband, thank you very much. I pointedly changed the subject.

'You think you might do a psychology course then?'

Will nodded. 'Might even do a degree.'

A degree? That was some undertaking. He'd been known not to commit to watching a TV series if it had more than six episodes, unless it was *The Sopranos*. 'Having two degrees would be impressive,' I said.

Will grinned. 'It'd look great on my CV when I apply for a job.'

My stomach twisted. I hadn't found the right time to tell him that he couldn't apply to a rival firm. Mainly because we hadn't been speaking much since Nap-gate. If he pursued a career in psychology, he'd never need to know.

'Need to find out how much it costs first.' He shot me a sideways look.

'Don't worry about that.' I placed a hand on his cheek. 'Spending money on your education is an investment in your future. And it won't take up as much room,' I added.

Will turned his face and kissed my palm. 'Sorry, didn't realise the summer house would come in so many boxes. I'll make a start on it soon.'

I ran my thumb across his cheek, enjoying the warmth of his skin. It was the most tactile we'd been for two weeks. I missed our closeness and vowed to make more of an effort to spend time together in future.

'Try to get it built before you start your course,' I said. 'You'll be busy studying then.'

Will nodded. 'I'm going to an open day at the college with Lauren tomorrow to find out more.'

First Miss Boast, now Lauren. Women were queuing up to spend time with my husband. Of course they were – no one could resist those deep brown eyes. I gave his cheek a playful squeeze.

'I'll have to meet her sometime,' I said lightly. Keep your friends close, and your enemies closer.

'Ow,' Will said, jerking his face away.

My playful squeeze had become a vice-like grip at the thought of meeting Lauren. 'Sorry.' I dropped my hand.

'You've already met her.' Will rubbed his shoulder against his cheek. 'She knows who you are, anyway. From reading time at school.'

I thought back to the two mornings a week when I used to go into Fred's class. I was always mentally scrolling through everything I needed to do, desperate to get through those twenty minutes so I could run, often literally, to my desk and start my working day. It had been hard enough to focus on Fred, never mind the other mums. Hopefully, that meant she wasn't particularly attractive. Even in my most distracted state of mind, surely I'd have clocked someone of Victoria's Secret model calibre in the room?

'It'd be good to meet her properly,' I said. 'Seeing as she's a new friend.'

Will's Adam's apple bobbed up and down. 'She's not a friend, exactly. The kids like playing together, so the parents are forced together and have to get on. Kind of like colleagues do. Like you and Tom do.'

'You're not being forced together tomorrow.' I ignored his reference to Tom. It was completely different. 'You're choosing to go to the open day with her.' A thought struck me and I frowned. 'Why is she going to the open day? She's already doing the course.'

'To catch up with her tutor.' Will shook his head. 'Don't make something out of nothing. I'm not questioning you going away with Tom.'

'I'm not going away *with* him,' I said. 'We're both going to a meeting with a client and it happens to be in another country.'

'Well, I'm going to an open day at a college where Lauren is also going.'

'Because she's taking you.'

'Are you and Tom taking separate planes?'

'Obviously not. We're going from the same place and need to arrive at the same time.'

'Same for us. What's the point in driving separately and going in convoy?'

I didn't say anything and Will placed a hand on my knee. 'We're just friends,' he said softly.

'You said you *weren't* friends.' I knew I sounded pathetic and needy, but I couldn't help it.

'Fine. We're adults who get on reasonably well because

135

we have to. Nothing more.' He squeezed my knee. 'Just like in *When Harry met Sally*.'

I pushed his hand away. 'Harry and Sally end up together. The whole point of the story is that sex got in the way of them being friends.'

'Do they?' Will frowned. 'Must have fallen asleep during that bit.'

'Becoming your trademark that, isn't it?' I crossed my arms tightly again.

Will didn't mention my negative body language for the rest of the journey, but he was straight back on it when we arrived at the airport.

'Know what that means?' he asked, as I smoothed my dress down.

I sighed. 'It means I want to look presentable, but you're probably going to tell me that I'm vain and self-absorbed.'

Will shook his head. 'Subconsciously, you're worried that you're overweight.'

I flinched. Knew I shouldn't have eaten all those leftover pizzas. They weren't even nice – either wafer-thin and burnt or so thick and doughy that you could insulate a loft with them. But I was too busy or tired to cook in the evenings, so it was that or nothing. Should have chosen nothing. It would have tasted better.

'How overweight?' I asked cautiously.

Will put his hands up. 'Ignore me. You look fine.'

Fine? Never mind body language, Will needed to brush up on the English language. Using the word 'fine' to describe someone's appearance was the biggest insult you could pay.

'I'm going.' I grabbed my case with one hand and extended my middle finger on the other. 'I'm sure you know what this means. If not, look it up in your body-language analysis book.' And with that, I strode off.

As farewells went, it wasn't the most romantic. Usually, we hugged tightly while I fought back tears. I hated saying goodbye, knowing that I wouldn't see him, even if it was only for twenty-four hours. He might get on my nerves for several of those hours, but there were enough of them when he didn't, and that meant I missed him when we were apart.

Racked with guilt, I wandered around the airport shops, half-heartedly picking up potential stocking fillers for Fred and Evie, putting them back when I saw the price, then picking them up again because I felt so guilty about leaving them for the night, and for how I'd treated Will. I loaded several jumbo-sized Toblerone bars into my basket. There was no excuse for my behaviour. Yes, he'd been annoying, and had suggested I was getting fat, but I should have been mature enough to say goodbye properly. If the plane crashed, his lasting memory would be of me flipping him the bird. Worse, if he died, I'd have to live with the guilt of how I'd chosen to say goodbye to the man I loved. I took my phone from my bag. I needed to call and apologise.

'Someone's hungry.' Tom appeared next to me and peered at the mountain of chocolate, sweets and Chupa Chups lollipops in my basket. He waved a Dutch dictionary at me. 'Or should I say: *iemand heeft honger?*'

'I don't know. Should you? Judging by past performances, you might well be telling me you smell of cheese.'

Tom swatted me with his book. 'I've been practising. Want to get it right this time.'

'Good for you.' I put my phone away. I'd call Will later. He'd be driving anyway and I didn't want to distract him. 'I'm going to put this lot back.' I indicated the basket. 'Evie and Fred will turn into gremlins if they consume this much sugar.' I took two of the Toblerone bars out. 'I'm keeping these, though.'

'Not worried you'll turn into a gremlin?'

'I already look like one first thing in the morning. Be warned.'

'I'll be careful.' Tom grinned and I felt my cheeks flush. Why had I said that? He wouldn't be seeing me first thing in the morning. Well, at breakfast maybe, but not as soon as we woke up. Thank God. My curls were off-the-chart crazy before I'd tamed them with serum and a blast from my new not-essential-but-if-you-want-it-back-you'll-have-to-prise-it-out-of-my-cold-dead-hands hairdryer. I wouldn't wish that sight of Medusa's significantly less attractive sister on my worst enemy.

'Have they announced our gate yet?' I asked, changing the subject completely.

Tom nodded. '*Laten we gaan.* Let's go.'

I held up the Toblerones. 'Unless you know how to say: "It was an honest mistake, your honour," in Dutch, I'd better pay for these first.'

Tom tapped his dictionary against his chin. 'I can say my friend has had an accident.'

I laughed. 'They'd think I'd wet myself. Which I probably would if I was arrested.'

'Can't have that. I don't know the word for incontinent.' Tom took the bars out of my hand. 'I'll get these.'

'No,' I said, but he was already heading to the pay desk. Bugger. Hope that didn't mean he expected me to share them with him.

'*Een zwarte koffie,*' Tom said to the flight attendant. '*Alsjeblieft.*'

'Of course, sir,' she replied with a smile. 'And for you, madam?'

Tom looked crestfallen, but I was relieved. I didn't want to seem ignorant and rude for not learning some basic vocab native to the country I was visiting. Especially as that was exactly what I was doing.

'A tomato juice, please,' I said.

'A Bloody Mary?' she asked.

I opened my mouth to say that, no, I wanted a straight juice, but Tom leapt in.

'Great idea,' he said. 'Cancel my black coffee. I'll have one too.'

'British people drink a lot,' the attendant said. 'I'll give you two each.'

Under normal circumstances, I'd have asked her if she'd consider moving to the UK and becoming my new best friend – Tonya would understand – but we were going straight to a meeting. Two alcoholic drinks at eleven in the morning on an empty stomach didn't seem like a good idea.

'Can we get some crisps, too, please?' I asked. That'd solve the problem.

Two microscopic packets of in-flight nibbles were placed on Tom's tray. I'd expected more generous portions from business class. They wouldn't exactly absorb much vodka. I'd ask for more.

'*Bedankt*,' Tom said, pouring out the first of the cans that she'd put in front of him. 'How's my Dutch, by the way?'

The attendant smiled. 'It is said *ber-dahnkt*. But very good.'

'*Ber-dahnkt*,' Tom tried.

'Very good,' she repeated.

The conversation was a little dry for my liking. As was my glass. I smiled encouragingly, and she got the hint and passed me my drinks. I opened my mouth to ask for more snacks, but Tom got in before me.

'Can you tell if someone's British?' he asked. 'Before hearing them talk, I mean.'

The attendant nodded. 'Yes. They always want more food and drink.'

I clamped my mouth shut. The snacks could wait.

'Cheers.' Tom tapped his glass against mine and winked. 'Here's to a successful trip.'

'Cheers.' I opened my teeny-tiny packet of nibbles. A pair of tweezers would have been useful. 'How do you think the team are getting on?' I wrestled a savoury snack free and popped it in my mouth. 'They never come and see me.'

Tom pulled a face. 'They're a funny bunch. Don't want to share what they're working on.'

'But we have to know what they're working on.' I went to eat another snack, but they were all gone. There were probably more calories in the celery stick in my drink than there were in the packet.

Tom passed me his packet of snacks. 'Want these?'

'Yes, please.' I took them gratefully. 'Let's have a team meeting when we get back. Reassure them we're on their side. That there's no shame in asking for help. It's how we learn and grow.'

Tom nodded. 'Good idea. I'll get Nancy to set it up.'

I bristled at the sound of her name. 'She doesn't speak to me anymore.' I scrunched up my already finished second snack packet. 'Still wonder if I should have confronted her.'

'You'd have made it worse.' Tom stirred his Bloody Mary. 'People like Nancy thrive on gossip. If you pull them up on it, they twist it to seem as though they're the victim and you're a bully. Better to rise above it and let it go.'

I thought back to the rumour circulating around the office earlier in the year that Nancy had helped Tom to get through his marriage break-up. I'd accepted it without question, but maybe it was as fabricated as her claim that I made Will leave work so I could become a Director. Had Tom heard the rumour, and heeded his advice of rising above it and letting it go? I nudged the side of my glasses up, desperate to ask him, but not sure I should. An announcement came over the tannoy that the plane was starting its descent. I decided not to ask Tom. It wasn't my business and I had something much more important to ask him: could I have my Toblerones now?

'*Proost*,' Dieuwke said, clinking her glass against mine, Tom's and Lars's.

'*Proost*,' we echoed.

That would be as far as I'd be venturing with the Dutch lingo after my earlier attempt. Instead of saying, 'Pleased to meet you,' I'd said, 'Well done.' It could have been worse, but congratulating someone for walking into a room was slightly overzealous. I was clearly not a natural linguist. I couldn't even get that one word right. My chances of ever being asked to host the *Eurovision Song Contest* were very slim.

There had been another tricky moment when I'd asked Dieuwke a question and she'd replied: 'Yes, whore.' My distress clearly showed, as she'd quickly explained that '*ja, hoor*' meant 'yes, of course'. Which was a relief. Last thing you want to hear when you're securing a work deal is that your client thinks you're a slag.

'To a long, enduring relationship,' said Lars, with a smile.

Tom nodded. '*Ja, hoor.*'

That was about the twentieth time he'd used the phrase. I was pretty sure he just liked saying *hoor*.

'Very good,' Lars said.

Tom smoothed his tie. 'Sorry about my appalling attempt at Dutch in the last meeting.'

'Why are you learning?' Dieuwke asked. 'We all speak English.'

'Good question.' Tom chuckled. 'I'll stick with marketing from now on rather than trying to be Superman and do it all.'

I frowned. Was Superman renowned for his Dutch conversational skills?

Dieuwke clapped her hands together. '*Ja, hoor.*' She seemed quite keen on saying it too. 'That is why you're so familiar. The actor in *Superman.*'

'Oh, I don't know about that.' Tom inclined his head. 'But thank you.'

I shot him a sideways look. Was it my imagination or had I heard all this before?

'Do you like *The Avengers* also?' Lars asked.

He and Tom launched into an in-depth conversation about which superhero powers were superior. I chose not to join in. Thor was clearly the best, but if I explained why then Dieuwke would be completely justified in calling me a *hoor*.

'Sarah Campbell,' she said to me across the table. 'Is it right to assume that you are related to Will Campbell?'

I nodded. 'I didn't mention it because—'

Dieuwke put up a hand. 'It is not relevant. I understand.'

I smiled with relief.

'Why did he leave the company?'

My smile wavered. 'He wasn't getting to see the children much. Thought it'd be good to take a few months out to readjust the work-life balance.' I felt my face flush. Did that sound plausible?

Dieuwke gestured to me. 'And how will *you* see your children if you are doing his job?'

By ditching everything else in my life. Racing home to put them to bed, then working late. Spending every weekend pandering to them, driven by guilt and maternal longing and, what was the other thing? Oh yes, more guilt. All with the aim of being a successful career woman and a doting mum. Both of which I was probably failing at.

'Tom's going to do the long-haul travel,' I said instead, deciding that was TMI.

'It is still a juggling act for you. Can you not both work part-time? This is common in the Netherlands when people have children.'

'Really?' I nudged my glasses up. 'Even in executive positions?'

Dieuwke nodded. 'Most parents do. My husband and I also. He works two days a week and I work three.'

I sighed. 'That sounds perfect. It isn't really a thing in the UK, though.'

'Perhaps you could make it a thing?'

Unlikely, as Will had been fired. I glossed over that.

'What does your husband do?' I asked, taking a sip of wine.

'He *fucked* horses.'

I choked on my wine. There must be some serious language breakdown here. 'Pardon?' I managed to squeak.

Dieuwke nodded. 'Yes, horses.'

I took a much larger mouthful of wine. Then another. 'That's a career in the Netherlands?' No wonder he only wanted to work two days a week.

'Yes. It is very fulfilling, but very demanding.'

'I er …' I trailed off. I had nothing.

'My husband – *hij fokt paarden.*'

Still nothing.

Dieuwke's brow furrowed. 'That's not right.'

She could say that again.

Dieuwke clicked her fingers. 'Breed. That is the English word. He breeds horses.'

Ah. *Fokt* meant breed. I stifled a giggle. '*Pardon* is Dutch for horse?'

'*Paarden.*' Dieuwke corrected my pronunciation. 'What is so funny?'

'Nothing.' I smiled. 'Nothing at all.'

The evening wound to a natural close – without any more references to bestiality, thankfully – and we said our goodbyes. Tom and I walked back to our hotel.

'Fancy a nightcap?' he asked.

It was tempting. Having a hotel room to myself wasn't as fun as I thought it'd be. Instead of relishing the peace and quiet, the room seemed cold and stark without Will to share it with. But an uninterrupted night's sleep without an alarm going off at five thirty would help compensate.

'Thanks, but I'm tired. Was up early prepping for the meeting.'

'Your prepping paid off. They loved you.' He gestured towards the bar. 'Just a small one? Celebrate your success.'

I dug deep and mustered up some self-control – shame I hadn't done the same when saying goodbye to Will. 'No,' I said firmly. 'I'd regret it tomorrow, when I get home and the children are hyper. They don't give hangovers the respect they deserve.' I pressed the button for the lift. 'See you at breakfast if you're up,' I said.

'Oh, I'll be up.' Tom grinned. 'See if you really do look like a gremlin first thing.'

I laughed. 'They wouldn't let me in the restaurant if I turned up without some serious maintenance first.'

'Spoilsport.' Tom winked and my stomach flipped over.

I stopped laughing instantly. Where the hell had that come from?

Chapter 20

Will

'Hi, I'm Jake, the tutor on the psychology course.' The man, who looked closer to Evie's age than mine, thrust a hand towards me. 'Are you looking to study for career purposes?' he asked.

I eyed him sceptically. Tutors were not called Jake. They were called Professor Plum or Franklin Finbar and they wore tweed jackets with leather patches on the elbows. There was a possibility Jake owned one, but he'd wear it in an ironic way, whatever the fuck that meant.

'Not sure yet,' I mumbled, desperately scanning the room to catch sight of an authority figure who looked as though they'd been born before Justin Bieber.

Jake nodded. 'People often study as a hobby. Are you interested in the certificate, diploma or degree?'

I gave up looking for someone with grey hair, a few creases around the eyes or tattoo-free skin and considered Jake's question. Certificates were all well and good as rewards for swimming twenty-five metres or cycling around a few traffic cones unaided, but they weren't going to display much kudos on my CV. And weren't diplomas for – what was the PC phrase? – thickos?

'The degree,' I said firmly. If I was doing this, I'd do it properly.

'Cool,' Jake said. Proper tutors did not use the word cool. 'Does the part-time or full-time option appeal more?'

I ran a hand over my head. My marketing degree had taken three years and I'd only had a few tutorials a week. If I knuckled down, I could rattle through this. 'Full-time,' I said. 'I'm on a six-month sabbatical, so that should give me enough time.'

Jake snorted. He covered it with a cough and scratched at his patchy beard. I held in a deep sigh. Bloody kids.

'A full-time course takes three years,' he said. 'That's with forty hours' study a week.'

'What?' I gave a hollow laugh. 'A normal degree wouldn't take that long if you cut out all the free periods and socialising. I was drunk or hungover most of the time I was at uni.'

Jake looked very disapproving. He was probably one of those kids who went to the gym instead of the pub and posted TikToks of wheatgrass smoothies.

'Did you pass?' he asked.

Bloody cheek. 'I got a First!'

'There's a much higher standard now,' Jake said. 'Forty hours is the minimum study time required to get a good grade.' It was the modern-day equivalent of 'things weren't like that in my day'. If he dared mention how lucky we'd been not to have theory driving tests, I'd point out that constant access to online porn versus the mortification of buying a copy of *Playboy*, then trying to hide it from your mum, more than compensated.

'If that's too much work, you could do the part-time course, which is twenty hours of study a week.' Jake scratched his patchy chin again. 'That takes six years to complete.'

'Six years?' I spluttered. 'I've got six months, not six years. There must be a way to fast-track it.'

'No, there isn't.' Jake smirked. 'You could do the certificate instead. That only takes a year of full-time study.' He didn't add, 'Because it's shit,' but that was the underlying message.

I looked him straight in the eyes. I'd show him. I'd do the

degree in less time than any student had managed before. That'd wipe the cocky smirk off his bumfluff face.

'I'll go for the degree,' I said evenly. 'Where do I sign up?'

Lauren appeared at my side. 'Hi Jake.'

'Hi Lauren.' Jake gave her a huge grin. Urgh. He clearly had a MILF crush. How unprofessional. 'Really impressed with your last paper. Just a few points I need to run through with you. We can do it now if you like?' He placed a hand on her arm and angled her away from me.

'I'm going to do the degree too,' I said.

Lauren spun round. 'That's so exciting. We can be study buddies.'

'Yes, we can.' I smiled broadly at her, ignoring Jake, who was glaring at me. 'Want to show me where I sign up?'

She nodded and we walked away. 'Thanks for your help,' I said to Jake over my shoulder. I didn't need a degree in psychology to read the 'piss off' vibes emanating from his body. Although at least he hadn't flipped me the bird, unlike my lovely wife the day before.

It had taken Sarah hours to call and apologise. Even then, it had felt like more of a formality to get out of the way, so she could witter on about how well the meeting had gone, and how she and Dieuwke had bonded, despite calling her a prostitute or something. She hadn't asked me anything about my day. Just wanted to speak to the kids, who were on top form when FaceTiming Mummy, eagerly telling her what they'd done at school. All I'd got out of them was, 'Fine,' at pick-up. They'd reverted immediately to inanimate objects on the sofa after hanging up. Sarah hadn't even asked to say goodbye to me. In too much of a rush to get ready to go out to dinner.

Lauren clapped her hands together and I pushed thoughts of Sarah's disinterest from my mind. 'It'll be so nice to have someone to talk to about the course,' she said. 'There are lots of online forums, but it's not the same, is it?'

I smiled. 'No, doing it in person is always nicer.'

'Said the actress to the bishop.' Lauren giggled.

My face grew hot. 'I mean—'

Lauren put a hand on my arm. 'I'm only teasing.'

I nodded, very aware of the warmth of her hand through my sleeve. 'Is that where I sign up?' I exaggeratedly raised my arm to point, so that her hand fell away.

'Yes. Come and grab me when you're done.' She turned and her glossy, black hair fanned out around her. This, and the invitation to grab her, did nothing to reduce my increased temperature.

I went over to a row of desks where smiley, friendly young people were talking to other smiley, friendly young people. Thank God this course was online. I could be as sullen and old as I liked, and no one would ever know.

'Hello,' said a friendly, smiley young woman. 'How can I help?'

'I want to sign up for the degree in psychology.'

Her smile faltered. 'The degree?'

'Yes.' I frowned. 'Isn't that what everyone else is doing?'

'Yes, but they're ...' She bit her lip. 'You're ...'

'A mature student?' I said, before she could utter the word 'old'.

She flushed crimson and nodded.

'The degree course,' I said firmly.

'Sure you wouldn't prefer the certificate?' She put her head to one side and gave me a kindly smile. Presumably because she doubted I'd live long enough to complete the degree course. For God's sake, I couldn't be the first mature student she'd come across. I glared at her. Her smile became less kindly. 'Will you be paying up front or in instalments?'

'Up front,' I said. 'How much is it?'

'It's £6,000.'

I swallowed hard. Slightly more than I'd anticipated. This would have to be it on the spending front. I'd got a bit carried away lately. While the cordless vacuum cleaner was a great addition to the household, we could probably have lived without the electric egg boiler. There wouldn't be time to watch the shopping channel when I started studying, so that'd help.

'You won't believe this, but degrees used to be free,' I said, further proving that I already had one foot in the grave.

The now-not-so-friendly-and-smiley young woman cleared her throat. 'That's for the certificate.'

God give me strength. 'I'm doing the degree, not the certificate,' I said, tapping my foot in frustration.

'OK.' She shrugged in an it's-your-life-albeit-a-short-one way. 'That's £20,000.'

My eyes watered. 'Maybe I will have another look at the certificate.' I picked up the prospectus and walked quickly away.

Did she just say £20,000? No wonder graduates had so much debt if that was the starting point, before adding the cost of accommodation, food, beer, wine and spirits. I scanned the room for Lauren. She was deep in conversation with smarmy Jake. I wasn't going to tell him I had cold feet. But seriously. Twenty grand and forty hours of study a week for three years was a much larger undertaking than I'd anticipated. Even if I could find forty hours a week, did I want to spend all of it studying? I'd barely touched the surface of my box set wish list, I had a summer house to build, and I was only on the beginner section of my pizza cookbook. Plus, I wasn't sure I could stomach dealing with know-it-all Jake. Not that I could stomach the beginner-level pizzas either. I chewed my lip. Sod the degree. I'd finish the body language book, but the rest of the study would have to wait. A retirement project maybe. I had more important things to focus on. Such as how I was going to assemble my new Lego Millennium Falcon without Sarah seeing it.

'It's almost Christmas,' I explained to Lauren as she drove us back. 'Then I've only got three months before my sabbatical ends.' By sabbatical ending, I meant new job starting, which I had to find. 'I don't want to start the degree without being sure I can finish it,' I added, omitting that, on reflection, I didn't want to start the degree at all.

Lauren glanced over from the driver's seat. 'Shame, it would have been fun. But I understand. I can still bore you with what I'm studying.' She laughed and I joined in. What she'd said hadn't been remotely funny, but who could resist that tinkly little laugh.

'You wouldn't bore me,' I said. 'It's an amazing subject. I'm learning so much from the book you lent me.'

'Plenty more where that came from.' Lauren indicated to turn into my road. 'At the moment I'm reading a fascinating book about how psychology follows the empirical method.'

She could keep that one. I steered clear of literature containing words I couldn't pronounce.

Lauren pulled up outside my house. 'I could come in and give you a quick demo of the pizza oven if you like?' she said. 'Got an hour before pick-up.'

I thought about the state I'd left the house in. Washing-up piled up by the sink. Laundry on the kitchen floor, on its way into the machine. Skid marks in the toilets.

'Thanks, but there's something I have to do,' I said. That didn't sound weird at all.

Lauren ran a hand through her hair. Each strand glistened, as it slipped through her fingers. 'It never ends, does it?' She smiled. 'I need to finish clearing our guttering.'

Clearing guttering? She was so capable. I hadn't even managed to keep our toilets clean for twenty-four hours. Although, when the kids got gung-ho with the toilet roll, it wasn't unlike clearing guttering.

I undid my seat belt and opened the door. 'Thanks for driving.'

'You're welcome. See you at the school gates.' She leant over and kissed my cheek.

I jumped, whacked my skull on the headliner, and slid sideways out of the car and onto the drive, landing heavily on my back.

'Will – are you all right?' Lauren called through the open door.

'Fine, thanks.' I sprang up immediately, as though nothing had happened, although inside I was whimpering and trying to remember where we kept the heat patches. 'See you in an hour.' I slammed the car door and limped towards the house.

Lauren had kissed me. It had been a chaste, meaningless kiss – the sort my sister would give me. But Tonya's kisses never caused my cheek to tingle the way Lauren's had. Throwing myself out of the car to get away had perhaps been slightly excessive, but it had solved the problem and it wasn't as if the car had been moving. It just felt like it had.

Three hours later, I took Sarah's lasagne out of the freezer. I should have got it out yesterday to defrost, but I'd forgotten, what with going through Fred's phonics and Evie's times tables, and washing the football kit and … Oh bollocks, I still hadn't taken it out of the machine. I'd do it once I got dinner on.

As I crowbarred the frozen-solid lasagne out of its Tupperware container into a microwave-proof glass dish, I tried not to be resentful that while I was dealing with all of the domestic shit, Sarah had been out with my clients. Dining in the restaurant that I should have been in. Staying in the hotel room that had originally been booked in my name. My attempt at not being resentful lasted less than the time it took me to remove the cellophane from the lasagne. It would have been me in Amsterdam if Sarah hadn't insisted on coming to the conference, I seethed, putting the dish in the microwave and switching it on to full power for ten minutes. If it wasn't defrosted after that then it would be cereal for tea. Again.

I was about to tackle the laundry, when Sarah walked in. My resentment dissolved at the sight of her. That smile had the power to take my breath away as much now as it had when we'd first got together. More so now that I knew how funny and kind and organised and good at buying Toblerones she was.

She wrapped her arms around me. 'Sorry about the way I said goodbye at the airport.'

'What was it again?' I asked. 'A bird, a plane, Superman? No, it was definitely the bird.'

Sarah cringed.

'I'm teasing.' I hugged her hard, inhaling the scent of her coconut shampoo, enjoying her soft cheek against mine. She turned her face and kissed me. A proper kiss that represented our decade-long love. Nothing like the very platonic peck on the cheek that Lauren had given me. I felt a stirring as the kiss deepened. See, that proved I had no interest in Lauren. The only hard thing I'd encountered with that kiss was the ground I'd fallen on.

'When's dinner?' Evie called from the living room.

'Not long,' I shouted, breaking away from the kiss briefly, then diving back in. The internal garage door was just inches away. Could we sneak in there without the kids noticing? I only needed a few minutes.

'I'm hungry,' Fred hollered.

Sarah stepped back, a rueful look in her eye. I'd take that as a promise for tonight.

'I've only said a brief hello to them,' she said, adjusting her slightly steamed-up glasses. 'I'll go and have a quick chat, then help with dinner, if that's OK?'

I nodded, adjusting my slightly steamed-up trousers.

She turned and whacked her knee on the open door of the washer-dryer. 'Ow,' she gasped, bending to close the door. 'Oh, it's full.' She reached for the laundry basket and started pulling all the dry clothes out of the machine. Fair dues. I'd have pretended not to notice. Actually, scrap that. No pretending would have been needed. I genuinely wouldn't have noticed.

'Yep, football kit all washed and dried, ready for tomorrow,' I said, feeling a little smug.

Sarah gasped again, much louder this time. 'No!' She held up a toddler-size strip. 'Evie can't wear this for her match tomorrow.'

OK, not feeling quite so smug now. 'It'll stretch,' I said, knowing full well it wouldn't.

'I told you they'd shrink in the tumble dryer.' Sarah took off her glasses and rubbed her eyes. 'I'll have to message the mums' WhatsApp group and ask if anyone's got a spare kit she can borrow.' She sighed. 'It'll be so obvious I'm only on there to ask a favour, after ignoring all the messages about baking half-time cakes or taking part in the charity car wash.'

My ears pricked up. 'There's going to be a bikini car wash?'

Sarah shoved her glasses back on and glared at me. 'Charity, not bikini. They don't sound remotely similar.'

'They do a bit.' They didn't.

The microwave pinged and I took the lasagne out.

'That needs to be reheated in the oven,' Sarah said. 'It won't get a nice, crispy top in the microwave.'

'Give me a chance. I'm defrosting it first.'

'Defrosting it? In the microwave?' Sarah couldn't have looked more disgusted if I were proffering raw monkey brains fresh from the skull. 'You can't do that. It could give them food poisoning.'

'How?' I was getting fed up with Sarah's insinuations that I didn't know what I was doing. I'd been looking after Fred and Evie for weeks now and hadn't killed them. Although I had come close when Fred knocked his juice over my two-hour-old phone.

'Bacteria multiplies on food when it's defrosted quickly. That's why I said to take it out of the freezer yesterday.'

'Sorry, it slipped my mind after taking you to the airport,' I snapped. 'Which I didn't get any thanks for.'

'I said sorry about how I behaved.' Sarah scraped her hair back into a topknot. 'Can you understand how frustrating this is for me?' she said in a low voice, her eyes darting to the living-room door to make sure the kids weren't listening. 'Work's full-on and I'm still responsible for everything at home. Even when I leave foolproof instructions, you get it wrong.'

'No, I don't,' I hissed.

Sarah held up the tiny football kit with one hand and gestured to the semi-defrosted lasagne with the other. 'What do you call this then?'

'Anyone can make a mistake.' I tutted.

Sarah wrung the football shirt in her hands, probably wishing it was my neck. 'It's constant mistakes,' she said through gritted teeth. 'And every one generates work for me, on top of the full-time job I'm doing.'

I dropped the lasagne dish heavily on the work surface. 'I've had enough of this. I'm doing my best and all you do is criticise.'

I paced up and down the kitchen. How was I going to get through the next few months? This wasn't fun. The kids' initial excitement of me being around had worn off. They were so grumpy most of the time that they made Mrs Manning seem only mildly unpleasant in comparison. My visions of bonding while building Lego or toasting marshmallows on an open fire or watching the classic films I'd loved as a kid – *Star Wars*, *Indiana Jones*, *Jaws 3-D* – had gone to shit. They fought over the Lego. The only film they'd watch was *Frozen Fever*, which ran for exactly seven minutes and was the most mind-numbingly inane animation ever created. Oh, and the toasted marshmallows. They shrivelled into lava-like pellets when I tried them in the pizza oven. Another reason I hadn't wanted Lauren to give me a demo. The blasted (literally) things were welded onto it now.

Sarah closed her eyes and inhaled deeply, then released a long, slow breath, puckering her lips as though blowing out a candle. I waited for her to let go of her negativity, realign her chakras and focus on what really mattered. Me.

'Sorry for snapping,' Sarah said. 'I know this is hard for you.'

The mindfulness breathing had actually worked! I'd never mock that chakra bollocks again.

'The biggest part of your life has been whipped away,' Sarah continued. 'You've had to completely readjust.' I nodded, touched that she understood. 'And you've got the added humiliation of me being promoted to a similar role to the one you did.'

She was going a bit far now. I wasn't humiliated – or at least I hadn't been till now. Should I be? Did I need to add degraded to the list of crappy emotions I was going through?

Sarah gestured to the lasagne dish. 'Let's not take any chances with this. We'll get the kids a McDonald's. They haven't had one for ages, so it'll be a treat and we won't have any washing-up to do.'

Would Evie and Fred mention that we'd had one yesterday? Probably, but it was worth it to move on from this fight. If we moved fast, Sarah's chakras might not have time to un-align themselves.

'Great idea.' I rubbed my hands together. 'Let's go now, then relax with a glass of wine when we get back.'

Sarah smiled, put a hand to my cheek and walked through to the living room. 'Who wants a McDonald's?' she called.

Moments later, we were about to pull out of the drive when a Tesco lorry pulled up.

Sarah looked impressed. 'Well done for organising a delivery. You deserve a lot more credit than I gave you.'

I considered lying and taking the glory – I hadn't done a Tesco delivery; the driver must have come to the wrong house – but it'd be obvious I'd bullshitted when the cupboards were bare, and Sarah's chakras only had so much give in them.

'Hate to disappoint you, but it's not for us. I'll tell him he's made a mistake. I'll do one for real when we get back.' I got out of the car and jogged over to the driver. 'Sorry, mate. There must be a mix-up.'

The driver held up a receipt. 'Don't think so.'

Clearly printed was my name, our address, and today's date and time of delivery. Underneath was a list of the items ordered. Twenty bags of satsumas and a £50 bottle of whisky. So that's what happened to that order.

Chapter 21

Sarah

'Miss Boast says our class is the best,' Fred said, kindly sharing a view of his half-chewed Weetabix with me. 'Miss Boast says we are extra-ordinary individuals.'

Miss Boast wouldn't have said that the night before, when Fred spent forty-five minutes vocally deliberating which flavour lolly he'd take to space if he were only allowed one. It was yet another tactic to delay going to sleep. I'd humoured him because it was the first evening that week when I'd been home in time to see him and Evie, and I'd intended to leave before they woke up.

However, an overnight storm had taken down some power lines and my train wasn't running. It couldn't be worse timing. Tom and I were doing one-to-one staff appraisals today and I couldn't miss them. I pressed refresh on my train app. All services still unavailable until further notice.

'Miss Boast made me Achiever of the Week.' Fred pointed to the gold sticker on his jumper.

'I know.' I cupped his cheek. 'Well done you.'

He shrugged me off. 'Miss Boast said she'd give it to me every week if she could, 'cause I work so hard.'

'Miss Boast says that to all the Reception kids,' said Evie, the world-weary Year Two.

'Miss Boast says it to me the most.' Fred waved his spoon in the air, spraying droplets of milk over my phone. 'Boast rhymes with most!'

'So does ghost,' said Evie.

'And toast,' shouted Fred. He tapped his spoon against his head. 'Miss Boast, Miss Boast, Miss Boast,' he chanted.

I wiped the milk from my phone and pressed refresh again. 'Can you think of another one, Mummy? What rhymes with Miss Boast?'

I thought for a moment. Cow-bag didn't qualify, unfortunately. 'Host,' I said.

'What does that mean?'

'The person who looks after their guests when they come round to play.'

'We could invite Miss Boast round to play,' Fred said.

Not on my watch.

'You're such a loser,' Evie said. 'No one invites their teacher round to play.'

'Post,' I said, before an argument could break out. 'There's another one.'

'Like the Christmas post?' Fred asked.

I'd been thinking more along the lines of post-mortem, but we could go with Christmas.

Will came into the kitchen, his hair glistening from the shower. 'Still no luck with the trains?'

I shook my head, refreshing the phone again. 'I *have* to get in for the staff appraisals. Maybe I could drive?'

Will shook his head. 'Not in this weather. Traffic will be a nightmare.'

I nudged my glasses up and looked out of the window. Rain pelted down and the plants in the garden were getting such a battering from the wind that it was a wonder they were still in the ground. I hated to admit it, but negotiating the North Circular and the frenzied drivers in the City scared the hell out of me. And that was without adding hazardous weather conditions into the mix. The only way I could confidently drive through London was as part of a royal procession, travelling at three miles an hour, with a police escort on horseback. Important as the staff appraisals were, it seemed unlikely taxpayers' money would be deemed well spent on such travel arrangements.

'What would you do?' I asked.

'Work from home,' Will said simply. 'You don't have any other choice.'

'But the appraisals—'

'The trains are cancelled. There's nothing you can do.' He took my hands and squeezed them. 'Rearrange the appraisals for next week. It's no big deal. Gives everyone longer to prepare.'

It sounded so obvious when he put it like that. I hated letting people down, but there wasn't much I could do about it.

'Thank you.' I kissed his cheek. 'I'll let everyone know now.' I hugged Evie and Fred. 'Have fun at school, guys. Love you.'

'Love you, Mummy.' Evie hugged me back.

'Miss Boast says—' Fred started.

'Gottogoloveyoubyeee.' I darted out the door and up the stairs. I'd had enough of Miss Boast for today and it wasn't even eight o'clock. How many sleeps until Fred finished Reception?

I rang Tom and he answered straightaway. 'Hi Sarah. Everything OK?'

'No. The trains are cancelled and I can't get into work.'

Tom groaned. 'How annoying. What is it this time? Leaves on the line? Wrong type of rain?'

'The storm's brought the power lines down. No idea when they'll be running.' I sat at my desk and turned the computer on. 'We'll have to move the appraisals to next week.'

'That's a shame,' Tom said. 'What about Zoom?'

'I'd rather not. Appraisals are personal. We should do them in person.'

'Good point.'

'There's lots of work for them to be getting on with,' I said. 'All the existing literature for Dekker's marketing needs refreshing. I'll email an apology about the appraisals and detail who can do what.'

'No need,' Tom said. 'I'll tell them, as I'm here. You said you could do with some quiet time to come up with ideas for Dekker's new campaign. This is the perfect opportunity. Put the phone on silent and get creative.'

'I can't do that.'

'Why not? I'll hold the fort here.'

I wound a curl around my finger. 'Doesn't feel right, abandoning my post and leaving you to sort everything.'

'You're not. We're a team, remember?' Tom said. 'Next time I need some time to focus, you'll do the same for me. Deal?'

I smiled. 'OK. Deal. But let me know if something major happens or someone needs to reach me.'

'It won't. Make the most of today and wow me on Monday with your award-winning ideas.' Tom's faith in me was inspiring. If he believed that what I produced would be good, then I'd make sure it was. 'Have a great weekend,' he added.

'Thanks. You too.'

We hung up and I opened my organiser to the page where I'd started making notes, feeling motivated and charged up. I transferred my notes to my computer and elaborated on them, my typing quickening with each sentence. The next hour flew by. Without the distractions of office life and Tom at his desk across from me, I could focus completely on the project. Ideas sparked other ideas and I eagerly wrote them all down, exciting myself at the way they developed. I was going to make this Dekker's best-ever marketing campaign and prove that I deserved to be a Director. I was so engrossed that I didn't register Will getting back from the school run and wasn't aware of his presence until he came into the study.

'Oh, hi,' I said, squinting up at him, my eyes adjusting their focus.

'Hi.' He smiled. 'How's it going?'

159

'Great, thanks.' I nodded at my screen, desperate to get back to it before I lost my momentum and my ideas evaporated.

'Made you a cup of tea.' Will placed a mug on top of my organiser.

'Thanks. That's really kind.' I moved the mug and withheld a tut at the tea stain on the page. Will had done a nice thing and didn't deserve to be criticised. I placed my fingers on the keyboard, poised as though about to start playing a piano concerto, and looked expectantly at Will. He looked expectantly back. Had I forgotten something? 'Thanks for the tea,' I said again, in case he'd missed it the first time.

He started humming a vaguely familiar song. He grinned, then launched into what I assumed was a serenade. He even knelt on one knee to sing, gazing into my eyes, as though he were in a Cliff Richard movie.

I politely smiled and nodded along, willing him to finish, so I could get back to my work. Eventually he did, and grinned earnestly. I clapped awkwardly.

'Very nice,' I said, trying to muster up the enthusiasm I reserved for the children after their eight-zillionth rendition of 'Rudolph the Red Nosed Reindeer'. Will pulled the arm of my chair so that I swivelled round to face him.

'Can I help you with something?' I asked, my face now just a few inches from his.

'Yes, you can.' Will grinned and burst into song again. Oh God, he wasn't going to ask me to help him put together an audition tape for *The Voice*, was he? I could save us both a lot of time by telling him here and now that no one would be turning their chair around for him. Not even I would have done, if he hadn't physically done it himself.

'Afternoon delight,' he sang, emphasising the words, then leant in to kiss me.

'Lovely,' I said, pulling away after a few seconds. The kiss had indeed been lovely – I'd married him for a reason – but now wasn't the time. I indicated my desk. 'I'd better get back to work.'

Will's face fell. 'What about afternoon delight?'

'What are you talking about? It's nine thirty in the morning.'

Will raised his eyes to the ceiling. 'Poetic licence.' He jiggled the arms of the chair so that I swayed from side to side. It was like being in a baby bouncer. 'We can go with morning delight if you're going to be pedantic.' He leant forward to kiss me again.

I stopped him with a shake of my head. 'What are you doing?'

Will frowned. 'I'm doing what we talked about. The day I lost my job, we went to bed and had some *afternoon delight*.' God, he was singing again. 'We said that one positive was that we could do it more often. This is the first time you've been home since you became Director, so let's make the most of it.' He wiggled his eyebrows up and down.

Ah, that's why he'd brought me a cup of tea. He'd clearly remembered that it had worked that time back in 2014 and thought he'd try again.

'Lovely idea,' I said tactfully. 'But I'm working. I haven't got the day off.'

'You're not in a meeting or on a call. You can do whatever you're doing now later.' Will nuzzled my neck.

I pulled away, then felt terrible when I saw the hurt expression on his face. 'I'm sorry.' I pressed my hands together. 'It's not that I don't want to, but I need to put this pitch together and I've just got going.'

'Then this is the perfect time, before you get properly stuck in.' Will wrapped his arms around my hips and tried to ease me out of the chair. 'I'll make it worth your while.'

I clenched my gluteal muscles. The knights of the realm stood a higher chance of pulling Excalibur from the stone than Will had of getting me out of this chair.

'I'm sorry,' I said again. 'Wish I could, but I haven't got time.'

'I'll be quick,' Will said. 'You don't even have to get out of the chair. And you can keep your top on.' He tiptoed his fingers up my thighs, towards my waistband. Should I go for it? He said he'd make it worth my while and he was always as good as his word in that department. But I was 'in the zone' with work and the ideas that had been bubbling out of me would fade quicker than a cheap hair dye if I didn't get them down. Plus, someone from work could ring at any moment. It was bad enough that I wasn't in the office; it'd be even worse if I didn't answer any calls.

I eased Will's hands away. 'I don't want it to be hurried, with me worrying about the phone ringing. Let's do it properly tonight, after the kids have gone to bed.'

'Yeah, right.' Will stood up and rearranged the crotch of his jeans. 'You'll be working or too tired later.'

'I won't. I promise tonight will be all about us.' I gestured to the scribbled notes spread out in front of me. 'Let me get this pitch sorted, then I can relax and enjoy our evening.'

'I'll believe that when I see it.' Will left the room, slamming the door so hard that tea sloshed out of my mug and over my organiser.

I picked it up and patted it dry with my sleeve. Great. Now I was feeling guilty about letting Will down, on top of feeling guilty about letting my team down. I took a deep breath. I'd talk to Will later. Right now, I needed to focus on Dekker's marketing message. I retraced the spider diagram I'd been making, trying to decipher what the random words I'd scribbled down represented and where they'd been taking me. A flash of the campaign's tagline had come to me at the exact moment Will had come in. I'd had that jolt of excitement when you know something's good (Daniel Craig emerging from the waves in *Casino Royale*, for example, or a BOGOF offer on Boots No7), but hadn't had a chance to write it down and now I couldn't remember what it was. I closed my eyes. That idea was in there somewhere. I could get it back. I just had to concentrate.

There was a bang and a screeching sound from the landing that I recognised as the loft hatch opening and the ladder being lowered down. A loud thud came next. And another, and another. Keeping my eyes shut, I massaged my temples. Come on, award-winning marketing message. Come back to me.

A few minutes later the loft hatch closed and Will's feet thudded downstairs. My eyes snapped open. The only thing that had come to me was the realisation that I was very hungry. I'd been up since five thirty and, with all the drama about how to get to work and words that rhymed with Miss Boast, I'd forgotten to have breakfast. And now I couldn't go downstairs without Will accusing me of making time for food, but not him.

A loud sawing noise came from the garden. Maybe Will had decided to make a start on the summer house. Under other circumstances I might have been annoyed that he was making such a racket when I was trying to work. Or that, once opened, there was no way of returning the summer house that he lacked the patience, skills and toolbelt required to build. But right now, I was thrilled that he was occupied outside. I could nip down to the kitchen, grab some basic supplies and retreat to the study to work.

I opened the door, eyeing the stairs to make sure Will wouldn't suddenly appear. And promptly fell over the Christmas tree. Thankfully, the sharp corner of a box labelled 'baubles' caught my fall or I might have hurt myself. Wincing, I hauled myself up and limped downstairs. My mission was to get some food and no festive-themed obstacles were going to stop me.

In the kitchen, I opened the fridge. I'd forgotten it was Friday and I'd used up the last of the week's supplies in the children's packed lunches. There wasn't even enough milk for a bowl of cereal. The fridge was far from bare, though. No, every shelf was filled with satsumas. Despite gifting a load to the school, there was still an orangery's worth left to get through. Our vitamin C levels certainly wouldn't be depleted this Christmas. Sighing, I took a couple, closed the fridge door and turned to sneak back upstairs.

'Thought you were too busy to leave your desk.' Will's voice came from the back door. I froze like a teenager being caught stealing a bottle from the drinks cabinet.

'Just grabbing some breakfast.' I held up the satsumas. 'I'm getting back to it now.'

Will grunted and lobbed a chisel across the room, into the sink. We both jumped at the clatter it made.

I glared at him. 'What was that for? You've probably dented the sink.'

Will shrugged. 'You don't mind denting my feelings. Is a sink more important?'

'Don't be so melodramatic.' I crossed the kitchen. Not only was there a chink in the metal sink, but the three breakfast bowls that had been left to fester were now in pieces. 'You idiot. You've broken the bowls.'

Will shrugged. 'They're only cheap ones from IKEA.'

Every nerve in my body tensed. 'That's a disgusting, entitled attitude. They were perfectly good bowls and now they need to be replaced. What a waste of money and time and resources.'

Will looked sullenly out of the window.

'The bowls shouldn't have even been in the sink,' I hissed. 'You should have put them in the dishwasher.'

'Here we go again,' Will muttered.

All the frustrations I'd been bottling up for the last month bubbled out of me.

'I wouldn't be going on about it again if you hadn't left them there for me to clear up,' I shouted.

'Sorry, Mom,' Will said in a bored, phoney American accent.

I inhaled sharply. 'You should be sorry. I do so much for this family and you can't even be bothered to put some bowls in the dishwasher, or care that you've smashed them.'

'You're overreacting. Don't take it out on me because you're stressed with work.'

'I wouldn't be stressed with work if I got support at home.' Anger coursed through me. 'I spend my weekends bulk cooking so the children have healthy dinners in the week. I make their packed lunches before I go to bed. I do the online food shop because it's the only way I can be sure we have something to eat that isn't a citrus fruit. I do all the laundry, and change the bedding, and clean the bathrooms. You didn't do any of those things when you were a Director. I'm working just as hard as you did – harder probably, because I'm proving myself – and I'm still doing the bulk of the housework. It's not fair.'

'Life's not fair,' Will growled. 'If it were, I'd have my job and a wife who wanted to have sex with me.'

I shook my head so hard that my glasses slid down my nose. 'Does any of what I've said mean anything to you?' I shoved the glasses back up. 'You should be ashamed that you leave the housework for me to do, not punishing me because I didn't drop everything to shag you when you had the urge. You could see I was working.'

'Why should I do the housework?' Will snapped. 'It's not my job and I'm already looking after the kids.'

My hands curled into fists. Will was very fortunate it was the satsumas that were getting squished in my palms, not his testicles. 'It *is* your job while you're the one at home. I've made it easy for you so far, but I've had enough. From now on, I'll put the same effort in that you did when you worked: bugger all.' With that, I tossed the decimated satsumas into the sink and went back upstairs.

I was shaking with anger. Will hadn't said it, but it was obvious that he viewed all jobs linked to running the home as my responsibility. I was, in his eyes, lucky that he looked after the children at all. No wonder he downed tools completely at weekends. He'd done his bit. And as for sulking because I hadn't dropped my drawers when he clicked his fingers,

165

that was pathetic. Beyond pathetic – it was worrying if he felt that was an acceptable way to behave when I'd spurned his advances.

I put my laptop and organiser into my backpack, clambered over the Christmas tree and jogged down the stairs. I'd go to a café, have something to eat and work. I'd be able to get on without any interruptions and it'd show Will that I wasn't going to tolerate his behaviour. I peered through the kitchen door. Will was back out in the garden. It looked as though he was wrestling with the pizza oven, and the pizza oven was winning. Should I tell him I was going out? No. Too great a risk it'd spark up the row again. I'd send him a text from the café.

I relaxed as I got closer to town. The storm had blown itself out, leaving a bright December morning. The sun was shining, the shop windows were full of festive cheer and a busker was belting out Christmas tunes. I crossed the market square and headed to Groundworks, which served the town's best brunch. Tonya and I used to meet there regularly, but I'd not been since going back to work full-time in September. And I hadn't seen Tonya since our cocktail evening a month ago. We'd barely even texted each other. A wave of sadness washed over me. I'd been so busy and I hadn't realised how much I missed her. I'd fix that. Now that I was handing the housework and chores over to Will rather than manically doing them all at the weekends, I'd have time to see Tonya again. I might even have time to start thinking about a mindfulness yoga class. Just thinking about it. No need to go crazy and actually do it.

The manager at Groundworks greeted me warmly and led me through the café to the back, where Tonya and I always used to sit. I gasped with delight when I saw Tonya sitting there, then faltered. She was with another woman.

For a moment I thought I was going to burst into tears, which was ridiculous. Tonya was allowed to have other friends. It wasn't as though she was cheating on me. But this was *our* café and this was *our* table. She could have had the decency to go somewhere else, or at least to sit at the table by the toilet. I eyed my competition warily. She had beautiful, auburn, wavy hair. I was pretty sure I'd taken photos of this woman into the hairdresser's and asked them to transform my frizz into those luscious locks, only to be met with a pitying look.

Tonya glanced up as I approached, then did a double take. 'Sarah!' She leapt up and hugged me. 'You should have told me you had a day off.'

'The trains aren't running, so I couldn't get in. This is me working from home.' I hugged her back. 'So good to see you.'

'You too. This is Zoë.' She held a hand towards the other woman. Not that she was the other woman. I really had to remember that Tonya and I weren't a couple. 'Zoë's the restaurant head. We're going over the Christmas menus.'

Relief washed over me. Zoë wasn't a friend. This was a work thing. Of course it was. Tonya would never bring someone else to our place.

'Lovely to meet you,' I said enthusiastically. I could display genuine warmth now that I knew she wasn't a threat. 'I'll sit somewhere else. Don't want to get in your way.'

'No, it's fine,' Zoë said. 'We're done now.' She smiled at Tonya. 'I'll see you later. Thanks for bringing me up to speed.' She stood up and I slid into her seat immediately.

'So lovely to see you.' I squeezed Tonya's hand across the table. 'How have you been?'

'The work parties have started and it's manic, but we'll survive, as we always do.' Her nails shimmered as she batted her hand. 'Never mind that. How are you? How's the job?'

I slipped off my coat. There was so much I wanted to tell Tonya. About how much harder everything was than I thought it'd be. I knew work would be full-on, but it was having to do everything else as well that was tipping me over the edge. The sensible part of me knew I should stop and let Will deal with it, as I'd threatened. But the thought of Evie and Fred opening empty lunchboxes, or not having any clean pants to wear, or dying of scurvy and/or constipation because their diet consisted solely of dense, doughy, disgusting pizza was too heartbreaking for me to bear. So, I kept cooking and cleaning and washing. And with every sandwich I made and every meal I froze and every school shirt I ironed, my resentment towards Will grew.

Then there was work itself. My team hated me. They clammed up when I asked a question, walked in the opposite direction if I approached them in the office, and all said they were busy if I suggested going to the pub. They must really hate me if they were willing to turn down a free drink to avoid spending time in my company.

Being so disliked at work magnified what I was missing out on with the children. I was jealous of Sinéad for spending more waking time with them than I did. I was jealous of Fred's crush on Miss Boast. I was jealous of Lauren and the other mums that Will hung out with. I was jealous of Tonya's colleague Zoë. I was even jealous of Zoë's hair. I was jealous of everyone and everything. Except maybe Mrs Manning. The caretaker was welcome to her.

And then there was that stupid stomach flip in Amsterdam the week before. I'd scuttled off to my room, skipped breakfast the next morning (thankful I'd reclaimed the Toblerones, as I wouldn't be getting any food on the plane if that same flight attendant was in charge) and tried to avoid being on my own with Tom since. Which was impossible, as we shared an office. The stomach flip hadn't happened again, though, so I was attributing it to indigestion after the meal, rather than Tom's twinkly-eyed wink.

'Are you enjoying the job?' Tonya asked and I realised a minute had passed since she'd asked the original question.

I opened my mouth. Where should I start? Or, more accurately, where shouldn't I start? I couldn't mention the stomach flip. I couldn't moan about not seeing the children enough when I'd been so keen to take the job. I couldn't complain about Will trying to have sex with me while I was working, because that would gross Tonya out. And I couldn't whinge about Zoë's perfect hair because I was forty-two and theoretically too mature for that.

'Will said you've been in Amsterdam,' Tonya observed.

I nodded. What could I say about the trip that didn't involve Tom? 'Did you know that the Dutch word for horse is *paarden*?'

'No, I didn't.' Tonya put her head to one side.

Could she sense there was more to Amsterdam than I was telling? In the same way she'd sensed when I'd had my first snog at the school disco with Clive Davies? Admittedly, she'd been at the disco, so it was less sensing and more spying, but even so. She had only to hint that she suspected something and I'd crumple like a cheap suit. Much like the polyester one that Clive Davies had been wearing at the disco. I decided to act innocent. Which I was.

'The client renewed their contract,' I said. 'Which is great and the whole point of going. It's their campaign that I'm working on today. Not that I'm getting very far with it,' I added guiltily.

The waitress placed two Americanos on the table. 'What else can I get you ladies?' she asked.

'The works, please.' I was in dire need of fuel. As soon as I'd eaten, I'd be able to focus on work.

'Me too,' Tonya said. 'I'm as hungry as a *paarden*.'

We giggled and chinked our coffee cups together.

'I've missed you,' I said. 'Work's so busy, but I need to make time to see you.'

'Missed you too.' Tonya tapped her nails against her cup. 'Are you enjoying the job?'

I shrugged. 'I like the work, but my team hate me.'

Tonya shook her head. 'That's crazy. You get on with everyone.'

'I used to, but with this lot, the more I try to improve the relationship, the worse it gets.' I sighed. 'They wouldn't even come out for a free drink with me the other night.'

Tonya put a hand up. 'Stop this, right now. If Evie and Fred were acting up, you wouldn't ignore it and take them out for ice cream, would you?'

'No,' I lied. I felt so guilty about not being around enough for them that I'd not only buy them an ice cream, but I'd also hire Ben and Jerry to personally serve it to them.

'So, don't take their crap either,' Tonya said. 'You're the boss lady. Kick-ass. What would Lucky Santangelo do?'

I smiled at her reference to my favourite Jackie Collins character. 'She'd sleep with them or have them killed,' I said. 'Possibly both. Possibly at the same time.' I sipped my coffee. 'I haven't enough energy, contacts or leopard-print outfits for those sorts of shenanigans. Plus, HR would probably claim I'd contravened health and safety regulations.' I tutted. 'Bloody red tape.'

Tonya laughed. 'Fair point. You'll have to give them a good old-fashioned talking-to instead.'

I squirmed in my chair. 'You know I hate confrontation.'

'Don't think of it as confrontation. That's too negative a vibe. You're addressing a situation with a view to improving it.'

She made it sound so easy. 'You're right. I'll talk to them.' I smiled. 'Thank you.'

The waitress arrived with our food. I was so hungry, I was already eating before she'd put the plate on the table. 'Didn't have time for breakfast this morning,' I explained to Tonya, holding my hand in front of my mouth so that I could talk without spraying her with food. A skill my children needed to learn.

'How come?'

'I was trying to figure out how to get into the office, then I was working ...' I hesitated, wondering whether to tell her. 'Then Will and I had an argument.'

'Want to talk about it?' she asked.

I swallowed a triangle of toast whole. Tonya could

probably see it travelling down my neck. 'This campaign for the Dutch client is really important. Today's the first chance I've had to prioritise it. The ideas were flowing and then Will interrupted me and I couldn't get that focus back afterwards. Probably doesn't sound that big a deal, but I'd never do that to him. Feels as though he doesn't respect my work.' He definitely didn't respect my work chair.

Tonya nodded. 'I get it. If I was trying out a new dish and someone interrupted me, I'd be annoyed too.'

A little of the tension in my shoulders eased. 'I told him how fed up I am that he leaves everything for me to do. He just thinks I'm nagging him.'

Tonya looked thoughtful as she chewed. 'I'm not taking sides here, just playing devil's advocate.' She dabbed her mouth with a napkin. 'I agree, Will needs to support you more. But he's trying his best. He's properly involved with the kids now. When I drop Evie back from ballet, he's got the dinner on and Fred's in his PJs. And Miss Boast was so grateful for all the satsumas he donated to the school. That was really thoughtful of him.'

I gripped my knife and fork tightly. Bloody Miss Boast again. Bet she'd loved having an excuse to fawn over Will. He wasn't thoughtful, though. He'd screwed up the online shop. I'd had to go to the supermarket the next day and battle with the Christmas-break stockpilers for some basic essentials to get us through the next week. And the dinner that Will had impressed Tonya with – I'd made that. And I'd washed the PJs and leotard that they wore. I shoved a whole hash brown into my mouth to stop myself challenging Tonya. This wasn't her battle.

'Fred loves that his daddy goes in and reads with him, too,' she continued. 'I remember you saying what a ball-ache it was, so it's great that he does it.'

Yes, it was a ball-ache, but I still did it, even though it made me behind with my work. Why wasn't it great then?

'I'm just thinking that Will needs some credit for what he's doing,' Tonya said gently.

Why? I wanted to shout. He was doing a fraction of what I'd been doing, and was *still* doing, yet Will was being likened to a decorated war hero.

Tonya smiled. 'The irony is that he'll probably get it all sussed out and know exactly what he's doing just as his six months end and he goes back at work.'

I swallowed loudly. I still hadn't told Will that he couldn't work for a rival firm. And I could hardly tell Tonya. He deserved to know first. The animosity that I'd been feeling towards Will was instantly replaced with guilt.

Tonya leant forward. 'What I'm trying to say is, I know you're having a tough time, and I'm not playing that down, but Will's struggling too.' She tapped her nails together. 'You need to get that team spirit back. Reconnect. I've got next Friday off. I'll have the kids so you two can go out.'

'Thank you. That's really kind.' An evening together would remind us that there was a life outside of the children and work. 'I know it's hard on Will too. Evie and Fred are full-on.' I sighed. They might be full-on, but I missed them. I'd get home for when they finished school so we could have some time together.

Tonya looked at her watch. 'I'd better go.'

I nodded. 'And I'd better do some work.'

I nipped to the loo before Tonya left, so I didn't have the tricky dilemma of either leaving my belongings at the table to secure my spot, and risk them being stolen, or taking everything into the toilet with me and losing my seat. Once Tonya was gone, I ordered a cafetière of coffee to get me through the next few hours, switched my phone off and tucked it into my bag, and took out my laptop and organiser. Now that I'd been fed and watered, I was able to concentrate and, within minutes, the campaign began to take shape.

I worked solidly, only pausing to order a mince pie to justify hogging a table for hours. Eventually I stopped, sat back in my chair and grinned. I'd done it. I'd come up with a new marketing campaign for Dekker that I was sure Dieuwke would love. The message had been in me the whole time; I'd just needed peace and quiet to eke it out. Now I could go home and spend the evening with my lovely family.

I looked up, surprised to see it was dark outside and the staff were tidying up around me. It was gone five. So much for being home to greet Evie and Fred when they got in from school. I packed my things away and switched my phone back on. There were two text messages.

The first was from Will: Bye then. He'd sent it shortly after I'd left home that morning. Guiltily, I realised that I hadn't messaged to tell him where I was and how long I'd be. I'd been so surprised to see Tonya that I'd forgotten.

The next message was from Tonya. So great to see you. Let's do it again soon. Forgot to tell you Will came in while you were in the loo. He said to say hi. x

I groaned. Will would never believe we'd met by chance. I pulled my coat on and headed out into the cold evening air. Time to face the music. And not the 'Afternoon Delight' variety.

Chapter 22

Will

'I can't get mine in.' Vicky held up her Christingle. The candle flopped over at a right angle rather than standing up tall and proud.

'Said the actress to the bishop,' Lizzie or Lisa said. I still didn't know which was which. They'd both given me a Christmas card, but at the same time, which was no help. And now I couldn't give one back. Not that I'd ever written a Christmas card in my life. Sarah did the family ones, but it probably wouldn't go down well if I asked her to do some for my friends. She wouldn't have time anyway, although she had time for brunch with my sister. Another thing that hadn't gone down well. Not that anything or anyone was going down. The actress would have nothing of note to report to the bishop if she lived here.

I laughed along with everyone. It was only five o'clock but I was already pretty pissed. Possibly because I'd only had a satsuma for lunch. I'd nipped into town with the intention of getting a takeaway bap from Groundworks, but had left immediately and stormed home when Tonya told me Sarah was in the ladies.

I couldn't believe Sarah. She'd made such a big deal about being too busy to take five minutes off for me – it had been so long that five minutes was a generous estimation – but had then met Tonya. She hadn't even told me she was going.

Sarah wasn't her usual thoughtful self anymore and I didn't like this new, inconsiderate, version.

'Just shove it in,' Lauren said, which led to more raucous laughter.

It wasn't just me who was pissed. Vicky was actually slurring. My fault for not providing anything more substantial than crisps to eat. I'd forgotten to get gluten-free ones, but thankfully no one had noticed.

I topped up everyone's glasses up and raised my own. 'It's my first time to host,' I said. They all cheered. I shook my head and held up my free hand. 'I can't take any praise. In fact, I must apologise. You always make amazing food and I've let the side down.' I was slurring as well. I should slow down. I had a sip of fizz while I considered this. 'So, I'm treating us all to a takeaway instead. What does everyone fancy?'

'Indian!'

'Mexican!'

'Thai!'

'Turkish!'

'Shall we let the kids choose?' I asked. I didn't want to be tight, but multiple orders to multiple restaurants was going to be pricey and I'd already wasted hundreds of pounds on the pizza oven that I feared was only fit for the skip. I'd scraped away all morning, but the sodding marshmallows wouldn't come off. I went to the door of the living room. 'Kids. What do you want for tea?'

'Pizza,' they all yelled back.

Lauren gestured to the garden. 'We could use your—'

'No, no.' I patted her shoulder. 'This is your night off. I'm not having you slaving over a hot oven. I'll order some from the place round the corner.'

The place round the corner was called The Best Takeaway In Town. There was always a pool of vomit outside on Saturday and Sunday mornings, which indicated that its takeaways were perhaps not the best in town, but it offered free delivery, so got my vote. I'd keep plying everyone with fizz, then they wouldn't be able to taste, or even care about, what they were eating.

'Do they do gluten-free bases?' Vicky asked. I nodded confidently, although I had no idea. It wouldn't matter anyway. Her enjoyment of the crisps proved that gluten didn't make any difference to the product. It was all a marketing ploy to get people to spend more money.

'I'll get the kids' orders.' Vicky went into the living room, bumping into the doorframe on her way.

'Mind if I use the loo?' Lizzie or Lisa asked.

'I need to go too,' Lisa or Lizzie said.

They might as well just be one person and be done with it.

'You can both go. There's one along the hall and another at the top of the stairs.' I sat down at the kitchen table next to Lauren.

'I love that you let Evie and Fred decorate the Christmas tree,' she said.

I frowned. *I'd* decorated the tree while they were at school.

'Will you or Sarah rearrange the decorations later, so not all the baubles are at the front, or leave it?' Lauren asked.

'I think it looks good as it is,' I said, a little affronted. 'But Sarah probably will. She's a perfectionist. Likes everything a certain way.' *Her* way.

'How's her job going?'

'Busy.' Not too busy for brunch, though. Not that I was harbouring a grudge.

Lauren wiped a smudge of lip gloss from the rim of her glass. 'Are you enjoying your sabbatical?'

Enjoy wasn't the word I'd choose. In truth, I was sick of Sarah accusing me of not pulling my weight; bored by the monotony of getting the kids up and to school every morning, and reading what was basically the same story, but with a different-coloured dog; daunted by the amount of paperwork they brought home that needed completing – and running out of places to hide it – and fed up with chauffeuring them to clubs, cooking dinner, making sure none of Fred's vegetables touched the rest of his food, and getting them into bed each night.

Each stage of the day was a battle. But instead of any victories, there was just the slight relief of survival till the next obstacle. It was like being a cast member in *Game of Thrones*, but without the gratuitous sex to make up for it. The only things that brought me any enjoyment at the moment were Fizz Friday, my Sunday morning lie-in and the TV trailer featuring Gal Gadot as Wonder Woman.

'It's fine.' I finished my glass and refilled both of ours from a new bottle. 'Looking forward to the Christmas break, though.'

Lauren took a sip. 'You're doing brilliantly. Raising kids is hard work. You're allowed to admit that.' She ran a hand through her silky, shiny hair and it rearranged itself delicately back around her shoulders. 'We should get together over the holidays,' she continued. 'Two weeks is a long time to keep the kids entertained.'

Two weeks! Fuck. I hadn't thought about that. Sarah would have a few days off, but there would still be many, many days to fill. And they wouldn't be going to Sinéad anymore after school in the new year. I'd have them every single day. What was I going to do with them? I stared at Lauren in horror and she laughed.

'Don't look so scared. We'll help each other out.' She put a hand on my arm. 'That's what friends are for.'

Her hand was so light and delicate that I could barely feel it. But I was also acutely aware of its presence. I should stop drinking. I should order some food. I should … There was a bang from the direction of the front door. I looked up to see Sarah walking across the hall. I should get Lauren's hand off me. Sarah paused at the door to the living room, flinched and came through to the kitchen, her cheeks red and her lips pressed tightly together. I jumped up, bashing my knee on the table and jolting my arm so that half my prosecco flew through the air and splashed over Lauren's head. She yelped and dashed to the sink. Bit extreme, but it had the desired aim of getting her hand off me.

'Sarah. Hi, you're home.' Nothing like stating the obvious. 'Just in time. We're about to order pizzas. What flavour would you like?'

Sarah set a large M&S bag on the table. 'I bought us dinner. Didn't realise you were entertaining.' Her eyes slid to where Lauren stood at the sink with her back to us, wringing out her hair and, I suspected, trying to pretend she wasn't there.

'It's Friday Fizz Club.' I pointed to my glass to prove it. 'My turn to host. Forgot to tell you. Sorry.' Wasn't Sarah the one who was supposed to be sorry? I couldn't remember now. 'Let me get you a drink.'

'Have you been in the living room?' Sarah asked.

Now that I came to think of it, I hadn't. The kids were quiet, which was all that mattered. Actually, they weren't quiet. They were laughing and shouting at full volume. But they weren't bothering us grown-ups. That was the bit that mattered.

'There's a woman asleep on the sofa,' Sarah said. No wonder Vicky had been gone so long. 'And snow spray all over the walls.' Her tone was so frosty, she could have blended into the Christmas scene.

'That was supposed to be for the windows,' I said. 'It's a stencil kit.'

Sarah crossed her arms tightly. 'Didn't it occur to you – or to anyone – that the children might need supervision with that?' She looked again at Lauren, who was now towelling her hair dry with an oven glove. It didn't look so shiny and silky anymore. Probably just as well.

Lauren must have sensed that we were both looking at her, as she turned around.

'Hi.' She waved a hand through the air. 'I'm Lauren. Nice to meet you properly.' She put the oven glove down and stepped forward, her hand outstretched. Before she could reach Sarah, she skidded on the pool of prosecco. I instinctively lunged forward to catch her before she fell. Her hands flew to my shoulders and, for a moment, I held her in my arms, her face millimetres from mine.

'What's going on?' Sarah growled. My eyes snapped away from Lauren's to Sarah's. 'There are about twenty kids vandalising our home, an unconscious woman on the sofa … and her.' She glared at Lauren, and I pushed her up to standing and as far away from me as I could.

'Your house is lovely.' Lizzie and Lisa wandered back into the kitchen. 'Hope you don't mind. We went on a little tour. Your wife has some very nice shoes. Oh, hello! We like your shoes.' They smiled at Sarah. Sarah did not smile back.

Evie came into the kitchen. 'Daddy, Vicky's been … Mummy!' She threw her arms around Sarah and buried her face in her torso. Sarah visibly softened. I chose not to point out that Evie had chocolate round her mouth, which was now smeared all over Sarah's pale blue, silk shirt. 'Can we have dinner please?' Evie asked. 'We're starving.'

Sarah stroked Evie's hair. 'I bought some food on my way home, but there's not enough for everyone.' She somehow managed to smile at Evie and snarl at me at the same time.

'Vicky won't want any,' Evie said. 'She's just been sick.'

Sarah inhaled sharply. 'Please don't tell me Vicky's the woman asleep on the sofa.'

'No,' Evie said.

Sarah released a slow breath.

'She's awake now.'

A choking sound came from Sarah's throat. It could have been tears or a battle cry. I didn't want to be around for either.

Lizzie and Lisa charged into the living room. Sarah shot daggers at me across the room as we listened to them comfort Vicky. 'Don't feel bad … Could happen to anyone … I'm sure it'll wash out … Probably not expensive … They can always get another tree.'

Lauren crept towards the door. 'I'll round the kids up.'

Vicky stumbled into the kitchen, looking very ashen. 'I'm so sorry,' she croaked. 'This usually only happens if I eat gluten.'

I cast an eye over the kitchen surfaces to make sure there wasn't a telltale crisp wrapper on display.

'I'll clean it up.' Vicky hiccupped. 'Got any Dettol wipes?'

I bent down to get some out of the cupboard under the sink.

'No,' Sarah barked. 'Everything needs bleaching thoroughly.'

'I'll do it.' Vicky took a step towards me, then did a swift about-turn and ran out of the kitchen, clutching her mouth. The toilet door in the hall slammed shut, followed by the gag-inducing sound of Vicky vomiting.

'Get these people out of here,' Sarah hissed.

I nodded, wondering if I could leave too. Just till Sarah had calmed down. Shouldn't take longer than a few months.

None of us said anything, as we ushered the kids into their coats and shoes. Lizzie and Lisa helped Vicky out into the cold and patted her back as she dry-heaved her way down the drive. Next door's dog would get anything she threw up. Shame I couldn't let him loose on the living room. I hadn't seen the damage yet, but it hadn't smelt pretty. Sarah's mulled-wine diffuser was going to be put to the test over the next few days.

Lauren tugged Jacob's and Max's hats down over their ears and crouched down to do up their coats. 'I'm so sorry,' she whispered up to me. 'Are you going to be OK?'

'Yeah, course,' I said.

'Sure?'

I ignored the question. I was far from sure I'd be OK, but didn't want to admit that. Or break down in tears of sheer terror.

'Have a great weekend.' I high-fived the boys and waved them all off. Reluctantly, I shut the door and walked across the hall towards the kitchen, dragging my feet as I went. Sarah had closed the living-room doors that led off the hall and the kitchen. Evie and Fred sat at the kitchen table, dunking carrot batons into a tub of hummus. A pan of water was on the hob, with a bag of fresh pasta and a pot of tomato sauce on the side, and it looked as though there was some garlic bread in the oven. I checked my watch. I'd only been outside two minutes. How had Sarah done all of this?

I leant over Evie and pinched a carrot stick. Sarah gave me a death stare. I put the carrot stick back.

'The bleach and bucket are in the garage,' she said. 'Let me show you.'

I meekly followed her through the internal door that led off the kitchen. The garage was freezing and I instantly started shivering. Sarah was trembling too.

'Are you cold?' I asked, wondering if giving her my jumper would be an appropriate peace offering.

'I don't know,' she said in a low voice. 'I'm so angry that I can't register any other feelings.'

It was going to take more than my jumper. 'I'm sorry,' I said. 'Don't know what happened. One minute we were having a normal, nice evening, the next it all went crazy. It's not like this usually.'

'You don't know what happened? I think I do.' Sarah pointed to the half-empty crate of expensive cava that she'd bought for Christmas.

I winced. 'Yes. Might have got a bit carried away. And we didn't eat, so …' I trailed off. Sarah's body language was a textbook display of anger – red cheeks, jaw tense, fists clenched, chest rising and falling. Under other circumstances, the heaving chest might have given me the horn, but not even a masochist would dare glance at Sarah's cleavage right now. 'Sorry,' I said feebly. 'Where's the bleach? I'll clean up.'

'Too right you will. And to my standards, not yours.' She thrust a bucket into my hands, then rummaged through a huge box of cleaning supplies. 'What exactly are you sorry for?' She noisily dropped a bottle of bleach into the bucket. 'Letting them trash our house?' Clang. In went a bottle of carpet stain remover. 'Not looking after the children?' Clonk. All-purpose cleaning spray. 'Forgetting to warn me?' A mere rustle from the pack of scouring pads. 'Drinking my cava?' I nodded with each point, staring at my shoes. 'Flirting with Lauren?'

My head whipped up. 'I wasn't flirting.'

Sarah glared at me. 'What would you call it then?'

'Talking.'

Sarah sidled up to me, touched my arm and looked up at me adoringly. I breathed a sigh of relief. She'd realised it had been one of those silly things that get out of hand and there was no need to be cross. No one had been hurt. It wasn't a big deal. We could go back to normal now.

'This isn't how friends talk,' she said softly.

I frowned. Sarah and I were a bit more than friends.

She squeezed my arm. 'This is how someone talks when they're trying to get off with you.' She blinked hard. 'Is something going on with you and Lauren?'

'No,' I said firmly. 'Why would you think that?'

'Because she had her hand on your arm and you were sitting together on your own.' Sarah's voice wobbled. 'Why weren't you with the children?'

I stared into the bucket, full of remorse. 'That's how Friday Fizz Club works. The kids play, and the parents hang out and unwind after a stressful week.'

'A stressful week?' Sarah dug her fingers into my arm and I winced. 'Are you joking? You do bugger all. I'm the one with all the stress.'

My remorse began to wane. I did not do bugger all. Just that afternoon I'd refilled all four soap dispensers in the house. Even the one in the en suite that no one uses. Although Lizzie and Lisa may have paid a visit.

'If you'd all been looking after the children, they wouldn't have sprayed fake snow up the walls and you could have stopped that stupid woman throwing up everywhere.' Sarah's eyes narrowed behind her glasses. 'You're irresponsible.'

Heat flushed through my body. 'We do look after them.'

Sarah gave a hollow laugh. 'If you believe that, then that's even worse. You can't be trusted. None of you can. Those women are never coming here again, and Evie and Fred are never going to their houses.'

I slammed the bucket down. 'You can't tell me who I can and can't hang out with. I'm not one of the kids.'

'Stop acting like one then.'

Sarah and I glared at each other. I desperately wanted to tell her to go fuck herself, but she'd no doubt use that as an example of how immature I was. Which I wasn't. I was a responsible adult who'd held the fort for weeks now while she swanned off to Amsterdam and for drinks in London and, and … and brunch with my sister. That's what I was pissed off with her about. My earlier emotional rollercoaster came rushing back. The hurt of being rejected by Sarah. The frustration of catching her in the kitchen when she'd claimed to be too busy for anything other than work. The disbelief that she left without saying goodbye. The tinge of contrition when I remembered how absorbed in projects I had sometimes got (although I'd never, ever been so absorbed that I'd turned down sex). Then the sting of humiliation when I discovered she wasn't working at all, but instead was out on a jolly with my sister. Not so much a slap in the face, as a swift hard kick in the nuts. I didn't care how immature Sarah accused me of being, I was telling her.

'Go fu—'

The door to the kitchen swung open. 'Water's jumping out the pan,' Evie said.

Sarah gasped. 'I forgot the hob's on.'

'How irresponsible.' I tutted with an exaggerated eye roll. 'Some people can't be trusted.'

Sarah's teeth ground together. 'I'll be right there,' she said in a strained voice to Evie, who nodded and went back in the kitchen. 'Clean the living room,' she hissed at me.

Furious though I was with Sarah, I knew I had no grounds to refuse to clean up. Begrudgingly, I picked the bucket up. 'Thank fuck this is only for a few more months,' I growled. 'The sooner I go back to work and things get back to normal, the better.'

Sarah's cheeks grew even redder. She stared at me, as though deliberating a retort, then followed Evie into the kitchen, letting the door slam behind her.

Chapter 23

Sarah

I flicked my computer on with a yawn. The trains were back on track, so I'd been able to get to my desk for seven thirty, giving myself an hour to catch up before people began to trickle in.

Despite the worst Friday evening of my life, which resulted in Will sleeping on an airbed in the study – for obvious reasons he couldn't take the couch, as he had done on occasion before – the rest of the weekend had been good. Desperate to escape the infusion of bleach and stale vomit, we'd gone out and, shock horror, done things together as a family. The local Christmas-tree festival and winter market were traditions for me and the children, but Will had never come before. To his surprise, he'd enjoyed it. The beer tent and hot-dog stand may have been contributory factors.

When the children went on the carousel, artificial snow sprayed out over them. Seeing the pure delight on their faces ignited something in me and I instinctively reached for Will's hand. Realising what I'd done, I went to whip it away, but before I could, his hand folded around mine. We smiled at each other sheepishly and, as always happens in the letters to the tabloids' problem pages, the next thing I knew we were making love. Well, not quite the next thing. First, we had to get home, give the kids tea, and get them bathed and to bed. But when we'd eventually done that, then we went to bed ourselves. And very nice it was too. Up yours, Lauren.

So, things were good at home again. Apart from the fact I hadn't told Will yet that he couldn't work for a competitor. Or pointed out that when the six months were up, things wouldn't be going back to exactly how they used to be, because my position as Director wasn't a trial: it was permanent. I also needed to figure out how to get more time with Evie and Fred than I currently had, without it detracting from my productivity at work. But apart from all that, and that last stubborn stain on the living-room carpet, things were good at home. Now I needed to get them good at work. The appraisals were the perfect place to start. An opportunity to sit down with each team member and find out what was going on.

My computer beeped and an invitation to a meeting with Clara at 10 a.m. popped up on my screen. I opened the online calendar to make sure the meeting didn't clash with the rescheduled appraisals. It was completely blank, apart from a half-day on Wednesday that I'd booked off to go and watch the children's Christmas show at school. I refreshed the screen. There'd been at least two client meetings in there, one of which was an important pitch to a new company. And where were the appraisals? I took my organiser from my bag. Despite having a calendar on my screen and phone, and despite Will's jibes that I was stuck in the eighties (not a bad thing in my view – if only for Harrison Ford), I still liked the old-fashioned, physical diary in my organiser. It was where I wrote all my ideas, too. Yes, I knew I could use the Notes app on my phone. I could also consume freeze-dried foods if I so desired. But writing on a clean page with a freshly sharpened pencil brought me pleasure. As did eating meals that didn't come in a pouch and have the consistency of sand.

The two client meetings were detailed in my organiser, so I hadn't imagined them. There was also a blow-dry appointment in my lunch break on Friday, ahead of my date night with Will, which I'd chosen not to share on the accessible-to-all online work calendar. Another reason why private diaries were invaluable.

A movement outside the door caught my eye and I looked up to see Nancy peering into the office. When she saw me, the hopeful expression on her face turned to one of annoyance. She turned away, threw her coat on the back of her chair and walked quickly towards the kitchen. I bolted after her.

'Morning,' I said, as we reached the kitchen. 'Good weekend?'

Nancy shrugged. 'It was OK.'

'That storm on Thursday night was unbelievable, wasn't it?'

Nancy yawned. I didn't blame her. She was in her twenties. Meteorology probably wasn't high on her list of interests.

'The client pitches I had booked in for this week aren't on the calendar anymore,' I said. Nancy looked even less interested in this information. 'What happened to them?'

Nancy shrugged again.

'Did they reschedule?'

Nancy sucked on her lower lip for a moment, then shook her head. 'No. No, they didn't.'

'They both cancelled, with no explanation?'

'Guess so.'

What did 'guess so' mean? It was a straightforward question that she should know the answer to. No guesswork was required. We weren't in an episode of *Spin the Wheel* and she'd landed on a category that wasn't her specialist subject. Hopefully, Tom would know what was going on. I'd worked hard to get those clients to agree to see us and had spent time putting the pitches together.

I took a deep breath. 'When are the appraisals taking place?'

Nancy frowned. 'What do you mean?'

I pinched the bridge of my nose as a cover while I smelt another flower and blew out yet another candle. 'Tom was rescheduling the appraisals that were supposed to happen on Friday,' I said slowly. 'I couldn't get in because of the storm. When have they been rescheduled for?'

Nancy shook her head. 'Tom did them on Friday afternoon.'

My stomach hit the floor. 'He what?'

'With Clara from HR.' Nancy smirked. 'Isn't that good then?'

No, it was not good. On a scale of nought to ten, ten being good and nought being bad, this was minus 357. As Director, and co-team leader and mentor, it was vital that I was in the appraisals. Not turning up would give the impression I didn't care about my team or take my role seriously. No wonder Clara wanted to see me. Nancy mustn't know any of this, though. It'd be round the office quicker than that meme of the American lawyer on a Zoom call with a cat filter on.

'It's absolutely fine.' I cleared my throat to hide the wobble in my voice. 'See you later.'

I hurried back to my office, my stomach churning. This was so bad. Sitting down at my desk, I took my glasses off and put my head in my hands. Pandora couldn't have regretted opening that stupid box as much as I regretted not coming into work on Friday. OK, Pandora released evil into the world, but her dad was king of the gods. She was always going to get away with it. I didn't have nepotism on my side, so would be getting away with nothing.

'Are you OK?'

I looked up to see Tom's silhouette moving towards me. My fear turned to frustration. Why had Tom gone ahead with the appraisals when I'd asked him to rearrange them? He knew how important it was that we were both there.

I put my glasses back on. 'You did the appraisals.' He reached my desk and put a hand on my shoulder. I shrugged it away. 'I told you I needed to be here. Why didn't you rearrange them, as I asked? I would never have done them without you.'

'I tried to.' Tom pressed his hands together. 'I called everyone together and explained about your train not running. Lin couldn't get in either. We were synchronising our diaries to see when we could reschedule, and Clara walked past and said that they had to be done that day or any salary reviews wouldn't be filed in time.'

I thrust my hands in my hair. 'Clara never mentioned a deadline before.'

'I know. First I'd heard of it too.' Tom tugged at his sleeves. 'Lucky she overheard, or they'd have missed out.'

'What about Lin? She's probably the only one who qualifies for an increase. Is it too late for her?'

'No, we did hers on Zoom.'

'I could have done them on Zoom.' I took my hands out of my hair and threw them in the air. 'I know I said I wanted to be there in person, but that was when I thought we could do them this week. Why didn't you call me?'

Tom's cheeks went pink. 'I did. Your phone went to voicemail.'

I groaned. 'I switched it off so I could focus on the Dekker campaign.' I covered my face. 'This is a disaster.'

'No, it's not,' Tom said firmly. 'It would have been a disaster if they hadn't happened at all. Yes, it would have been better if you'd been there too, but I was representing us both. We're a team, remember?'

'Yes, and should show a united front.' I clasped my hands together on the desk. 'They're going to think I don't care about them.'

'No, they're not.' Tom placed a hand over mine and gave them a squeeze. 'The appraisals needed doing. They got done. The Dekker campaign needed to be put together. That got done.' He gave me a nervous glance. 'Didn't it?'

'Yes!' I felt a flutter of relief. 'I think I managed to get the message that they want to convey across in an exciting way. I've got some new ideas about how to market it too.'

'That's brilliant.' Tom grinned at me. 'See, teamwork – together we achieved our goals.' He gave my hands another quick squeeze before releasing them, grabbing his own chair and pulling it over next to mine. 'Can I see the presentation?'

'Of course.' I took the memory stick containing the presentation from my bag and plugged it into my keyboard.

'I love it,' Tom said when I'd finished talking him through it. His eyes shone as he grinned at me. It was a good pitch and we both knew it. He winked. 'They'll love it too. It's perfect.' His face was mere inches from mine. I felt a flutter, similar to the one I'd felt in Amsterdam and much lower down than I was comfortable with. Not again.

I turned swiftly back to my computer, breaking our eye contact. 'I'll get Nancy to set up a meeting with Dieuwke and Lars.' I closed the file and put the memory stick back in my bag. 'That reminds me. Two clients cancelled meetings with us this week. Any idea why?'

Tom wheeled his chair back to his desk. 'First I've heard of it. Did they go through Nancy?'

'Yes, but they didn't say why, apparently.' I flicked through my diary to the note I'd made when I last spoke to the new client. 'I don't understand it. We'd got on well and she seemed keen.' I tapped my organiser with my pencil. 'I'm going to call her and find out.'

'Want me to ask Nancy about it first?' Tom asked. 'If I offer to make her a coffee it might jog her memory.'

'Worth a try. Thanks.'

Tom crossed the office and opened the door to the open-plan office space.

'Oh Tom,' I called after him. 'While you're talking to Nancy, can you ask her to arrange a team meeting for as soon as possible, please? Preferably today. I need to apologise to everyone.'

'No worries,' Tom said, leaving the room.

Nancy's head bobbed up as he walked towards her. He said something and she nodded, then followed him in the direction of the kitchen.

I waited until they were both out of sight, sat back in my chair and whimpered. Where the hell had that flutter come from? I didn't fancy Tom. I didn't. I couldn't. I was happily married. Or married, anyway. The happily bit varied day to day. But our weekend had been good, once we'd got past Friday. And I loved Will, I really did. Yes, we were going through a bit of a rough patch as we adjusted to our new roles, but that didn't cancel out the last twelve years. And certainly didn't cancel out the way his deep brown eyes warmed me from the bottom of my toes right up to my front bottom. So why the pathetic, teenage-like tummy flutters when Tom winked at me? I thought back to the time in Amsterdam. That had been easily explained away by a large meal. But today? It wasn't even ten o'clock. I hadn't eaten yet. Aah – that must be it. Hunger pains, not desire. A little snort of laughter escaped me. What a relief. All I needed was some breakfast. My stomach gurgled loudly in agreement.

I checked my watch. Fifteen minutes until my appointment with Clara. If I was quick, I could dash to the canteen and grab something before the meeting. I picked up my organiser and was walking past Nancy's desk, when her phone rang. Usually, I'd let it go to voicemail, but given the two cancelled meetings recently, I didn't want to risk losing any more potential business.

'Ballas & Bailey Marketing. Sarah Campbell speaking,' I said into the receiver.

'Sarah? It is Dieuwke from Dekker. Why are you answering the phone?'

'Hi Dieuwke,' I said warmly. Thank goodness I'd picked up the call. 'My PA's stepped away from her desk for a moment. I was going to ask her to contact you anyway to arrange a meeting. I've put together your campaign and am very excited to show it to you.'

'I am excited to see it also,' Dieuwke said. 'My schedule is very full before the New Year, but could we do it on a Zoom?'

'Definitely. When's good for you?' I opened my now empty diary.

'December 27th would be perfect. Then we can launch the campaign in the new year.'

I turned the page. That week was empty deliberately. 'I'm off work between Christmas and New Year.' I flicked back a page. 'Do you have any gaps at all to squeeze me in before then?'

'No.' Dieuwke sighed. 'I am on holiday for two weeks in January, so this is an extremely busy time for me. That is a shame about the 27th,' she added.

I looked again at the Christmas week in my diary. I'd be at home on the 27th, recovering from two days of non-stop gorging. I could easily nip into the study for an hour to Zoom with Dieuwke. She wouldn't need to know that I had pyjama bottoms on under the desk.

'Let's do it,' I said. 'I'll Zoom from home and see if Tom can, too.'

'Thank you,' Dieuwke said. 'I look forward to it. Until then, *vrolijk kerstfeest*.'

'Thanks. *Vrolijk kerstfeest* to you too.' Presumably that meant Merry Christmas, not anything to do with amorous liaisons with farmyard animals. I hung up and wrote down the time and date in my organiser. I'd enter it on the computer system later. At least Dekker was on track. I'd worry about the other clients after my meeting with Clara.

At exactly ten o'clock I knocked on Clara's open door and stepped in.

'Hi.' I smiled. 'How are you?'

Clara didn't return my smile. She looked at the banana skin in my hand with distaste.

'Breakfast,' I said, holding it up. It was all I'd had time for after speaking to Dieuwke and I'd had to eat it in the lift up to Clara's floor. 'Mind if I put it in your bin?'

Clara took a wastepaper basket from under her desk and held it out. She wrinkled her nose as I dropped the banana skin in. Her fondness for everything being neat and tidy must extend to the contents of her bin.

'Thanks for overseeing the appraisals with Tom on Friday.'

I sat down opposite her. 'Obviously I wish I'd been there, but the trains—'

'You could have done them by Zoom,' Clara said. Her tone wasn't unfriendly exactly, but it definitely wasn't warm.

'I felt I should be there in person.' I clasped my hands together. 'I thought we could reschedule them for this week, but unfortunately we couldn't.'

'That is unfortunate.' Clara tweaked the position of her keyboard by a millifraction. 'On a general note, how do you feel the job's going?'

Should I admit that the hours were draining, I hated being away from Evie and Fred so much, it was a strain on my marriage, and my team despised me? No. Not unless I wanted an instant demotion. I was less than two months into the role. All of those elements would get easier with time. I needed to focus on the positives, such as the buzz I'd got when I completed Dekker's campaign. That part of the job, the creative part, was brilliant.

'I love it.'

Clara picked up a very sharp pencil. 'How are you getting on with the team?'

'Tom and I work really well together.' No need to let on that everyone else despised me. 'We're good at working to our individual strengths.'

Clara prodded the point of the pencil. 'What would you say are your strengths?'

What was this? An interview?

'Creating innovative marketing concepts and delivering them.' I usually waffled on about what a great people person I was, too, and how I loved motivating and mentoring, but I wasn't confident about that anymore.

Clara placed the pencil carefully on the table. 'How do you think your team feel about you?'

Honestly, I dreaded to think. Mrs Manning would probably rank a higher popularity score. 'I'm not sure,' I said carefully. 'They're not open or approachable. A couple of them need to up their game, but are resisting my guidance. Don't know why. I've never had any issues before.'

'No, you haven't.' Clara leant towards her computer screen. 'Your staff and peers have always been full of praise. It's one of the assets that made you stand out as Director material.' She narrowed her eyes. Hopefully because she needed reading specs, not because she was on the cusp of turning evil. 'Which is why it's such a shock that four members of staff have lodged formal complaints about you.'

My stomach clenched so tightly that I gasped out loud. 'Who has? What have they said?'

'Jed.'

It would be that git, wouldn't it?

'And Rebecca and Dean.'

But they'd barely spoken to me. 'What am I supposed to have done?' I asked. Oh God, I hadn't accidentally flashed them that time my shirt button came undone, had I?

Clara read from her computer. 'You were very unprofessional recently in a meeting. Your phone kept ringing, you left halfway through and didn't participate when you rejoined.' No mention of the bra. At least that was something. 'You're distant, keeping yourself tucked away in your office, and never ask how they are or how they're getting on with their projects. They feel that you don't value them or their work and have no interest in helping them further their career trajectories.' That must have come from Rebecca or Dean. Jed wouldn't know what trajectory meant. 'Not turning up for their appraisals, without a phone call or email explaining and apologising, reinforced their concerns.' Clara finished and sat back in her chair. 'What is your initial reaction to these comments?'

My initial reaction was to label the lot of them hypocritical, work-shy jobsworths. But this probably wouldn't help to quash the accusation that I was an uncaring, unnurturing cow of a boss. Coming a close second in the reactions department was a strong desire to run to the toilets and have a good cry. Again, unlikely to help. Instead, I took a deep breath, inhaling several bouquets' worth of flowers, and blew out the equivalent of the Towering Inferno.

'I'm very shocked and upset to hear this.' I nudged my glasses up. 'I do value them. They're an asset to the company. I was aware that they weren't approaching me. In fact, they seemed to be actively avoiding me whenever I tried to go and talk to them. I'd hoped to get to the root of this during the appraisals.' I should have found a way to get into work. Missing the appraisals was inexcusable. I took a deep breath and forced myself to go on. 'They seem to have formed good bonds with Tom, so he has been more hands-on with the team, while I focused on the projects. In hindsight, I should have dealt with this sooner. I certainly don't want any of them to think I don't care, because I do.' I didn't care too much about Jed, but kept quiet on that point.

'The meeting that they're referring to ...' I continued. 'I felt terrible when my phone rang. It was a call from the school because the children hadn't been collected. I was worried something had happened to Will, so left the meeting to find out what had gone on.'

'Was he all right?' Clara asked, her professional guard dropping for a moment, and a chink of her former human warmth showing.

'Yes, thank you.' I didn't elaborate. No need to sully his name further by admitting that he'd been snoozing on the sofa after blowing his Christmas bonus on unnecessary rubbish. Apart from my hairdryer. 'But I was shaken up and wasn't really with it for the rest of the meeting.'

Clara nodded. 'OK, I think we can let that one go.' She adjusted her engagement ring so that the stone sat in the centre of her finger. 'Stepping back from your team and allowing Tom to liaise with them, rather than dealing with them jointly, is a problem, though. As is the lack of contact about the appraisals.' She looked at me directly. 'You had no control over the trains. But you had control over how you handled it. You should have held a team meeting by Zoom and asked them if they were comfortable with you doing the appraisals remotely. I understand that you'd prefer to be there in person, but virtually is better than not being there at all.'

I nodded. 'You're right. I made a mistake. One I intend to correct. Involving myself with the team is going to be my priority now. I'll start off by apologising to them all in a meeting. I'll hold weekly one-to-ones to monitor their progress and mentor them too.'

Clara nodded thoughtfully. 'That sounds like a good plan. These complaints will go on your record and will be reviewed in a month, but I'm confident that you've taken on board my comments and will rectify them.'

'I will.' I sat up straight. This was a far from ideal situation, but I could turn it around. 'I've already asked Nancy to arrange a team meeting for as soon as possible.'

Clara plucked a pen from a pot on her desk, examined it and put it back. 'I said four people had lodged a complaint, but I've only detailed three of them so far.'

My posture sagged. I'd forgotten there was another person. 'Who's the fourth?' I asked quietly.

'Nancy,' Clara said.

My mouth dropped open. 'But I'm ridiculously nice to her, even though she's a—' I stopped myself. 'What complaint has she made?' I asked through gritted teeth.

Clara flushed. 'I need to get her to elaborate. She emailed me her complaint and it's lacking in detail.'

'You do know she's the office gossip?' I pushed my hair off my face. 'And a liar. I overheard her telling a colleague that I'd made Will leave to further my career.' My face was burning. 'I should make a complaint about *her*.'

Clara ignored my comments, but gave me a sympathetic smile. 'As her complaint stands, it doesn't hold any water. It won't be going on your record unless she can substantiate it.'

My shoulders were up by my ears. I forced them to relax. 'What has she said?' I asked, my voice shaking with anger.

'She's accused you of inappropriate behaviour in the workplace.' Clara squirmed in her chair. 'Sexual harassment.'

'What?' I laughed, not that there was anything remotely amusing about this situation. 'I'm married. Even if I wasn't, I'm straight.' I shook my head. 'Even if I was gay and unmarried, I wouldn't sexually harass her, or anyone.' Especially not Nancy, though.

Clara cleared her throat. 'She's not claiming to be the victim.' She glanced in my direction, then quickly looked away. 'She said she witnessed you sexually harassing Tom Page.'

Chapter 24

Will

'Have fun,' I said, waving. Not that Evie and Fred noticed. Far too busy running off to meet their friends. The days when they hugged me goodbye were long gone. I'd transitioned from novelty factor to run of the mill in less time than it would take them to say: 'Go home, Daddy, you're embarrassing us.' Which was no time at all, because they couldn't even be bothered to say that.

Someone wolf-whistled behind me. Not something you usually heard in a playground. Perhaps the caretaker had spotted Mrs Manning and couldn't help himself. I turned to see Lauren walking towards me.

'Where are you off to all dolled up?' She ran a fingertip down the arm of my dark grey coat.

'Christmas shopping in London.' I shuffled from foot to foot, partly to keep warm and partly to create a little distance between me and Lauren. It was probably my imagination, but I felt she'd been a bit flirty since the week before, when we'd all got so pissed. I'd worried Sarah's behaviour would turn the Friday Fizz Club against me, but they'd been even nicer than usual, texting and asking if I was OK, and whether I wanted some company. I hoped they didn't think I was in an abusive relationship.

'You're dressed very smart for Christmas shopping. Those sales assistants are in for a treat.' Lauren laughed daintily.

'Sarah and I are going for dinner afterwards. My sister's

picking the kids up and having them for the night.' I gave a small smile. 'So, I won't be at Fizz Club tonight, I'm afraid.'

Lauren's face fell. 'But it's the last one before Christmas. I'm doing mulled wine and pigs in blankets. I've even got tree-shaped crisps.'

'Don't let me anywhere near the mulled wine.' Vicky appeared beside us. 'Although,' she added with a grin, 'it's easy to say that at eight thirty in the morning. Might have changed my mind by home time.'

'Will can't come.' Lauren thrust her hands into her coat pockets. 'He's out in London.'

'No!' Vicky looked as though she'd just been told Father Christmas wasn't real. 'But it's the best one of the year. You have to come. There'll be crackers and charades and Christmas tree-shaped crisps.' She turned to Lauren. 'You did manage to get the gluten-free ones, didn't you? They were sold out when I tried.'

Lauren nodded and Vicky looked slightly mollified. Christmas, it seemed, was not entirely ruined.

'Sorry,' I said. 'Can't we do all of this next Friday? I'll be here then.'

'They break up at lunchtime next Friday,' Vicky said. Just as well we'd had this conversation or I'd have been getting another call from Mrs Manning. She wouldn't have reacted well to her Christmas bonus from the caretaker being delayed. 'We're heading straight off to my in-laws in Rotherham for the break, and Lizzie and Lisa have got an Airbnb in Devon with all their family.'

'Can't you go to London another night?' Lauren asked. 'We owe you a good evening after last week.'

I contorted my face as though mulling it over, which was purely for their benefit. No mulling was required. If I told Sarah that I was cancelling dinner to go to Friday Fizz Club, I may as well pack my bags and start looking for somewhere else to live now. Besides which, I didn't want to. Sarah and I hadn't been out for ages, and she was always good fun when she'd had a few drinks. And usually up for afternoon delight too, although obviously that was a bonus, rather than the evening's main objective. Obviously.

'Sorry, I can't,' I said with a regretful shrug when I'd deemed enough mulling had been done to appear authentic. 'Have a great time.'

Vicky stuck out her lower lip. 'This is my fault, isn't it? You're not allowed to see us anymore because I was sick in your house.' She winced. 'Sorry again about that. Can't understand why it happened.'

'No. Must have been a bug.' My face grew hot. 'Thanks for the chocolates and candle. Sarah appreciated them.' It was true: she had – she'd regifted them to Evie's teacher. Poor Miss Boast didn't seem to have a present yet. I'd have to remind Sarah. I rubbed my hands together. 'Got to go or I'll miss my train. Have fun tonight. See you Monday.' Lauren and Vicky nodded and waved. I felt ridiculously guilty. As though I was dumping them because I'd had a better offer. Or cheating on them with my wife, which was ludicrous. Out of the corner of my eye, I saw Lizzie and Lisa approaching. As I hurried away, I heard a gasp, followed by: 'Did you not tell him about the Christmas tree-shaped crisps?'

At six o'clock that evening I sat in the upstairs bar at St Pancras station, waiting for Sarah to arrive. We'd decided that meeting at one of the bars near Ballas & Bailey ran too high a risk of bumping into someone from the office and I had no desire to do that. Not one of them had been in touch to see how I was. All that back-slapping and camaraderie had been superficial. My so-called friends hadn't wanted to risk being tainted by association. Admittedly, I hadn't contacted Jasper when he'd been fired, but that's because he was a twat. I mean, what sort of moron loses a work laptop when sober? I'd been pissed when I'd done it, so had an excuse.

I watched the commuters as they popped up from the

underground escalator and crossed the station, impatient for Sarah to arrive. Since the big blow-up last Friday, we'd got on better than we had for ages. That had clearly been needed to clear the way. Now we were back to saying goodbye with a hug and a kiss, looking pleased to see each other when she got home, and snuggling up as we watched TV. Apart from when Spurs were playing. I loved Sarah with all my heart, but every marriage had boundaries, and mine was Sarah trying to canoodle as I howled with frustration when they were losing.

A drop of condensation trickled down the bottle of Veuve Clicquot I'd bought in preparation. I was gagging for a glass, but was chivalrously waiting for Sarah. My day in London hadn't been much fun. As I'd already bought all the presents, and the shops were rammed and about a hundred degrees, I'd decided to walk along the Thames to take in the sights and enjoy the tranquillity of the open water. It had been enjoyable for about three minutes, till an Arctic breeze swept in from the river and threatened to freeze my nuts off. With hours to kill and nothing to do, I'd gone to the cinema and watched a newly released Christmas comedy. I'd have been within my rights to get my money back under the Trades Description Act, because it wasn't funny in any way. Although, in fairness, nothing would ever come close to the Coca-Cola belch scene in *Elf*.

Just as I was deliberating whether to start the champagne without her, Sarah came up the escalator. At least I thought it was her. I could see the same bright red coat, but instead of a wild mass of curls, her hair was in soft waves and she was with someone. A man. Her shoulders wiggled as she laughed at something he said. They turned to make their way towards the stairs leading up to the bar where I was sitting. I frowned. The man with Sarah was Tom.

Sarah's laugh echoed up the stairwell. Tom's hearty chuckle rang out next. Knob. Except that he wasn't, was he? He was actually a decent bloke who'd tried to help me out. OK, he'd failed spectacularly, resulting in me losing my job, but that didn't make him a knob. Just useless.

I leant back in my chair and scrolled through my phone, pretending I was unaware of them walking towards my table.

'Ooh champagne. Thank you,' Sarah said.

I looked up with a start. 'Oh, hi.' I stood and gave her a quick kiss, then held my hand out to Tom. 'Long time, no see.'

Tom shook my hand warmly. 'I'm meeting some friends in a bar near here, so thought I'd say hello.' He let go of my hand and smiled. 'How are you doing?'

'Great thanks.' I nodded energetically. 'You?'

'Great,' Tom echoed. Difference was, he probably wasn't bullshitting. He tugged at the cuffs of his coat. 'Sorry about how everything turned out.'

'Don't be,' I said. 'One of those things.'

There was an awkward silence. I looked to Sarah for help, but she was downing a glass of champagne. So much for waiting for each other before tucking in.

'Sorry.' She gave me a guilty smile. 'I needed that. It's been quite a week.'

Tom exhaled loudly. 'You can say that again.'

'Why?' I asked. 'Has something happened?'

'No,' Sarah said quickly.

Tom gestured towards the stairs. 'I'd better go.'

I nodded. 'Thanks for stopping by.'

'No worries. Good to see you.' He turned to Sarah. 'See you Monday.' He leant down to kiss her cheek and his coat fell open, revealing a glimpse of an Arsenal pin on his jacket beneath. My jaw clenched. I wasn't sure which I disliked more – him kissing my wife or his blatant love of Spurs' biggest rivals.

Sarah waved him off, then turned to me and held her empty glass up. 'Thanks for this.'

I obligingly filled her glass, then my own. 'Thank fizz it's Friday.'

Sarah gave a tight smile. She'd rightly assumed that that was the Fizz Club's motto.

'What's going on at work?' I asked before she could cast her mind back to last week's fizz fiasco.

'Nothing.' Sarah drained the contents of her second glass of champagne. This could turn into a very expensive evening if she kept this up.

'You just said it's been quite a week.'

Sarah nudged the side of her glasses up, which was very amusing to watch, as she was wearing contact lenses. 'Oh, the usual manic run-up to Christmas. You know how it is. Everyone panicking because the City's going to shut down for a few days. You'd think they were preparing for Armageddon rather than a national holiday that happens every year.'

She was wittering, which suggested she was nervous. This date clearly meant a lot to her. She'd made a special effort with her appearance too. A red dress with a drapey bit at the front. She'd once asked if it showed too much cleavage. As if there was such a thing!

'What do you think of my hair?'

With a jolt I realised I was staring at her tits. I whipped my eyes up to her face. I should have mentioned her hair as soon as I saw her. I'd been so busy pretending I hadn't noticed her and Tom arriving that I'd forgotten.

'It looks great,' I said enthusiastically. 'Really great.' Sarah's face fell. Shit, I'd gone too far. She'd seen me react in the same way when Fred drew a picture in which I resembled a root vegetable. Not even one of the nicer-looking ones. I put my hands up. 'Seriously, it looks really nice.' Better not ask if that was a result of the zillion-pound hairdryer. Might reignite memories of my day of splurging, followed by failing to pick the kids up. Not my finest hour.

'Thank you.' Sarah seemed mollified. 'You look nice too.'

I nodded my appreciation and we smiled at each other over our champagne flutes, before taking a sip. Then we smiled at each other some more.

'Thanks for getting the Veuve,' Sarah said.

'You're welcome.'

There was a long pause.

'Your hair really does look nice,' I said.

'Thanks. Got it done at lunchtime.'

My cheeks began to ache. Sarah's smile had switched from natural to fixed, too. Fuck, this was awkward. We needed to get some conversation going before rigor mortis set in. I opened my mouth to speak, but nothing came out. In the past we'd agreed not to talk about the kids or work when we went out, so that we could recreate our early dates, when we'd been eager to find out as much as possible about each other. Well, Sarah had been. I'd gone along with it in the hope of getting a leg over. But we knew everything about each other now. I could hardly pique her interest in my bad-boy phase by relaying yet again the story of throwing a can of baked beans into the fire on a Scout trip to see if it'd explode. It did, in case you're wondering. Thankfully, no Scouts were harmed as a result of the experiment. But if the kids and work, which I'd already asked her about anyway, were off the table, what else was there?

I drained my glass and picked up the bottle. 'Ready for a top-up?'

'Please.' Sarah looked relieved. Surely we could get a conversation going from here. 'What year is it?' she asked.

Christ, she was as desperate as I was.

'Er ...' I scanned the label. 'A fine year: 2022.'

We both laughed and then fell into silence again. I chewed my lip. What did we talk about at Friday Fizz Club? The chatter was non-stop, but I couldn't recall a single topic. Vicky barely paused for breath and ended most sentences with: 'Said the actress to the bishop.' Lizzie and Lisa echoed what everyone else said. Lauren asked me lots of questions about myself, so I'd never had to put much effort into it. Conversation just happened.

'What time's the table booked for?' Sarah asked.

'Sorry, what?' I asked, feeling guilty for thinking about Lauren, even though it had been in a purely platonic way.

'The table?' Sarah said. 'Just wondered when we should head over.'

I frowned. 'You were booking the table.'

Sarah's smile and eyes widened so much that she looked like Wendolene in *Wallace and Gromit*. But with better hair. 'Please tell me you're joking.'

I swallowed hard. 'I thought you said you were booking it.'

The smile vanished and was replaced with a steely stare. Now she looked like the evil penguin. 'No,' she said. 'Definitely asked you to do it.' Her grip tightened on her glass. 'It's almost Christmas. All the restaurants will be rammed.' She downed her champagne, closed her eyes and took a deep breath. Then another. I shuffled awkwardly in my chair. It was like sitting opposite a Tibetan monk. Hopefully, without the vow of chastity, although there were no guarantees now that I'd screwed up the restaurant booking. I racked my brains. Had she asked me to do it? I couldn't remember, but that meant nothing. I couldn't remember what I'd given the kids for dinner the night before. Oh yes, I could. Fish fingers, potato waffles and beans. The same meal they'd had every night since Sarah had stopped cooking and freezing meals to get us through the week.

Eventually, Sarah opened her eyes. 'Who needs dinner?' She shrugged. 'We'll enjoy our champagne, then grab a kebab to eat on the train home.'

I pushed the thought of the fine cuisine I'd been looking forward to out of my mind and raised my glass. 'Here's to kebabs.'

Sarah clinked her flute against mine and then paused, the glass halfway to her mouth. 'Just to clarify: by kebab, I mean Leon.'

Thank fuck for that.

* * *

An hour later the conversation was flowing. Largely because we'd ignored our vow not to talk about kids or work. I was happy to ignore all vows, especially those made by Tibetan monks.

'Do you mind me talking about work?' Sarah tried to spear an olive with a cocktail stick, but it jumped out of the bowl. She picked it up and ate it. Must be pissed to do that without first running an anti-bac wipe over the table. 'Don't want to seem as though I'm rubbing it in.'

'I know you wouldn't do that.' It was true. One of the things I loved about Sarah was her considerate nature.

'Thank you.' She sighed. 'The team haven't responded to me very well.'

I reached over the table and took her hand. 'It's early days. Bound to be a period of adjustment. The team's twice the size it was when Jasper and I ran them separately. They're getting used to each other, as well as you and Tom.'

'True.' She attempted to harpoon another olive with her free hand but they swam around the bowl, evading capture. 'I tried to hold a team meeting to sort things out, but the only time everyone else could do was the afternoon of the school Christmas show.'

'You said yourself it was manic at the moment. Maybe wait till the new year. Get Nancy to set up—'

'Nancy's a bitch,' Sarah snapped.

I hadn't expected that. Nancy had been uninterested and made no secret of the fact that PA wasn't her career of choice, but she'd done a decent enough job and had never been rude.

Sarah studied the cocktail stick as though it were faulty in some way. 'She's making stuff up about me,' she said quietly.

'What stuff?'

'Saying I made you leave so I could take your job.'

'What a bitch.'

'I know! And I can't say anything because ...' she waved the cocktail stick in the air '... you know ...'

I nodded. Poor Sarah. Out of loyalty to me she was having to suck it up. 'What else is Nancy saying?'

Sarah looked up sharply. 'What do you mean?'

'You said she was making stuff up. Is there more?'

Sarah cleared her throat. 'Oh no, that's it. But that's enough, isn't it?'

'Yes, it is.' I tapped the table. 'Have you talked to Clara?'

'No!' Sarah yelped. 'I mean, no,' she said more calmly.

'Talk to her,' I said firmly. 'You're within your rights to make an official complaint against Nancy.' Sarah flushed. 'Now isn't the time to be nice and give her the benefit of the doubt like you usually do,' I continued. 'Nail that bitch to the wall.'

Sarah stared glumly into her glass. More than ever, I regretted leaving my laptop on the train. If I hadn't, Sarah wouldn't be going through this crap. Things would have stayed as their hunky-dory selves.

'I'm sorry.' I put my arms around her. Sarah rested her head on my shoulder. 'Just a few more months till I go back to work and then we can go back to normal.'

Sarah stiffened. 'What do you mean?'

'I mean that you won't have to keep slogging away like this when I'm working again. I can see how much you miss the kids. They miss you too.' And eating something other than fish fingers, potato waffles and beans.

Sarah pulled away. 'Unless something goes really badly, I'll still be a Director in a few months. It's a permanent role.'

I smiled. 'We'll cross that bridge when we come to it.'

Sarah tried to nudge her non-existent glasses up again and almost poked herself in the eye. 'I don't want to spoil our evening, but you need to understand that—'

I put a hand up. 'Don't worry about me. I'll find a job easily. Come January I'll be on a mission.' I nudged her. 'No pinching my marketing ideas when we're rivals.'

Sarah tried to pour herself another glass, but the bottle was empty. 'Why not try something different?' she said.

'You were so keen on psychology. This is the perfect time for a new start.'

I shook my head. 'More studying than I'd realised. And I like marketing. Know where I am with it.'

Sarah pulled her hair off her face, disrupting the soft waves. 'What about doing marketing for a small firm instead of going to one of the big corporations? With your experience, you could turn a company around. Really help and make a difference. Build a bond rather than juggling lots of clients.' Her hair was starting to get its frizz back.

'Enough work talk.' I took her hand. 'Let's have a shot. What do you fancy?'

Sarah opened and shut her mouth a few times, clearly deliberating what to go for. She was wise to. It was an important decision. Choose the right shot and you were in for a cracking night. Choose the wrong one and you'd have your head down the toilet all the way home on the train.

Eventually, she stopped her goldfish impression and nodded. 'OK, no more work talk. Line up the shots.'

Three hours later, we stumbled through our front door. The shot had led to two more, which led to another bottle of champagne, which led to us being wasted. The evening had cost almost as much as the pizza oven, but it had been good fun and neither of us had thrown up or left anything of value on the train – except possibly our dignity, which hadn't been very present when eating our Leon takeaways out of the bag.

When Sarah was drunk, bedtime went one of two ways. She either behaved like a sex maniac who'd been deprived of carnal pleasure for the past decade, or she fell asleep. There was no middle ground. Obviously, I always hoped for the former. Although I had been known to pray for sleep to take her on particularly exuberant marathon sessions. Falling asleep myself usually put an end to things when they'd gone on too long.

Happily, tonight Sarah was in full-on sex-starved-slut mode and we got down to business the moment the front door was shut.

'God, you're sexy,' I said in between kisses, as she untucked my shirt from my trousers. I tried to undo her dress, but the drapey wrap thing at the front thwarted me, so I hitched it up instead.

'I love you,' she slurred, attempting to unbutton my shirt, abandoning the job and unbuckling my belt instead.

'Love you too.' I whipped my wallet out of my pocket before my trousers fell to the floor and took out a condom.

'No, I mean, I *really* love you.' Sarah placed her hands either side of my face and looked at me intently.

'I know. Same.' I kissed her and laid her back on the stairs.

She wrapped her legs around my waist. 'No matter what happens with work, we'll love each other just as much.'

'Yep.' I slipped the condom on.

'Because it's just work.' Sarah guided me in. 'You and me and the children, that's what matters. Not work.'

'Can we stop talking about the kids and work?'

'Yes. Sorry.'

Normal duties resumed and we made the most of having the house to ourselves. It wasn't until we eventually fell into bed that we realised the condom had disappeared.

'Nooo!' Sarah knelt up on the bed and spun around, looking over her shoulder as though chasing a tail. 'Where is it? When did it come off?'

I placed my hands on her shoulders to slow her down. 'Don't worry. Practically impossible to get pregnant at our age.'

'I still have periods.' Sarah covered her face with her hands. 'I can't be pregnant. Did you definitely come?'

'Yes,' I said, a little hurt that my cry of 'I'm coming' hadn't had more impact.

'Why is all this bad stuff happening?' Sarah began to cry. 'It's one thing after another.'

'Don't be sad.' I wrapped my arms around her. The booze must be making her melancholy. I mean, what was the worst that could happen? A baby, that's what, and babies were a gift. Now that I thought about it, it'd be quite nice to have another baby. Life had been a lot simpler when Sarah was on maternity leave. I'd gone to work and done my thing, and she'd stayed at home and done her thing. The sleepless nights hadn't been ideal, but once my back had got used to the airbed in the study, they had got easier.

I kissed the top of Sarah's head. 'You know what? Maybe this was meant to happen.'

'What?' Sarah's voice was muffled against my shoulder.

'A baby wouldn't be the end of the world,' I said softly. 'You're a great mum.'

Sarah looked up, confused. 'I can't cope with work and two children, let alone a baby as well.'

I laughed softly. 'You wouldn't have to work, you silly thing. You'd stay at home while I worked.' I warmed to my theme. 'No more worrying about deadlines, or getting the team to like you, or Nancy being a bitch. All you'd need to think about is the kids.' I stroked her hair. 'You leave all that silly worrying to me, and focus on the family.'

I did not see that punch coming.

Chapter 25

Sarah

This was so bloody typical. Will had messed up putting on the condom, but it was me who had to sort it out.

At the chemist's, the day after the incident, I'd had to wait outside the head pharmacist's office for forty-five minutes, desperately praying no one I knew saw me and asked what I was doing. I'd explained the mortifying situation to the very handsome, very young, equally mortified head pharmacist, Mr Raju, who couldn't prescribe the morning-after pill because I couldn't remember when my last period had been. I'd never forgotten before, but life was so manic at the moment that I barely had time to have a period, let alone note down the date and duration.

Mr Raju had suggested I tried the family planning clinic. The clinic was closed over the weekend, so I'd had to go first thing Monday morning – citing an emergency dentist appointment at work – and was told that the only way of guaranteeing against pregnancy was to get a coil fitted. The doctor in charge of fitting coils (bet that made for an interesting business card) wasn't available, and the next available appointment was Wednesday morning.

So, on Wednesday morning, there I was: knees spread, forceps wedging my fanny open, a doctor foraging away like a fox delving down a rabbit hole, telling me to relax, while she attached what felt like a bulldog clip to my cervix. The world didn't contain enough flowers to inhale or candles to blow out to stop it fucking hurting.

And while I was going through this, Will was sulking at home because I hadn't gone along with his idea of taking a chance and maybe having another baby. What parallel universe was he living on that made that seem like a good idea? Oh yes – the one in which life reverted to him doing what he wanted, when he wanted, while I stayed at home, raising children and dealing with everything.

Bugger that. Yes, I wished I could be around for Evie and Fred more, but having a baby was not the way to do it. Especially as all the nappy changing and feeding and sleepless nights would take everything out of me. I'd have even less left for them than I did now. Besides, I was forty-two. Which, while not ancient, was getting on a bit to have a baby. That was before I even thought about my career. I was clinging on to it as it was. Taking a third lot of maternity leave and potentially coming back part-time would definitely be the end of the Director's role. Possibly Senior Manager, too. I whimpered at a sharp stabbing sensation deep within my vagina. Was the doctor fly fishing down there? I gritted my teeth. Better this than the alternative.

'All done.' The doctor sat back, unpeeled her gloves and handed me a sanitary towel the size of a lilo. I would not be using that. I was wearing a thin wrap-around dress. VPL was enough of a concern without a giant pad showing, too. The doctor stood up and retreated to the other side of the curtain. 'You'll bleed for a while and may be quite tender.' Tender wasn't the word I'd use. That was like describing labour as smarting a bit. Still, I reminded myself, the whole point of this torture was to avoid labour. 'Take a painkiller if you need to,' she added. 'And try to rest.'

Rest was not an option. I had to get to work immediately, then we had our Christmas party tonight. Unable to pin any of my team down in the office, I'd decided the best approach was to befriend them at the party. Show them my fun side and assure them that I was there for them. I couldn't do that if I was curled up in a corner, hugging a hot-water bottle.

'I will,' I lied, wiping myself with the paper towel she'd left me. My eyes widened at the amount of blood that came away. Perhaps I would use the mattress-thick sanitary towel after all. Let's be honest, it was unlikely anyone would be looking at my bum anyway. I rolled off the bed and stood up. My knees buckled and I grasped the bed for support.

'You might feel a bit woozy,' the doctor called through the curtain. 'Sit and wait in reception till you feel better.'

'OK.' Another whopper. I'd rather pass out struggling to the train station than sit in reception, watching *Homes Under the Hammer* with all those sexually inept losers. Too much of a reminder that I was one too.

The party was in full flow and so was I. Amazing what a codeine and a few glasses of fizz could do. The codeine had been gifted to me by one of my old team, who had asked if I was OK when she'd found me walking very slowly and carefully along the corridor to the ladies. I'd blamed my frailty and ashen face on some root-canal work. Instead of questioning why this affected the use of my legs, she'd offered me the painkiller, left over from when she'd had a minor op, which I'd taken gratefully.

I'd spent the next couple of hours catching up with my former team. My lovely team whom I got on brilliantly with and who'd never complained about my lack of care or fictitious sexual advances. Tom had told Clara that Nancy's complaint was pure fabrication on the very same day it had been received, but I still felt uncomfortable about it.

Much as I wanted to spend the entire evening with my lovely former team, that'd only add fuel to the accusation that I didn't care about my current one. After a codeine, several glasses of fizz and four HR complaints against me,

I cared more about the plight of the vine weevils than I did about my team, but had to put on a front.

Tom was chatting to Jed, Rebecca and Dean. My three accusers. I should join them. Worst-case scenario, they'd scarper as soon as I arrived. Or was that the best-case scenario? I wasn't sure. Only one way to find out.

Downing the remainder of my drink and exchanging it for a full glass, I walked over to the group. Tom flashed me a smile, but the others carried on talking as though I wasn't there. Dean was telling a skiing-trip story and I realised that he was a natural raconteur, witty and concise rather than waffling on, enjoying the sound of his own voice. It was shameful that I hadn't discovered this before. I really needed to get to know everyone better. Jed leapt in with his own anecdote, which wasn't funny or concise. Not so keen to get to know him better, if I was honest.

Jed eventually came to the end of his story and I spoke up, eager to participate.

'I've never been skiing. Sounds like I'm missing out.' Silence. I persevered. 'Where would you recommend a complete novice went? Or have I left it too late to start? Can you teach an old dog new tricks?' My nervous giggle faded away. The look on Jed's face suggested that there was only one trick he'd like to teach this old dog and that was to roll over and play dead. Without the play element. My cheeks burnt. They hated me. Had I really neglected them to such an extent that they couldn't bring themselves to talk to me?

'Never too late,' Tom said. I shot him a grateful smile. 'The skiing's only a small part of it anyway. The après-ski's the main appeal.'

'I could manage that part OK.' I held up my glass. 'Cheers, everyone.'

Rebecca and Dean muttered a very quiet 'cheers' without glancing in my direction. Jed exhaled loudly and looked around the room.

'Cheers.' Tom chinked his glass against mine.

The five of us stood in silence for a moment. I had to address the elephant in the room. The elephant being me.

'I'm really glad you're all here, as I've been wanting to talk to you,' I started. Rebecca and Dean exchanged a look. Jed's jaw tightened. 'I'm very worried by what Clara told me. The last thing I want is for you to think I don't care, because the opposite's true. Your work and your career progression are very important to me.' I put a hand to my chest and encountered flesh. Glancing down, I realised that my wrap-around dress was gaping open. Instead of this being a heartfelt gesture, I was groping my semi-exposed breast. Gasping, I tugged the dress together and tried to resume my apology speech. 'What I'm trying to say is, you're wrong. I do care.'

'We're wrong, are we?' Jed tutted. 'Bloody typical.'

My stomach sank. 'Bad choice of word. I meant that you're mistaken.'

'Still all on us, though.' Jed rolled his eyes at Tom and strode off.

I turned to Rebecca and Dean. 'That's not what I mean. I'm really sorry if that's how it seemed. I want to make this right. Please can we talk properly in the office tomorrow?'

Dean shuffled from foot to foot. 'I'm not in tomorrow.'

'Friday then,' I offered.

Dean gave a reluctant nod.

'How about you, Rebecca?' I asked. 'Can you do tomorrow?'

Rebecca's eyes fluttered, as she mentally Rolodexed through a list of excuses. 'I need to check my diary,' she said eventually.

'Of course.' I nodded enthusiastically. 'Let me know when's good for you. Dean, I'll send you a meeting invite for Friday. Thank you.'

Rebecca gave me a curt nod. 'See you later.' This was directed to Tom rather than me.

'Yeah, see you,' Dean said, seizing the opportunity to run.

I put a hand to my head and groaned. 'What a disaster. Everything came out wrong. Have I made it worse?'

Tom shook his head. 'Not at all. Not that anyone will remember anything tomorrow anyway.' His eyes flitted to my chest and I realised that I'd let go of my dress without securing the wrap part of the wrap-around back into place. Nancy strolled over, presumably to talk to Tom, and when she saw me, her eyes narrowed. She clocked my bra on display, shot me such a look of hatred that it was a wonder I didn't burst into flames, and then carried on walking.

'No,' I wailed, holding the front of my dress together.

'What's wrong?' Tom asked, oblivious to Nancy's appearance.

I thrust my glass into his hand. 'I need to go to the ladies and sort my dress out,' I said.

'OK.' He smiled. 'I'll keep your drink safe for you.'

'Thanks.' I hurried off to the toilet, registering, as I passed the buffet, that I hadn't eaten anything yet. No wonder my feet weren't going exactly where I was trying to place them. I hadn't had too much to drink – I'd had too little to eat.

Inside the loo, I inspected my appearance in the mirror. The belt of my dress had come loose, causing the front to bag open and reveal one lace demi-cup. I sighed heavily, tying the belt in a double knot. I wiped a smudge of eyeliner away and was about to reapply my red lipstick, when Nancy came out of one of the cubicles. Our eyes met in the mirror. She pursed her lips and walked to a sink as far away from me as possible.

'Hi Nancy,' I said, trying to put aside my anger at her accusations and appear as nonchalant as I could. I sounded as nonchalant as a drill sergeant.

She turned the tap on, blanking me completely.

'Nancy?'

'I talk to you at work because I'm paid to,' she said tightly, washing her hands at lightning speed. 'I don't have to in my free time.'

'Fine,' I said. 'But just so you know, your complaint against me was pure speculation and it's been withdrawn.' Nancy pursed her lips. I sliced the air with my hand. 'This isn't a game. You could have ruined my career. I've never done anything to you, so I don't understand why you have this vendetta. Can you explain it to me? Because I'd really like to know.'

Nancy switched on the hand dryer, drowning out my last sentence.

I folded my arms and waited for her to finish. The hand dryer switched off. 'We need to sort this out, Nancy.' The hand dryer went back on again. I watched her rubbing her clearly dry hands together. She was chewing her lower lip and, now that I looked closely, her hands were shaking. Shit, had I scared her? I reassessed my standpoint. She was only about twenty-five. I was almost twenty years older than her, and needed to use my maturity and experience to rectify the situation without her feeling threatened.

The hand dryer eventually switched off. I waited until Nancy stepped away from it before trying again. 'Please help me understand the situation.' I clasped my hands together. 'I want us to have a good working relationship, but it's hard to fix when I don't know where any of this has come from or why.'

Nancy's defiant expression softened and she looked momentarily vulnerable, before snapping back to her default position of contempt. 'I've been told not to talk to you outside of work.'

I held my hands up. 'OK. I'll catch up with you tomorrow in the office.'

Nancy's glare in response indicated that catching herpes would be more appealing.

She walked out and I turned back to the mirror to reapply my lipstick, then paused. What was the point? None of my team wanted me to be here. Admittedly, I'd only spoken to three of them so far, but the others weren't exactly lining up to talk to me. I checked my watch. Only nine o'clock;

if I left now, I'd be home by ten thirty. I could get a decent night's sleep and start afresh tomorrow. Get to the root of what was going on with everyone and sort it out before we broke up for Christmas. Yes, that's what I'd do. Putting my lipstick back in my bag, I left the ladies and headed to the cloakroom to get my coat.

'Sarah.' Tom called my name as I crossed the room. 'Your drink.'

I turned. 'Thanks, but I'm going to head off.'

'You can't go,' Tom said. 'Got another three hours of free drinking ahead of us.'

'I know, but the complaints, Nancy's particularly—'

'Is bullshit,' Tom said. 'Clara's discounted it.'

I gave him a grateful smile. 'I know. Thank you. But the others still stand and I'm shattered. That root canal this morning took it out of me.'

'God, of course. I'd forgotten about that.' Tom handed my glass back to me. 'One more for the road? Please. I've hardly seen you tonight.'

His blue eyes stared into mine, before dropping to my mouth, and my stomach did its treacherous flip.

Averting my gaze, I knocked my remaining fizz back. It was warm from where he'd been holding the glass and tasted as though it had contracted a yeast infection in the time I'd been in the toilets. If there had been any teeny-tiny part of me that had wondered what it'd be like to be kissed by Tom – there wasn't; this was a purely hypothetical musing – the tepid fizz eradicated it. Aside from the obvious morality issues, and the fact that Tom was not, I repeat *not*, my type – Will was my type – my breath must now be as fragrant as a septic tank in a heatwave.

'No, I'm going to call it a night.' I placed the glass on a tray, as a waiter passed by. 'I need to sleep.'

Tom gave me a rueful smile and nodded. 'Fair enough. Text me when you get home, so I know you're OK.'

'Thanks. I will. Enjoy the rest of the night.'

* * *

Just over an hour later, the train pulled into my station, and I got off and limped to a cab. It wasn't a long walk and usually I preferred the fresh air to inhaling pine-scented air fresheners and being blasted with a forty-degree heater, but I was exhausted and my sanitary towel-cum-portable mattress was too heavy to lug any further.

Once home, I opened the front door, closed it quietly to avoid disturbing the children and tiptoed across the hall. The kitchen door was closed and behind it I could hear Will's muffled laugh. Maybe he was listening to a podcast? I pushed the door open. Will was reclining in a chair at the kitchen table. Wearing his favourite teal jumper, a relaxed and easy smile on his face, an empty bottle of red wine in front of him. His eyes widened and his smile froze when he saw me. It wasn't a podcast that had made him laugh. It wasn't a podcast that was leaning towards him, angling its body so that it mirrored his in a classic body language 'I want you' pose. It wasn't a podcast that had a hand on his arm. No. It was the person sitting next to him. And that person was Lauren.

Chapter 26

Will

I stared in disbelief at Sarah standing in the doorway. The Christmas party would be in full swing right now. She should be in London swinging along with it. Well, not swinging – definitely not swinging – but having a nice time with her gal pals. Catching up on the latest gossip, having a bop to Take That, photocopying her boobs to put in a frame to give me for Christmas. That kind of thing.

'What are you doing here?' I blurted out.

Sarah's eyes narrowed. Possibly because she didn't have her glasses on and couldn't see me as well through her contact lenses. But, possibly, because I was in very close proximity to a very attractive woman and very clearly hadn't expected my wife to be home for some time.

'I live here,' Sarah said coldly. 'Remember?' Her narrow-eyed glare focused on Lauren's hand, which was on my arm. Shit, not again. How long had it been there? Why was it there? I honestly couldn't remember. Red wine always made everything hazy, especially two bottles' worth, but I needed to explain why Lauren was here and why her hand was on my arm.

'Not wool,' I said slowly and clearly to Lauren, in the same way Fred's teacher spoke when explaining something baffling to the class, such as why it wasn't a good idea to go to the toilet in your trousers. 'Good guess, though.' Lauren, understandably, looked as bewildered as if I'd announced that *I'd* just been to the toilet in my trousers. I lifted my arm and stroked the fabric of my sleeve. 'My jumper is in fact made from recycled plastic bottles.' I went over to Sarah and put my arm around her. 'Lovely to see you. Just wondered why you're back so soon. Wasn't the party fun?'

'Your jumper's from M&S,' Sarah said, with a glower. 'It's polyester.'

'Knew it began with a P.' I fake laughed.

There was a delicate tinkle of a laugh from the table. Sarah and I turned as one, with me gripping her shoulder as though we were part of a chorus line.

Lauren gave a little wave. 'Hi. Sorry to say I'm a bit tipsy again.' She raised her shoulders to her ears and giggled. 'I'm not always drunk, honest.'

'Don't worry about it.' Sarah crossed her arms, a move that instantly made me worry. 'I find Will much better company when I've had a drink too.'

I laughed as forcibly as the studio audience of an American sitcom, stopping just short of mopping tears of laughter from my eyes.

Sarah gave me a look of disdain. I stopped laughing.

'Has Friday Fizz changed to Wednesday Wine?' Sarah's tone was light, but her body was so rigid that I could have flipped her over and used her as an ironing board.

'No, but I think that could catch on.' Lauren smiled. 'I'll suggest it to the rest of the gang.'

Sarah gave a tight smile in return. 'Where are the rest of *the gang*?' she asked, managing to make *the gang* sound like a group the Krays would be wary of. 'Throwing up in the living room again or trying on my shoes upstairs?'

Lauren cringed and her shoulders shot up to her ears. 'So sorry about that. We all felt awful.'

'Hmm,' Sarah said. She waited a moment then asked again. 'So, where are they?'

'Oh, it's just me tonight.'

I'd thought Sarah was tense before, but she'd been almost zen-like in comparison to how stiff she was now. Forget using her as an ironing board. She'd make a sledgehammer seem limp.

Lauren picked up a brightly coloured, family-size bag of crisps and dangled it between her thumb and forefinger. 'Will missed the last Friday Fizz because you were out in London. I couldn't let him miss out on these too. I was passing on my way back from college, so thought I'd drop them in.'

Sarah couldn't have looked less enamoured if Lauren had held up a bag of Anthrax. 'How kind,' she said. 'But Will *has* had crisps before.'

'Not Christmas tree-shaped crisps, he hasn't.' Lauren rustled the bag. 'These are a limited-edition range. Sold out within hours, so no chance of getting any more.'

'Thank you for thinking of us. We'll be sure to enjoy them on Christmas Day,' Sarah said stiffly.

Lauren pulled her shoulders up to her ears again. ''Fraid we've eaten them. Sorry. They're very moreish.'

'Yeah. Sorry about that,' I mumbled, giving Sarah's shoulder a squeeze. 'Very moreish.'

Sarah shrugged me off. 'Great.' She picked up the empty bottle of wine from the table – mercifully leaving the one that still had some left in it, as I wouldn't have dared try to grab it back – strode to the recycling bin and dropped it inside. Then she made a grand display of gathering up the empty crisp wrapper and the other detritus, and threw that away too. 'It's getting late, so …' She trailed off and looked pointedly at Lauren.

Lauren smiled and nodded. 'I understand. Don't feel you have to stay up just because I'm here.'

Sarah's mouth fell open. I was as surprised as her at Lauren's lack of awareness. She was the one doing the psychology degree. How could she not have picked up that Sarah's body language screamed: 'Will you fuck off please?' Though, without the 'will you'. Or the 'please'.

I yawned loudly and stretched my arms wide. 'Feeling a bit sleepy myself. Think I'd better turn in too.' There was no chance of me winning an Oscar for that piece of acting, although the way Sarah was glaring at me, a Will Smith-style slap round the face might well be awarded before the night was out.

'Oh, OK.' Lauren finally took the hint and stood up, clutching the table for support. 'I'll go then.'

'I'll call you a cab.' Sarah took her phone from her bag and opened an app. 'An Uber will be here in two minutes,' she said, mere seconds later.

'Thanks.' Lauren picked her coat up from the end of the table and knocked a pile of Christmas cards, which Sarah had asked me to post, onto the floor. I crouched down to retrieve them, my eyes darting around for somewhere to hide them till I could sneak out to the postbox the next morning.

'Let me know how much I owe you for the cab,' Lauren said to Sarah.

'No need,' Sarah said, in a way that suggested there was no need for them to ever communicate again. 'Use the money to buy yourself some more crisps.'

'Thanks.' Lauren unhooked her bag from the back of her chair. The chair teetered on its back legs and would have fallen heavily to the floor if it hadn't handily landed on my head, as I gathered up Christmas cards.

'Aaah,' I yelled, rocking back and landing on my arse.

'Will, I'm so sorry.' Lauren knelt down and placed a hand gently either side of my face. 'Are you hurt?'

'No,' I lied, my head throbbing.

'You should put some ice on it.' Lauren peered at my scalp, her chest millimetres from my eye level. I swallowed hard.

'Cab's here.' Sarah yanked Lauren up by her arm and frogmarched her out of the room.

'Bye, Will. See you tomorrow,' Lauren called over her shoulder, her feet scampering across the hall floor. Seconds later, the front door shut.

I eased myself up, rubbing my head. Sarah walked back into the kitchen, her face like thunder. I should have stayed under the table.

Sarah crossed her arms. 'Are you two having an affair?'

'What?' That hurt more than a slap. 'No! How could you think that?'

Sarah blinked hard. 'Why was she here then? It's one thing seeing her with the others or going to the open day at the college. Spending the evening drinking together is something else completely.'

I shook my head. 'She brought those crisps round, like she said.'

'What sort of a stupid excuse is that?' Sarah was blinking so hard that she was in danger of dislodging a contact lens or possibly even an eyeball. 'She could have given them to you tomorrow at school drop-off. Why the urgency? Did you tell her I was out tonight?'

I hesitated. Yes, I had told Lauren, but it was just conversation. She wouldn't have thought anything of it.

Sarah's eyes widened. 'Did you invite her?'

'No! I didn't know she was coming.'

Sarah eyed me up and down. 'Why are you wearing your best jumper then?'

I put a hand to my chest. Everything else needed washing, but if I admitted that I hadn't done any laundry this week, she'd hang me out to dry. There would be plenty of room on the line. 'Coincidence,' I said instead.

Sarah tutted. 'There's no such thing as coincidence.'

'So, it's not a coincidence that the bloke you fancy from *Bridgerton* just happens to have his arse out every time I walk in then?' I said indignantly.

Sarah's cheeks flushed. 'That has nothing to do with why *Lauren*,' she said her name as though it were an infectious disease, 'was here when I was out and you thought I wouldn't be back for hours.'

'She's a friend,' I said, my irritation growing. 'I'm allowed to have friends round. You wouldn't be bothered if she were a man.'

'I would if he was practically sitting on your lap. What would have happened if I hadn't come home then?'

'Nothing,' I snapped. 'I'm married to you, remember?' For better, for worse. In sickness and in health. In shit times when neither of you seems to like each other much and there's a hot woman who maybe, just maybe, fancies you and, if you're completely honest, you kind of fancy her too, but have to pretend you don't.

I did what any man in my predicament would do. I threw it back at her. 'I'm not having an affair, but for all I know, you are.'

Sarah opened and closed her mouth a few times. 'What are you talking about? Who with?'

'Tom,' I snapped. 'I wasn't going to mention it, but in London he practically had his head on your shoulder as you came up the escalator.'

Sarah's cheeks instantly turned a vivid shade of red. 'That's pathetic. Trying to offset your guilt by blaming me for something.'

Her astuteness just riled me more.

'Pathetic, am I? That explains why you act as though I'm beneath you.' I paced up and down the kitchen. 'Ever since I lost my job, you've behaved as though you're better than me and I'm some stupid errand boy that you can boss about.'

'I don't boss you around,' Sarah said bossily. 'I just ask you to help out around the house. Not that you do.' She picked up the fruit bowl and pointed at the pile of Christmas cards I'd hidden behind it. 'You walked past the postbox four times today on the way to and from school, and you couldn't even post the cards. Cards that I was up until midnight writing.'

'What's the big deal?' I tutted. 'I'll post them tomorrow.'

'Today was the last day for guaranteed post before Christmas.' Sarah thumped the bowl back down. 'When you were at Ballas & Bailey, I know you worked hard, but

225

you could switch off when you got home. When I get home, I have to sort out all the chaos you've created.'

I tensed.

'I miss being with Evie and Fred,' she continued. 'I want to be able to spend the little time I have with them playing and reading and being a mum. Instead I'm cooking and cleaning and doing life admin and writing cards that you can't be bothered to post.' She thrust her hands into her hair. 'It isn't fair.'

I stared at her flushed face, her glistening eyes and her crazy hair that was sticking out at right angles. 'You know what's not fair?' I snapped. 'You complaining about work when I should be there.'

Sarah inhaled sharply. 'Where should I be then? At home with the kids? A submissive little housewife, because that's all women are good for?'

'I didn't mean it like that.' I paced up and down the kitchen. 'I'm not saying you shouldn't work because you're a woman. You're good at your job, I know that. But I'm crap at being at home. I belong in the office. You're good wherever you are, so it makes sense for you to be here.'

'You're just saying that to justify it to yourself,' Sarah said through gritted teeth. 'It's obvious what you really think. You can't stand the fact that I'm working with Tom and—'

'Can't resist bringing his name up, can you?' I snapped.

'For God's sake,' she snapped back. 'I am not having an affair.' She hesitated and took a breath. 'Be honest with me. Are you?' She looked up at me questioningly, a mixture of fear, hurt and hope in her eyes.

My anger subsided. Frustrated as I was with her, my instinct was still to reassure her that I loved her and hadn't cheated on her. 'No.' I stepped towards her. 'There's nothing going on, I promise.'

Relief spread across Sarah's face, but she put a hand up and I stopped in my tracks.

'Good,' she said. 'Even when things aren't going great,

I like to think we wouldn't betray each other.' I shook my head solemnly. 'That we'd talk to each other and sort whatever was wrong out.' I nodded enthusiastically. Did this mean everything was OK? Could we go to bed now? Could make-up sex be on the cards? So long as Sarah didn't dwell on the unposted ones. I took another cautious step forward.

'However,' Sarah said. I faltered. 'I think that you resent me working.' She took another deep breath. 'What happened with your job wasn't my fault. It's not fair that you take your frustrations out on me. Or that you expect me to do so much at home when I'm working so hard.' Tears filled her eyes. 'I'm exhausted. I can't do it all. I've tried to and it just means I'm failing at everything.' Her voice cracked, and I crossed the short distance between us and wrapped my arms around her. 'I'm failing,' she said again.

Guilt flooded through me as she sobbed into my shoulder. Sarah seemed so capable. I hadn't realised she was struggling.

'It's OK,' I said, stroking her hair. Well, I tried to stroke her hair, but she had so much product in it, it was like stroking a toffee apple. 'You're not failing.'

'I am,' Sarah cried. 'Everything's going wrong at work.'

'I'm sure it's not,' I soothed. 'It seems like that because it's so hectic in the run-up to Christmas. It'll be better in the new year. You'll have had a break and you'll be halfway through.'

'Halfway through?' Sarah's voice was muffled.

I nodded. 'I'll be working again in three months. We don't need two Directors' salaries. We can manage with you as a Senior Manager again. Or, better still, go back to being part-time.'

'No, I—' Sarah started.

'Shhh.' I gave up on the hair stroking and patted her back instead. 'The important thing is that you're not so stressed. That it's not all on your shoulders anymore. I'm sorry I didn't realise sooner.' I was going to get a Husband of the Year Award for this level of understanding.

'No, you don't understand,' Sarah said, whipping the award away before I'd even seen it, let alone picked out a trophy cabinet to place it in. She pulled back and wiped her cheeks. 'I don't want to go back to being a Manager or part-time.'

'But you miss the kids.'

'I do.' Sarah clasped her hands together. 'But I'd spend more time with them if I wasn't doing all the work at home by myself. I enjoy the level of responsibility I'm getting at work. I've earned it and want to make a success of it.'

I ran a hand back and forth across my head. 'OK, let me get this right. You want to keep being a Director, even though it's stressing you out and you don't get as much time with the kids?' Sarah nodded. 'Why?' I asked. 'Why do you want to make life hard for yourself?'

Sarah took such a deep breath that she could have swum to the bottom of the Pacific Ocean and back and still had oxygen to spare. 'It wouldn't be so hard if you were prepared to do more.' She nudged up her glasses that weren't actually there, and looked at me with a mix of nervousness and defiance. 'That's what I need – more help at home, not less time at work. More help from you.'

Oh, here we were again. No matter what I said or did, it always came back to this. I should be doing more. Regardless of whether I was working my arse off in the office, looking after the kids, running the household – which, as far as I could gather, mainly entailed stacking the Tupperware so it didn't fall out of the cupboard when the door was opened – whatever I did, it wasn't enough. I could have always come home one drink earlier. The kids always needed a more thorough wash or teeth clean. And the water bottles always tumbled out of the cupboard, no matter how far back I hurled them.

'I'll be working flat-out and travelling again soon,' I said coolly. 'How do you expect me to help more then?'

Sarah clasped her hands together. 'You wouldn't have to work such long hours or travel if you took a marketing role with a smaller firm, rather than with one of the big companies.'

Blood rushed to my head. She had it all worked out. She'd keep the glory job, while I took a massive step down and carried on my Daddy Daycare duties. 'Here's another idea,' I snapped. 'Why don't *you* get a job with a smaller firm?'

Sarah looked taken aback, as though I'd suggested she quit marketing and become a scullery maid. 'I just said I want to make a success of my role,' she explained.

'The role you're failing at.'

Sarah winced. I knew that was a mean thing to say, but she couldn't expect me to roll over and agree to the crappy end of the deal, when that had never been part of the plan.

Sarah pulled herself up tall. 'Running away when it's not going as smoothly as I hoped wouldn't make me feel good. I'd rather make it work if I can. It doesn't make sense for us both to be job-hunting and starting again anyway. You have time to look for another job; I don't.'

'Sure it's not that you can't bear the thought of not working with Tom anymore?' It was a childish retort, but I was fed up. Fed up with being treated like a loose Jenga piece that could be pushed out and repositioned, when I'd always been the key, grounded piece that held everything strongly together. Well, apart from the time I fell asleep on the train. 'I've seen the way he looks at you,' I added.

Sarah's cheeks flushed scarlet. 'Don't be stupid,' she snapped. 'He doesn't look at me any way. Even if he did, you wouldn't see it, because you're not there.'

I glowered at her. 'That's right, rub it in. You can't resist an opportunity to remind me that I'm no longer part of Ballas & Bailey, can you?'

Sarah put her hands over her face. A muffled wail filtered through them. 'This is going nowhere. Let's talk tomorrow.'

'There's nothing else to talk about.' I sat back down at the kitchen table and readied myself to have another drink.

'After Christmas, I'll be speaking to the other big marketing firms. By Easter I'll be back in employment and things will go back to normal.'

Sarah lowered her hands 'What do you mean by normal?'

'I mean me working again and doing whatever the job requires, and you …' I studied the table.

'Me what?'

I picked up the remaining wine bottle and emptied the last trickle into my glass. I wasn't going to repeat myself. I'd already suggested that she go back to a less stressful position, which was clearly the most obvious solution.

Sarah threw her hands in the air. 'You don't care, do you? All you care about is what *you* want to do. There's no way we can both work the number of hours the Director role requires. One of us has to stand back to let the other do it. In your eyes, there's no question as to who steps back, is there? It has to be me. My career has to take second place to yours.' She snatched up the glass I'd just poured the meagre few remaining drops of wine into and downed it. 'Why is your career more important than mine?'

She plonked the empty glass down. I stared at it in disbelief. That had been my wine. She was always telling the kids off for taking what wasn't theirs, and now she'd done it to me. I stood up, strode to the garage, leant in and took a new bottle from the wine rack.

'I asked you a question.' Sarah slammed a hand down on the table. 'Stop ignoring me.'

I picked up the corkscrew and sliced open the foil. Sarah's eyes narrowed when she realised I'd gone for a premium bottle, rather than our usual plonk.

'You can't drink this. It's for Christmas,' she snapped, taking it off me.

I took the bottle back. 'Don't tell me what I can and can't do. I'm not one of the kids.'

'Stop acting like one then.' She yanked the bottle out of my hands. 'What about my job?' she shouted.

Heat rushed through me. 'I don't care about your job.' I tried to wrestle the bottle from her, but she held on tight. 'Do what you like.'

'I *can* do what I like.' Sarah tucked the bottle under her arm in an attempt to wrench it out of my grasp. 'You're the one who can't.'

'Yes, I can.' I darted round the other side of her and yanked the bottle free. 'I've got a glowing reference and years of experience. Getting another Director position will be a cinch.' I held the bottle up triumphantly, extending my arm as she reached up to grab it. Lowering it, then lifting it higher, just to taunt her.

'You're pathetic.' Sarah stood back. She was visibly shaking. 'Keep your bottle. Enjoy your victory over me. Doesn't matter how glowing your reference is. You can't get a job with Ballas & Bailey's rivals.'

'Yes, I can.' I lowered the bottle, my heart pounding. 'I'll get a better one too,' I added. 'So, up yours.'

'No, you won't,' Sarah said in a low voice. 'None of them will employ you because I work for their competitor. It's a conflict of interest.' She glowered at me. 'So, up yours.'

The bottle slipped from my hand and smashed onto the floor.

Chapter 27

Sarah

The loud crash of the bottle hitting the kitchen tiles alerted my senses more quickly than those of a middle-class housewife being alerted to Boden's end-of-season sale. And not just because I knew it'd be me clearing it up if I wanted to be certain there weren't any shards of glass left for the children to tread on. No, it was the way the smashing glass emphasised the look of shock and betrayal on Will's face.

'What did you say?' he gasped.

I put a hand to my mouth, wishing I could take my last sentence back. He'd needed to know, but I should have imparted the news in a calm, rational way that conveyed regret and compassion. I definitely should not have concluded with the words 'up yours'.

'I'm sorry,' I said. Glass crunched under my shoe, as I stepped towards him. 'I didn't know how to tell you. When you were thinking about a career change to psychology, there didn't seem any point. It wouldn't have been an issue.'

Will glowered at me. 'That was ages ago. How long have you known?'

I tried to nudge my glasses up, but of course I wasn't wearing them. 'A while.'

Will was quivering with rage. 'A while? As in the whole time?'

'No,' I said firmly. Ninety per cent of the time wasn't the *whole* time. I pressed my hands together. 'I really am sorry.

But it sounds worse than it is. The Big Five aren't the be-all and end-all. They just think they are. There are loads of smaller marketing firms. You could be a big fish in a small pond instead of the other way around.'

Will looked at me with such disdain, you'd think I'd suggested he go and live in an actual pond. 'I want to be a *big* fish in a *big* pond,' he said through gritted teeth. 'Which I was, till you got involved.'

I wasn't going down that train track again. 'Or you could do marketing for a company internally,' I continued. 'No more juggling different accounts or having to pitch for new business. You could use your expertise to work with a company you like and believe in. Such as ...' I racked my brains to think of his interests. 'A brewery,' I said. 'That'd be really fun and you might get freebies.'

Will glared at me. 'I ran McMullen's marketing campaign when I was at Ballas & Bailey. I was already doing something I liked and believed in.' He prodded my chest with his finger. 'If it's such a great idea, why don't you go and work for a smaller marketing company and be a fish?'

'I already told you,' I said evenly. 'It'd be difficult for us both to look for new jobs. Makes more sense for me to stay where I am, bringing in a guaranteed income, while you take the time to find something that's right for you.'

Will eyed me for a moment, seemingly absorbing what I'd just said. I allowed myself a glimmer of hope that he was recognising this course of action as the most sensible. Which it was, as any fool could see.

'Are you joking?' he spat. Any fool apart from Will. 'My career was exactly where it was supposed to be. Next step was Partner. I'm not walking away from that.'

'But we can't both work for one of the Big Five. They're rivals.'

'No, we can't.' Will's nostrils flared, as he looked at me pointedly.

My heart rate quickened with a sense of dread. 'Are you saying what I think you're saying?'

'I'm not a mind reader,' Will snapped. 'If you think I'm saying that you should do the decent thing and leave Ballas & Bailey, so I can get back the career I worked my arse off for, then yes, you're spot on.'

My blood went cold. Will wanted me to leave work so he could pursue his own career. He genuinely believed that he was more important than me. That my prospects were irrelevant and could be shunted aside to make way for his own, far superior ones. He was like all those other pre-#metoo era, chauvinistic, sexist, egotistical gits in the media. And, quite frankly, I didn't want to be with someone like that.

My hands clenched into fists and I backed away, ignoring the glass crunching beneath my feet. I'd clear it up later. Right now, I couldn't be anywhere near Will. 'That's it,' I said breathlessly. 'I've had enough.'

'So have I,' Will roared. His face was contorted with rage. He didn't look like my husband – the man I loved and always thought would be there for me.

'I think we need some time apart.' I surprised myself by how calm I felt and sounded, now that a decision was being reached. 'We'll get Christmas out the way, then you can stay somewhere else for a couple of weeks. Give ourselves some space to assess how we really feel.' I gave an authoritative nod, as though addressing a work project, not my marriage.

Will's mouth dropped open. '*I* can stay somewhere else? Why me?'

I frowned. 'I need to be here with Evie and Fred.' That was obvious.

'Why?' Will asked.

'Because I'm their mum. I can't leave them.'

'I'm their primary carer.' Will jabbed at his chest. 'I'm the one who gets them up in the morning, does the school runs, takes them to their clubs, gives them tea. I'm not moving anywhere.'

I gritted my teeth. He was right. He needed to be here, unfortunately.

'I'm going to bed,' he said. 'You know where the airbed is. Make yourself at home in the study.' Turning, he walked out of the room, leaving red wine footprints across the kitchen tiles.

Fuming, I went to the garage, took out the dustpan, brush and mop, and began cleaning the floor.

Chapter 28

Sarah

'Did you have a fun Christmas?' Dieuwke asked.

'No' was the short answer. No, it had not been fun pretending that everything was good between Will and me, when I'd rather have spent the festive period with the Grinch. No, it had not been fun pasting on fake smiles for Evie and Fred. No, it had not been fun sleeping in the study on an airbed, which deflated every night. No, it had not been fun juggling the emotions of guilt, anger and grief because my marriage was in tatters. I missed our banter and the feel of his arms around me, and his off-key singing in the shower. But I was also so angry that if he'd tried to do any of those things, I'd have accused him of violating my human rights.

'Yes, thanks,' I said pragmatically instead, rummaging in my bag for my organiser and the memory stick containing Dekker's presentation. 'You?'

'Christmas isn't a big thing in the Netherlands,' Dieuwke said. 'Is Tom attending the meeting?'

I froze. Tom didn't know about the meeting. I'd arranged it with Dieuwke right before Clara had told me about the complaints made against me. I'd written it in my organiser, but forgotten to log it on the system. Tom probably wouldn't have been able to come, as we were officially off, but I should have given him the option.

'Unfortunately, he can't make it,' I said, hoping my flushed cheeks wouldn't show up on screen. 'The office is closed today.'

'You have left your home to come in specially?'

'I really don't mind,' I said. She had no idea how heartfelt that statement was. The Archbishop of Canterbury's Christmas message was unlikely to have been as sincere. 'How about Lars?'

'No,' Dieuwke said. 'He doesn't work Tuesdays. He will be at the meeting next week, when I am away.'

I hadn't realised there was a meeting booked in for next week. I'd better make sure Tom knew about that one.

'I remember you saying Lars and his wife both work part-time,' I said. 'You and your husband do too, don't you? How's the horse breeding going?' I messaged Tom under the desk while Dieuwke answered.

In office. Meeting with Dieuwke. Sorry not in the calendar. Will ring after.

'Winking and urinating are common signs …' Dieuwke was saying animatedly.

Presumably this was something to do with horse breeding, but it could equally apply to one of the Friday Fizz Club's get-togethers.

'… That the mare is ready to accept the teaser,' Dieuwke finished.

Again, very possibly a Friday Fizz Club activity.

'Goodness. So much to know about horses.' I plugged the memory stick into my laptop. 'Ready to start? I think you're going to love this campaign.'

The icon showing that the memory stick had connected came up on my screen. I clicked it, ready to share the presentation that I'd painstakingly put together. It opened to reveal … nothing. The folders that had been in there when I'd last looked a few days ago had vanished.

I turned to Dieuwke, aghast. 'The presentation was on here. I don't know what's happened.'

Dieuwke frowned. 'This is very unsatisfactory.'

'I'm so sorry.' My hand shook, as I closed the icon and reopened it. Still empty. Why the hell hadn't I made a copy? I'd been so focused on getting through Christmas, I'd forgotten the most basic of rules – always back up your work.

'We should reschedule,' Dieuwke said.

'No,' I yelped. Today had to go well. Everything else in my life was falling apart. One positive thing had to happen. I grabbed my organiser. 'I'll talk you through the marketing campaign. It's a shame we don't have the visuals but, trust me, I can still paint a good picture.' I opened my organiser. I could do this. I *had* to do this.

An hour later, we said goodbye and I released my breath. I'd done it. My enthusiasm and belief in this campaign had come across, and I'd delivered my vision, despite the lack of imagery. Dieuwke was as excited about it as I was and couldn't wait to put it in place in the new year.

A huge smile on my face, I picked up my phone to call Will, eager to share my good news, then remembered we weren't talking. Disappointment coursed through me. Instinct had driven me to reach out to him, but that instinct needed to be curtailed. Like the instinct to do something for your child instead of letting them discover they can do it themselves. Or go on ASOS after consuming a bottle of wine.

I noticed a missed call from Tom, plus a message.

What meeting? Call me!

I rang and he answered immediately. 'The office is closed. Why are you having a meeting?' He spoke so quickly, it was impossible to tell if he was annoyed, had run to the phone or was auditioning to read out the T&Cs in a radio commercial.

'It was the only day Dieuwke could do before February,' I said.

'Why wasn't it in the calendar?'

'Nancy can't have put it in there.' I pushed my hair off my

burning face. It went completely against my nature to blame another person for my own mistakes, but Nancy wasn't a person. Nancy was a cow. 'Dieuwke said there's a meeting with Lars next week,' I said. 'That's not in the calendar either.'

There was a moment's pause. 'No, it isn't.' There was an edge to his voice. 'Nancy had better get her act together.'

Never mind her act. Getting the personal items in her desk together and buggering off somewhere else would be a much better outcome.

'How did the meeting go?' he asked.

'Great, actually.' I smiled. 'Dieuwke loved the marketing campaign and—'

'You did the presentation?' Tom interrupted. 'But …' He trailed off.

Guilt flooded through me. 'Yes, sorry. It would have been better if you'd been here too, but if she hadn't liked the vision … I needed to know now, so that I could change it. Luckily, however, she loved it.' The warmth I felt after doing a job well returned and I couldn't resist adding: 'Yay!'

'That's great,' Tom said slowly.

My smile wavered. What was with the flat, monotone response? Where was *his* 'Yay!'ing? This was the biggest marketing campaign we'd put together since becoming Directors and it had got the thumbs up. It would reflect really well on us. He should be pleased, not reacting as though he'd just won a colonic irrigation treatment.

'Yes, it is,' I replied equally flatly, slightly miffed that he wasn't congratulating me. We'd both get the credit for this after all, and it had been me who'd done all the work. 'Especially as I had to do it without the PowerPoint presentation.'

'What? Why?'

'My memory stick was blank.' I shuddered at the memory. 'So mortifying to open it up and find nothing on it. And I stupidly hadn't made a copy.'

'No! What a nightmare.' Tom was back to his usual engaged self. 'Was it near your phone? Mobile signals sometimes interfere with other things. Bank cards, for example. Could be that they affect memory sticks too.'

'Really? I do keep them in the same pocket in my bag.' I glared at my bag, as though it had been complicit.

'How did you do the presentation without the PowerPoint?'

'All the info's in my organiser.' I patted the book in front of me affectionately. That was two fingers up to everyone who thought I was archaic for using pen and paper instead of mindlessly tossing all my work up into the cloud. Obviously, I wasn't against technology – I'd be lost without my phone and if anyone tried to take my new hairdryer, I'd club them to death with it – but relying on it completely wasn't a safe bet.

Tom whistled. 'Wow. Impressive.' He chuckled into the phone. 'We need to celebrate. I'll come and meet you at the office.'

'Everywhere's closed. We'll do it next week, with the team.' I was determined to be a better boss, one that the team respected and felt comfortable with. Plying them with free drink seemed like a good place to start.

'No, we have to celebrate now,' Tom said. 'There's a bar near me that's open. It's opposite the station. You go past it on your way home.'

'I don't know.' I took my glasses off and rubbed my eyes. 'I should get home.'

'It's two o'clock, it's the Christmas holidays and your pitch has just got the green light, even though you had to present it using old-school notes.' Tom laughed. 'If that doesn't deserve a drink, what does? Just have one.'

I hesitated. The mum part of me wanted to get back to Evie and Fred. To snuggle up with chocolate coins and watch *Miracle on 34th Street*, or some other film featuring a handsome man (Dylan McDermott, not Richard Attenborough, just to clarify). I slid my non-rose-tinted glasses back on. In reality, they'd already be watching CBBC and wouldn't let me change channels, or let me snuggle up with them, or eat their chocolate coins.

'Go on,' Tom said.

What would Will do, if the roles were reversed? Would he race home after a victory at work or would he see a celebratory drink as an essential part of the process?

'OK,' I said. 'Just one, though.'

'I'll have it waiting for you.'

Chapter 29

Sarah

Thirty minutes later, I walked into the bar. It was trendy, but cosy, and housed exactly the right number of people. Not so few that you assumed there was a food-hygiene issue, but not so many that you worried there wouldn't be any paper left in the toilets.

Tom was at a table in the corner and waved me over. Standing, he gave me a huge hug.

'Well done. What a great start to the new year.' His arms were warm and firm around me. I realised, with sadness, that this was the most physical contact I'd had for a while. Evie and Fred's cuddles invariably ended up with an elbow in the face – my face, obviously – or with the other one getting jealous and climbing on too, resulting in two elbows in the face. And Will and I weren't speaking, let alone hugging. There was more chance of Johnny Depp and Amber Heard getting touchy-feely than us.

'Thanks.' I pulled away. 'I'm so relieved Dieuwke likes it.'

'It's a brilliant concept,' Tom said. 'There's no way she wouldn't.' He took my coat as I slipped it off and gestured for me to sit down. 'Hope you don't mind, but I took the liberty—'

'Tom!' I gasped, clocking the bottle of champagne on ice. 'You shouldn't have. I said I could only have one.'

Tom picked up one of the flutes. 'Shall I swap this for a pint glass?'

I laughed. Something else I hadn't done for a while. 'Thank you for this. I mustn't stay long, though.'

'We'll drink fast.' Tom winked and filled both flutes. 'Here's to you smashing the Dekker account.'

'Here's to us,' I corrected. 'And the whole team.'

'To us,' Tom said.

As with all good intentions, I failed spectacularly. Before I knew it, we were two-thirds into a second bottle – it seemed rude not to buy one back – and I was very tipsy. Tom was easy company, making me laugh with tales of his childhood. He'd been so naughty, it was a wonder his parents hadn't pretended to be negligent so social services would take him away.

'What time is it?' I asked, when I'd finally stopped laughing.

Tom picked up his phone. 'Five o'clock.'

'What?' I grabbed my own phone to double-check. 'I should have left ages ago.'

Tom shrugged. 'If you work till six, you'll have completed a full day and can claim it back as holiday.'

I pushed my hair away from my face. It bounced straight back again. 'That's a great theory, but this isn't exactly work.'

'Let's talk about work then.' Tom cleared his throat. 'The Dekker PR campaign is successful because it offers both a hook and a solid offer.'

I giggled. 'You sound like a marketing lecturer.'

'I'll stop then, before I feel the need to put on a tank top and saggy, faded chinos.'

Involuntarily, my eyes scanned what Tom was actually wearing. Relaxed dark denim jeans and a fitted blue jumper. All of a sudden, I felt like stroking it to see if it were made from recycled plastic bottles.

I put my glass down firmly. 'I really have to go. I haven't eaten and I'm starting to feel woozy.'

Tom picked up a menu. 'Let's order some food. I'm starving too.'

'Sorry, I can't.'

'Please don't make me eat alone. I've nothing at home and can't face a supermarket.' Tom read from the menu. 'Sharing platter – sourdough with beetroot hummus, mushroom arancini—' My stomach rumbled loudly and he grinned. 'Come on, let's have this to soak up the booze. You don't want to be negotiating your journey home half-cut.'

He made a good argument. Last thing I wanted was to get the wrong train. Asking Will to pick me up was unthinkable. Mainly because it'd involve speaking to him.

'OK.' I reached for my bag. 'I'll order it, then nip to the ladies.'

'Thanks,' he said with a wink.

My stomach flipped over. Oh no.

Blaming the stomach flip on another bout of famine, I messaged Will while on the loo. We might not be speaking, but it seemed courteous to let him know where I was and how long I'd be. I hesitated before writing. I didn't want to let him know exactly where I was – in a bar, quaffing champagne with Tom, whom he'd accused me of having an affair with, would go down as well as the film adaptation of *Cats* – but I also didn't want to pretend I was at the office. Lying was wrong. I couldn't look Evie and Fred in the eyes and lecture them about the importance of being honest, if I wasn't honest myself. More importantly, Will might look up my location on Find My Friends and know I'd fibbed.

Still in London. Trains running a slow service. I'll message when I know what time I'll be in. Love to Evie and Fred. X

I included the kiss automatically and had pressed send before realising. Bugger. He might see that as an acceptance of his chauvinistic attitude, which I did not accept at all. I'd sooner accept a free cut and blow-dry from Boris Johnson's hair stylist.

In the mirror, I tried to calm my curls down, firstly with my hands, then with a stern talking-to. Neither approach worked.

It didn't look too bad, though. Springy rather than spongy. My eyes were bright and shiny behind my glasses and my skin glowed. Not in a shiny, end-of-the-day, makeup's worn off and I need a wash way. No, in an exuberant, glowing, healthy way. I needed to nail marketing pitches more often if this was the result.

Tom was looking at his phone and I watched him, as I walked back to our table. A muscle pulsed in the side of his cheek. That meant he was concentrating. I'd got to know him well while sharing an office over the past three months. We talked constantly. He knew more about what was going on in my everyday life than my husband did, including the complaints made against me. The way things were between me and Will at the moment, he might well call Clara and add a complaint of his own. But Tom was there for me, having my back, liaising with the team when they were avoiding me, making sure Nancy's allegation was withdrawn. Without his support, I couldn't have kept going. He'd become much more than just a colleague. He'd become a friend. Tom glanced up and grinned when he saw me. My stomach flipped over again. Where was that bloody food?

'So, tell me,' he said as I sat down. 'How exactly did you do the presentation without a physical presentation?'

'Like I said, with my organiser.' I took it from my bag and turned to the pages detailing Dekker's campaign. 'It's all here, just not in a presentable way. I don't recommend we stop using PowerPoints.'

Tom laughed. 'Do you always use your organiser for client work?'

I nodded and flicked through the pages, showing him some of the projects he was familiar with and many more that I was playing with, but hadn't fleshed out yet. 'I write all my ideas in here too. Not all of them come to anything, but lots do.'

'So that's why you're always scribbling in there,' Tom said. 'I thought it was a diary.'

'It has a diary section. That's how I knew some of our meetings had been cancelled.' I waggled my organiser at him. 'Nancy thought she could get away with it, but she didn't know about this.'

'Just when I thought you couldn't impress me any more.' Tom took the organiser out of my hand, placed it on the table and handed me my glass. 'This deserves another toast.' His blue eyes sparkled as he clinked his glass against mine. 'To you. You're incredible.'

He held my gaze. The fluttering in my stomach grew so intense that it was a wonder it didn't upturn the table. This wasn't good. I needed to go.

'Food's here.' The large platter I'd ordered was placed between us.

I smiled my thanks to the waitress and started shovelling the food into my mouth. The sooner it was gone, the sooner I could leave.

'How do you get your ideas?' Tom asked.

I shrugged, unable to talk with so much food in my mouth.

He misinterpreted my reluctance to speak and put a hand up. 'Sorry, enough work talk.'

I swallowed hard. 'Carry on. I don't feel so guilty being in the pub if we talk about work.'

Tom gave me a quizzical look. 'Will wouldn't mind you going to the pub, would he? He was always there when he was with the company.'

'Of course he wouldn't.' I put down the piece of bread I was about to eat, no longer hungry. Will definitely would mind that I'd left him home alone with the children while I went to the pub. So hypocritical when he'd gone out regularly without a second thought. Tom's gaze was full of concern. I checked the time to avoid meeting those piercing blue eyes and jolted. 'It's almost five thirty. I'm going to have to run to get the next train.'

'You can do it.' Tom scooped up our coats and handed me my bag. 'I'll get the doors.' He sprinted ahead, weaving between customers as deftly as a Formula One driver. I hurried behind, trying to mirror his smooth manoeuvres, but the afternoon's booze rendered me as deft as a dodgem car. I stumbled through the door that Tom held open and shivered as the cold, dark air hit me.

'Come on.' Tom grabbed my hand and pulled me across the road.

Squealing like a schoolgirl, I ran with him, through the smattering of people carrying heavily discounted decorations and goodies, and into the station.

'You're going to make it.' Tom led me towards the turnstiles, but slowed to a halt as we drew near them. 'Shit.'

'What is it?' I followed his gaze to the board displaying the train times. But there were no train times. Just a simple message: no service.

This time my squeal sounded less playful schoolgirl, more piglet being slaughtered.

'Don't worry,' Tom said calmly. 'We'll talk to someone. Find out when the trains will be running again.' He looked around. There weren't any staff on duty. Of course there weren't. It was Twixmas Tuesday. Unless there was an extremely good reason to be out – seventy-five per cent off panettones seemed to be the key one – any sane person was at home, in the warm, with their family.

My heart sunk. Why hadn't I left earlier? If not straight from work, then after one drink, as originally intended?

'I live two minutes' away,' Tom said. 'Let's go back to mine and keep checking the trains.' He squeezed my hand. I hadn't realised he was still holding it. It was warm and reassuring. Reluctantly, I eased my hand free. Warm and reassuring it might be, but it didn't belong to my husband. Although, I'd rather hold turkey giblets than Will's hand right now.

'Thank you,' I said. 'That's really kind of you, but I'll get a cab.'

'You can't. It'd cost a fortune.' Tom put his coat on and

I did the same, then opened my bag to take out my woolly hat and gloves.

'I know,' I said. 'But I really need to get back and—' I gasped and rooted through my bag. 'No,' I said. 'No, no, no.'

'What is it?' Tom asked.

'My organiser.' My heart pounded in my chest. 'I left it on the pub table.'

'Don't panic,' Tom said. 'We'll go back and get it.'

I turned and ran out of the station and back to the pub, tipsily ricocheting off every obstacle in my way, and many that weren't.

The table Tom and I'd been at was still vacant, although the empty plates and glasses had been cleared away. I hurried over to it, with a growing sense of dread. My organiser wasn't there. Dropping down, I scoured the floor, then ran my hands over the banquette sofa, easing them in between the cushions. Apart from a few balls of dust and a beer mat, I found nothing.

I eased myself up, my legs trembling. Tom was at the bar, talking to a member of staff. Please, please, say it had been handed in. I went over, my fingers tightly crossed. As I got closer, I could tell by the grim expression on Tom's face that it hadn't been. The bartender lined up two shots. Wordlessly, Tom handed one to me, lifted the other and we both downed them. I felt physically sick. My organiser was as precious to me as the Bible was to a priest and social media was to a Kardashian. I put my head in my hands.

'I'm so sorry,' Tom said quietly. 'I feel responsible. If I hadn't thrown your bag at you and grabbed the coats, you'd have seen the organiser on the table.'

That was possibly true, but I couldn't blame him. Tempting as it was.

'It's not your fault,' I said, signalling to one of the bar staff.

'He's already asked us, love,' the woman said. 'No one's seen it.'

'Can I leave my number? Someone might have picked it

up by accident or one of the cleaners might find it.' I wasn't confident about either scenario, especially given the amount of dust I'd found down the sofa, but it was worth a shot. Speaking of which: 'And two more of these, please.'

The woman refilled our glasses while I wrote my number down. Tom and I downed our shots. I leant against the bar. 'I write everything in that organiser. Work ideas, addresses, birthdays, anniversaries, appointments.' Without it, I had no idea when the children's dental check-up was, or when parents' evening was, or when the book club I didn't have time to attend was. I didn't even know when my next period was due.

I did up my coat purposefully, desperate to see Evie and Fred. One of their cuddles would make me feel better. I'd probably have to pay them for it if they were in the middle of a game, but so be it.

'I'm going home,' I said. 'If the trains still aren't running, I'll get a cab. It'll be crazy money, but I have to get back to the children.'

Tom nodded. 'I'll walk you to the station.'

In the few minutes we'd been in the pub, snow had begun to fall. The floor at the entrance to the station was wet and I almost slipped over. Tom put an arm around me to steady me and my treacherous stomach fluttered. Gently extracting myself, I checked the departure board. Still no service. I dreaded to think how extortionate a cab home would be, but at least the City was quiet so we wouldn't be slowed down by the usual rush-hour traffic. On a normal working day, it'd be quicker to walk home.

We left the station and both gasped audibly. The smattering of snow had escalated, and flakes fell heavily. The few people still around grinned up at the sky. Under other circumstances I'd have been oohing and aahing along with them, but as the trains were cancelled, I'd lost my organiser and my marriage was on the rocks, I was not in the right frame of mind to gaze in wonder at nature's beauty.

A solitary cab sat in the taxi rank. I shuffled over and the driver lowered his window a centimetre.

'Can you take me to Huntonbrook, Hertfordshire, please?' I asked.

'Are you having a laugh?' the cab driver spluttered.

No, I was not having a laugh. I was trying very hard not to have a cry.

'Have you seen the snow?' he asked. As my glasses were coated with flakes, I could see it more than most. 'It'd be reckless to drive in this.' He tutted.

I ran a gloved finger over my lenses. 'Why are you here then?'

'About to clock off,' he said. 'Thought I'd give it a minute in case anyone needed a lift.'

'*I* need a lift,' I hissed through chattering teeth.

'A short lift,' the cabbie specified. 'A short, on-my-way-home lift.' He sniffed. 'Safety first.'

I straightened up. 'I'll give my money to someone else then.'

'Good luck with that. No one in their right mind'd go that far.'

He sped off – so much for safety first.

Tom rubbed his hands together. 'We need to get out of the snow.'

I shook my head. 'You go. I'll wait in case a train comes.'

A loud clattering behind us made us look round. A man in a high-vis jacket was pulling shutters across the station entrance.

'Wait,' I shouted.

The man yanked the shutters shut and disappeared behind them.

I tucked my chin into my chest to hide the tears I could no longer hold in. Tom pulled me into his chest. Possibly to comfort me, but equally possibly to muffle the loud, snorting noises emanating from me, lest they scare passers-by. Either way, it felt nice. Too nice.

'I'm OK.' Stepping back, I took off my glasses and wiped

my face. As my glove was drenched from the snow, it was as effective as dipping my face into a puddle.

'Come back to mine,' Tom said gently.

I stared at the shuttered station miserably.

'We can dry off and figure out how to get you home.' Tom wrapped his arms around his torso. Even without my glasses on, I could see that his lips were blue.

I felt a stab of guilt. He was being so kind. What did I think would happen if I stubbornly stayed out here? That the blizzard would magically stop, and the trains and taxis would spring into action, as though nothing had happened? There was more likelihood of a winged horse swooping down and carrying me home.

'OK. Thank you.' I slid my glasses into my pocket. The snow was falling so fast, there was no point putting them on. Tom cocked his elbow and I slid my arm through his. The hug had felt too intimate, but linking arms was innocent – and essential, as I could barely see without my glasses on.

'We'll work something out,' Tom said, as we trudged through the snow.

With every step I took away from the station, I felt a growing unease. The main something I needed to work out was how to tell Will that I was at Tom's house, with no obvious way home.

'It'll all be OK,' Tom said.

I wished I could be as sure.

Chapter 30

Will

Still in London. Trains running a slow service. I'll message when I know what time I'll be in. Love to Evie and Fred. X

My jaw clenched. I couldn't believe Sarah had gone to work when she was supposed to be off. It wasn't that I wanted to spend time with her – after her revelation that I couldn't get another job because hers took priority, I'd rather hang out with Hannibal Lecter the day after meat-free Monday. Or, worse still, Adam Sandler – but I looked after the kids *all* the time. It was her turn now. Despite her claims that she missed them, that it was breaking her heart to be away from them, she'd dumped them and legged it to the office more eagerly than a disgraced politician going to the jungle. The office wasn't even officially open. She must have sweet-talked security into letting her in.

I read the message again, my frustration growing. Obviously they were running a slow train service. No one commuted between Christmas and New Year. People who went to the City were there for the sales or to watch a show and the only thing they were in a hurry for were the bargain rail or the toilets in the interval.

There was a loud crash and a wail from the living room. Evie and Fred had been fighting all afternoon over everything, from who had the most chocolate coins left to who was the most annoying. I couldn't pass judgement on the coins, but they were neck and neck in the annoying stakes. As if to prove the point, they launched into their usual inane argument.

'I hate you.'

'I hate you more.'

'You're ugly.'

'You're fat *and* ugly.'

'Your bum stinks.'

'Your breath stinks.'

Life stinks, I thought dismally, my head in my hands at the kitchen table. Was four o'clock too early to have a beer? It *was* Christmas, and while it wouldn't stop the kids fighting, it'd stop me caring. Fuck it, I was doing it. I stood up and a movement outside the window caught my eye. Being the manly man that I was, I shrieked and leapt a foot into the air.

'Daddy?' Fred and Evie appeared in the doorway, their argument forgotten. Had I known that the threat of a murderer at our door was the way to instil tranquillity in the house, I'd have signed up to the Horror Channel years ago.

'It's OK.' My voice came out several octaves higher than usual. I cleared my throat. 'Nothing to worry about. You two wait here while I—'

'It's snowing,' Evie gasped.

We all went to the window. She was right. Snow, I could handle. I mentally cancelled the Horror Channel subscription. It would have given me nightmares anyway.

'Let's go outside.' Fred ran to the back door and flung it open.

I pulled him back and shut the door, locking it swiftly. 'We'll go to the park.' No point taking any chances, just in case there was a crazed axeman lurking in the pitch-black garden. Or axe-lady. I wasn't a misogynist, as Sarah had claimed.

Two minutes later we were on our way. I smiled smugly to myself at the speed of our exit. If Sarah had been home, it would have taken ages while she packed water bottles and snacks, and made everyone change into appropriate clothes and go to the toilet. Once, she took so long getting ready that it had not only stopped snowing by the time we left, it had also melted away.

'I need a wee,' Fred said.

OK, maybe going to the toilet would have been a good idea.

Fred weed behind a tree, and we giggled at the patterns he made in the snow and the steam rising. My smugness remained intact. This was much more fun than doing a standard wee at home. I stopped giggling when he pissed on my trainers. The supportive sponge heel wasn't such a USP then.

'My feet are cold,' Evie said, three steps later.

OK, should have got them to put wellies on. At least they didn't have Fred's urine on their trainers, though.

'I'm thirsty,' Fred said.

'And hungry,' Evie added.

My smugness evaporated.

'Eat some snow,' I said. 'Not the bit behind the tree, though.'

That kept them entertained and there were no more complaints in the three minutes it took to get to the park. The snow was coming down thick and fast, and the play equipment was completely covered. It would have been eerie had it not been for the other three million families who'd clearly also been desperate to entertain their stir-crazy kids. All around us children were indulging in good wholesome fun – building snowmen, sledging, kicking snow in each other's faces.

'There's Jacob and Max,' Evie said, pointing.

My throat tightened. If Jacob and Max were here, then Lauren must be too. I hadn't seen her since Sarah had thrown her out, for the second time. What must she think of me? Henpecked, spineless and pathetic probably. Fred had bigger balls than me and that took into account his exposure to the sub-zero temperature. Before I had time to decide how to handle it, Evie and Fred had dashed over, and Lauren was waving at me. Her long, dark hair was in a plait over one shoulder and her petite frame was encased in a long, cream, caterpillar-type coat that made her look cute and adorable. I walked across to where they were standing. Why was my heart pounding? Was it working harder than usual to maintain my body temperature in these arctic conditions? Or was it because, much as I tried to deny it, I fancied the arse off Lauren? And all the other bits too. Not that I wanted to be crude about it, but I'm a man and we have base instincts.

'Hi.' I stuffed my hands deep inside my pockets to ensure I didn't do something highly inappropriate like tuck the stray strand of hair that was blowing about behind her ear.

'Hi.' Lauren beamed at me. 'Isn't this weather amazing?' She spread her arms and spun around, her head tilted to the sky.

'Yes, it is,' I said, unable to take my eyes off her as she twirled in front of me, the snowflakes settling on her silky, dark plait. Joy radiated out of her. She was like a living snow globe. One of the posh John Lewis ones, not the Poundland version featuring a deformed polar bear, which only generated three flakes of glitter even after you practically dislocated a shoulder to shake it. I couldn't believe Sarah had bought that for Fred's teacher. It was almost as though she wanted to jeopardise the relationship we'd established.

Lauren took a deep breath and released a contented sigh. This 'I'm in the moment' breath was a far cry from Sarah's 'smell the flower, blow out the candle' technique that she employed in lieu of shredding a cushion or punching a hole through a wall. Or my intestine, depending on what had riled her in the first place.

Lauren put her head to one side. 'How are you?'

'Completely shit' was the honest answer. I couldn't get my

head around the fact that Sarah knew I couldn't get another Director job and hadn't told me. Or that she expected me to be OK with taking a smaller role, after having worked for years to get to where I was. She moaned constantly about missing the kids, but when it came to it wouldn't consider taking the smaller role herself so she could spend more time with them. She seemed oblivious to how I felt and I had no idea how we were going to get past this.

'Good Christmas?' Lauren prompted.

No, Christmas had also been completely shit. You could have cut the atmosphere with a knife. Which was more than could be said for the stuffing balls. Sarah had insisted on cooking dinner single-handedly, and consequently bitten off more than she could chew. Again, something the stuffing balls couldn't be accused of. We'd fooled no one with our frosty exchanges over dinner. Well, Evie and Fred were fooled, but they believed Dumbledore ran the town's organic veg shop, so their perspective of reality was rather warped. Tonya and my parents could definitely tell something was up, though. The easy banter that usually flowed over dinner was non-existent. Silent retreats were probably rowdier.

'It was fine,' I said.

'Fine?' Lauren pulled a sad face. She was so sweet. 'Christmas should be better than fine.'

'I blame the lack of tree-shaped crisps,' I said, and was rewarded with Lauren's tinkly laugh. 'The kids loved it. That's the important thing. How was yours?'

'Quiet, but lovely,' Lauren said. 'Just me and the boys. We played with their new toys, went for a long walk, then chilled out.'

If Sarah and I broke up, what would our Christmases be like? I'd still see my family, I supposed, but every other year it'd be without Evie and Fred. I'd miss out on their excited shrieks throughout the night, asking if he'd been yet, before giving in at five o'clock and letting them open their stockings, then having two overtired, overexcited, overbearing kids to deal with. As appealing as a quiet, calm Christmas sounded, I suspected the reality would be too harsh a contrast.

A snowball hit me hard on my ear. Mustering all of my self-control, I managed not to yelp in pain.

'Got you, Daddy!' Evie called.

Another snowball landed by my foot. I much preferred Fred's aim.

'We're being ambushed.' Lauren laughed, as Max and Jacob got in on the action and pelted snowballs at us both. Before long, a full-blown snowball fight was in full swing. Us throwing balls gently at the kids; the kids throwing theirs with a force that'd win them a place on the Olympics shot-put team. My face stung and my hands throbbed, but I gamely carried on. If Lauren could keep up with them, so could I. Eventually, after what could only be described as abuse, Lauren held her hands up.

'We surrender,' she said with a laugh. I'd never felt so relieved in my entire life.

The kids cheered triumphantly. 'What's our prize?'

Lauren shook her mittened hands and chunks of snow flew off. 'Hot chocolate back at ours.' She grinned at me. 'I'll put some Amaretto in ours.'

Before I had time to consider, she was off, calling out: 'Race you!'

The kids charged after her. Unless I was prepared to abandon my offspring (tempting, I'd admit), I had no choice but to follow. A kernel of guilt niggled at me. Sarah had looked genuinely upset when she'd asked if we were having an affair. I didn't want her to doubt my loyalty and I certainly wouldn't like it if she went round to Tom's house. I pushed the guilt away. It was an innocent play date.

A few minutes later I arrived at Lauren's house. They were already sat around a log burner in the living room. Their coats, wellies (Max and Jacob) and inappropriate footwear (Evie and Fred) were dumped inside the door. I bent to pick the coats up.

'We'll sort that out later,' Lauren said. 'Come through to the kitchen and pour us a drink while I make the hot chocolate.'

I stared dumbfounded at the pile on the floor. Sarah would never leave them like that. Wet shoes would be lined up on newspaper, and coats would be hung over radiators the moment we got in the door. Sometimes before the kids had taken them off.

Lauren took the coat I was holding and dropped it back on the floor, wrapped a hand around my wrist and led me to the kitchen. 'Beer, wine or spirits?' she asked.

The kernel of guilt was back, as I asked for a beer. I honestly didn't know what was making me feel uneasy – being at Lauren's, drinking with Lauren or leaving wet clothing to fester.

Three bottles of beer later, the kernel had been ground to dust. The kids had been fed and were playing Twister, and I'd sneakily hung the coats up when Lauren wasn't looking, so that was off my mind.

'I've got some leftover turkey that I'm going to make into a stir fry, if you'd like to stay for dinner,' Lauren said, toying with the end of her plait.

I hesitated. I was in no hurry to get home, but things couldn't continue as they were. Sarah and I needed to sort things out, and initial peace talks would be the opposite of peaceful if we were at Lauren's when she got back.

'You'd be doing me a massive favour,' Lauren said. 'Max and Jacob have decided they don't like turkey anymore and I'm struggling to get through it.' She pressed her palms together. 'Please. I need help.'

I ran a hand over my head, torn over what to do. Go home to an atmosphere as chilling as that of a medieval dungeon, or stay for dinner and go home to an atmosphere so chilling that a medieval dungeon would seem cosy and inviting.

'I, er—' My phone rang, which was a blessing, as I had no idea what to say. I slid it from my pocket. Sarah's name was on the screen. I no longer felt blessed. 'Sorry, I'd better answer this.' Lauren nodded and left the room. I accepted the call. 'Yes,' I said guardedly, waiting for a barrage of abuse as to why we weren't home waiting to greet her.

'It's snowing,' Sarah said.

I frowned. Even in the early 'can't get enough of you' phase of our relationship, we'd never felt the need to ring each other with the tedious minutiae of our days. We swore that if we ever became one of those couples who phoned to ask what the other had had for lunch, then it was time to go our separate ways.

'What did you have for lunch?' I asked.

Sarah was silent for so long that I thought she'd got my coded message and hung up.

'Nothing exciting,' she said eventually. There was a clink down the phone as she pushed her glasses up. 'It's snowing,' she said again.

I gritted my teeth. Did she think my intelligence levels were so low, I couldn't identify the white stuff falling from the sky? 'I know. The kids and I have been to the park.'

'How lovely.' She sounded disappointed, but that was her fault. She could have been here if she'd wanted to be, but she'd chosen to go to work. 'How are they?' she asked.

'Fine. They're playing Twister.'

Sarah sighed softly. 'That's nice. Give them my love.'

'You can give it to them yourself when you get home.' I looked at my watch. It was seven o'clock already. 'When will that be?' I'd make sure I was back before her to avoid any Lauren-related confrontation.

'That's the thing,' Sarah said. 'It's snowing.'

If she said that one more time, I'd shove the snow where the sun didn't shine. Although as the sun didn't shine when it was snowing, I wasn't sure the usual principle applied.

'All the trains are cancelled and I can't get a cab. No one will take me.' Her voice wobbled. 'I really want to come home, but don't know how.' She sniffed and I couldn't help but feel sorry for her. It wasn't her fault she'd had to go into work and it certainly wasn't her fault she was now stranded because of the weather. 'I'm hoping it'll stop soon,' she said in a small voice.

I looked out of the window. The snow had progressed to a blizzard that would have the Abominable Snowman looking for shelter. I wasn't sure how I was going to get the kids home from two streets away, let alone Sarah getting back from London. 'Can't see that happening, to be honest. It's falling heavily here.'

'I really want to come home,' Sarah said again, her words slow and sad.

'I get it.' As pissed off with her as I was, it was no fun being let down by the trains. It had happened to me a few times over the years, and I'd had to check into a cheap hotel and go into work hoping no one noticed/smelt that I was wearing the same clothes as the day before. 'You might have to stay in London. Hopefully, the trains will be running in the morning.'

'But I haven't seen Evie and Fred. Can I FaceTime them?'

'No,' I said quickly. Sarah's sorrow would be replaced with anger if she knew where we were. 'They're tired and grumpy. Seeing you would send them over the edge.'

'Thought you said they're playing Twister.'

'They are, in a tired and grumpy way. It's pretty much a scene from *Squid Game*.'

Sarah sighed. 'Tell them I miss them.'

'I will. You can spend lots of time with them when you get home tomorrow.'

Sarah nodded. I couldn't see her, but I could sense it. We'd been together so long that I could visualise her mannerisms even when she wasn't there. And I cared about her, even though I was angry with her. I guessed this was what marriage was about. Getting through the ups and downs. The thick and thin. The wax and wane. I frowned. Was that from the wedding vows or was I reciting a poorly crafted sex scene?

Either way, perhaps it was time to sort this argument out and come to a compromise. Sarah's distress at not being able to get home proved that that's where she really wanted to be. For the first time since our argument, I felt a glimmer of hope for our future.

'Sorry about this,' Sarah said haltingly. 'I really want to be at home.'

She seemed to be reaching the same conclusion as me. Things were looking up.

'It's OK,' I said. 'It's hardly your fault.'

Sarah sniffed again. 'Please tell Evie and Fred I miss them.'

I frowned. Was this conversation playing on a loop?

Down the hall a toilet flushed. Lauren would be coming back any second. I needed to get off the phone fast. Our reconciliation negotiations would go a lot more smoothly if the starting point wasn't another accusation that I was having an affair.

'Thanks for ring—' I started.

'How are they playing Twister?' Sarah asked at the same time. 'If there's only two of them. Who's spinning the arrow?'

'Me. So I'd better get back.' Down the hallway, Lauren came out of the cloakroom and went into the living room, where the kids were. 'Will you be OK getting a hotel?'

'I don't need to,' Sarah said slowly.

I wished she'd speed up. 'Don't be silly. You can't sleep on the office floor.'

'No.' There was another clink as she pushed her glasses up. 'Tom's said I can stay at his.'

It was as though she'd hit me over the head with a cartoon-style mallet. My head felt like it was going to explode and white stars flashed before my eyes. 'He's what?'

'He says I can have his spare room.'

I glowered at the snow through the window. Men like Tom didn't have spare rooms with a neatly made-up bed and lavender posies on the dressing table. Their second bedrooms were makeshift gyms, so any invitation to stay there was a ploy.

'Don't go back to his,' I said, forcing myself to stay calm. 'There's a hotel round the corner from the office. I've stayed there in the past and it does the job.' A piss-poor job – it was clearly geared up for people who were desperate, or would only be using the room for an hour at most, so wouldn't notice that the teabags were fourteen years out of date. Not that there was a kettle to make an out-of-date cup of tea anyway.

'The thing is,' Sarah said. 'I'm already at Tom's.'

'You're what?' My calm façade dissolved. 'Why? Why are you there? You're supposed to be at work.'

'I was,' Sarah said. 'But then it started snowing. I'm sorry. I really want to come home.'

Why did she keep saying the same thing over and over? She usually only repeated herself when she was drunk. Another cartoon mallet whacked me over the head. That's why she was speaking so slowly. Not to stop herself crying – to stop herself slurring.

'Have you been drinking?' I snapped.

'Pardon?' Sarah gave a nervous laugh. 'Did I tell you the Dutch word for a horse is—'

'You're pissed, aren't you?' My jaw clenched. I'd been feeling sorry for her, while she was on a jolly with Tom. 'Have you been to work or have you been at his all day?'

'Yes, I've been to work.' Sarah sounded hurt. 'The presentation went so well that Tom said we should have a drink to celebrate and then it started snowing.' Her voice grew small. 'Really wish I'd come straight home. It's horrible being away.'

A door creaked in the background, then I heard Tom say: 'A glass of Sancerre for the lady.'

'Doesn't sound very horrible from this end,' I hissed.

There was a shuffling noise, followed by the door creaking again, before clicking shut.

'He's just being nice,' Sarah whispered.

'Bet he is,' I bellowed. 'He's not going to get you into bed by being horrible, is he?'

'That's not going to happen,' Sarah said in a low, but firm, voice. 'We're colleagues. You wouldn't be reacting like this if I were staying with Clara.'

'Clara doesn't think with her cock,' I shouted. 'Tom does.' Sarah started to protest, but I cut her off. 'Don't be naïve. He's a man and that's what men do.'

Lauren darted into the kitchen, a concerned look on her face. 'Are you all right?'

I sent Lauren a telepathic request to be quiet so that my wife wouldn't know I was at another woman's house, while I berated her for being at another man's house. My telepathic request was not received.

'Were you just shouting?' Lauren asked. 'It was hard to tell over the kids' screeching.'

I shook my head and held up two fingers. 'Give me two minutes,' I mouthed.

Lauren nodded to show she understood and left the room.

I held my breath. There was silence. Maybe Sarah hadn't heard.

'Who was that?' she asked quietly.

Could I claim it was the TV?

'Is it Lauren?'

Claiming Lauren was now an actress appearing on prime-time TV would be pushing it.

'Is she at our house?' Sarah asked.

'No.'

'Are you at hers?'

'Yes,' I admitted. Not much else I could do. The kids would spill the beans anyway. They spilt everything else.

'Why?' Sarah asked.

'It's snowing,' I said. If that excuse was good enough for her, it was good enough for me.

'That doesn't explain anything.'

I sighed. 'We bumped into them at the park. She invited us back for hot chocolate and the kids said yes. We're about to go home.'

'Hot chocolate?' Sarah sounded doubtful. With good cause. On the two occasions she'd encountered Lauren, we'd been drinking everything other than hot chocolate.

'Yes,' I said indignantly. 'Not all of us feel the need to consume alcohol on a Tuesday afternoon.'

'Want another beer or shall we start the wine?' Lauren asked, appearing from nowhere.

I shook my head furiously and gestured to the phone. She formed a silent 'oh' and retreated to the living room.

'Funny-sounding hot chocolate,' Sarah snapped. 'Why is she offering you a drink? Thought you were about to go.'

'She's being nice,' I said, copying exactly what Sarah had said about Tom. 'You wouldn't be reacting like this if I were with a male friend.'

'But all men think with their cocks, remember?'

I gave a hollow laugh. 'Lauren hasn't got a cock.'

'No, but you have,' Sarah screeched. 'You're the one who told me not to be naïve. You're a man and that's what men do.'

I tutted. 'I didn't mean me.'

'So, you're the one exception to the rule?' Sarah's voice was bordering on hysterical now. 'Rubbish. You have a go at me for being with Tom, but you're with Lauren. I'm here because I can't get home. You're there because you want to be.'

'Because the kids want to be,' I said in a low voice. 'Freezing my nuts off in the park wasn't top of my wish list, but I did it because I'm a good dad. And when they wanted to go back to their friends' for a hot chocolate afterwards, I took them because that's what good dads do. Got a problem with that?'

'No,' Sarah said, her voice shaking. 'I've got a problem with you and Lauren fancying each other.'

'What?' I spluttered. 'That's pre—' Well, I tried to say preposterous, but the shock of her accusation, and the beers I'd had, resulted in me stuttering: 'That's pre-pre-pre … stupid.' I sounded guilty as hell, so I threw it back in her face. 'If anyone fancies anyone, it's you and Tom.'

'That's pre-pre-pre … stupid,' Sarah stuttered.

We inhaled sharply simultaneously, as we both realised that we'd pretty much admitted that, yes, we did fancy someone else. My blood ran cold. What now?

Chapter 31

Sarah

I clutched the phone tightly. Was Will saying that he fancied Lauren? I closed my eyes. Of course he did – she was beautiful, giggly and borderline alcoholic. What's not to like? As for Tom – just because he was handsome, thoughtful, caring, fun and my stomach flipped over when he winked at me didn't mean I fancied him. I closed my eyes. Bugger. It wasn't hunger, or excess alcohol, or any of the other flimsy excuses I used to explain away my stomach churnings. It was lust. My eyes snapped open. I needed to remove myself from this situation.

'I'm going to try the station again,' I told Will with renewed determination. 'If I can get home tonight, I will.'

'OK.' Will sounded resigned. As though he'd accepted I'd be sleeping with Tom tonight and made peace with it. Was that because he didn't care about me anymore or so he could sleep with Lauren without feeling guilty?

'I'll text and let you know.' I hung up before he could reply.

There was a light tap on the door and Tom poked his head round. 'Everything all right?'

I nodded, picked up the glass of wine he'd brought in earlier and took a sip. Well, the aim was to sip it. After the stressful conversation I'd just had, I ended up practically downing it. Tom refilled my glass before I'd even put it down.

I smiled my thanks. 'Mind if I connect to your Wi-Fi?'

'Sure.' Tom took out his phone. 'I'll Bluetooth the details. Password's Kryptonite.'

I suppressed an eye roll. Under normal circumstances I might have teased him, but there was nothing amusing about tonight. The train app revealed that all services were cancelled for the foreseeable future.

'Not surprised.' Tom nodded towards the window. 'It's not safe in this.'

I followed his gaze. Snowflakes the size of ping-pong balls were hurtling past the glass. I hadn't seen anything like this since a foam party I went to in the early 2000s, and certainly no one had been driving that night. Sinking back into the sofa, I pressed my lips tightly together to stop myself from crying. I shouldn't be at Tom's. Will shouldn't be at Lauren's. The children shouldn't be in the middle of an emotional minefield. My organiser shouldn't have gone missing. I shouldn't have had four complaints against me at work. Unable to hold the tears in any longer, I placed a hand over my face, twisted away from Tom and sobbed.

Tom placed a box of tissues in front of me and put a hand on my shoulder. He didn't say a word, but let me cry, his hand reassuring and comforting. I cried like I hadn't cried for years. Probably not since the final scene in *Coco* when the family reunites and sings together and everyone's happy. The thought of this made me cry even more, as my family couldn't be less united or happy. And our singing was so out of tune that if we tried to belt out a heart-rousing number, we'd be mistaken for rabid, wild dogs and shot.

Eventually my sobs subsided, and I blew my nose, wiped my cheeks and cleaned my glasses. By the time I'd finished, there was a mountain of balled-up, snot-filled tissues in my lap.

'Sorry.' My voice was coarse, as though my larynx had gone through a pepper grinder. One of those huge, phallic-shaped ones the waiting staff proffer at pizza restaurants, causing the guests at the table to either wince or sigh wistfully.

'Nothing to apologise for,' Tom said softly.

I scooped the tissues up. 'Can I use your bathroom?'

'Second door on the left.'

'Thanks.' I sidled out of the room. Despite my anguish, I was still vain enough to keep my face away from Tom, as it no doubt resembled a blotchy, melted candle.

In the bathroom I threw the tissues in the bin, then braved the mirror. Bloodshot eyes, smeared mascara, mottled skin, and hair that managed to stick out *and* hang limply. My only consolation was that Tom couldn't have caught sight of me, because he would have instantly turned to stone if he had. I wiped away the smeared makeup and cleaned my teeth, glad I always carried a toothbrush with me. Given the concoction of drink and food I'd had, I was not only in danger of stripping paint with my breath, but also of dissolving the foundations of the building. My hair was beyond salvaging, so I pulled it up into a topknot, and then went back to the living room.

Tom was in the same place on the sofa. He'd changed into navy joggers and a fitted, blue T-shirt with a large yellow 'S' on it. A giggle escaped me.

'Really?' I pointed at the 'S'.

Tom glanced down at his chest and grimaced. 'Wasn't thinking when I put this on. My ex bought it. Bit of a joke. Some people think I look like Henry Cavill, the *Superman* actor.' He patted the space next to him on the sofa. 'Make yourself comfy.'

I sat down, suddenly feeling awkward. To avoid meeting his eye, I looked around the living room. Everything matched perfectly and was laid out to minimalist perfection, as though it had been airlifted from a John Lewis shop floor. There were no suspicious-looking splodges on the deep green sofa. No piles of school forms to fill in. No shoes in the middle of the floor. It was these fragments of everyday life that made a house a home, though. Without the clutter and debris that Will and the children left in their wake, the room felt stark and soulless.

'You OK?' Tom asked.

I gave a half-hearted nod. 'Sorry about crying. Silly to get so upset over an organiser. It's not as though I've lost something of real value, like one of my children ... Chance would be a fine thing,' I added. 'I can't even go to the toilet without one of them following me in.' Another sob escaped me. I'd give anything to have them follow me into the toilet now.

Tom gave a small smile. 'I envy you,' he said.

Seriously? It wasn't great if you had a shy bladder.

'Having children,' he continued. 'My wife and I broke up before we got to that stage. Didn't see it coming at all. Thought we were happy and about to start trying for a family. Next thing I knew, she was kicking me out.'

I inhaled sharply. 'She kicked you out?'

'It was her house. I'd moved in when we got serious, because it was bigger.' Tom waved a hand around the room. 'Luckily, I'd kept hold of this place as an investment. Bit depressing coming back.'

'That's awful.' I cringed at how negative I sounded. I should be focusing on the positive aspects of Tom's life, not being the voice of doom. 'I mean, the way she treated you. Your apartment isn't awful. The décor and colour scheme are gorgeous.' What was worse? Being the voice of doom or the voice of Laurence Llewelyn-Bowen? I wasn't sure there was much in it. I ploughed on. 'And work's going brilliantly. You must be one of the fastest-ranking Directors of all time.'

'Doesn't feel like I am.' Tom looked down. I followed his gaze, realised I was inadvertently gazing at his crotch, and quickly redirected my attention to his face. Thankfully, he hadn't noticed and continued talking. 'I should have been at that presentation today to support you and I wasn't.' He tutted. 'Can't believe Nancy cocked up and didn't put it in the calendar.'

'She's not putting anything in the calendar,' I said, conveniently omitting that it was me who'd cocked up in this instance. 'In fact, she's taking things out, as though she wants me to miss meetings and look bad. And there's her complaint ...' I trailed off, too embarrassed to mention her claim that I sexually harassed Tom, especially when I'd just accidentally checked out his crotch. 'It's as though she's trying to sabotage my career.'

Tom frowned. 'Why would she? How would that benefit her?'

I realised how ridiculous it sounded. Nancy might have a personality so devoid of charm that she made Piers Morgan seem empathetic, but that didn't mean she'd risk her own job to bring me down.

'You're right. She risks being worse off if I leave. My replacement might expect her to do unreasonable things, such as be civil.' I drank the last of my wine. 'I'm overthinking it. Ignore me.'

'You need a distraction.' Tom clicked his fingers. 'I know. Let's brainstorm the marketing ideas you had in your organiser.'

I yawned. 'Not sure my brain's up to it.'

'Doing something productive will make you feel better.' Tom sprung up. 'I'll get some more wine.'

I shook my head and the room swam. 'I've had more than enough. I ought to go to sleep.'

Tom nodded. 'No worries. You have my bed and I'll kip on the sofa.'

'I'm not kicking you out of your bed. Didn't you say you have a spare room?'

'I do, but it's a study-slash-gym. The sofa is comfier.'

'Then that's where I'll sleep.' I held a hand up. 'No arguments.'

Tom frowned. 'Doesn't seem very gentlemanly, but if you're sure?'

'I am,' I said, hiccupping slightly. 'Can I borrow a T-shirt to sleep in, please?'

Tom nodded. 'I'm sure I've got something.' I hoped fervently that the 'something' wasn't as snug as the Superman T-shirt he was sporting.

Tom left the room and I picked up my phone with trepidation. Did Will believe me when I said I couldn't physically get home? It was the truth, but if I'd left when I was supposed to, I wouldn't have ended up in this predicament.

It was too late to ring, so I sent a text: No trains. Will get back tomorrow as early as I can.

I pressed send, hoping it wouldn't wake him if he was asleep. Would he be passed out on the sofa or have gone to bed? I clicked on my Find My Friends app. No idea why. It wasn't as though it'd pinpoint his exact whereabouts in the house. The circle thingy whirred for ages and I was about to close the app, when it zoomed in on his location. I froze. Will wasn't anywhere in our house. He was at Lauren's. The children wouldn't be up at this time, so they must all be sleeping there. I couldn't physically get home, but he could. He'd physically chosen to stay with Lauren.

'You OK?' Tom stood in the doorway, holding a pillow and duvet.

I blinked furiously, desperately fighting back yet more tears. My body was going to look as though it had been vacuum-packed if I carried on excreting water at this rate. I bit my lip. No, I was not OK. My husband was with another woman.

'Yes,' I squeaked, blowing my nose.

Tom dropped the bedding and walked out. Possibly in search of yet more tissues. A moment later he was back, with two glasses and a bottle of Baileys. He poured a generous measure into each glass and handed one to me. I didn't need another drink, but took it anyway, with a watery smile of thanks.

'Talk to me,' he said, sitting down. 'Anything you say will be in the strictest of confidence.' I swallowed hard. It'd be a relief to talk about it, but the small shred of professionalism that remained between Tom and me would be obliterated if I told him what was going on. Especially the bit where Will accused me of fancying him.

271

'Is everything all right with Will?' Tom asked gently. 'I couldn't help but hear some of your earlier conversation. Something about a woman called Lauren?' I sipped my Baileys to avoid replying. 'In the office, there have been a few fraught conversations too,' he continued. 'I honestly don't listen in, but sometimes it's hard not to overhear. Sounds to me as though Will's not being as supportive of your career as he should be. And if he's cheating on you …' His hand curled into a fist. Through my watery eyes, I clocked his biceps bulging. Despite my distress at Will's betrayal, I managed to appreciate the aesthetics. Multitasking at its best.

A muscle pounded in Tom's jaw. 'You're working so hard, but Will doesn't appreciate it. He expects you to do everything at home, even though you're working full-time.' For someone who didn't listen in, he remembered more about our conversations than I did. 'It's not fair on you, Sarah. You don't deserve to be treated like this. You deserve better.' There was an intense look of sincerity and tenderness on his face. He cared about me. I could see it in his eyes. He really cared.

'Earlier I said I envy you,' he said softly. 'But it's Will I envy. Not because he gets to spend all day with the children.' He took my hand. 'Because he's got you.' My head swam. This was like something out of a romance novel. 'I like you, Sarah,' Tom whispered. 'I've tried to ignore it because of Will, but he's not making you happy. I would. I'd do anything to make you happy.' My body trembled as he leant closer. His blue eyes searched mine. 'I've never connected with someone the way I have with you.' He cupped my face. 'Give me a chance. Please.'

Blood coursed around my body, igniting every nerve ending, making me tingle from head to toe. This handsome, kind, thoughtful, fun man liked me. Over the past few weeks he'd seen me at my best, at my worst, at my average. He'd witnessed blood, sweat and tears (the blood had only been from a paper cut, but still counted). And none of that had put him off. Just as none of what I'd seen in him had put me off him. He was perfect. Tom's thumb grazed my cheek. Perfect. But he wasn't Will. Admittedly, that was another point in Tom's favour at the moment, but it didn't justify cheating on Will. I couldn't do it. Will might be massively annoying, and we had a hell of a lot to sort out, but I wanted to try. Plus, I had no idea when I'd last had my bits waxed.

I sighed inwardly. Out of respect for Will, my marriage and my bikini line, I wouldn't do this. Although the thought of kissing Tom was creating a stirring so intense it was a wonder the sofa cushion beneath me wasn't vibrating, I wouldn't give in to temptation. I'd do the right thing and speak to Will. Hear his side of the story. Maybe he wasn't even at Lauren's. He could have left his phone, so although his location showed him being there, he was actually at home. I needed to give him the benefit of the doubt rather than assume he was with her.

'Sarah,' Tom said breathlessly, his lips full, his pupils dilated.

I had to stop this before it went too far. 'Tom, I ...' My phone beeped and I jumped. 'Sorry, I'll just get this. Might be about Evie or Fred.'

My hands were shaking so much, it took several attempts to open my phone. It was a message from Will.

Text when you're on your way home.

My throat tightened. He was definitely with his phone, then. Any hope that maybe he'd left it at Lauren's evaporated. He was at Lauren's and had chosen not to tell me. The only information he wanted from me was an ETA for the next day, so he knew when to be home by. I dropped the phone into my bag and clasped my hands together. I'd been battling against the attraction I felt for Tom in order to do the right thing by Will, but he wasn't extending that courtesy to me.

No, as soon as the coast was clear, he was straight in there, like a rat up a drainpipe. My stomach churned. The thought of Will with Lauren made me feel physically sick.

'Sarah.' Tom wrapped his hands around mine. 'There's a constant sadness behind your eyes. I want to take that pain away. I want to make you happy.' His hands slid slowly up my arms, warming the skin beneath my shirtsleeves. 'I want you.'

I gasped, as a shiver of anticipation ran through me. Sex with Tom would be amazing. Not because he was incredibly hot, but because he genuinely cared about me. The incredibly hot factor wouldn't exactly hinder the experience, though.

Tom slid one hand behind my head and caressed my cheek with the other. Each touch sent a jolt of longing through me. I had feelings for him too, I realised. Had done for some time, but I hadn't allowed myself to acknowledge them. Just as I hadn't allowed myself to acknowledge the truth about me and Will. We were over. Everything had started to fall apart the moment I got promoted. He didn't support my job. He resented it. And now he was with Lauren. There was no way past this lack of respect for me, my career or our marriage. Why martyr myself for someone who didn't care, when I could be with someone who did?

'Sarah,' Tom whispered, his eyes boring into mine.

I gave an almost imperceptible nod, and he lowered his face to mine and kissed me.

Chapter 32

Will

No trains. Will get back tomorrow as early as I can.

I fired a non-committal text back, then paced up and down Lauren's kitchen while she checked on the kids. They'd all passed out on the sofa halfway through *The Polar Express*, so Lauren had suggested they stay. I'd come back and get them in the morning.

My hands curled into fists as I strode up and down. Sarah was at Tom's. For the whole night. He was probably making his moves on her right now. Plying her with wine. Showering her with compliments. Massaging her feet. Ugh. Fucking Tom. I'd known he wasn't to be trusted. I'd warned Sarah that night of the conference that he was flirting and she'd said I was being stupid. But I'd been right. Ha! Who was the stupid one now? I paused. They were together and I was looking after the kids. Crap, I was the stupid one.

My jaw clenched so tightly that my teeth ground together. Was this even the first time? It could have been going on for weeks. Perhaps they'd got together in Amsterdam. Was this why she'd been so keen to get the coil fitted? I emitted a low growl. They must be laughing their heads off at me. Gullible, clueless Will, running around after the kids while they fucked each other's brains out. Because that's what it'd be. A proper pounding. Men like Tom viewed sex as a workout. No point doing it unless it burnt calories and incorporated resistance training. Not that Sarah would be resisting. No, she was a little goer in the sack. She'd happily let him hoist her up against a wall, so that he could improve his strength and stamina while giving her a good seeing-to. Bet he was competitive about how many times she came, too. I tensed. He'd better not top my record of three times. It had only happened once, in the very early days, but it was still one of my finest moments. Some men spoke wistfully of seeing their newborn for the first time, or their partner walking down the aisle, or John McClane defeating Hans Gruber. My glory was Sarah's three consecutive orgasms. Yep, *consecutive*.

My brief moment of pride crashed and burnt when I remembered why I'd been reminiscing about that night. The dread that Tom was about to steal my thunder, as well as my wife. *My* wife. Had the man no scruples? You just didn't do that. Hans Gruber was pure evil and he didn't try to steal John McClane's wife. Kill her, yes, but not jump her.

I placed my hands on the work surface and leant forward, gripping the worktop edge tightly. I was so angry, I'd rip it out from the wall if I could. Fortunately for the kitchen, I didn't have the strength.

'Will.' Lauren's voice was soft behind me. 'What's wrong?'

I couldn't speak until I got rid of this rage burning inside me. A run should do it. I could go all Rocky and power my aggression into a gruelling endurance feat. Except that the pavements outside were coated in slippy, slidy snow. And I couldn't run more than a few metres without getting a stitch.

'Talk to me, Will,' Lauren said. 'Maybe I can help.'

Unless Lauren could teleport herself to Tom's flat, kick him in the nuts so hard they permanently dislodged, and bring Sarah back, she couldn't help. But would I want that anyway? (The bringing Sarah back part; I'd definitely be up for Tom's castration.) It took two to tango. Tom was undoubtedly the seducer, but Sarah was at his flat voluntarily. She didn't *have* to stay there; there were plenty of hotels in London. It was bad enough that she'd put her job before her family. Now she'd put Tom before us, too. I clenched my jaw.

'Will.' There was an urgency in Lauren's voice. 'Please. You're worrying me.'

She placed a hand on my arm and I glanced down. It was a lovely, small, delicate hand. My knob would look massive in Lauren's hand.

I pulled myself up tall. Sarah had accused me of having an affair. Might as well be hanged for a sheep as for a lamb.

'Things aren't good with Sarah,' I said gruffly, turning to face Lauren.

'Sorry to hear that,' she said. She didn't look very sorry. There was a glint in her eye. Was it lust or a dislodged contact lens?

'Do you wear contact lenses?' I asked.

She giggled her pretty, little laugh. 'No. Where did that come from?'

'Just checking.'

Lauren looked up through her eyelashes, toying with a necklace at her throat. The pendant hung just below the V of her top, in between her breasts. I swallowed hard.

She was so pretty and delicate and petite and different to Sarah. With her long legs, athletic build, and drive and ambition, Sarah had always been out of my league. She'd never needed me – she was far too independent and resourceful for that – and now it seemed she didn't want me either. Unlike Lauren, who was gazing up at me as though I had the power to make all her Christmas wishes come true. She was the perfect antidote to everything that was shit in my life. Lauren could make everything right.

Lauren tilted her head up and her beautiful, soft lips parted slightly. It couldn't have been clearer what she wanted me to do if she'd been wearing a kiss-me-quick hat.

Fuck it. I was going in. Leaning forward, I brought my lips down on hers.

Chapter 33

Sarah

As Tom kissed me, my thighs all but burst into flames with desire and I started to worry about the flammable upholstery on the sofa. We tentatively explored each other's mouths, savouring the feel of one another after weeks of growing feelings.

He ran his hand down my face and I leant into him. Moments later, that same hand was plunged between my legs and I inwardly recoiled. I hadn't expected him to treat me with the tenderness of deflowering a virgin – in fact, I was all up for a bit of wanton passion – but I also hadn't expected him to be so basic. As he clumsily kneaded my crotch through my skirt and tights, I couldn't help but compare his actions to my first encounter with Will. That had been electrifying. We'd been so in sync, desperate to touch and kiss every part of one another, but equally unwilling to rush it, wanting to prolong the anticipation and intensity for as long as possible. We'd truly appreciated and delighted in stimulating and satisfying each other.

By contrast, Tom seemed intent on numbing my labia rather than arousing me. Edward Scissorhands' technique would be less invasive. Tom's tongue now felt wet and cloying in my mouth, and I pulled back, pushed his hand off me and turned away, folding my arms protectively around my body.

'Sorry,' I stuttered. 'Thought I could do this, but I can't.'

'Sure about that?' Tom edged towards me. 'Don't want to blow my own trumpet, but I can guarantee you a good time.'

He might not want to blow his own trumpet, but I had a sneaking suspicion that part of this guaranteed good time would involve me blowing said trumpet, and the prospect turned my stomach. Instantly, I realised what a massive mistake this was. The alcohol combined with his attentiveness, and the monumental hurt and despair over my marriage, had momentarily confused me. I'd mistaken my sadness, frustration and loneliness for desire. And now I had to break the news to Tom and his roaming hand, which was trying to find a way into my shirt.

'Tom.' I clasped his hand, placed it firmly on his lap and withdrew my own sharpish, in case its proximity indicated an urge to touch his trumpet. 'I'm so sorry, but this isn't right. I'm married and—'

'He's cheating on you with Lauren,' Tom said quietly.

I winced at the words. 'I don't know that for sure,' I said, although I was pretty convinced. 'Even if he is, we're still married and it doesn't feel right doing this. Sorry if I led you on. I didn't mean to.'

Tom looked crestfallen, and I added feeling guilty about hurting his feelings to the enormous list of other things I already felt guilty about.

He gave a small nod. 'I understand.' He stood up, gathered the bedding from the floor and placed it on the sofa, avoiding my eye.

'I'm so sorry,' I said again. 'I hope we can still be friends.'

Tom nodded. 'Definitely. I'll always be here if you want to talk about Will or work or brainstorm any ideas.' He smiled. 'Don't rush off tomorrow morning. I'll make you breakfast and help you remember the ideas for pitches you'd outlined in your organiser.'

I put a hand to my head. Amid my potential marriage break-up and my overwhelming desire to be with Tom, swiftly followed by my overwhelming desire to be nowhere near Tom, I'd forgotten about my organiser.

'Know what the most frustrating thing is?' I sighed. 'It wouldn't be so bad if Will hadn't lost his laptop. All my notes for the ideas I had are on his desktop.'

'Why his and not yours?' Tom asked.

'We took the children to a trampoline park and Will couldn't resist going on with them.' No need to mention that I'd gone on, too, and wet myself within minutes. Tom might consider an insight into the weak state of my pelvic floor as an invitation to reignite his earlier explorations. If anything was going to finish my pelvic floor off, it was his foreplay technique. 'I had nothing to do, so Will lent me his laptop. I'd been meaning to write up my notes for ages and that was the perfect opportunity.' I hugged a pillow to my chest. 'What a waste of time.'

Tom tapped the side of his head. 'It's all up here. I'll help you retrieve them in the morning.'

I nodded. 'Thanks.'

'No worries. Sleep well.' He winked and left the room.

His wink didn't induce any flutters. The attraction I thought I'd felt was gone. It had been nothing more than a distraction from the crap going on in my life and now that I'd identified it as such, I knew I'd never be tempted again. My labia breathed a sigh of relief.

I shook out the duvet and lay down on the sofa with all my clothes on. Tom had forgotten to bring a T-shirt through for me to sleep in – perhaps assuming I wouldn't need one – and I didn't feel comfortable stripping down to my underwear, in case I needed to go to the loo in the night and bumped into him. I stared at the ceiling, wishing I was anywhere other than here. Actually, that wasn't quite true. Tom's living room was preferable to being in a disease-infested swamp or the queue for the toilets at Glastonbury, but apart from that, I'd rather be anywhere else. Ideally, at home. Ideally, before any of this had happened – to a time when frustration about lack of time was my biggest problem; when Evie and Fred turned to me rather than to Will or Miss Boast when they needed something; when Will and I were a proper couple, with the usual niggles and annoyances, but solid and still very much together.

I ran through the different elements that had forced this massive wedge between us. Clara encouraging me to apply for the Director's job. Will being fired. Me working crazy hours. His resentment. My exasperation at running the house with a full-on career. The complaints at work. Will's reaction to being unable to work for a competitor. Me spending more time with Tom. Will spending more time with Lauren. Lauren. Lauren. Lauren.

I pressed my hands to my eyes, trying, unsuccessfully, to suppress yet more tears. He was with Lauren now. He thought I was with Tom. Why wouldn't he go for it? After all, I'd kissed Tom. It didn't matter that I'd halted proceedings and stopped things going any further. The damage was done. I'd cheated on Will and nothing could be done to change that.

My stomach tightened with fear. Was he cheating on me right now? I covered my mouth to muffle the racking sobs. How would I cope if he was? How would I cope if he and Lauren got together and I had to see them as a couple, hand in hand, with our children? How would I cope without him, full stop?

Chapter 34

Will

'Will,' Lauren murmured, as our lips met.

The way she said my name was soft and delicate; so different to Sarah's low, throaty tones. Brian Blessed sounded like a prepubescent choirboy in comparison. Actually, that wasn't true. Sarah had a very sexy voice. It was the first thing that had caught my attention. I'd not been at Ballas & Bailey long, and was by the water cooler, when I heard a voice so smooth, it could have had a lube named after it. Like a hound tracking a scent, I followed the husky laugh, peering around cheese plants and over dividing screens till I found its owner. And there she was, perched on the edge of a desk, chatting to her team, as relaxed and warm as a beer garden on a summer's day. I'd gasped. It was Sarah Brown. I hadn't seen her for years. Growing up, she'd been my annoying kid sister's annoying friend, and I'd done my best to avoid both of them. I didn't want to avoid her now. Her smile was wide and genuine, her eyes bright and animated behind blue-rimmed glasses, and her mass of curls was so alluring that I longed to reach out and thrust my hands in her hair.

Sarah had spotted me loitering and walked over, a huge smile on her face. 'Will Campbell! I don't believe it.' Laughing, she kissed me.

The touch of her lips on my cheek sent a jolt of excitement through me so intense, it reminded me of the first time I'd watched *Baywatch* as a youth.

'What are you doing here?' she asked.

'I've just joined the company. Used to be at RHT.'

Sarah burst out laughing. 'Tonya's useless. When I asked her what you did, she said she didn't really know, but it was something to do with the menopause.' She shook her head. 'We need to catch up properly. Let's grab lunch.'

Grab lunch we had. Every day for two weeks till we progressed to grabbing dinner, and then grabbing each other. Tonya was grossed out at first, but she melted when I explained how the first time I held Sarah, I knew I never wanted to let her go.

Yet here I was, kissing another woman.

Or was I? Our lips were touching, but neither of us had moved. Our mouths hadn't parted; there were no tongues, no entwined limbs or heavy breathing. It was the kind of kiss that kids give their parents when they're so young, they still kiss on the lips. I opened my eyes. Lauren's eyes were wide and full of alarm. I drew back.

'Sorry.' I cleared my throat. 'Shouldn't have done that.'

Lauren's laugh wasn't as tinkly as usual. 'That's not how I imagined it would be.'

Just a few minutes ago the knowledge that she'd imagined kissing me would have given me the almighty horn, but now it felt wrong. What was up with me? She was hot. So very, very hot.

I sank down at the kitchen table. 'I'm sorry,' I said again. 'It's not you, it's me.' I cringed at the cliché.

Lauren sat next to me. 'Want to talk about it?'

Yes, actually. I did want to talk. To someone other than my sister, who always saw Sarah's viewpoint, or Howard the local barman, who saw me every week, but still introduced himself each time.

'Long story short,' I started, 'I was a Director. Sarah was a Senior Manager. When I lost my job—'

Lauren frowned and I remembered that she thought I'd taken a sabbatical.

I held my hands up. 'I was too embarrassed to tell you. I lost my laptop and they made an example of me. I'm on six months' gardening leave and can't work during that time. Sarah was offered a promotion to Director and said it made sense to take it, so we had a good income coming in.' My words tumbled out. 'The power went to her head. She's working all hours, neglecting me and the kids. Now it turns out she knew I couldn't get a job with a rival firm and – get this – expects me to take a lower-level role with some small firm while she keeps the Director one. I said no, that wasn't the plan, so we're at loggerheads.' I paused for breath. Sod it, I'd tell her the whole story. 'And, tonight, she's staying with Tom, her colleague-slash-friend-slash-whatever.' Something inside my stomach twisted. 'No idea where we go from here. If we can go anywhere.' The pain in my stomach intensified.

'That's a lot to deal with,' Lauren said quietly.

At last – someone who understood.

'Put Tom to one side for now.' I'd like to do more than put him to one side. I'd like to put him out of his misery. 'Whatever's going on there – *if* anything's going on – is symptomatic of the existing problem in the relationship. That problem being, your wife throwing herself into her career, then refusing to give it up when you're able to re-enter the workforce.'

'Exactly.' I slapped the table. 'Except that she doesn't have to give it up. She can do what she expects me to do – take a marketing role within a small company.'

Lauren nodded. 'Humour me here – why is it better that she does that, rather than you?'

'She's only been a Director for a few months. I was one for years.'

'So, you're more important than her?'

'Yes.'

Lauren put her head to one side.

'I mean, no.' I wasn't a fan of these quick-fire questions.

I didn't have time to think about my answer. 'We're equals as people,' I added. 'It's just my job that's more important.'

'Why's that?'

'Because I'm the breadwinner.'

'Can't Sarah be the breadwinner?'

'No.'

'Why not?'

'Because I'm the man.'

The words hung in the air. I wished I could grab them and hide them and pretend they'd never been said. Sarah had accused me of being a misogynist. Was she right? Was I the feminist's equivalent of the bigots who started sentences with: '*I'm not racist, but …*' No, I thought. Expecting my wife to be the primary carer, and for her career to be secondary to mine, wasn't sexist. It was the norm. It wasn't as though I demanded she stay at home. Of course she could work if she wanted to. Just in a smaller role.

I replayed my words in my head, then put my head in my hands. For someone who wasn't sexist, I was doing a good impression of someone who was. I'd not only subscribed to the stereotypical male breadwinner scenario, but I'd also pretty much asked where I could sign up. I didn't want to be that person.

'I don't mean that.' I sighed heavily. 'Or I shouldn't mean that.'

'What do you mean then?' Lauren asked quietly.

I pondered her words. 'I'm pissed off about what's happened to my career,' I said eventually in a quiet voice. 'There's a possibility that, because of that, I haven't been as supportive or understanding as I could have been.' It was the understatement of the year. Not only had I let – no, expected – Sarah take over doing everything at home the moment she walked through the door, but I had also blamed her for me losing my job, which was ridiculous and so unfair. I, and I alone, had lost it.

Lauren gave me the same kind of smile that Sarah gave

the kids when they realised that if they picked up their toys, the floor wouldn't be a mess.

I dropped my eyes, too ashamed to look at her. Why had it taken me so long to realise how unreasonably I'd behaved? Now that I had, it was too late. Sarah had had enough of taking the rap for my ineptitude and was off with Tom, who would never make her accountable for his mistakes. Not that he'd make any, because he was so fucking perfect. My stomach twisted again at the thought of them together.

'It doesn't alter the Tom situation, though,' I said. My behaviour might have been a factor in driving Sarah to Tom, but she was the one who'd got in the car and driven off. 'How can I trust her again? Without trust, there's nothing.'

'You need to talk to her.' Lauren fiddled with her pendant. I wasn't tempted to look at her breasts this time. The dynamic between us had changed completely. I was even calling them breasts, rather than tits. Get me – I'd be reading Germaine Greer next. 'There's a strong possibility nothing's going on,' Lauren continued. 'Just as there's nothing going on between us.'

Heat flooded my face. 'Sorry about earlier. I don't know why nothing happened.'

'I know why.' Lauren gave me a wistful smile. 'Nothing happened because you love your wife.'

I gave a resigned nod. She was right. In spite of everything, I still loved Sarah. The question was, did she still love me?

Chapter 35

Sarah

I woke with a crick in my neck. I'd lain awake for hours, so wired and upset I doubted I'd ever sleep again. I'd be like Sleeping Beauty in reverse, cursed to lie awake for evermore because the so-called handsome prince had kissed me. But I'd obviously dropped off at some point, so the curse thankfully had a shorter expiry date than Princess Aurora's.

I fumbled for my phone, desperately hoping for a message from Will. The phone was dead. Bugger. With everything else going on, I hadn't thought to charge it. My head pounded as I got up, slid my glasses on and checked the time on my watch. Six thirty. Would trains be running yet? If they were running at all. I shuffled over to the window and pulled the blind back. The good news was that it was no longer snowing. The bad news was that it had snowed a hell of a lot before stopping. Everything was crisp and clean and pure. The view couldn't have been more of a contrast to my current situation. There was nothing pure about my behaviour.

I tiptoed to the kitchen, drank a pint of water, then tiptoed to the bathroom and threw it up, stifling my retches to create minimum noise. Last thing I wanted was to wake Tom. I needed some distance from him for a while. Last night's eagerness to remain good friends now felt naïve. I wasn't convinced we'd ever go back to the carefree banter we'd enjoyed before. The thought of him near me made me shudder. Although, given my hangover, even the thought of Instagram-friendly kittens made me shudder.

I cleaned my teeth so thoroughly that the enamel probably came off, looked longingly at the shower and decided against having one. The longer I stayed, the more likelihood there was of Tom waking up and me having to interact with him. I did need to charge my phone, though. I checked the living room and kitchen, but couldn't find a charger. I was about to give up when I remembered the study-slash-gym. I crept into the hallway and eyed the two doors I hadn't been through yet. One would be to Tom's bedroom, which I definitely didn't want to enter, lest he woke up and thought I was up for it after all. In my mind, he was reclining on a heart-shaped waterbed, below a mirrored ceiling, wearing Hugh Hefner-style silk pyjamas. I shook myself. This was ridiculous. Tom wasn't anything like that. They'd be Superman pyjamas, for sure.

One door was slightly ajar and I pushed it gently, exhaling with relief when I saw a desk with a charger on it. I plugged my phone in and looked around the room while I waited for it to boot up. A rowing machine, cross trainer and pyramid of free weights dominated half the room. Tom's coat from the day before was balled up in the corner. The mum in me sprang into action and I picked it up. It was wet through from the snow and I spread it across the bars of the cross trainer to dry. Something fell out of an inside pocket and landed heavily on the floor. I froze, staring at the door, hoping it hadn't disturbed Tom. After a few seconds had passed without any noise coming from the direction of his bedroom, I looked down to see what had fallen to the floor.

It was my organiser.

Gasping with delight, I swooped down, picked it up and hugged it to my chest. Thank God. Without it, I was like the healthcare system without the NHS. The legal system without a jury. Claudia Winkleman without her fringe.

I stood up slowly, a sudden thought tainting my euphoria.

Why did Tom have my organiser? I pushed my glasses up with trembling fingers. He wouldn't have taken it, would he?

I shook my head, instantly dismissing the idea. Of course he wouldn't have taken it. There was no reason. My personal info was dull and interesting to no one other than me. Some of the time not even to me. And there was no benefit to be gained from stealing my ideas, as I happily shared them with him anyway. Plus, we were friends. If I hadn't turned him down last night, we'd be more than friends.

My throat tightened. Had he taken it to get back at me for rejecting his advances? No – it had gone missing before that. My brain felt as though it was trying to expel itself from my skull, as I attempted to figure out what was going on. There had to be a simple explanation. I thought back to when we'd left the pub. We'd been in a hurry to get to the station. Tom had grabbed everything as I'd run ahead. He must have picked up the organiser with the coats and it had worked its way into his pocket. I smiled, relieved I'd worked it out. This crazy paranoia was nothing more than a side effect of my hangover. The important thing was that I had my organiser. Nothing else mattered. My phone beeped and flashed on the desk. At last. Enough charge to get me through the journey home. I hesitated. Home. What would happen when I got there? I supposed that depended on Will. If he was there. I opened the Find My Friends app, then closed it immediately. I couldn't deal with that right now. I could barely deal with breathing.

Five minutes later I let myself out of Tom's apartment with the stealth of a cat. A cat that had been drinking so heavily the day before, there was a possibility it was still drunk. The snow was thick and fresh on the ground, so I was able to walk without fear of falling over. Under other circumstances, I'd have appreciated the satisfying crunch beneath my boots and the beauty around me. But under my current circumstances – I'd annoyingly realised that I still loved my husband, who was with someone else, and was both starving and on the verge of throwing up – the snow's aesthetics did little to lift my mood. In fact, if the trains still weren't running, the snow could go fuck itself.

I entered the station and my heart sunk even lower at the sight of the departure board. Service delayed. A whiteboard advised that trains would be running later in the morning and travellers into the centre of London could use the nearby Tube. I groaned. It was only seven. I didn't want to hang around here for hours and there was no way I was going back to Tom's.

A few doors down from the station was an independent café. The smell of fresh coffee wafted up the street and I headed towards it. Caffeine and food would kill some time and help me feel, if not better, then slightly less wretched.

There were a few people already in the café, which surprised me until I remembered that today was actually a normal working day. Just because I'd booked it off didn't mean the rest of the UK population had. I sat at a table and picked up a menu.

'What would you like?' the waitress asked.

'A full English and a large coffee, please.' This was kill or cure.

Taking my organiser from my bag, I stroked it lovingly, then turned to the diary section. With the exception of the meeting with Lars next week, there was nothing in there. I sighed. This wasn't right. Surely someone somewhere wanted to speak to me.

'Hi Sarah.'

I jumped. I hadn't meant *now*. Not in the state I was in, emotionally, mentally and, worst of all, physically. Not only was I wearing the same clothes I'd worn the day before, but I was also wearing the same clothes I'd slept in. My makeup was left over from yesterday, too, and my hair was in a topknot usually reserved for the shower. A meteor shower.

I looked up into Lin's face. Her expression wasn't particularly friendly – I doubted there'd be an open invite to a New Year's Eve party – but she wasn't snarling or running in the opposite direction, so I considered that a win.

'Hi Lin,' I said warmly. 'What are you doing here?'

'I live round the corner.' Lin gestured in the opposite direction to Tom's apartment. 'What are *you* doing here?'

'I was in the office yesterday. Called in to see a friend and got stranded. I'm waiting for the trains to start running so I can get home.' I wasn't lying. Just hadn't mentioned that the friend was Tom. 'Sorry for looking so awful.' Definitely not lying. 'I hadn't planned on staying over.'

Lin nodded. 'Doesn't look as though the overground trains will be operating for a while. I'm going to get the Tube to work.'

I hesitated. 'I'm glad we bumped into each other. I want to apologise for missing your appraisal.'

Lin's mouth formed a thin line.

'I'm so sorry I wasn't there,' I said. 'I've been trying to catch up with everyone since, but you're all so busy.'

Lin's eyes narrowed.

'Which is great,' I added quickly, so it didn't sound as though I was criticising. 'You're clearly all using your initiative and getting on with it.'

'Don't have much choice,' she muttered.

'Have you got time to talk now?' I asked. 'Let me treat you to breakfast.'

Lin's eyes darted between me and the door. She was probably wishing she'd skipped her morning latte.

'I'd really like to hear how you're getting on,' I said.

Lin shrugged non-committally, but sat down.

'Great,' I said enthusiastically. 'Order some food first and then let's talk.'

Lin ordered a fruit pot, which made me feel like a right greedy cow, but I didn't let it sway me – the hangover was doing a good enough job of that. I went into work mode, talking about the projects she was working on, the skill sets she wanted to focus on and her future aims. Over breakfast I learnt more than I had in the past two months.

'Let's put a plan together for the new year,' I said. 'These goals are more than achievable. Book a meeting in with Nancy for next week.'

Lin's smile turned into a frown. 'Aren't you all booked up till February or something?'

I frowned back. 'No. Where did you hear that?'

'Nancy. I wanted to ask you about one of the projects the other day and she said you were too busy.'

My mouth fell open. Why would Nancy say that? And who else had she been saying it to? 'I'd never be too busy to talk to you or any of the team. That's my job.'

Lin popped a grape into her mouth. 'It did seem strange. I'm friends with Megan, you know, from your old team, and she always said you were brilliant to work with. I was really pleased when you took over from Jasper, but then ...' She trailed off.

'Go on,' I said gently.

'You kind of shut yourself off. Always in your office rather than on the floor. Nancy never let us book meetings or pop our heads in to ask you something. Said you'd told her you mustn't be disturbed.'

Heat rushed to my head and my heartbeat hammered against my ribcage. 'That's bull—' I stopped myself. 'That's not true.'

Lin smiled. 'It's OK, you can swear. I won't report you.'

My stomach flipped over. With all the reports already against me, I was thankful for one fewer complaint. 'I don't know what's going on,' I said, 'but things will be very different from now on.' I checked the time. It was only eight o'clock. I couldn't get home for a few hours. May as well put that time to good use. I smiled at Lin. 'I'll come into the office with you. We can put that plan together now if you like?'

I paid the bill and we headed to the Tube station. 'How long have you lived here?' I asked.

'A couple of years,' Lin replied. 'It's so handy for work. Quite a few people from Ballas & Bailey live around here. Tom ...' My stomach turned. 'Isla in analytics, Brady in tech, Nancy—'

'Nancy?' I looked around in alarm. I really didn't want a run-in with Nancy. My hair couldn't handle it.

'I think so. I've seen her getting off the train a couple of times.'

Thankfully, we didn't encounter Nancy, and Lin and I talked animatedly all the way into work. The conversation continued in my office, and by ten o'clock, we'd come up with a strategic plan that Lin was excited about and which gave her lots of opportunities for growth and progress.

'Thank you,' she said, shaking my hand enthusiastically. 'Megan was right. You're great to work with.'

She left my office with a spring in her step and I sat down, a huge grin on my face. This was the part of the job I loved and that I'd missed. I didn't want to only do the marketing campaigns and pitches; I wanted to be involved in developing the team too. I was a people person and, for some unknown reason, Nancy had been sabotaging the team's attempts to reach me. I'd have to find out what was going on there.

I stared out across the banks of desks. If I was going to properly interact with my team, I needed to be among them. I'd speak to Andy and ask to have a desk set up out there. Not conventional for a Director, but it was where I'd be able to give my best. Nancy wouldn't manage to block me if I was there for everyone to approach. I didn't know how Tom would feel about that. He might like having the office to himself or he might want to join me on the floor. That would be his decision. Mulling it over, I realised that I hoped he'd stay in the office. Thinking of Tom made me, firstly, want to get in a shower and scrub myself clean and, secondly, realise that I'd left without saying goodbye.

I tapped out a text to Tom. **Sorry for dashing off. Couldn't sleep, so decided to head home.**

I needed to message Will, too. But first, I had to put on my big-girl pants – anything was better than the ones I'd slept in – and find out where he was. I clicked on my Find My Friends app and squinted through my glasses at the phone, hardly daring to breathe while the app found Will. His location popped up and I inhaled sharply. He was still at Lauren's. He *had* stayed the night. Hope deflated from me. We could find a solution to the work issue. We couldn't find a solution to him being with Lauren. Tears trickled down my cheeks and I swiped them away. I'd do my crying when I got home. Right now, I needed to be professional. As professional as someone wearing yesterday's underwear could be.

My fingers trembled as I typed out a message to Will. **Trains not running yet. I'll be home as soon as they are. Will let you know when I'm on my way. We need to talk.**

That sounded ominous, but it was the truth. I was dreading this conversation more than any other I'd ever had. My phone beeped and I looked at the message, wondering what Will's response would be and if he'd admit to being at Lauren's. The message wasn't from Will, though. It was from Clara and it simply read: **Please call me. We need to talk.**

My stomach dropped. That was ominous with knobs on.

Chapter 36

Will

A message from Sarah came through as I arrived at Lauren's house.

> Trains not running yet. I'll be home as soon as they are.
> Will let you know when I'm on my way. We need to talk.

I puffed out my cheeks and exhaled, my breath creating clouds in the cold air. That didn't sound good. People never said: 'We need to talk. I've won the lottery and want to give you a million pounds.' Or, 'We need to talk. Would you like curry or pizza tonight?' It was always: 'We need to talk. I've got a gambling addiction and have lost the house.' Or, 'We need to talk. I'm in love with my co-worker and am leaving you.'

I reread the message, trying to decipher any hidden meaning. Eventually, I concluded that the trains weren't running yet, but Sarah would let me know when they were and she was on her way home, and that she wanted to talk. Any subtext about how amazing Tom was in the sack and how many orgasms he'd given her was thankfully lost in translation.

'Morning,' Lauren said brightly, opening the door. 'How are you?'

I thrust my phone in my pocket. 'Fine,' I lied. 'You?'

'Great.' She took my coat once I was in the hall. 'We had pancakes for breakfast.'

My stomach rumbled. My breakfast choices had been leftover turkey with pickled onions, or Christmas cake. Pickled onions optional. I'd decided to go without.

Lauren smiled. 'I'll make you some. Evie and Fred won't mind staying a bit longer.'

As Evie and Fred had yet to come and say hello, I suspected she was right.

'Hi kids,' I called out, following Lauren into the kitchen.

'They're in the garden, building snowmen,' she said, cracking eggs into a bowl.

How did she do it? At home they complained when they had to leave the sofa for the dining table or toilet. Under Lauren's care they were one with flipping nature. I watched Lauren whip up the pancake mix and pour it into a pan. Everything she did seemed effortless. At home Sarah was always racing around, doing twenty things at once, stress oozing from every pore. I picked at a bit of loose nail on my thumb. Was that because I wasn't doing enough? If I got involved more, reduced the twenty things that needed doing to a more manageable ten, would Sarah be calmer, more relaxed and happier, like she used to be?

'What's your secret?' I asked Lauren. 'How do you manage to look after two kids, run a household, study, do all of this,' I gestured to the pancakes, 'and be so chilled out?'

'I make the kids play outside as much as possible. It wears them out and gives me time to study.' Lauren poured orange juice into a glass and passed it to me. 'I don't clean or care that the house is a mess.'

'Your house isn't a ...' I started, then trailed off. Now that she'd mentioned it, the house *was* a mess. The bottles of lager we'd worked our way through the night before were still on the table, Christmas cracker remnants were all over the floor, and my glass had lipstick on the rim. I drank from the other side.

'Life's too short to spend it tidying.' She rinsed a knife and fork under the tap for me, failing to remove the food that was coated on them. I decided to eat with my fingers. 'A cleaner comes in twice a week and blitzes the place,' Lauren continued. 'She does the laundry too. Changed my life. We used to live in squalor, but now you could eat your dinner off the floor.' Lauren flipped a pancake onto a plate and passed it to me. I tried to wipe a smear of leftover tomato sauce from the side of the plate. It refused to budge. Would she take offence if I asked to test that theory and actually eat off the floor?

'Have you spoken to Sarah yet?' Lauren asked.

I stared down at my plate. 'No. She messaged to say we need to talk.' All of a sudden, I wasn't as hungry as I thought I was and it was nothing to do with the congealed second-hand ketchup.

Lauren put another pancake on my plate. 'She's right. You should talk.' She put her head to one side. 'Want to leave the kids here to give you some space?'

'No,' I said quickly. The kids being with Lauren wouldn't be a good starting point for negotiations. I'd get a better reception if I told Sarah I'd exchanged them for some beans. 'Thanks, but it'll be better if they're there.'

Would it, though? If she was going to tell me she was with Tom, nothing in the world could make it better.

Chapter 37

Sarah

'Hi Clara.' I forced my voice to sound light and breezy down the phone, even though I was petrified she'd received another complaint about me, or I'd done something else wrong. 'Good Christmas?'

Clara wasn't getting drawn into small talk. 'I know you're off, but something's come up that I thought you'd want to know about.'

That was debatable. If she had a spare ticket to see Harry Styles then yes, I definitely wanted to know about it. If I was being fired, then that news could keep.

'I'm supposed to be off, but I'm actually in the office. Long story.' One that I would not be sharing with the HR Director.

'Perfect! Come on up.' Clara hung up, then immediately rang back. 'Don't tell anyone,' she added, before putting the phone down again.

My stomach churned. This was all very strange and, I suspected, didn't involve Harry Styles in any way. I walked towards the lift, taking my coat and bag with me so I could go straight home afterwards. If indeed it was still my home. Lauren might have designs on it. I was so deep in thought that I didn't realise someone was coming towards me until I literally collided with them. I gasped audibly when I saw it was Nancy. My face grew hot, recalling Lin's revelation that Nancy told everyone I was too busy to see them. Nancy scowled and sauntered off. I'd ask Clara for her advice on how to deal with that situation. Hopefully, it wouldn't be my last request.

'Sarah, come in.' Clara gave me a tight smile, but there was a spark in her eyes. 'Shut the door behind you.'

I did as she asked and sat down opposite her. 'Is there a problem?' I asked, nudging my glasses up.

'Not a problem – a development.' Clara smoothed down the A4 notepad in front of her. 'IT has received an alert from Will's laptop. Someone's logged onto it, for the first time since he lost it.'

I gasped. 'So they can locate it?'

'Possibly.' Clara laced her fingers together. 'The timing indicates that it was sold on and given as a Christmas present. Hopefully, it would have been cleaned before being sold, but we need to know for sure. They're trying to trace it now and will keep me updated.' Clara looked at her desk phone eagerly. This was clearly more exciting than the usual issues of someone taking too much time off sick or pinching stationery. 'Want to hang on to find out where it is?' Clara asked.

I hesitated. 'No' was the honest answer. I'd be more than happy for her to call me with the details, but after the complaints made against me, I desperately wanted to get back on Clara's good side, so I nodded. 'Did they give any indication of how long it'll take?' I tried to say this in a way that conveyed I was eager to find out, rather than eager to get out.

Clara shook her head. 'It's like being in *Law & Order*, isn't it?' She grinned.

'Haven't seen *Law & Order*,' I admitted. I didn't add that this phone-watching encounter wasn't making it a must-see for me.

'It's an American crime series with Benjamin Bratt in it,' Clara said.

OK, maybe I'd give it a try.

'While we're waiting …' Clara moved her phone an inch closer, in case she somehow missed it ringing. 'How are things with the team?'

'Not great,' I said. 'But I think I know why.'

Clara's expression grew progressively grimmer as I detailed Nancy's behaviour, my cancelled appointments and blank diary, and Lin's revelation that they all felt rejected by me. I took my organiser from my bag and showed her all the crossed-out meetings.

'I don't want to seem as though I'm being overdramatic,' I said, 'but first there was the ridiculous harassment allegation, and now Nancy's jeopardising relationships with the team and my clients. The *company's* clients,' I emphasised. 'She's not just damaging my career and reputation, she's also preventing me from making money for the firm.'

'This is outrageous.' Clara scanned the notes she'd made while I spoke. 'I need to talk to Nancy about this. Before I do, do you have witnesses or proof? I'm not doubting you, but if she denies it, then it's her word against yours.'

I nodded. 'Lin can confirm what Nancy's been doing. And it wouldn't take too much investigation to find out from the clients who cancelled our meetings.'

Clara sat up straighter at the word investigation. This usually quiet Twixmas day had certainly perked up for her. 'Is Nancy in today?'

I nodded and Clara's hand hovered over her desk phone, then moved to her mobile. 'Don't want to block the landline in case IT ring,' she explained, keying Nancy's number into her mobile. 'It's ringing,' she mouthed, excitement oozing from every pore. 'Nancy, it's Clara,' she said. 'Can you come up and see me, please?' There was a pause. 'I'll explain when you get here. See you in a few minutes. Thanks.' She hung up, turned to a new page on her notepad, removed the lid from a ballpoint pen and placed it neatly on the paper. It was the office equivalent of preparing for battle. She gave my tatty organiser on the desk a sideways look. It was very much a poor relation compared with the order and neatness of her stationery.

My heartbeat quickened as we waited, although I hadn't

done anything wrong and it was Clara who'd be doing the bulk of the confrontation. I hoped. My phone beeped in my bag, making me jump.

'Sorry.' I took it out and switched it to silent. It was a message from Tom, saying he was sorry he'd missed me and that he'd just got into the office. I fired back a reply, telling him that I was already here, as the trains hadn't been running.

I wasn't being paranoid about Nancy, I typed. We're in HR. I'll fill you in later.

Three dots appeared on the screen, but before Tom's reply came through, Nancy knocked on the door and I shoved the phone into my bag.

'Come in,' Clara called. Nancy visibly jumped when she saw me.

'Sit down,' Clara said calmly.

'What's this about?' Nancy asked, panic in her voice.

'We understand that you've been preventing Sarah's team members from seeing her when they've requested meetings.' Nancy's cheeks went scarlet. 'Also, meetings have been removed from Sarah's calendar and rescheduled without her being informed.' Nancy shuffled in her seat. 'We'd like to hear your thoughts on these claims.'

Nancy's eyes darted between the two of us. The expression 'a deer caught in the headlights' sprang to mind. Except that deer were beautiful, innocent creatures. Nancy was a manipulative, lying bitch.

Clara picked up her pen. 'Have you ever told Sarah's team members that she's too busy to see them?'

Nancy stared miserably at the phone on Clara's desk, as though seeking inspiration.

'This isn't *Who Wants to be a Millionaire?*. You can't phone a friend.' Clara's eyes flicked my way before returning to Nancy. I got the impression she was quite pleased with that line. 'It's a straightforward question. Have you ever—'

The office door flew open and Tom tumbled in.

'Don't listen to her,' he panted, flinging a hand in Nancy's direction. 'It's all lies. She'll say anything to cause trouble.'

Nancy's cheeks flushed puce.

'Tom,' Clara said sharply. 'This is a private meeting. You can't just barge in.' She gripped her pen tightly, clearly loving the drama.

'But she's feeding you a load of bullshit. I'm trying to save you time.' Tom stabbed the air. 'You can't trust a word that comes out of her mouth.'

Clara made hushing motions with her hands. 'A word hasn't come out of Nancy's mouth yet.'

Tom froze. 'What?'

Clara looked at Nancy, who shrank back in her chair, then up at Tom. 'What bullshit had you anticipated her feeding us?'

Tom smoothed down his tie and did a little double take, as though he'd just strolled into the room and was surprised to see us there. 'Pardon?'

I opened my mouth, then closed it again. This was not the time for the horse story.

Clara was clasping her pen so tightly that her knuckles had turned white. 'Why did you think Nancy was going to lie to us?' she asked Tom.

'Because she told everyone that Sarah forced Will to quit so she could have his job.' Tom placed a hand on the back of my chair, as though posing for a family portrait. I resisted the urge to flick it off. 'Everyone hates Sarah now,' he added.

Everyone? How many people had Nancy told? And why did they all believe her?

Clara glanced at me. 'Sarah's already told me about this.' She turned to Nancy, whose face was now so red, it looked as though she'd been on a spit roast for several days. 'Why did you say this?' she asked.

Nancy shrugged. 'That's what I'd heard.'

'Bullshit.' Tom tutted. 'Only us and Andy know the truth.'

Ignoring him, Clara addressed Nancy. 'Who did you hear that from?'

Nancy glanced up at Tom. I swivelled round in time to see him shake his head.

'What's going on?' I asked.

'This isn't getting us anywhere,' Tom said. 'We're wasting time.' He turned to Nancy. 'Say you're sorry and we can all move on.'

'Excuse me,' Clara snapped. 'I'm running this meeting, not you.'

Tom gripped the chair behind my head. 'Yes, sorry. Getting frustrated on your behalf.'

'I can get frustrated on my own behalf, thank you.' Clara narrowed her eyes at Tom, then turned to Nancy and softened her features. 'Who told you that Sarah made Will leave so that she could have his job?'

Nancy closed her eyes. 'No one. I made it up.'

'Told you.' Tom released my chair and clapped his hands together. 'Can we get back to work now?'

'You can,' Clara said. 'Sarah and I still need to talk to Nancy.'

Nancy looked up at Tom, misery oozing from every pore. He met her eyes briefly, then looked away. His gaze landed on my organiser on Clara's desk and his eyes widened.

'You got your organiser back. That's great.' He grinned broadly. 'Did the pub phone you?'

Clara and Nancy both frowned.

'You two were in the pub?' Nancy said.

'Just a quick drink after a client presentation,' I said.

Tom winked at me. Thankfully, Clara didn't see, but Nancy did and she glowered at us both.

'Are you two …' She trailed off, as though she couldn't bring herself to say the words. Clara looked at me incredulously.

'No,' I said firmly. 'Definitely not.'

Tom shook his head in agreement, but winked again, making it look as though we were teenagers fibbing to our teachers.

Nancy's hands flew to her face. 'You're cheating on me with *her*?'

Clara's mouth fell open.

'No, he is not,' I said indignantly, increasingly thankful that was the truth. Hang on. Cheating on Nancy? Did that mean …

'You told me to pretend she was harassing you!' Nancy wailed. 'I didn't think you'd go along with it.'

'Shut up,' Tom said. 'You're talking nonsense.'

He put a hand on her arm but she shrugged him off. 'I did everything you asked and you've gone off with *her*.' She shot a look of disgust in my direction.

My head was pounding. What did all of this mean?

'This is all a stupid misunderstanding.' Tom tugged at his collar. 'Nancy's claims that—'

'Stop talking and sit down,' Clara said coldly. She turned to Nancy. 'Did Tom tell you to claim you'd seen Sarah sexually harassing him?'

'No!' Tom interrupted. 'Nancy and I had a bit of a fling and she's saying this to get back at me for breaking it off.'

Nancy's eyes welled up with tears. I started to feel sorry for her. 'A bit of a fling? You said you wanted to be with me, but we had to wait till you were more established before we got serious.' She shot a poisonous look my way. 'Did you just say that so you could be with Sarah?' She grimaced. 'She's so old.' I stopped feeling sorry for her.

'Tom and I are not together,' I said firmly. 'Whatever's going on with you two has nothing to do with me.'

A muscle pounded in Tom's cheek. 'This is all bullshit. She'll say anything to get back at me.'

Nancy stared at him, pain etched across her face. Tom steadfastly ignored her, his eyes focused on the window. Nancy gave Tom a last wounded look, then pushed her shoulders back and turned to Clara.

'He got me to cancel Sarah's meetings,' she said quietly. 'And pass new enquiries on to him instead of her, and tell the staff that she was too busy to talk to them.'

I inhaled sharply. I'd been right. Nancy had been sabotaging my career. Not out of malice, though. She'd done it because Tom had told her to. My head spun. No wonder he'd always been so quick to jump in and offer to talk to her or the team. If I'd spoken to any of them, I'd have found out what was going on. But why? We were a partnership. It didn't make any sense.

Nancy's eyes were trained on Clara. 'And he told Sarah you'd insisted the appraisals take place the day her trains weren't running, so she'd miss them.'

Clara pursed her lips. 'What do you have to say about all this, Tom?'

Tom lifted his hands and let them drop onto his thighs. 'Why would I do any of this? The sooner you stop listening to her lies and tell her to go, the better.'

'Tell me to go?' Nancy's head whipped round. 'You want to get me sacked too?'

I frowned. 'What do you mean "too"? Who else is getting sacked?'

Nancy gave me a withering look. 'You, obviously. As long as you're here, you'll get the better deals. Tom wanted to learn everything he could from you, then get you fired so he could take over and get the big clients.'

I felt as though I'd been punched in the stomach. That's why Tom took such studious notes and asked so many questions. That's why he panicked when he missed the Dekker presentation. And why he kept me away from the team and got my meetings cancelled. That's why he took my organiser. I'd been a fool to think he'd picked it up by accident. He'd stolen it to get my ideas. But when it became obvious that my notes were practically in code, he'd needed more information. He'd needed me to elaborate on them. A thought struck me and bile swirled around my throat. Was that why he'd tried to seduce me? Not because he cared about me, but because he needed me to stay around long enough to get all of my marketing ideas so he could use them himself. And I'd fallen for it. I'd been taken in by his charm and compassion and Superman T-shirt. How could I have been so stupid? I'd ruined my marriage for this narcissistic, power-hungry, selfish man. Possibly, my career too.

Clara turned to Tom. 'What do you have to say about all this?'

Tom pulled at his collar. 'The harassment charge. Sarah flashed her bra at me on two occasions.'

I inhaled sharply. 'By accident. The buttons on my shirt came undone once and then my wrap dress at the Christmas party came loose.' I turned to Clara. 'It wasn't intentional.'

Clara nodded. She'd seen my wardrobe malfunctions enough times. I needed to invest in some new clothes or at least a couple of safety pins.

She tapped her pen against her pad. 'What about the other allegations? Nancy's claims that you got her to cancel meetings and prevent the team from seeing Sarah. There have been three complaints against Sarah, which back up this theory.'

'Yes – theory. Not fact.' Tom waved a hand in Nancy's direction. 'She's out to get me for reasons I've explained. Don't know why she dragged Sarah into it.'

Nancy shook her head venomously.

Clara hooked a finger across her chin. I wondered if that was *a Law & Order* pose. 'You deny it all then?'

'Yes, I do.' Tom slapped the table. 'Who are you going to believe? An established member of the management team or a PA with a vendetta?'

I pressed my lips together. I hated him. He was a horrible, horrible man. The knowledge that I'd had feelings for him, no matter how short-lived, filled me with shame and disgust. Nancy sat beside him, looking distraught. Not only had she been unceremoniously dumped, but she'd also been thrown under the bus. And he'd tried to get me sacked! He'd acted with malice and disregard for the feelings of everyone involved, not caring whose career he destroyed in his desire to get to the top. He mustn't be allowed to get away with this. But how could we prove what he'd done?

Clara slid open her desk drawer and peered in. I wondered what she was looking for – some guidance on what to do next, either from an HR manual or Benjamin Bratt himself?

The phone on her desk rang loudly and we all jumped. She slammed the drawer shut and grabbed it, an excited flush creeping up her neck. With all the drama from Nancy and Tom, I'd forgotten about Will's laptop.

'Yes, yes,' Clara said, writing something on her notepad. 'And that's definite?' A pause. 'No, I don't recognise it, but hopefully someone will. Well done.'

She hung up, placed her pen down neatly and frowned at her notepad.

'Was that about the laptop?' I asked, wringing my hands.

Tom sat upright. 'What laptop?'

'Never mind,' Clara said sharply. 'That's a separate issue and doesn't concern you.'

She tilted her notepad away from Tom's prying eyes. But my prying eyes could see perfectly what she'd written. Just three words – *Network name: Kryptonite.*

Chapter 38

Will

The front door closed and Sarah's keys clinked as she hung them up on the rack. I abandoned the washing-up and went out into the hall. We gazed at each other warily.

'I didn't sleep with Tom,' she said. A rush of relief swept through me so powerfully that my knees buckled. I sank down onto the stairs.

Sarah clasped her hands together. 'Did you—'

'No,' I said quickly, ashamed that I'd left her dangling. I'd been so happy that Tom's dangling hadn't been involved, I'd forgotten to reassure her about Lauren. 'The kids fell asleep and I left them there, then went back this morning.'

Sarah made a noise that was somewhere between a sob and a laugh. 'Thank God.' She looked around. 'Where are they?'

'Tonya's taken them to the panto.'

'That's nice.' Things were serious if she wasn't going down the 'oh no she hasn't' route. Sarah nudged her glasses up. 'Tom and I did kiss,' she whispered. My jaw tightened. 'I regretted it straightaway and really wish it hadn't happened.' Sarah visibly shuddered. 'I'm so sorry. It was horrible.'

Shallow as it might sound, the news that Tom's kiss was horrible went a long way towards making it easier to forgive Sarah. And who was I to judge anyway? I'd kissed Lauren.

'I er …' I stared at my hands and tapped my thumbs together. 'Same here.'

'You kissed Lauren?' Sarah's voice caught in her throat.

'It wasn't a kiss exactly.' I looked up at her. 'Our lips touched, but all I could think about was you.'

Sarah gave me a watery smile. 'You were all I could think about too.' She crossed the hall and knelt in front of me. 'I know we have a lot to sort out, but I want to sort it out. I don't want us to break up.'

'Neither do I.' My voice broke this time, and we pulled each other close and held on as tightly as we could. 'I'm sorry,' I said eventually. 'You were right about everything. I didn't support you the way I should have. The way you've always supported me.' I kissed her, then pulled back. 'I'm ashamed of how I've behaved. You were right, I did resent you. Thought it wasn't fair that your career flourished while I festered at home. I shouldn't have felt that way and I definitely shouldn't have expected you to deal with all the house and kids' stuff on top of that. You were already doing one job. You shouldn't have had to do another one when you got home. I've been a shit husband and I'm really, really sorry.' I stared into her eyes, hoping the extent of my regret was clear for her to see. 'I don't know why I felt I had to be the breadwinner. That you being the main earner was undermining my masculinity or something.' I shook my head. 'Ridiculous. I honestly don't believe that a woman's place is in the home or that your career should be secondary to mine. None of that matters. What's important is that we're working together as a team and supporting each other. I'm sorry it took me so long to figure that out.'

'I'm sorry too.' Sarah sniffed. 'I got too caught up in work. Yes, it's important, but you, Evie and Fred will always come first. I lost sight of that for a while.'

We smiled at each other. She was so beautiful and thoughtful and caring and all-round amazing. How could I have risked fucking this up?

'I thought I'd lost you,' I whispered, my throat tight.

'Same,' she whispered back. 'I was so scared you'd got together with Lauren.'

'Never.' I wrapped my arms around her. 'There'll never be anyone but you.'

I hugged her tightly, feeling closer to her than I had for a very long time. 'I'll look for a marketing position within a company, like you suggested,' I said. 'No need to work for one of the big fish. It was my ego telling me I had to.'

'God, you don't know.' Sarah pulled away and gripped my hands. 'Tom took your laptop.'

I sat bolt upright. 'What?'

Sarah nodded enthusiastically, her topknot bobbing up and down with the motion.

I shook my head, confused. 'Why would he take it?'

Sarah's grip tightened. 'When you told Tom about Jasper being fired for losing his laptop, he hid yours so you'd get fired too. With two Director positions going, he knew he'd definitely get one of them. He wasn't happy about me getting the bigger clients, though, so he tried to get me fired.'

'What?' I exclaimed. 'How?'

'He turned the team against me, and got Nancy to cancel loads of meetings. Four people made complaints against me.' Sarah's voice wobbled. 'It's been horrible a lot of the time.'

I pulled her to me, my heart aching for her. 'Why didn't you tell me?'

'I didn't want to complain about work when you were so down about *not* working.' Sarah sniffed into my shoulder. 'Tom did loads of other stuff too. He wiped clean my memory stick that had Dekker's presentation on it. He even stole my organiser to get my marketing ideas. Then I told him my notes were pretty basic, but that I'd written them up in detail on your laptop. Do you remember I borrowed it when we took the children trampolining?'

I nodded, even though I didn't.

'Because I'd said that,' Sarah continued, 'Tom logged on to your laptop to try to find my notes. IT got an alert and traced it to his network, Kryptonite. The vain prick used it as his password for everything.' She sat back, smiling and crying at the same time. The facial equivalent of a rainbow in a downpour. 'With Nancy's and the team's statements, Clara has everything she needs to get rid of him.' She let out an almighty sigh. 'I can't tell you how relieved I am.' She shook her head and her topknot sprang free of its bobble, firing her curls out in all directions.

I loved that hair. I loved this woman. And I loved that Tom was being told to do one.

Sarah's phone rang and she pulled it from her bag. 'It's Clara,' she said. 'She's FaceTiming.' She accepted the call, squeezed in next to me on the stairs and held the phone up. 'Hi Clara.'

'Hi Sarah. And Will! So lovely to see you.' Clara was more animated than I'd ever seen her. A few strands of hair were out of place and her shirt collar was slightly twisted. 'What a morning,' she said, rubbing her hands together. 'Has Sarah filled you in, Will?'

'I gave him the abridged version,' Sarah said. 'I'll give him an in-depth version later.' Her thigh pressed against mine and my heart skipped a beat.

'Great.' Clara smiled broadly. 'In that case, Will – when can you come back?'

'What?' Sarah and I said in unison.

'I've spoken to Andy and we're in agreement. With Tom gone, and your name cleared, the job's yours again. We'd like you back asap.'

My name was cleared? My job was mine again? This was incredible. I was getting another chance. My life could go back to the way it used to be. Instead of the hassle of looking for another job, I could slot back in as though I'd never left.

'Sarah, the complaints against you have been withdrawn,' Clara said. 'Andy and I will tell the team what's been going on and you can start afresh. Without Tom here to do the long-haul travel, you'll need to factor that in, but I'm sure you can figure it out.'

Sarah nudged her glasses up. Her hand was trembling.

'Can you give us five minutes?' she asked Clara. 'I'll call you back as soon as we've had a quick chat.'

Clara looked taken aback. So was I to be honest. Surely this was a no-brainer?

'Sure,' Clara said, smoothing her hair behind her ear. 'Take as long as you like.' She paused. 'But five minutes would be better.'

'Thanks.' Sarah ended the call and exhaled. 'I can't believe it,' she said.

'Me neither.' I wrapped my arms around her. 'We're both Directors. This is incredible.' Sarah didn't hug me back as enthusiastically as I was hugging her. Shit. Was she still annoyed about Lauren? 'What's wrong?' I asked. 'Aren't you pleased?'

'Of course I am. It's only right that you get your job back.'

'And that you keep yours.' I pulled back and gazed into her eyes, which was easier said than done. Her glasses were so smudged, it was like looking through frosted glass. 'Once the team hear how Tom and Nancy targeted you, they'll be behind you all the way.'

'Not sure Jed will. He was very much Team Tom.' She shrugged. 'Doesn't matter anyway. We can't both be Directors.'

'Yes, we can.' I gripped her shoulders. 'This is what we've worked hard for. We deserve this.'

Sarah gave a small smile. 'Evie and Fred don't deserve it, though. One of us needs to be around some of the time for the children. They can go back to Sinéad's a couple of days a week after school, but no more than that.' She put a hand to my cheek. 'I'll do it. I missed that time with them. Important as my career is, they're more important.'

I shook my head. 'That's not fair on you. I want my job back, but not at the detriment of yours. Your career shouldn't play second fiddle to mine. You've earned that position. Sacrificing it so that I can carry on where I left off isn't right.' My cheeks grew warm as I acknowledged an uncomfortable truth. 'Not so long ago I'd have accepted – expected even – this outcome, but not anymore. We're equals. We need to find a compromise that's fair to both of us.'

Sarah's eyes grew so large, it was a wonder her glasses could accommodate them. She threw her arms around me. 'Thank you. Hearing you say that and knowing you value me means so much. More than the job, to be honest.'

I felt a glow of pride. I was doing the right thing. Not just to win brownie points, but because I genuinely felt that way. Get me! I was behaving like a mature, responsible adult. *And* I'd used the word detriment in a sentence. This was possibly my finest moment ever.

'There has to be a way we can both do the Director's job,' I said, springing up from the step. Well, not so much springing, but standing with as much vigour as my back would allow. 'Our job is to come up with concepts and solutions. Often for the most mind-numbing products imaginable.' Sarah gave a throaty chuckle. I'd missed that laugh. It spurred me on. 'If we can make software sound appealing, we can definitely come up with a solution to this dilemma that appeals to both Ballas & Bailey and us.'

'You're right.' Sarah took her organiser from her bag. 'Let's brainstorm ideas.' She opened to a page covered in scribbles, with Dekker underlined at the top. She turned the page, paused and then turned back. 'In the Netherlands couples often work part-time. They share the work and the childcare. Makes it fairer and less stressful.' Her face lit up. 'Maybe we can job-share? Neither of us would have to give up the Director role then.' She blinked up at me. 'What do you think? Share the stress and time with the children?'

I ran a hand across my head. My instinct was to say no, I didn't want to job-share. I wanted to take full ownership of my role, to be involved in every element, both with the clients, the team and my colleagues. How would it look on the days I was off if someone was desperate to get hold of me, only to be told I was on the school run or taking my kids to the dentist? And what would everyone else at work think? The other Directors might view me as inferior to them, not committed or mentally strong enough to handle the role on a full-time basis. I'd miss out on what was going on in the office on the days I was out, from pitches coming in, to how my team were coping, to beers after work when it was someone's birthday.

It wasn't until I kicked one of Fred's discarded trainers that I realised I was pacing up and down the hall. I looked down at the trainers, embellished with images of Minecraft. I'd taken Fred to get them fitted. He'd grinned up at me in delight when I'd said he could have them, even though they cost more than the usual, standard trainers he got. As he'd held my hand tightly all the way home, I'd felt exhilarated to have made an everyday event into something exciting for him. It had brought me unexpected pleasure to be involved. If I worked full-time I couldn't do things like that anymore. I'd go back to being on the periphery of Fred's and Evie's days. Experiencing their lives second-hand through Sarah's anecdotes or theirs. I realised with a jolt that I didn't want that. I wanted to be a part of their lives. Admittedly, not all of it – cleaning dog's muck off the Minecraft trainers, I could do without – but I certainly wanted to be around more than I would be if I was a full-time Director.

Sarah was eyeing me nervously. I wanted to be around more for her too. And I wanted her to have the job she deserved, not the one she had to take so that I could have mine.

I grinned at her. 'Let's do it.'

Clara's expression was unreadable, as Sarah outlined the proposal for our job-share. We'd called her back from our study, where we could use the computer, rather than squeezing together to see her on Sarah's phone. The airbed that Sarah had been sleeping on leant against a wall. I'd deflate it the moment we got off the call. I might even puncture it.

'Will and I have worked together before, so that won't be an issue,' Sarah said. 'You could speak to Dieuwke or Lars at Dekker if you'd like a testimonial of how effective working part-time is.'

I reached under the desk and took Sarah's hand. Clara had to see that this solution was perfect. It ensured she'd have two loyal, hard-working, team players who would devote themselves and their experience to the company, instead of a stressed out, unhappy Director and Senior Manager.

Clara laced her fingers together. 'I hear where you're coming from.' Next to me Sarah released a shaky breath. 'A Director's role is demanding and all-consuming, so I see why you'd like to share the responsibilities.' I squeezed Sarah's hand. This sounded good. 'But …' That didn't sound so good. 'The salary justifies those demands. We need Directors who are prepared to make sacrifices, work long hours, travel whenever necessary and do what it takes.'

'We'll do all of that,' I said. 'On our working days we won't need to think about anything other than work because the other one will be taking care of the kids. We'll be completely focused on the job.'

'What about when the travel takes you to the other side of the world?' Clara asked. 'Will you fly home halfway through the trip because your two-and-a-half days are up? Or if the client wants you to check in with them at the end of the week? Not very professional to say you don't work that day, so they'll have to wait until you're next in the office.'

'We'll be flexible,' Sarah said. 'We'll plan out who needs to be where and make it work so that none of the projects are compromised.'

Clara smoothed her hair. 'I hear how desperately you want this to work, but I'm afraid it goes against our company policy. If we do it for you two, we'll have to do it for everyone. The blanket rule is that Director roles are full-time, no exceptions. I'm sorry.'

Sarah gave a resigned nod. She glanced at me, then back to Clara. 'Will can start back next week. I'll step down as Director and go back to being a Senior Manager.'

I opened my mouth to object, but Clara cut in.

'We'd love Will to come back straightaway. But I'm afraid there isn't an opening for a Senior Manager at the moment.'

Sarah's face fell. 'I'll have to leave then,' she said in a small voice. 'I'll email you my letter of resignation.'

'No,' I said firmly.

Sarah turned to me. 'We can't both be Directors.'

'I'll find something else then.'

She shook her head. 'You're not doing that.'

'Well, you're not doing that either.'

Clara cleared her throat. 'Never mind what you're *not* doing.' She hooked a finger across her chin. 'What are you actually *going* to do?'

Good question.

Chapter 39

Sarah

Six months later

'I did not trust him, Sarah. He was a *pronk*,' Dieuwke said.

I frowned at her image on my computer screen. Did she mean prick? As she was talking about Tom, that description was spot on, but I wasn't sure if Dieuwke's English, excellent though it was, extended to such English colloquialisms.

'*Pronk?*' I asked carefully.

Dieuwke nodded. 'What is the word in English?' She clicked her fingers. 'A *pronk*. A show-off. Pretending to be Superman.' She tutted. 'Lars is *pronk* also. Thinks he is Spider-Man.'

As Lars was about twenty years older and twenty feet taller than Tom Holland, I couldn't see why, but I let it go.

'Well, we don't need to worry about working with those *pronks* anymore,' I said, raising my mug of coffee. 'Here's to our new jobs.'

I'd lucked out big time with Dieuwke. I'd had no idea, when dealing with her at Dekker, that she was in talks with another company. She'd contacted me as soon as she started working there and asked if I'd do their marketing. I'd never have been able to work with Dekker. They were Ballas & Bailey's client and if I'd approached them, or any of Ballas & Bailey's other clients, they'd have sued me. Or had me shot. Either way, it was enough to deter me.

The moment I told Clara I was leaving, and that Will and I would be setting up our own marketing company, I was put on three months' gardening leave. If Clara could have helicoptered to our house and seized my laptop and computer, she would have done, but helicopters for hire were thin on the ground at Twixmas. Instead, she accepted my word that I wouldn't sabotage or steal any company information. Will and I took everything back the following morning and were frogmarched straight into an HR meeting. Clara highlighted the clause in our contracts that stated we couldn't work with any of Ballas & Bailey's clients for the next gazillion years. She used actual highlighters, which magnified the seriousness of the situation, as she didn't like disrupting that neatly arranged row of pens if it could be avoided.

Will and I used our fully paid-up leave to set up our new company – Campbell Consulting. We'd been in the industry for years and knew plenty of people who, like Dieuwke, had moved to other companies that weren't represented by Ballas & Bailey. Others had let their contract expire because Ballas & Bailey were charging too much, or they didn't like the *pronk* running their account (probably Jed). Happily, Will and I weren't classed as *pronks*. They'd clearly never seen us on the dance floor after a few drinks.

So, here we were, newly open and ready for business, with several clients already lined up for us to work with. Will and I had set up a rota for taking Evie and Fred to and from school and their clubs. They were going to Sinéad's twice a week to give us both two full working days. Evie and Fred didn't mind, as they liked playing with the other children, although they'd already asked me to talk to Sinéad about upgrading the toilet paper. I would not be raising this matter with Sinéad. I was so thankful she was able to fit them in, I wouldn't have questioned it if she made them go in the garden.

Dieuwke and I said our goodbyes and I ended the Zoom

call, enjoying the buzz of a successful pitch. The study door opened and Will came in.

'All good?' he asked.

'Yes!' I grinned. 'Dieuwke's pleased and has given me the go-ahead.' Will high-fived me. 'How was reading time?' I asked.

Will grimaced. 'Those tiny plastic chairs are ridiculous. Sitting on a bread knife would be more comfortable.'

The chairs didn't bother me when I read with Fred. The daggers Miss Boast shot me were more of a concern.

Will looked at his watch. 'What time shall we go to London for the Wired meeting?'

I checked my organiser. 'Need to get the two o'clock train. Tonya's picking Evie and Fred up from Sinéad's, so we don't have to rush back. Hopefully, we'll have earned a celebratory drink.'

Will crossed his fingers. 'Let's have a drink anyway. Doesn't have to be celebratory. Although, I'm sure it will be. They loved the concept we pitched.'

We exchanged a smile. Working together was going better than I could ever have hoped. When Will had initially suggested it, every instinct screamed no, although out of love for him, I hadn't actually screamed. He'd allayed my 'never mix business with pleasure' fears by reminding me of how well we'd used to work together. Brainstorming with Will was fun and I hadn't realised how much I'd missed it until we started again. Working with Tom had been completely one-sided, I now realised. I'd come up with all the ideas and he'd made notes, then passed them off as his own to the rest of the team. Will and I fed off each other and grew our concepts together. It was sparky and fun and, as a result, our relationship was sparky and fun too.

It wasn't all smooth, of course. We'd started off working in the study together, but it quickly became apparent that we needed a little space from each other. My daily chats with Tonya distracted him (he wasn't as into Love Island as we were), and his constant foot tapping and humming grated more than a *Love Island* contestant's talon-like fingernails being dragged down a chalkboard. Now I worked in the study and Will worked in his summer house. He had, at last, got around to erecting it. Or paying someone who had the necessary skills required to erect it. Lauren.

I'd been reluctant to get to know her at first – call me old-fashioned, but the fact she and my husband almost had an affair didn't exactly endear her to me. But Will had assured me that nothing would ever happen and he didn't think of her in that way anymore. To her credit, Lauren had approached me in the school playground and apologised for her previous silly drunken behaviour. I took this to include kissing Will, although that was never mentioned. We wouldn't ever be friends, but things were amicable. I declined joining the Friday Fizz Club. Will still went, but I couldn't handle the lack of gluten or the phrase: 'Said the actress to the bishop.'

Now that we had separate working spaces and could discuss reality TV shows/be a one-man band without bothering each other, things were great. We bickered sometimes about whose turn it was to run back to school with a forgotten musical instrument/PE kit/classroom hamster (mainly because we were both scared of Mrs Manning), and other domestic nonsense, but work was fantastic. We valued our clients and got a kick out of delivering a great service to them. We could go to Evie's and Fred's sports days or assemblies without having to beg for time off. We didn't need to panic about how we would look after them if they were off ill. We didn't have to deal with malicious, back-stabbing colleagues. I could use as much stationery as I liked without fear of dismissal. And Will wouldn't be fired if he left his laptop on a train. Although sexual favours would probably be withheld for a while. Speaking of which …

'I don't have any calls for a while.' I grinned up at Will.

His eyes lit up. 'Are you free for the next, I don't know, fifteen minutes?' he asked.

I nodded.

He crossed the room and knelt before me. 'In that case can I tempt you with …' He paused and I stiffened. If he sang 'Afternoon Delight' then the only thing he could tempt me with would be a decree nisi.

'With a change of scene?' Will asked.

I breathed a sigh of relief. 'Yes please,' I murmured, as he pulled me to my feet and led me towards our bedroom. I sighed contentedly, a complete contrast to the way I'd felt for most of the past year. It had been such an emotional rollercoaster that it was a wonder Disney hadn't been in touch requesting we become a permanent fixture at their Orlando site. We'd been through the full gamut of emotions, from shock to disbelief, bitterness to jealousy, distrust to fear.

It scared me to think how close we'd come to breaking up, to losing sight of the things we loved about each other and trying to find them elsewhere. It was almost as though we'd needed to teeter on the edge of separation to see what we had and appreciate its value.

The change in Will's outlook was phenomenal. He no longer viewed jobs around the house or involving the children as mine, or felt that the working week was primarily his. He saw me as his equal now and I'd never loved him more. We'd achieved that rarest of things – the perfect work-life balance. Provided he didn't sing.

We reached the bedroom and grinned at each other before falling onto the bed. Will had been right. Mixing business with pleasure could work.

Chapter 40

Will

Afternoon delight!

THE END

A Note from the Author

Dear Reader,

THANK YOU for reading *Would You Ask My Husband That?*. I hope very much it made you smile or even laugh out loud (LOL some say, but I can't see that catching on).

The book was inspired by friends who have done exactly what Sarah and Will have done – she's the high-flying, high earner, while he's the stay-at-home dad (you never hear anyone talk about stay-at-home mums, do you?!). The dads, without asking for it, get much more kudos for raising the children than the mums do. 'Isn't he good to do that,' is a common response, at his noble sacrifice for the good of the family. Yes, he is good to do that, but so are the millions of women who do the same thing without recognition. Can you tell this annoys me? It's up there with 'Is dad babysitting tonight?' No, he's just looking after his own children! Another thing I hate hearing is: 'We're out of coffee and walnut cake', but that's a completely separate issue.

To hear more of my random wittering, as well as receive updates and news of my writing and events, please sign up to my newsletter https://www.kathleenwhyman.com/contact-me. Please also feel free to get in touch via Twitter, Instagram or Facebook if you'd like to talk about the book, or anything else. I'd love to hear from you.

Finally, if you have time to write a review of *Would You Ask My Husband That?* wherever you bought the book, or on social media, I'd be very, very grateful. It doesn't have to be long. Something along the lines of: 'The best book I've ever read' would be perfect. Ha! No, whatever you write would be fantastic, thank you. You have no idea how happy reviews make writers. Well, the good ones anyway. The bad, not so much! ;-)

Thank you again for reading this book. There are many distractions out there – social media, the Internet, a zillion TV channels, the buttocks scenes in *Bridgerton* – so I really appreciate you investing your time and look forward to catching up via my newsletter or on social media.

Until then, take care and happy reading!

Kathleen x

www.twitter.com/KathleenWhyman1

www.instagram.com/kathleenwhyman1

https://www.facebook.com/kathleenwhymanauthor/

Acknowledgements

Top of my list of acknowledgements has to be my wonderful agent Emily Glenister at DHH Literary Agency. Emily and I met during lockdown at a DHH Pitch Day. Despite the meeting being via Zoom, such was my eagerness to impress that I ditched the PJ bottoms and wore actual clothes on my lower half, even though they'd never be seen. Emily and I hit it off instantly and even more so when we eventually met in person the following summer and she bought me my first ever Aperol Spritz. How I got to that point in my life without such nectar I'll never know. Thank you for the introduction, Emily, and, more importantly, for being such a supportive, caring, hard-working cheerleader of my work. I feel #blessed to have you as an agent. And you know how much I hate hashtags.

Emily's enthusiasm for my writing was matched by Cara Chimirri, editorial director at Embla Books. Her email expressing how much she loved *Would You Ask My Husband That?* and would like to publish it was so complimentary and flattering that I almost didn't show anyone, as it felt too vain. Putting it on a T-shirt wasn't too showy-offy at all though! Thank you, Cara, for loving my book as much as Emily and I do and for all your help and guidance in getting it to the best place it could be. And thank you to all the Embla team, including Emilie Marneur, Anna Perkins, Daniela Nava, Hannah Deuce, Katie Williams and Paris Ferguson, for your hard work and for making me so welcome. Beth Free – I love, love, love your cover design. Thank you for making Sarah strong, savvy and speccy.

I need to give a huge shout-out to the Comedy Women In Print Prize (www.comedywomeninprint.co.uk), set up by the absolutely fabulous Helen Lederer. It's a voluntary organisation, run by incredible people with the aim of celebrating, supporting and encouraging witty women writers. I feel truly honoured to be a part of the CWIP family, having been shortlisted in the unpublished category in 2020. I've made some wonderful friends, particularly Faye Brann, Nancy Peach, Kirsty Eyre, Hannah Dolby, Rebecca Rogers and Maureen Stapleton. Although I shouldn't like them, as they're all much wittier than me.

Other organisations (all voluntary – a massive thank you to the extremely kind and generous people who give up their time to run them) that have given me a much-needed helping hand/kick up the arse with my writing are: www.writershq. co.uk – an amazing resource of workshops and writerly advice with the best slogan ever – Stop F**king About & Start Writing; www.theunstoppableauthor.com – honest advice on building resilience, which writers need in abundance and, ideally, in chocolate form; www.romanticnovelistsassociation. org – an endless source of encouragement and warmth, with fun and fizz thrown in; and www.womenwritersnetwork. com, and www.booksbywomen.org both of which promote awareness and visibility of female writers.

My next thank you is to my beta readers. The official definition of a beta reader is: a test reader of an unreleased work of literature. I'm not sure my rough drafts qualify as works of literature, so I'm extremely thankful to these people for wading through the dross and giving me their honest feedback: my generous, kind, inspirational mum, Susan Fisher, who, despite being my number-one fan, loves me and my work enough not to foist it on her book club in case they don't like it (very diplomatic and wise); Zoë Folbigg, my Groundworks ('Are you sure this is oat milk?') / library writing / book talk ('Why did we agree to this?') partner; Catherine Bennetto, who managed to read the book despite having brain surgery (I'm assuming the two are unrelated); and Brigid Gannon – I love you even more for finding time to read the book with everything you've had going on. I'm both sorry and astounded I haven't cured your insomnia, although just an hour in my company should do the job.

I wouldn't be who I am without my amazing family and friends, and I wouldn't be able to write if it wasn't for their support, care, belief and motivational chats, meet-ups and messages. A massive THANK YOU to all of them, particularly my in-laws, *Strictly* gals, Socially Isolated crew, the Readers Wives book club, RNA group chat, and my school friends who can't escape me, Becky, Marie and Tonya. I love you all so much and am very lucky and grateful to have you in my life. Admittedly I'd get a lot more writing done if it wasn't for all the motivational chats, meet-ups and messages, but please don't stop!

Additional thanks go to: Linda and Jed Whyman for being the best in-laws ever (it's official, I checked); Vicky Bradford and Kate Lowe, who provided cake and cocktails and chauffeured my daughters to countless dance classes and competitions so I could catch up with ~~box sets~~ my writing; Sarah Tomlin, who, as a great wit and an exceptionally knowledgeable nutritionalist proves that laughter is the best medicine; Clara Nicoll, who selflessly emigrated to the Netherlands so she could provide me with Dutch phrases and colloquialisms – I have her to thank for the horse breeding story; Sarah Johnson and Lizzie Rooney for the fizz and fish 'n' chips; Lisa Haskins for the moniker The Author; Jill Dawson for being a gold star mentor and friend; and Jo Carnegie, future partner of Crap Blogs Services if the author career bombs.

Thank you to Fran Boast, HR aficionado, for all the info, so that I could ensure Will got sacked correctly. I've named one of the characters after her as a sign of my appreciation, but must stress that the character is completely fictitious. The real-life Fran Boast has not had any incidents involving soiled nappies, as far as I'm aware.

Thank you Ruth and Magda for the Hermitage Rd Café Writers' Room, the coolest place to write in town with, unfortunately, the coolest cakes. Closely followed by Hitchin Library, which I'm very fond of, even if it is a bit lacking in the cake department.

Thank you Jane Wenham-Jones for your wit and wisdom. And Louise Pyper for being a ray of sunshine. I'm so very sorry you're no longer with us. You're missed by many. Sadly, as we get older, so do our parents. My beloved dad, John Fisher, died in 2010 and has unhappily been joined by some of my friends' parents. They were all wonderful people and will never be forgotten. I like to think they're all having a drink together somewhere, reminiscing about their full lives and debating which Beatles song was the best. Whatever they're up to, they'll always be in our hearts.

As you can probably gather from these acknowledgements, I'm a big fan of women supporting women. But there are a couple of men who deserve a mention. My 'little' brother Adam (he's six-foot-six), who I am full of love, pride and admiration for, but who I would like to stop ageing, as it makes me feel well old. And my incredible husband James. I'd never have been able to follow my dream without his support and encouragement and I'll forever be grateful for that. He also gave me my beautiful, wonderful, incredible, spirited (now teenage) daughters Eve and Elena. The sheer force of my love for them blows me away every day. Although a particularly enthusiastic door slam can have a similar effect.

Last, but definitely not least, thank YOU, lovely reader for buying / borrowing / being gifted and feeling obliged to read *Would You Ask My Husband That?* I hope you enjoyed reading it as much as I enjoyed writing it. ☺

About the Author

Kathleen Whyman is an author, a journalist, a knackered mum and an Espresso Martini fan. These may be linked.

Kathleen wrote her first novel at the age of ten. Despite the accompanying illustrations, *The Ghost of Cripple Creek* was rejected, as were the short stories she submitted to *Jackie* magazine in her teens (probably for the best), but this didn't deter her from a life of writing.

Working as a magazine journalist, Kathleen longed to be a novelist, but got slightly side-tracked over the years by work, children and *Mad Men* box sets. It was her daughter's words – 'Stop talking about writing a book and just write one' – that gave her the push she needed to enrol on a writing course with Jill Dawson and get on with it.

Kathleen's debut novel, *Wife Support System*, was shortlisted for the Romantic Novelists' Association's Joan Hessayon Award 2020 and the Romance Comedy Novel of the Year 2021. Her novel *Second Wife Syndrome* was shortlisted for the Comedy Women in Print prize 2020 in the unpublished comic novel category.

Kathleen lives in Hertfordshire with her husband and two daughters – one of whom is expecting 10 per cent of any profits.

About Embla Books

Embla Books is a digital-first publisher of standout commercial adult fiction. Passionate about storytelling, the team at Embla publish books that will make you 'laugh, love, look over your shoulder and lose sleep'. Launched by Bonnier Books UK in 2021, the imprint is named after the first woman from the creation myth in Norse mythology, who was carved by the gods from a tree trunk found on the seashore – an image of the kind of creative work and crafting that writers do, and a symbol of how stories shape our lives.

Find out about some of our other books and stay in touch:

Twitter, Facebook, Instagram: @emblabooks
Newsletter: https://bit.ly/emblanewsletter

Printed in Great Britain
by Amazon

26218323R00192